LEECH MOB

A Novel about a Connecticut Gang

LEECH MOB

A Novel about a Connecticut Gang

John Harwood

Cover Illustration Copyright ©2013 by John Harwood
Cover Design Copyright ©2013 by Jeff Cordova

ISBN-13:978-0-989057-00-4
(Hard Core Publishing, an imprint of Harwood Publishing, LLC)

This novel is dedicated to
Mom and Chris
and
Rachel, Eliza, and Makayla

CONTENTS

LEECH MOB
A Novel about a Connecticut Gang

Chapter 1: Welcome to Riverview High

SEPTEMBER 1990

Fair Hills Psychiatric Hospital was an ancient nuthouse with a maze of concrete tunnels running underneath the joint to keep the patients from seeing the light of day. All I remember was going to that crazy rave and getting tear-gassed by the cops who then pulled us out, choking to death. Or maybe it was just me who was dragged out. Anyway, I must have taken something. I just don't remember what it was and, the next thing I knew, the cops hauled me into Crisis Intervention where the doctors held clipboards and stared at me through plexiglass windows.

One doctor looked real evil, like he was planning on lobotomizing me the first chance he got, and then I was being transferred to State Hospital where I was escorted by the frowns in white.

Now we were walking up this caged-in staircase with *ADOLESCENT WARD BUILDING F* stenciled in blood on the cracked and water-stained walls.

"Why F?" I asked the tall orderly with a Jamaican accent and a sideways name tag which said *Bunny*.

"You don't like F's, mon?"

"Nah, I got too many of those in school," I mumbled and Bunny cracked up.

"Ain't nothing to warry about. Dose letters don mean anyting. Each division has its own share of complicated issues." Bunny spoke in a sing-song voice before lowering his tone, "Especially hee-er!" He hit the buzzer on the outdated security system.

"Ward F," came the static reply.

"Open the bamba-clot, mon!"

The intercom screamed and the door swung open. *STAY CALM* was stenciled high on the moldy pale green walls with rusted metal grates covering every window.

The building looked gothic with hissing radiators and buzzing fluorescents which lit the place up in a sickly yellow hue. Two dim hallways stretched in opposite directions: *MALE ONLY* and *FEMALE ONLY* and in the middle, glassed off, was a bullpen with *NURSES STATION F* covered in signs:

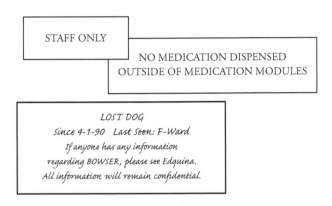

"Here's da new patient, Doctor G."

From his paper-stacked desk, the doctor, with tufts of white hair floating above each ear, gazed over his thin reading glasses. He was a black man in his mid-fifties.

"Oh yes. I've been expecting this young man."

"I'll be at me desk," Bunny nodded and stepped out, leaving the door slightly ajar.

"I've already reviewed your file. My name is Doctor Gildmore. Go on and take a seat. So this is what–the third time you've been arrested?"

"Something like that."

"So why don't you tell me about this group you've been hanging around with? The Leech Mob. Your mother brought in this newspaper article."

I leaned forward, shaking my head, which was still swimming in chemicals that made my eyes run.

"Leech Mob Arrested after Fight at School," I read and looked up sheepishly. "What's there to say? I don't want to get them into trouble or anything and, besides, I don't rat!"

The doctor chuckled. "I wonder about you kids sometimes. So what's a day in the life of the Leech Mob like? What do you guys do? Visit the elderly–that sort of thing?"

"Yeah, sometimes, but usually they just call the cops."

Gildmore lowered his voice. "You've also lost some friends, I see. You want to talk about them?"

"Which ones?" I folded my arms.

"Have their deaths put a lot of stress on you? Were they a part of this Leech Mob, too?"

"I think I missed their funerals."

Now that got me depressed and when I get depressed, I don't feel like doing anything, especially talking. And that's all adults want me to do–to confess what I've done. "I plead the fifth. I know my damn rights."

"That's right. You do have patient rights and, if you're like most of the others, you aren't too happy being stuck in here–but few understand that I'm their ticket out."

"What's that supposed to mean?"

"It means that if you choose to talk to me–and I don't care what you've done– I've heard things that would make your head spin. All I care about is getting you better and then out of here, and how do we do that?" he asked but didn't wait for my answer but went on to tell me anyway. "We start by talking through your issues. But if you clamp up, which most kids do, you might be in here for a long, long time. So it's up to you. Now, should we start again?" Gildmore smiled.

"Your file says your parents divorced, and you and your mother moved to Connecticut just last year." He scanned the page and then looked up. "Riverview, huh? The river, a covered bridge, lovely homes nestled in the woods. It seems like an ideal place to live. Why don't you tell me about it?"

"Yeah, it seems like a nice place."

"Then your grades began to drop." Gildmore leaned forward to read the file closely. "You started getting into trouble. You had fights at school. So what happened? You didn't like your teachers? Pissed off at your parents? What?"

"I rode the tard-cart."

"The tard-cart?"

✦

ONE YEAR EARLIER

Horseface turned, eyeballing me as I walked down the aisle of the mini-school bus at 6:45 on the first day of school.

"Well?" she croaked. "What's your name?"

"Kelly."

"Call me Lucille," snorted the bus driver in a voice that matched her looks.

"Yeah!" a kid named Roger said in a deep and guttural voice, staring wildly through his strapped-on, magnifying glass lenses. I smiled at a girl in the back of the van, who rolled her eyes and turned up her headphones. Lucille grabbed the lever, slammed the door, and drove down the steep narrow road that a regular bus couldn't handle. She honked when we got to the next stop. The screen door bashed open and a kid ran out, leaping over the potted plants on the front porch like he was storming a military obstacle course, and then dove into the seat across from me. Toby's wavy hair looked plastered to his skull with fistfuls of gel, and a half-dozen razor scrapes boasted that the fourteen-year-old already needed to shave.

On the way to school, Toby started to flip out with flashbacks from playing video games, so Horseface howled into her rear-view mirror for him to calm down. After a ten-minute ride, our little van pulled in front of the school, grinding to a stop alongside the line of ten regular school busses. When she opened the door, Toby scrambled forward, leaping off the minibus first and then charging toward the side entrance where a special ed teacher was waiting. I made a real fine target for the Preps, who were getting out of their busses, as we all walked into the school together. They talked junk and tried to get in my way.

"Help! I'm too retarded to ride the bus!" they joked. "Hey, aren't you supposed to go in through the side door with the rest of the tongue-chews?"

They circled me like a gang of vampire preps so I picked up my pace.

"Hey Gator, Look! A lost retard!" They broke into hysterical fits of laughter. "Check out those velcro sneakers–Corky doesn't know how to tie his shoes!"

"I don't care what I wear."

"Yeah and it shows!" Gator responded and, after the next round of laughter faded, a blinding red slap stung the side of my face.

"Oooooohhhhh! Get em, Sean!" The yelling got louder as we turned in circles, facing each other with doubled fists.

"Fight! Fight! Fight!" The Preps began to chant, low at first, and then working themselves into a frenzy. I knew I'd gotten stuck. There was no way out of this now. They inched forward, getting more excited by the second, all dying to see a fight and thrilled that it wasn't them in the center ring because that would have scared the hell out of any of them.

The racket brought dozens more, just as bloodthirsty, running in from all sides and bunching in around us. Out of the corner of my eye, I saw Gator sneaking around the edge of the pit until he was out of sight. Then I was violently shoved toward Sean. We grabbed each other, only letting go of our grasp to land a few punches. I could taste salty blood as I stumbled to the side but was caught by the inner ring of students and shoved back into him. I saw flashes of their faces, ugly and howling. Gator continued to weave in and out of the pack, using the others as camouflage as he pushed us into each other so we'd have no option other than to brawl.

Sean gritted his pointy teeth and rammed his fists into my face. I tried to back away, only to be shoved into a left hook. We tangled up, Sean fighting dirty and reaching out to gouge my eyes or rip my face with his dirty ragged fingernails. The inner ring grew tighter as more students ran and jumped on each other's backs to get a glimpse of the action, compressing us into a tighter and tighter circle. We locked up, shoved each other's faces back, and took tight swings.

Then someone yelled, "Teacher! Teacher! Teacher!" and like a well-planned drill, the students turned and calmly walked away. I looked into the distance and saw a pudgy man, squinting and waddling toward us. We were almost down to the innermost ring, the original kids who started the fight, when Sean saw his chance to snuff me real good with a sucker punch to the nose, bleeding it, and then he took off with his cronies.

I tried to get out of there, too, holding my nose and trying to stop the blood from leaking all over my sweatshirt when the teacher called out, "Hey! You! You in the blue! Freeze! Wait! Wait right there, buddy boy!"

I stopped walking, knowing he meant me, and waited for the pudgy guy to chug over. I leaned forward, breathing hard, spitting and dripping blood from my nose and lip.

As he got closer, he checked out my scraped and bloodied face disgustedly and roared, "FOLLOW ME!" He shuffled towards the school building, breathing as heavily as me. "Come on, hurry up, *huff*, haven't got all day! Lots of other kids have, *huff*, come for a proper education and here you are, *huff*, going around disturbing everyone!" The teacher spun around and reached for the door, glaring at me as he held it open.

"But I didn't do anything wrong."

"Tell it to the principal, not me."

"What about the others?"

"What others? I didn't see anyone else. At least no one else covered in blood!"

"What do you think–I was fighting myself?"

"Don't play smart with me! You're new this year, aren't you?"

"Yeah."

"Where from?"

"New York."

"City?" he asked with widened eyes.

"Yeah."

"Doesn't surprise me."

Once in the main office, the principal opened his door and motioned me in. "Do you want to go to the nurse?"

"Itsjustanosebleed," I said into my shirt.

"What?" he raised his voice.

I lowered my shirt and spoke slowly. "No thanks. It's just a nosebleed."

"Well, you're going anyway." For a moment, he looked almost impressed.

"Must have been a doosy of a fight."

"Not really."

"Tough guy, eh?"

"No," I answered and he frowned.

"Who were you fighting?"

"Don't know his name. This is my first day."

"Ah, new to Riverview and already in a fight. Not off to a good start, now are you?"

"No," I agreed, thinking he might be cool after all, but then he glared, like I'd just reminded him that he should've been pissed off.

"I hope you aren't going to be a problem for this school because of some adjusting issues you may have."

"No, I won't be a problem. It's no big deal."

"No big deal?" he repeated as if he couldn't believe what I had said. "Well, yes it is! Fighting is a big deal and is grounds for being expelled!"

"That's not what I meant."

"I hope that you can stay with us because if this starts to become a behavior problem for you, I'd have no problem kicking you out of my school."

"I won't make any more problems for you."

"That's what I want to hear." He smiled. "I have faith that you can make it through your first year without any more issues, but that's going to be entirely up to you. In other words, the ball is in your court."

"Then I'm gonna slam dunk it."

"Excuse me?" The principal glared, nervously shuffling papers.

"Nothing. I mean, I won't be a problem."

"I'll give you the benefit of the doubt. I hope we understand one another."

"Yes," I said, "and thanks!"

"You know, I find you slightly odd but even so, I'm still going to take it easy on you but only this one time. So here are your options. Either one-week detention or a three-day home suspension. The choice is yours."

The next day I told Mom I was staying after school with some friends I didn't have to do a history project that didn't exist. At lunch, this kid named Andrew sat hunched over, polishing his glasses while Toby grinned into his bag of Doritos, shoving handful after handful of orange goop into his face and chewing with his mouth open. Then Roger smashed his fist into the middle of his sandwich.

"Dead meat," he growled in his burnt voice.

This was called the *loser table*. So I took a deep breath and walked with my tray past them. Andrew cocked his head interestedly and watched me head for a table that appeared more neutral in the ninth grade infrastructure. These particular kids looked baffled but didn't object when I grabbed one of the empty seats. Then more kids rolled up and stood behind me, nervously fidgeting and holding their trays. I ignored them and tried to eat a slab of bleached rubber chicken.

"Hey, you're in my seat. I sit there everyday," one kid said almost politely so I slid over.

"Nice try, but now you're in my place," echoed another.

I looked over at two teachers, standing about five feet away as they manned the outer perimeter of the mess hall. They took no notice of the room but chatted to each other instead.

"If I get up, then where can I sit?" I asked.

"How about over there?" one snapped back, pointing.

"Yeah man, you can't just . . . sit wherever you want!"

The kids who were safely planted began to turn on me, so I was forced into following a local delegate who ushered me to the table that apparently always had plenty of open chairs. As he tried to make introductions, Andrew ignored him, removed a crumpled tissue out of his pocket, and blew his nose.

"I know their names," I told him.

"That's right, you do! Cause you sit here everyday."

"We've been in school only two days," I sighed, hearing him receive some applause as he walked away.

"Don't worry about it," Andrew said. "You new this year?" but he already knew my answer. "Me too." He extended a floppy hand, which I shook, looking into his intelligent but sad and watery eyes.

At the other table, a burst of laughter boiled up as the kid was now dusting off his hands as his boys patted him on the back for a job well done.

✦

Carlie, the prettiest girl in the whole ninth grade, strolled by our classroom door as all the boys leaned forward to get a better look. She had long, blonde hair and these blue scopes for eyes. I raised my hand and asked the teacher if I could get a drink of water. By the time I got out into the hall, she'd dipped into the girl's room so I hung back near the water fountain and waited. A moment later she came out, throwing her yellow tresses over her shoulder and leaning to drink from the fountain. The water splashed against her mouth, and then she stood up, wiped her lips slowly and whirled back in my direction.

"Where have you been?" she asked when she got a little closer.

Was she talking to me? "Uh," I said, nervously running a finger around my collar. "I've been around."

"What was that? I couldn't hear you."

She tilted her head and suddenly a voice boomed from behind me.

"Why? Did you miss me?"

"Always, baby!" She walked past me and briefly hugged Gator, who grinned over her shoulder as he breathed into her ear. "Are you going to the Party Zone this Friday?"

"Maybe."

"So you gonna dance with me?"

"Yeah, sure, but don't forget to ask," she said coyly.

"Do you want something, loser?" Gator narrowed his eyes at me as Carlie turned and smiled.

Back in the classroom I slumped into my chair. The teacher was handing back tests. She slapped mine face down. I flipped it over and read *F*.

After class was lunch and not wanting a repeat of yesterday, I went straight to the half-empty table and sat down.

"What happened? What's wrong with you? You're not acting like yourself today," Andrew asked over our trays of slop.

"I'm failing math."

"So," he told me, "study harder."

"I saw Carlie Petros out in the hall. I thought she was talking to me but she was talking to Gator and I felt like such a dumb ass."

Andrew cackled. "I knew something was up. I always see you staring at that girl. She dissed you, huh?"

"Yeah." I frowned.

"Ah, so what? I'm in all honors classes with them and they diss me all the time—until they forget to do their homework. Then I'm their best friend."

The teachers started to clap their hands, yelling for us to throw out our garbage and go outside for the remainder of our lunch period. Once outside, I got a basketball and started shooting hoops while Andrew stood watching me and blinking his watery eyes.

"Come on, Andrew." I motioned for him to get on the court but he shook his head sternly, wanting nothing to do with the sport of basketball. "At least help me catch the rebounds or something?" I pleaded, so finally he stood under the basket. After a minute I passed him the ball. "Take a few shots."

At first he refused but then changed his mind and dribbled for a minute, staring down at the ball like any coach's nightmare. He took a deep breath, concentrated on the hoop, tossed the ball up, but it fell short of the net. We didn't realize that we were being watched until Gator, Sean, and the Night of the Living Preps began to laugh hysterically, their big joke being that Andrew was black but sucked at basketball.

"Don't worry about them, Andrew," I said, passing the ball back to him.

"I know that!" he snapped and reset his glasses. "I told you I didn't want to play!" He dropped the ball and stormed off the court.

◆

"You got into a fight on the first day of school?"

"Something like that."

Dr. Gildmore removed his glasses and polished them on his shirt. "Going to a new school is tough I imagine, especially when you're a teenager." He sighed and called to the door. "Bunny, are you still around? I'm sorry but I'm going to have to stop you there because I have a whole list of patients to see."

A moment later the tall man stepped back into the room.

"Can you show Kelly his way around the dorm before you take him to…What's going on now anyway?"

"Conflict Resolution Group, I tink. I find out." The two of us began to walk out when Gildmore called from his desk.

"That was a good start! Keep it up and you'll be out of here before you know it."

We zigzagged out of the office halls, out to the dorms where Bunny finally announced, "This here's you room. And you know about the two halls. The boys are not allowed down the girls' wing and the girls are not allowed down the boys' wing, you understand me?"

"Yeah."

"If you have a problem with that sort of ting, you'll wind up in Seg."

"Nah man, no problem."

"Al-reet. The smoking lounge is here and the day room is there and all the windows are fitted with double-reinforced plexiglass. So if you throw a chair or someting, it will just bounce off, so don't even try it, right?"

"Right."

"That's the front door. When it opens, some kids try to escape. They run down the hall and right into another locked door, all wired to a security system. You'll just wind up in four-point restraints, so that's a big no-no, okay?"

"Okay."

"If you get thoughts about running, it's best to let the staff know."

"I won't run."

"You'll see some of the patients wearing hospital style clothes but you can also wear clothes from home but no provocative clothing will be tolerated. Over there is the medication room. We hold our group meetings in the conference room, where most of the kids should be right now." Bunny looked at his watch. "They still have a little time left so I show you in."

Chapter 2: The Program

When high school started, me and the others who hadn't fit into the regular curriculum were thrown into something called the *PROGRAM*, designed for outcasts, screwballs, and kids with mild learning disabilities. We were all grouped together like some sort of virus the school system needed to quarantine, while safely registered in high level classes that their parents, counselors, and coaches had chosen, the preppy elites were nowhere to be seen. If I really wanted to go looking for them, I had to cross into the kingdom of trophy cases and school banners, where classrooms sequestered the royalty who laughed at their teachers' dry jokes.

But back in the corners of the high school where the Metal Chicks skipped class, where the restrooms reeked of cigarette smoke and graffiti colored the stalls, the Program stumbled on. Here is where six-foot tall, 300-pound special young ladies with hairy arms and combat boots wove the halls with mullet-headed burnouts in flannel shirts and ripped bleached jeans.

Resource Study Group was my second period class of the day and met in a room where the retarded kids usually were for periods three through six. The alphabet bordered the ceiling, and numerals hung on the wall. The goal of Resource was to get help with our homework but Mr. Allen began by giving us only two rules.

"You can't talk to each other or sleep."

Mr. Allen had a sad look to his tired eyes and seemed like he'd given up on teaching long ago. There were four of us, each isolated at our own circular table, two sorta slow kids, a big, shysty Latino dude, and me.

Everyone began reading except Flip, who didn't bring any books and sat looking around the room with a big grin on his face. At the sound of the bell, Flip went to work on Mr. Allen until the balding man threw down his pen. "Back in my day, do you have any idea what our principal did to correct problem students? To give you a hint, it involved a wooden plank!"

"What?" Flip grinned. "How did he do that?"

"It's true." Allen nodded. "The principal was allowed to discipline the trouble makers by spanking them but I'll tell you one thing," Mr. Allen held up his finger, "not too many kids stepped out of line."

"You hear this?" Flip asked. "This perv used to spank little kids with a wooden plank!"

Mr. Allen's left eye began to twitch and then he began to stutter, as he tried to get his words out. "N-No Flip! I n-never hit any of the kids with the plank! I s-said the principal had tha-tha-that job."

"You know, you sound just like Porky Pig sometimes? Beep-bee-bee-bee-beep-beep, That's all folks!" Flip threw back his head and laughed as Allen's eyes dropped into his book and, for a time, Flip was forced into picking on the others instead. "Ben, how ya been man! How was your summer? You know, I forgot just how big that head was of yours! Damn! Maybe it grew! You must look at yourself in the mirror sometimes and say, 'Damn! I got a big fucking head!'"

"Flip!" shouted Allen.

"What? I'm just being honest and while we're on the subject Ben, you really should clean out your ears once in a while cause you got like cheese dripping out of those things!" Flip made a twirling gesture by his ear. "You should go to work with a Q-tip sometime and really dig those suckers out one day, and I bet even you'd be surprised at what you find!" Flip glanced at Allen who rolled his eyes and went back to his papers. "You know Ben, it's really disgusting to look at your earwax. You really are one nasty …"

"Flip!" Mr. Allen raised his voice.

"What?" Flip asked, raising both his palms innocently. "I'm only trying to help the kid out with his hygiene. You must admit that's very important!"

I couldn't help smiling, which Mr. Allen zoned right in on.

"If you think that's funny, you go and visit Flip in about ten years from now! Then you'll see something really funny!"

"Yeah, okay Allen." Flip smiled crookedly. "And while we're on the subject of jokes, if you really want to get a good laugh, you can ask Allen about all the space men he knows, isn't that right, Allen?"

"What?" I asked smiling, as Mr. Allen's right eye started to shudder, a hundred blinks a minute.

"Oh, I didn't tell you?" Flip slapped his thigh and slid back his plastic chair. "Mr. Allen is famous. My older brother told me all about him! Allen is always calling the newspapers, telling them how he sees space aliens driving UFO's around his house, beaming him up to the mother ship, and taking him for spins around the solar system. Isn't that right, Allen?"

"Mr. Allen!" he corrected

"Yeah, Professor Allen over there is always in the *National Enquirer* talking about moon-men landing and making first contact. Then the school got an anonymous tip from somebody and they called him down to the office to find out if he had all his shit together. You want to know something else, Allen?"

"Enough Flip! You want to get kicked out of here the first week of school?"

"No really, all jokes aside. I'm being 100% completely serious right now, okay Mr. Allen? I need to tell ya something really important. Now this is a true story. I was in the mall the other day, sitting in the food court, getting something to eat, and you know how they have that glass ceiling?" Flip began.

"Yeah," sighed Allen.

"Well, I just happened to look up and saw this huge, floating spaceship and written on the side of it, in huge letters, was *ALLEN INCORPORATED*!"

"Flip, I'm giving you this one last chance to shut your mouth!"

"Hey Ben, did you go yet?" Flip turned his attention toward Ben. "Psst Kelly, yo Kelly, peep this. Did you know that Ben got caught jerking off in the middle of history class so they dumped him in the Mastery Program and gave him a permanent pass to the nurse's office to, you know, take care of business in private if he ever get the urge to smack his unit around a bit."

"Flip! This is your last warning!" Allen glared and Flip nodded his head and straightened up, waiting for Allen to get caught up in his book again before leaning forward.

"Hey Ben!" Flip gleamed, turning so red it looked as though he were about to sprout horns. "Ben, did you go down there yet? You use your pass to the nurse?"

"Not another word, Flip!" Allen looked up from his papers but Flip ignored him.

"How many times have you skipped on down there today, bro?"

"Flip! One more word and you're out of here!" Allen shouted, his voice echoing out into the hall.

"Hey Ben, does the nurse ever join in on the fun and give you a hand when you go down there or at least tickle your balls or something?" Then Flip stuck his tongue out and acted like he was jerking off with both hands.

"Flip, get the hell out of here!" Allen stood up, knocking his chair over with a loud crash as Flip ran out into the hall. Mr. Allen started to chase him down but changed his mind and moped back in.

◆

Period 3 Science. I strolled in and saw four Skaters glaring at me with laser beam eyes, wearing tee shirts advertising: *INDEPENDENT TRUCKS*; *ELEMENT BOARDS*; *SLUDGE WHEELS*; and *PROJECT BEARINGS*. They hunched together in the back of the room as our science teacher scrawled his name, *MR. RYAN*, in capital letters on the chalkboard and then turned around, staring through Coke-bottle glasses, eyeballs pingponging at us. He was bald with a thick salt and pepper beard, yellowed around his lips, with his front row of teeth jutting forward as though they were being squeezed out of his mouth.

"Oh, no you don't!" He waved his short arms in the air. "You guys, in the back of the room! I want all of you split up and sitting up here in the front! You there! You over here! And you and you! Up front in these four desks!"

The Skaters grumbled as they got up.

"What's this dude's problem anyway?"

"We didn't even do nothing yet," a huge, pale kid complained. He had short blonde hair and sharp blue eyes.

"You, what's your name?" Mr. Ryan asked him.

"Jonah."

"Jonah, I want you sitting right there behind him!" Mr. Ryan pointed at me. Jonah dropped into the desk behind me, knocking my chair.

"Who's the new kid?" Jonah shoved me again. "Turn around, bitch!"

Mr. Ryan grimaced. "As some of you may be able to read, my name is Mr. Ryan. I'm new to this school system but I am not new to teaching! Let me assure you I've seen everything! I know your types and won't hesitate to kick anyone out of my class who interrupts others who want to learn."

"We want to learn!" a kid with bleached spikes announced.

"Shut up, Ezra," said Jonah.

"What? I'm totally serious."

Mr. Ryan twisted his lips. "Yeah, we'll see."

✦

The first major fight of the school year happened during the second week. The system that had always separated these two students mistakenly placed Sonny, from the Mastery Program, next to Nate, from honors classes, in the same study hall. It was the first time they'd seen each other since the fifth grade. The two began arguing and by lunch that day they were squaring up behind the school. Nate, a six-foot tall, 200-pound lurking jock, smugly wearing his football jersey, stared at everyone with a look on his face like he just smelled a fart. Yet at only five feet and 100 pounds, Sonny had charisma. He was a tough, ugly little son-of- a-bitch who was a skater but looked more like some 1950's greaser with Elvis Presley sideburns. Sonny's face was covered with a bubbly layer of acne, and his small but muscle-bound arms were covered with webs of thick blue veins. Ropey scars shined on his legs, boasting old injuries from falling off skateboards.

Nate stood, sneering down at Sonny, as if he was better than most kids, especially Sonny or anyone else in the Mastery Program. Nate seemed more than happy to make an example out of Sonny, though only half his size. The Jocks stood on one side and the Skaters on the other, both cheering for their boy. The Skaters groaned when Nate threw the first punch, hitting Sonny squarely in the chest and knocking him back. Sonny grimaced and danced back in, swinging and trying to get close enough to return some punishment, but Nate used his longer reach to keep the fight cheap and pounded jabs down on Sonny's face from a distance. Sonny tried to swing back but couldn't get close enough to reach the larger boy, and Nate went on to pummel Sonny for another thirty seconds.

"It's alright Sonny, you still got this!" Jonah tried to talk him through it.

"That kid is so dead!" someone growled.

"Shut up or it's gonna be you and me next!"

When Sonny looked dazed enough, Nate saw his chance and shot forward, picked the smaller guy up and tried to toss him over a short fence that ran along the edge of a twelve-foot drop onto the maintenance driveway below. With his body hanging halfway over the fence, Sonny hooked a leg on each side and squeezed them together to keep himself from being shoved over the embankment. Nate gritted his teeth and pushed upward, straining to end the fight by dropping the kid onto the cement below, but Sonny wasn't about to let go. Nate glared up and then took a step forward, trying to wedge his body completely under Sonny but, as he changed his footing, he slipped, falling to one knee.

That was all Sonny needed. He pushed his body straight up and hopped to the ground like a gymnast. Quickly, Sonny fought his way to the inside, moving his arms like two lightening fast cobras on the strike. When he got close enough, he began to hop, landing two jabs on every pounce. One-two, one-two, one-two. Sonny threw lefts and rights and landed sixty punches in thirty seconds. Nate was stunned. He thrashed about like a stupefied Frankenstein, no longer protecting himself but throwing punches in slow motion compared to his tiny opponent. The Skaters went crazy as the Jocks faded back.

"HISS-HISS. HISS-HISS!" Sonny went, every time he threw a flurry of punches.

"HISS-HISS. HISS-HISS!" was all we could hear besides the dull slaps to Nate's face, which was beginning to puff up with big red welts. Eventually knocked senseless, he held his arms down by his side as Sonny bounced up and down, hissing and punching the bigger guy's head like it was a speed bag.

The Preps, who gathered for the show, began to yell at Nate. "Come on Nate, you lazy fuck! Get back in there!

"Don't go out like that!" shouted his jock buddies. Nate was making them look bad. They booed while the Skaters cheered, but then a stoned-out cretin ran out and stood between them.

The hippie pointed at Nate, "Are you done?" Nate nodded his head and Sonny raised his fists triumphantly as our cheers rang out.

But the majority of the school didn't like seeing a jock in a football jersey getting his ass kicked by a skater.

"How did that happen? You're ten times the size of him!" The Jocks complained and turned their backs to him when Nate slumped over speechless. Meanwhile, the Skaters grabbed Sonny and congratulated him while Jonah tried to pick him up.

"We thought you were in trouble for a minute there!" Jonah smiled. "I thought I was gonna have to jump in!"

"Yeah, I was wondering when you were gonna stop fucking around and kick his ass for real!" said Ezra.

"Watch this!" Sonny walked over to Nate and admired the damage he'd caused. Nate's lips puffed out and his left eye was half-closed. "Now you watch what you say! About me or whatever class I'm in!"

✦

Period 4 Spanish class. There was a knock on the door and a student told Mrs. Nowak that she had an emergency phone call down in the office. She panicked, put a student in charge of our class, and ran out of the room. That must have been the way they still did things in Poland cause Mrs. Nowak was part of the Foreign Teacher Exchange Program. I looked around the room, sensing the lack of authority. I had to make my move sooner or later to show the Skaters what was up.

The student put in charge of our class was a girl who spoke in class only when Mrs. Nowak called on her, and then she'd always blush and whisper the correct answer. I had been waiting for a chance to make my move and now seemed to be it.

"Anybody ever read *Lord of the Flies*?" I asked, getting up and looking at the Skaters.

"Yeah sure," said Sonny.

"Sit your ass down," said Jonah. "Nobody wants you to teach class."

"I read that last year in English and it sucked," said Ezra.

"Naw, it wasn't bad," Flip admitted.

"Are you kidding? It was great!" I climbed up on top of the tall radiator box, so I could reach the sliding windows that ran high along the wall. "There were no adults on the island so all the kids went crazy." I stood up and looked out to see the view.

"Are you gonna jump?" Jonah laughed.

Our classroom was on the second floor of our school building. Across the way were the sports concession stand and the football field bleachers. Since there were no screens on the large windows, I decided to look for things to throw out. First, I started small and threw out some pens, and then moved on to the chalkboard erasers, and finally grabbed a box of Spanish audiotapes and began to chuck them out, one at a time. The Skaters looked at each other, not exactly knowing if they were impressed. I could tell I needed to do something more attention getting, so after I ran out of tapes, I threw the tape player out, too. The tape player bounced off the concession stand's roof and shattered on the concrete below. I looked back at the class to see half of them grinning while the nerd girl and the others looked completely horrified. The Skaters began to pound on their desks.

"Throw something else!" a dark-haired skater named Brody yelled. I did a little dance, spun around once, and then looked around for more things to throw.

"Lord of the Flies!" I shouted and then went for the box of Spanish VHS tapes.

"These were boring. I'll have to get rid of them!" I threw the whole box out at once. Next, I unplugged the VCR.

"You don't have the balls," Flip said but Sonny disagreed.

"No, he's gonna throw it. Watch."

That also shattered into a hundred pieces below. I threw out some textbooks but they were boring in comparison, so I scanned the room and my eyes landed on a large globe.

"No, he isn't," laughed Sonny. "This kid's crazy!"

I picked it up over my head and Flip and Ezra jumped up and stood on the radiator so they could peer out the windows to get a better look. I carried the globe across the room and placed it on the windowsill. I climbed up, gave it a shove, and watched it hurtle down and then collapse like a giant egg on the concrete below. I jumped back down and snatched the dusty, overhead projector out of the corner of the room and then chucked that out, too.

Meanwhile, in the science building across the courtyard, a class saw the many things flying out of our window. They started pointing to each other until the teacher noticed and got on the intercom with the main office, who must have figured out pretty quickly the classroom in question.

I looked around the room for one last thing that I could throw. I had actually picked it out from the beginning but hadn't worked up the guts until now. The class television was the right choice for the grand finale.

"Damn Kelly! Not the TV!" grinned Sonny.

"Yeah!" laughed Ezra. "Whatever you do Kelly, don't throw the TV!"

"Oh yeah? Give me a hand lifting it up!" I said, and we carried it over to the radiator and set it down.

The kids either gasped or cheered me on as I climbed up, picking it back up and placing it on the ledge of the window. I raised it off the ledge and then turned it sideways before tilting it through the opening and watching it drop. It fell fast and then exploded on the ground with a loud sonic "BOOM!"

"Holy shit!" I exclaimed, hands covering my surprised face, momentarily scared at what I had actually done.

"Shit! They're coming! They're coming!" Brody hissed, who'd been playing lookout at the door.

I slammed shut the window and we all hurried back to our seats, just as a group of teachers, the assistant principal, and the principal bolted into our room, looking around, very panicked.

The class sat dead quiet, almost frozen. The good kids held their breaths and stared down into their books while pretending to read. There was no sound but dead air, not one kid turned a page or dropped a note on their blank worksheets. I sat there, like the others. The adults were rather confused but slowly filed back outside and huddled together in the hall. From time to time, one returned to nervously peer back into the room, completely baffled as they whispered to each other.

A moment later, our Polish exchange teacher bounded up the stairs, ran up to the administrative group, and froze. Her big blue eyes bulged and her curly hair never looked so tight. The adults scanned the room for any gesture that might give any one of us away. After a while they left abruptly, except for Mrs. Nowak, who took a deep breath and smoothed the front of her dress. Then she walked to the front of the room, trying to hide her horror as she proceeded with the lesson exactly where she had left off.

The Skaters stole glances at each other as the rest of the class pretended that nothing out of the ordinary had happened. No, someone had not just thrown half of the classroom out the window. When Brody caught Ezra's eye, the two of them began to crack up, then Sonny, and then Flip. Jonah refused to give in, staring blankly at Mrs. Nowak. He glanced back at me with a hard look, until finally we both cracked up as Mrs. Nowak continued to ignore us.

That day at lunch, Jonah motioned me over.

"Sit with us, Kelly."

"Yeah, that shit was off the hook!" said Sonny.

"I can't believe you got away with that." Brody shook his head. "They just acted like it never happened."

"That's how I roll."

✦

Sean walked out of the school with his head thrown back, shoving his way through the crowd like he was eight feet tall. A little nerd scurried in front of him, and Sean reached out and slapped him as he climbed into the school bus.

"Ow." The dork rubbed his head, glanced back at Sean, but then slipped off the bottom step.

Sean laughed. "Have a nice trip?"

The little nerd scrambled up the steps and ran past the bus driver to grab a seat.

Sean continued to laugh until I bumped into his shoulder.

"You better watch it!" Sean lowered his eyebrows and tried to look tough.

"What are you going to do about it?"

"Hey Sean, get in the bus and stop giving those kids hell!" The fat bus driver laughed, scratching his beard and pushing back his long, greasy hair under his red bandanna.

"I hate that kid!" Sean flicked me off. "Go get on your retard cart! Check this kid out, Dennis. He rides the handi-van. Somebody get him a helmet!"

Dennis wheezed, his fat rolls shaking with laughter as he bent over his steering wheel. I shoved Sean sideways and he fell against the bus.

"Hey!" Dennis shouted. The kids jumped out of their seats and pressed their faces to the windows as the bus driver began rocking his body, trying to wrench himself from behind the steering wheel.

"Hey!" Dennis hollered. "Hey, knock it off!"

"Shut up, fat man!" I barked as Sean jumped to his feet and started swinging. We moved along the side of the bus, trading punch for punch, clobbering each other as the kids stuck their heads out the windows and screamed. The other bus drivers blared their horns, trying to signal the school, but the bus attendants had already gone back inside the building. Dennis managed to free himself from behind the wheel and jumped down the steps, bouncing the bus up and down. I kept my fists doubled, faked left, and hit Sean with a right cross.

"Get em, Sean!" Dennis sucked wind and Sean fired a hook to my jaw. I danced backwards to stay on my feet with a ringing sound in my head. "Hit him, Sean!" When Sean glanced over his shoulder, I stepped on his foot and shoved him backwards.

"Hey you!" Dennis yelled. "That's enough. You get over here!"

"Hell no!"

"Did you hear me? Get the hell over here!"

"Uh-uh," I said and jogged through the diesel fumes of eight or nine busses waiting to depart. The farther away I got away from those who witnessed the scuffle, the better off I was.

At the front of the bus line, I boarded the van where our red-faced driver, Horseface, wailed, "What the heck is going on back there?" She stared at me cross-eyed, her short black hair in spit curls.

"Beats me," I shrugged. "A fight or something."

She jerked her head back and forth, twisting to look out the window behind her. "What's with all the honking?" She waved her hands at the driver behind her. "Jesus, alright already!" She put the van into gear and then led the bus procession out of the parking lot.

✦

"You want me to slap your fucking teeth out?" A football player with tobacco dip shoved into his lower lip twisted my shirt into a knot and then lifted me off the ground like I was a bag of potato chips. "You think I'm gonna let you get away with that?" Behind him were the banners for Friday's big game:

GO BOBCATS!
KILL THE WOLVES!

"Get away with what?" I asked.

"You think you can rough up my little brother?" he shouted in my face with his putrid, chewing tobacco breath. "You got nothing to say now!"

"Who? Sean?"

"Yeah!"

"He's a piece of shit who picks on midgets."

Marc knocked my head back against the wall.

"Whip his skinny ass, Marc, and let's go to lunch. I'm starving!" his friend, a big, bald footballer said.

Marc twisted my shirt into a tighter knot. "Let's see how tough you are! Outside!" The bell rang and students filed out of the gym with two coaches behind them. Marc dropped me onto my feet.

"What the hell is going on here?" a woman coach shouted, twirling a whistle on a lanyard.

Marc grinned embarrassedly. "Nothing–nothing, I swear to God!"

"Yeah, what the hell is this, Marc?" The man took off his sunglasses. "Do you want to miss another game?"

"Hey, Coach Wilson, I, uh, we were–I was–," he stammered.

"You alright, kid?" the woman coach asked me.

"Yeah."

"Good. Then beat it," she said.

"He's fine, Coach Denver," Baldy tried to smooze her with a smile. "We were just messing around with the stupid freshman. Come on!"

"Sure you were," Denver said.

◆

"So then what?" Dr. Gildmore asked.

"I walked away."

"Yes, and then?"

I leaned forward. "What would you have done, Gildmore?"

"I would have told the teachers right there on the spot."

I rolled my eyes. "I knew you'd say that."

"But you didn't."

"I didn't what?"

"You didn't tell the teachers."

"Nope." I shook my head.

"Because you're not a rat?"

"Something like that."

"You shouldn't have started more problems with that kid."

"Sean the Moron was in the honors class! Honors, can you believe that?"

"So?" Gildmore asked. "What do you want me to say?"

"I hated him!"

"And that bothered you that he was in the honors class?"

"Yeah, because he didn't *earn* it. He was just one of the elite."

"Well you can't blame him for everything," Dr. Gildmore sighed. "And what did you do next?"

"I went home and looked for a weapon."

"I bet that solved everything."

◆

My mother collected antiques, but the only thing that got my attention was this old billy club. It was a police baton, the type English cops carried a hundred years ago. It was made of wood, with its center drilled out and filled with heavy lead. A leather strap, attached to the grooved handle, could be wrapped around the wrist. My mom kept it around as a decoration but now I needed it for what it was made–protection. I dropped it into my backpack but it stuck out the top, so I had to hang my baseball cap on it and that's how I carried it to school. At the end of the day, I went to the boys' restroom before detention started and washed my hands. *89-90 Varsity Football Kicks Ass* had been written on the wall in big, black letters, but painted over it in sharp graffiti style was **LEECH MOB STOMPS**.

"Hey kid! I've been looking all over for you." A faded Stoner in a black Zeppelin shirt stood in the doorway. "Marc says he wants to talk to you."

"Yeah," I said, tensing for the baton.

"Easy kid, I'm just a messenger."

"Where is he?"

"Outside. I'll walk you over."

"I don't know." I hesitated. "I have detention."

"Just go and hear what he has to say. There's no use hiding from him."

I followed the skinny kid through the old smoking lounge and out behind the gym. Every so often he'd turn around to make sure I was still there. We rounded the corner where Marc and Baldy were standing, already suited up for football practice, their helmets on. Maybe they'd heard about the weapon. After all, we were meeting where all the fights took place. When I got closer, Marc smiled and extended his hand.

"Hey, how ya doing there, buddy?" he asked in an overly friendly voice. I automatically reached out and shook his hand as the smile faded from his face. He began to clinch his fist, to hold me with one hand and hit me with the other.

I sprang back as he tried to punch me in the face, reached for the weapon, and clubbed Marc in the head. As he stumbled back I saw that I'd knocked his helmet sideways across his face but the last surprise was my own. The billy club bounced off Marc's helmet and ricocheted through the air, flying like a helicopter blade, hitting the ground and rolling down the hill. As Marc stumbled around, I went after the club, slipped on the grass, and went sliding down the hillside with Baldy dead on my heels. As it came within reach, I scooped up the baton and leaned to the side, winding back as Baldy stormed in from above. At the last moment, I swung the club as he jumped overhead and smashed him across his shins. He flipped through the air, landed on his back, tucked his legs in and screamed.

"Hey Baldy! Baldy, are you alright over there?" Marc straightened his helmet and yelled down to his friend.

"Naahhh," Baldy groaned. "I think he might've chipped something!"

"That's the best fullback in the region. If you fucked his leg up, I'm going to kill you!" promised Marc.

"Leave me alone or I'll break your arm next!" I warned him.

Suddenly thunder sounded in the distance as the rest of the team barreled out of the locker room and pounded towards the field, taking no notice of us. Marc took off his helmet and let it fall to the ground and roll away. He reached up slowly, touched his ear and then looked at the blood on his hand. He seemed to sway for a moment, his eyes wide and bugged with fear. "My ear's bleeding," he said, sounding more like he was asking a question.

"Are you alright?" I asked, stepping toward him.

"Fuck you!" he screamed. "Stay away from me!" A group of football players heard him yell and started to jog over. I hid the weapon in my backpack as I ran back into the school.

✦

"Was anyone seriously injured?" Doctor Gildmore asked and I shook my head. "You're lucky you didn't really hurt those boys."

"Fuck them."

"Now what was happening to your old buddy Andrew in all of this?"

"With him in the honors classes and everything, I didn't see him around too often. So while I got cooler with the Skaters, he got tighter with the Preppies by trading homework or something."

✦

"Where you been?" Andrew asked.

"I got suspended."

"For what?"

"Fighting."

Andrew shook his head, removed his glasses, and wiped his eyes. He seemed jittery about something. "Kelly, next Friday there is going to be this party and I know that you're gonna want to go along with me, right?"

"A party?" I couldn't believe my ears. "You want to go to a party?"

"Yeah, I want to meet up with this girl I've been talking to."

"What's with that necklace?" I pointed at the leather medallion around his neck, a round, black talisman with the shape of Africa in the middle, in stripes of red, black and green.

"It's a conscious band. It means a free South Africa. You heard what's going on down there?"

"No," I admitted.

"It's really messed up there."

"Can I try it on?"

"Yeah sure. It's attracting way too much attention anyway. You can even borrow it for a while."

✦

Back in science class, the Skaters greeted me, having heard bits and pieces of the rumor that was getting worse by the day.

"Mr. Hayes," Mr. Ryan interrupted my chatter to the others. "Since you are in such a talkative mood today, why not tell us why the animal cell's mitochondria are so important? I know you've probably been up all night studying and are now suffering from an information overload, but why not give it a try."

"Mitochondria are like–little red spiders or something."

"That would be a *no*, not even close."

"Hmm."

"Do you see little red spiders, Kelly?" mocked Ryan.

"Yeah, I guess sometimes I do."

"Oh, I see. Do you see them crawling all over the place maybe?"

"No, but I see them crawling all over you."

Down in the principal's office, Mr. Murphy's eyes bugged out. "You again? You were just in here! Those in-school suspensions haven't seemed to teach you a thing!"

I shrugged.

"You seem to becoming more of a problem every day."

I stared at him.

"Don't you have anything to say for yourself?"

I raised my index finger up to the side of my head and pulled the trigger.

"Yes, my feelings exactly! Get in here," he grumbled. "Don't you think I'm getting tired of this, too? Frankly, I'm sick of seeing your face in these situations!" He added, "I was just on my way out to a meeting with the Board of Ed and now I'm going to be late–again!"

"Sorry," I said, which he ignored.

"So why are you here today?" he asked and then sighed when I told him.

"I was just joking about the bugs," I maintained. "I don't really see little red bugs crawling on Mr. Ryan."

"I should hope not." He frowned. "Alright, since you were straight with me, I'll give you another week's detention, but this is your last break before I give you another out-of-school suspension. You've already had one and, according to school policy, if you get three suspensions in one year, your next problem might just be solved by expelling you from school for good. Do you understand this break I'm cutting you?"

"Yeah," I said meekly.

"Now go and sit with Mrs. Flannigan in the attendance room until your next class.

"Yeah, alright."

"And what are you wearing around your neck?" Murphy asked, putting on his glasses.

"It's a conscious band."

"A conscious what?"

"A necklace that symbolizes a free South Africa."

"I didn't know you were so political, Mr. Hayes."

✦

When students were late or missed school, they always reported to the attendance room, which also served as the in-school suspension room. The only staff member who ever manned the room was a secretary called Midge, a little old lady with a Q-tip haircut. I walked into the crowded attendance room and Midge looked up, squinting above her reading glasses that were attached to a gold chain around her neck. She stopped typing at the sight of me, letting her glasses fall from her face, and then leaned back in her chair.

"Oh my! Look who's back again–and so soon. Did you miss me, Mr. Hayes? Cause if you did, I'm sure you could find a better way to arrange to say hello."

"Yeah, I know."

"What did you do this time?"

"I told Mr. Ryan that I saw bugs crawling on him."

"Is that it?"

"Yeah."

"Well, it sounds like bullshit to me, so why don't you tell me what really happened?" Midge frowned, shook her head, and then quickly went back to typing as the Stoners began to chuckle. Most of them were older, the last of the Dead Heads, sporting tie-dyes, sandals, and floppy hats. They were glassy-eyed and permi-grinned.

Most tried to hide their walkmans under their long hair, but Midge wouldn't bother taking them away anyway. Two burnouts were rambling to each other, uninterrupted by Midge, who often took part in the conversations she allowed all day long in the in-school suspension room.

"No way, dude. I don't believe you!"

"No, really man, really! When they tried to send someone to the moon the first couple times, they ended up burning up. So the first set of moon pictures were all fakes to fool everyone into thinking we were all great and powerful."

"So you're saying we never been to the moon?"

"I didn't say that! Now they got bases on fucking PLUTO, MAN!"

"And some of you, smoking your whacky tobacky, are right there taking up permanent residence," Midge added, looking over her glasses. "Take a chair, Hayes." She raised her voice, "What are you waiting for–a host to come and seat you?"

A moment later, the door swung open and Principal Murphy walked in behind two older Skaters, telling them, "This isn't some damn country club where you two can drop in and out whenever you damn well please! You can't just drive off school grounds whenever you want. I don't care if you're hungry. That's why we serve lunch, wise-guy!" he bellowed. "I want both of you in my office first thing tomorrow morning and then I'll deal with each of you personally! Do you hear me?"

Vick turned around and fixed on the principal with his sharp eyes, one of them blackened from some recent fight, and slowly nodded his head.

"Mr. Murphy, do you remember your big meeting today?"

"Yes, Mrs. Flannigan. I just can't seem to get out of here today, with the best and brightest of Riverview to contend with, and nobody," Murphy warned the group, "better give Mrs. Flannigan any of your junk, if you know what's good for you!"

"Whatever man, we love Midge!" said Vick, who acted as though he were about to hug her. "We treat her better than you do!"

"I've heard about enough out of you, mister!"

"They'll be fine or I'll whip their hineys!" said Midge. "Now don't miss your meeting dealing with these knuckle-heads! They won't know what hit them, Mr. Murphy!"

Mr. Murphy smiled and then looked at one of the burnouts. "Wake him up! You wake up!" he shouted. "This isn't kindergarten. There's no nap time here!" Mr. Murphy walked out but then turned to glare at Vick and Casey. "Sit down!" he commanded and shut the door, but they didn't pay him any mind and instead hovered around Midge's desk as the burnout fell back asleep. Vick started to pick up a photo on her desk but Midge slapped his hand away.

"I just want to look at your daughter. She's so hot I can't help it!"

"Vick! Don't start with me, not today. I'm not in the mood. I got a lot of work to get done!"

"Sorry Midge, you know I love you."

"Yeah, yeah, yeah, but only because I let you all get away with murder." The room mumbled in agreement.

"Now take a seat. You don't want to get me fired, do ya?"

"Hell no, Midge!"

Vick looked around for a place to sit and since there was none nearby, grabbed the sleeping kid up, yanking him out of his puddle of saliva and shoveling him away. Midge stared at him with a shocked expression.

"Vick! What do you think you're doing? That was very rude!"

"What? He was drooling all over the place and Murphy told us to wake him up!"

"Vick!"

"So! He doesn't care. He can sleep anywhere!"

The kid shrugged and slumped into another desk where he dropped his head down again.

"So what's up, Midge? How's you and yours been?" asked Casey.

"Busy and overworked! As usual!"

"You still working that other job?" Vick asked.

"Sure am, boys!"

"That's not good for you. You should be taking it easy!"

"What, and leave it all to my husband so he can go for his third heart attack?" Midge answered and then went back to her typing.

Casey glared around the room and the Stoners instantly got busy doing something else. Then Casey looked at me. "What the hell are you looking at?"

I went back to my book and when I looked back up, both of them were staring. Casey held his hand up over his mouth and whispered something to Vick who asked me, "Do you know what you're wearing?"

"The conscious band?" I asked, thinking that he was just messing around.

"It's not funny, bro. You better take that shit off!" Casey threatened, pointing at my chest.

"Why? If you're a racist, that's your problem," I said.

"You're calling me a racist? You fucking poser!" Casey shouted, becoming enraged. "You don't know nothing about Africa! Black people don't want you wearing that!"

"Casey!" Midge slammed her hands down on either side of her typewriter. "Knock that off and sit down! Have you two lost your minds?"

"You probably don't even know what it means!" Vick said.

"Free South Africa," I said.

"Free from who?" Casey asked.

"From posers like you!" Vick shouted at me.

"Vick!" Midge snapped.

"What?" Vick responded in a joking manner.

"Both of you leave that boy alone!" Midge raised her voice, reached for the phone, picked it up and then slammed it back down. "He can wear that if he wants!"

"No he can't! Hill Top Posse said no whites should be wearing those things! And if we can't wear em, what makes him think he can get away with it?"

"I don't care! You boys are gonna leave me no choice–I don't want to call down to the office but I will!"

"Hill Top Posse?" I asked. "A black guy let me borrow it!"

"I don't give a damn! You wanna fuck with Hill Top?" Casey raised his voice, looking at me as if I were stupid.

"You'd wind up dead!" Vick shouted, looking as though he wanted to start brawling right there in the in-school suspension room.

"Alright Vick, Casey, get the hell out of here!" Midge screamed. "Go to the library. I'll write you both passes but don't make me call down to the office because this time, you will be expelled and that's the last thing you two boys need!" Midge was shaking as she grabbed the pass book and began to scratch out their passes, her wrinkled and boney hand moving three thousand miles an hour. "Here, take these and get the hell out!" she commanded when she had completed the two passes in record time, but they both held still, mad dogging me. "Do you boys have wax in your ears!" Midge shouted, releasing the tension and making the duo crack up.

The two sauntered over to the exit. As they passed in front of me, Casey leaned over my desk and said, "Next time I see you, I don't want to see that thing hanging around your neck, cause it looks real stupid on a white boy like you."

"Casey!"

"Sorry, Midge."

"Yeah, I bet," she said as Casey snatched the pass from her hand and stormed out.

"Thanks, Midge," said Vick as he gracefully accepted his while winking at the lady, but Midge continued to stare angrily up at him and followed him with narrow eyes as he moved out the door.

After they'd walked out, the burnouts began smiling again. "Wow man, you got some guts to stand up to those guys!"

"It's nothing. You should try it sometime."

"What's your name, man?"

"Kelly."

"So you know Vick and Casey?"

"Not really."

"Oh man!" one of the Stoners said. "Like wow man! This is better than TV!"

"Well, it was like nice knowing you, dude!" chimed in the other.

"Why?"

"Cause if I were you, I wouldn't want to get on their bad side, man."

"Oh brother!" moaned Midge, going back to her typing. "You all are worse with your rumors than old ladies on bingo night! They're just a couple of normal boys like you all. Or maybe now that I think about it," she added after a moment's thought, "none of you are normal, but they're just the same as you are anyway!"

"Maybe they're sweethearts to you cause you don't treat em like every other adult does in this school. But out there," the kid gestured to the hallway, "out there it's a different story."

Midge rolled her eyes and went back to typing.

"No really, Midge," one of the hippies continued, "most of the teachers not only don't like them but some of them, well, are kind of scared of the Leech Mob."

"The Leech Mob?" I questioned and noticed the name alone seemed to make them uneasy.

"Yeah, those kids you just mouthed off to. Wait," one laughed, turning to his friend, squinting his eyes and displaying two rows of perfectly straight but yellowed teeth. "You really don't have any idea who they are, do you?"

"Oh, this is like blowing my mind, dude!" said the little Stoner who'd been jerked out of his seat by Vick. He had remained quiet until now and was rocking back and forth and shaking his head unbelievably.

"Wait, what's you name again, dude?"

"Kelly. What's yours?"

"Ted."

I nodded my head and his boy asked, "Kelly what?"

"Hayes."

"He's that kid I heard about from fucking Norton!" he told Ted. "The bat, the kid with the fucking bat! BAM MAN!"

"Watch your mouth, Billy!" Midge warned.

"BAM MAN!" Ted echoed as they both grooved out in their heads with squinted eyes.

"Well maybe you ought to think about bringing that bat back in," Bill laughed dryly.

"Oh no you don't!" warned Midge. "I'm gonna pretend that I didn't ever hear this conversation!"

"See, that's why we love you, Midge!" said Ted.

"I must be losing my mind," she answered as she tore a sheet from the typewriter.

Chapter 3: The Keg Party

"Kelly, come on! You got to go with me. I don't want to go alone."

"Dude," I exclaimed, "you're only going there to meet what's her name."

"Lori," Andrew grinned.

"And then you're out, right?"

"Yeah."

"So what do you need me around for?" I asked, already knowing the answer. Andrew was nervous about going to this keg party alone. Besides, his parents were strict and didn't let him stay out late, so he had to say that he was sleeping over my house.

"I'm just meeting her there, on the down-low. You know what the down-low is, right?"

"Don't be stupid, Andrew."

"Right," he said, looking a bit embarrassed as he searched for the words to explain himself, with his watery eyes shifting back and forth as if he were reading a book.

"Why is she even like that?"

"Cause she's white and fine and I'm black and fat." Andrew started cackling as I slowly shook my head.

"What?" I raised my voice.

"She just doesn't want anyone to know right now."

"That's messed up," I said but he didn't care, as long as he might be able to score with this tall, blonde-haired, blue-eyed sophomore. I didn't like the secret meeting bullshit and because of that I didn't like her, but when I finally agreed, relief spread across his face. I guessed the party wouldn't be that bad, which went to show how little I knew about what was about to go down.

A group of high school seniors scored three kegs of suds and designed a party flyer that said, "DRINK TILL YA PUKE! FIVE BUCKS!" It was a little out of our league–me and Andrew had just turned 15 and neither of us had ever gone to a real party before, but when my mother went to bed, we snuck out and started hiking it. We cut through the woods, got lost in the neighborhood for a while, and then followed the music to a long stretch of cars.

As we got within sight, we saw the action. Guys howled at the moon and chased friends into the woods. Girls puked into bushes, holding back their hair. Gangs of kids were scattered everywhere, leaning against trees, making out, rolling in the leaves. Andrew went through his backpack and checked out his supplies: a thin blanket, a box of lubricated condoms, a porno mag, sex-lotion, two candles, a tiny pillow, and a flashlight. He then wickedly held up a steel ring.

"What's that?"

"It's a cock-ring," he answered.

"How do you use it?"

"I don't know. You just put it on, I guess." He giggled and dropped it into his backpack. "You think there's anything I forgot?"

"Are you sure she wants to do all this?"

"I think so. I mean, she's not a virgin and we've been talking like every night on the phone since we met. She made it sound like tonight's the night."

"Well good thinking on the blanket and the condoms, but lose the rest of that shit."

"Why?"

"Cause honestly, it makes you look like a pervert."

Andrew started cracking up again with this weird laugh he did, sounding as if he were gargling mouthwash.

I looked at him funny. "Where did you find that dick ring?"

Andrew stared at me, with all seriousness before confessing. "I found it in my dad's underwear drawer." He then started cackling again, so I pushed him away.

"Damn dude, that is some nasty shit!" I said as Andrew went into hysterics. "You'd probably use it, too!"

"Well if she asks, but I don't want to tell her it's mine!"

"Who are you gonna tell her it is, dumb ass? Duh, it's my dad's!"

"I hadn't thought of that."

"Dude, let me see that!" I said, and he rifled through his bag and then held the ring up again for me to see. Quickly I grabbed it and chucked it into the woods and wiped my hand on his shirt.

"Hey! What the fuck, man!" Andrew swore, which he rarely did. "That was my dad's! I was going to put that back, and what if he knows that it's me who took it?"

"That thing was gonna cause you more trouble than you know how to handle and, if you're smart, you'll ditch that porn mag and that weird sex lotion shit while you're at it!"

"Well, she told me to bring that stuff–told me where to order it from and everything!"

"I should have guessed," I said, shaking my head. "That girl's as horny as you! You better watch out. She'll show up wearing spiked underwear and a Lone Ranger's mask!" I warned as Andrew cackled. I then spotted the keg of beer twenty yards off. "How much money you got?"

"Seven dollars," Andrew said.

"Let's go buy some beer."

A line of kids were already waiting to fill their red plastic cups that some older guy sold on the sideline.

"Alright," Andrew said, composing himself. "I might need some if I convince her to go into the woods. I'll start thinking about bears and wolves and ..." He looked at the shadowy trees and shivered.

"Look at that kid chugging beer!" I blurted out.

We silently watched one heck of a show unfold. The skinny kid finished his cup in record time only to cut into the line to fill it up again. He tilted his head back so far as he drained off the last of the suds that he lost his balance, fell backwards, and dumped the rest of his beer on his face before sitting up, dumbfounded. He drunkenly peered into his cup, checking to see if any beer remained. An older guy walked down from the porch, tossing a can of beer over his shoulder, gripped the drunk's arm, and pulled him to his feet.

"What the hell is this? You can't make a drunk ass out of yourself and then blame us when you drive into a telephone pole!" the guy yelled.

"What are yoou–the breer police?" the skinny drunk slurred.

"We're going inside so you can sign a statement saying that no one got you drunk and whatever happens is your own damn fault!"

"But yoou wanted to see if I could match yoou breer for breer!" the kid complained.

"Nah, that wasn't me!"

"Hell yeah it was!"

"Nope, in your drunken stupor, you got it *all wrong*! Now for that contract!"

"Check out this sorry son of a bitch!" another jock said, rolling up in a Riverview football jacket. "I think we should charge him for two cups since he got himself pissed! Look at this dumb ass. He can barely stand up."

The Beer Cop grinned, shaking the kid until he was about to hurl. "So what do you have to say for yourself, fuck ball?" he asked, entertained.

"Jus-wa-more-an-I'll-begone!" the kid muttered, his eyes rolling back.

"You're already gone!" The Beer Cop shoved him away but shrugged as if he were thinking about the kid's request.

The kid caught his balance, steadied himself and then, like a magnet, was drawn back to the keg, where he cut the line again, gripped the handle and gave it a few pumps. That was when the Beer Cop's eyes bugged out. He lunged for the kid's wrist, spilling his beer and holding his hand in the air.

"This isn't even one of our cups!" the Beer Cop shouted as he and his football cronies began to shove the kid back and forth, playing catch. A moment later, the kid began to puke and the others jumped back. A thick orange oatmeal spray covered the edge of the driveway and, in anger, the Beer Cop kicked the drunk in his ass and sent him tumbling onto the grass.

"Hey Nick, get me one of the cups we're selling!" the footballer hollered over to his cup merchant.

"Why?" Nick yelled back.

"Just get me one, you fat lazy fuck!" the jock screamed back.

"Alright, take it easy already."

"Just what I thought!" The Beer Cop compared the two cups. "This punk brought this cup from home and's been drinking our beer all night without chipping in a measly five bucks!" he shouted angrily to his friends.

"Thas da one dey gravy–*hiccup*–I mean–gavey–gave me!" the kid slurred, trying to defend himself from the ground, wiping the orange oatmeal from his face.

"Well cough up the five bucks then, Spanky!" shouted the Beer Cop. "And we'll forget the whole thing ever happened!"

The kid clumsily shoved his hands in his pockets and with some difficulty retrieved his wallet, until they pulled him onto his feet and snatched it out of his hand.

"Let me see that, dickless!" the Beer Cop said, smiling and peeling open the dollar flap. "Now look at this shit. This loser doesn't even have a buck to his name!"

"So what are we going to do with him?" asked one of the Beer Cop's boys.

"Make him clean up his puke!" another answered.

"Yeah and make him pay up on Monday!" suggested Nick.

"Both! You hear that POO-BUTT? You gonna pay up and you gonna clean up! Shit for brains!" the beer guy announced, loud enough for everyone to hear. "Now go plant this loser somewhere and let him sleep it off!"

The others carried him halfway across the yard and then dropped him, where he lay with his face in the grass. A moment later another drunken soul, female, came out and sat Indian-style next to him. She held her red beer cup up over his head and drizzled her beer into his hair. He didn't move.

Unnoticed, Andrew and I had moved in closer to get a better view of the action. After all, this was our first keg party and it was proving to be far more interesting than either of us expected.

Back at the keg, kids clung to their legal red plastic, waiting for their turn to fill their cups with suds. That was when I saw Flip standing there and flirting with this cute sophomore chick. Just as she turned to pass the nozzle to him, a big, disgruntled-looking senior cut the line and snatched it out of her hand. He pumped the knob twice before aiming the tube into his cup, filling it lazily and draining off the extra yellow suds onto the ground.

Nobody in the long beer line said a thing cause Rick Brown was responsible for the entire beer supply. Now most people would've just let this incident slide on by, but most people just weren't Flip either. The longer Rick took filling his cup, the more certain Flip became that he had to do something, especially in the presence of this hot sophomore he'd been talking to. She now appeared somewhat apologetic if not embarrassed.

"Don't worry about it," she whispered.

Flip stood there, shaking his head and drinking in the situation before piping up. "Yo!" he said with a smile on his face but Rick ignored him. "Hey! I'm talking to you!"

"What!" Rick turned around and eyeballed Flip, who laughed dryly.

"Just take your time with that, you cutting bastard!"

The girl turned, surprised, as the nearby crowd grew tense and silent. Flip grinned, glancing back and forth between the girl and Rick, who contemplated his next move, raising the cup slowly to his lips and taking a drink.

"Didn't your mother ever teach you any manners, you selfish bastard?" Flip added, still grinning.

"What did you say?" Rick's eyes bugged open in surprise.

"I think you heard me!"

Rick tried to look entertained to hide his shock and glanced over at his jock buddies, before grilling this short, Puerto Rican kid. "Yeah, I heard you. I just couldn't believe you're so damn stupid!"

"You don't walk up and cut everybody! That's some flat out, rude ass shit, man! God-damn!"

"Shut the fuck up, faggot! The only reason your little punk ass is drinking beer is because of me. Who the hell ya think got these kegs here, asshole?"

"Let me guess. You?" Flip answered.

"That's right, you fat little fuck, I did! That's why everyone is drinking and feeling good tonight and that's why I get to cut anybody I want, cause it's my beer, freshman!"

Rick's eyes bugged out, appearing dangerously close to losing it, but Flip just exclaimed in a high voice, "What! We don't owe you shit! We all paid for this beer and from what I see, you're making a lot of dough off us, so you should be glad we showed up!" The crowd laughed as Flip continued to run his mouth. "So get your ass in the back of the line like everybody else! You ain't special!" Flip looked around at everyone as he chuckled, amusing himself as much as the crowd, who laughed more freely.

"If you don't like it, why don't you try scoring your own booze and throw your own goddamned party!" Rick spit.

"Shit!" Flip drawled slowly, never knowing when to shut up. "I drink whenever I damn well please! I can get liquor to fall down from the sky! All I got to do is a little liquor dance like this, UH! Like that, AH!" Flip began to dance. "Are you seeing these moves I got? Are you taking notes, you old motherfucker?" Flip shadowboxed in circles in front of the astounded Rick. "What are you gonna do? You might be all big and bad around your sucker friends but you ain't shit to me!" Flip said, gesturing at all the football players who jumped off the porch and circled around.

"What the fuck, bro?" A big, acne-covered steroid cretin stepped forward.

"No, I got this one, Gary." Rick held up a hand.

"Shut him up, Rick!"

"Yeah, kick his ass, Rick!" shouted another, as Rick whipped off his all-star, varsity jacket.

"That's some tough talk for such a fat, little shit! That's right, I cut you in line, Pillsbury Doughboy, so deal with it!"

Rick shoved Flip, who stumbled back but then danced forward, bobbing his head and attempting to fake Rick out. Rick lined his fist up and then fired a straight jab at Flip, who sidestepped it and then swung one of his own. It was wide and only caught air, but he followed it up with a quick left fist, hitting Rick as he returned a weird hammer punch. Flip shook it off, staying light on his feet as he threw a couple of jabs. He connected, ducked a hook, dipped around an uppercut, and started looking pretty good out there. But Rick suddenly raged forward, accepting a few hits before tackling Flip. A loud thump sounded when their flesh collided against concrete. They reeled off the driveway onto the grass, as a swarm of drunk kids came running from all sides, circling the two. Clawing one another to catch a better glimpse, the crowd drove Andrew and me back. Between their clamors for more violence, I could hear Rick and Flip grunting and gasping for air.

I wondered if Rick wasn't killing Flip, so I ran past the huddle of kids and jumped on the porch to see over everyone's heads. Rick had straddled Flip and was taunting him in between punching him in the face, but Flip continued to fight, even in this predicament. Flip could barely jab, but kept on trying as Rick easily pounded down on Flip's face every few seconds.

"Are you done?" Rick screamed.

Flip muttered, "Not–even–close." So Rick hit him again, then again.

Finally an older kid pulled Rick off Flip saying, "Alright, that's enough! You got him, Rick!"

When Rick stood up, I saw that Flip had marked him good. Rick's left eye was starting to close up and his lip was bloodied. I wish I could say Flip held his own and walked away with that smile still on his face but, for all Flip's showmanship and guts, the audience turned on Flip as fast as they had encouraged his rebellion.

Flip looked up from the ground, confused upon seeing their quick reversal. He painfully rose to his feet, dusting off his pants, wiping the blood from his eyes, and searching the crowd for a friendly face. When none could be found, he turned from the wild-eyed goons and began to limp away, as the crowd now cursed him for all the bravery he had shown. A handful descended on him like vultures, getting in the warrior's bruised face and screaming at him to get the hell off the property.

"That's so messed up," I thought and followed Flip as he trudged away, down the driveway and onto the dark street, "Flip! Hey Flip!" I ran up behind him and he spun around with fists raised until he recognized me.

"Oh, what's up, Kelly?" Flip mumbled through tight lips. His left eye had already swelled shut and his nose trickled blood. "I didn't see you down there."

"Hey man—you got him pretty good! His eye is all cut to shit!"

"For real?" Flip asked, smiling.

"Hell yeah, man, that's messed up. All those kids back there, they're stupid!"

"Fuck em," said Flip.

"Yeah, fuck em," I said, not knowing what else to say.

Flip looked at me, raising his eyebrows but I couldn't really measure his expression through his one good eye. "Look man, I got to go," he said, not wanting me to notice the tears that stung his eyes.

"Yeah alright, I just wanted to tell you, good fight, man!" Flip nodded and then turned and continued down the road. "See you in class," I called out but he didn't reply.

Back at the party, I saw that Lori had found Andrew and they'd moved into the shadows at the edge of the woods. She was swaying on her feet, holding onto him and whispering in his ear. Then she ran off to join a group of girls as Andrew scanned the crowd, saw me, and walked back over with this huge grin plastered to his face.

"So, I guess you're leaving."

"Yeah, after she talks to her friends."

"You're one lucky kid! She's hot!"

"I know," said Andrew, cackling again. "Here she comes."

"Andrew, if you really want to, uh, get lucky, try not to laugh until it's over."

He grinned and I watched them disappear into the night. Then I was alone.

I decided to head back to the keg, where a guy sat posted in a folding chair, guarding the stash of red plastic cups.

"All I got is three dollars," I told him, "but I won't drink that much."

The older kid looked at me for a moment, then shrugged, and handed me a cup. "I was your age once," he said, sounding as if he was my grandfather or something. "Save it for some gum or something—trust me, you'll need it."

I approached the keg, picked up the nozzle, and pressed the lever but nothing came out. I held it up and looked at it. "It's empty or something."

"Ya got to pump the beer!" the guy slurred.

"Here, I'll show you." A girl walked up and smiled, grabbed the knob and gave it a few pumps. I stared at her until she raised her eyebrows. "It's all set now, boy." She took the spout and directed it toward my cup and poured the frothing beer in. I hit it, not realizing how thirsty I was until I had guzzled it down. "Thirsty?" She laughed and then helped herself, but when I began to talk with her, she lost interest and stumbled off. I went for another and downed that too, before filling my cup up a third time.

"Hey kid, get away from dere!" the guy smeared his words. "You're gonna get sick!" He then motioned for me to sit down beside him. "Besides, you're disturbing my—customers," he belched.

I sat in the empty chair beside him and finished half my beer. "Do you think cows get high when they eat grass?"

The kid looked at me, contemplating what I asked and, after taking a drink, laughed as the beer poured out of his mouth and ran down his chin.

"Is this your first beer?"

"Yup!"

He nodded his head slowly. "I remember my first beer," he said, talking like he was eighty years old again. "I remember."

I sauntered over to the keg to pound another beer and then stumbled towards the woods to take a leak when I saw the cops cruising in. I walked back to the keg and sat back down in the folding chair. I tapped the guy who now was almost passed out and pointed to the two shadowy figures heading up the driveway, holding their flashlights. He jumped up and took off running, overturning his chair as he booked away.

Now the scene turned 180. Kids started screaming and running around— either giddy or terrified, not knowing where to turn. Some banged on the door to the house, begging to be let inside so they could hide. Others took to the woods. But I just sat there, watching. The cops strolled into the light, shaking their heads at all the commotion their presence caused.

"Party's over!" one cop yelled towards a group of older guys sitting on the porch. "Frankly, we're getting sick of the complaints from the neighbors!"

"Hey you!" Another cop pointed at me. "That wouldn't be beer, would it?"

"No." I shook my head, looking down drunkenly into my half-filled cup. "It's apple juice."

"Apple juice?" the cop snickered before slapping it out of my hand.

"Hey!" I slurred. "Now you owe me five bucks!"

"Kid, if you paid five bucks for that, you shouldn't be drinking in the first place."

I shrugged and the cop motioned for me to stand up. "Alright kid, you're free to go."

"What?"

"Get going to wherever you're going!" the other cop snapped and shoved me out toward the road.

I glanced around, seeing more cop cars at the front of the house, so I held back in the shadows near the far edge of the driveway. A crowd of older kids were slowly making their way down to their cars

"It's going on midnight!" a cop's voice boomed. "You've had your fun. Go home and sleep it off but you better not drink and drive! Cause we'll just pull you over and take you to jail!" he warned.

Then a voice shouted from somewhere in the crowd, "Make up your god-damned mind! Do you want us to stay, or do you want us to drive home drunk? Asshole!"

"Who said that?" a young rookie cop screamed. He jumped into groove, shining his flashlight and charging around to find the culprit, picking out the drunkest kid he could find as a scapegoat.

"Let's break this party up, kids. Please meet up with your designated driver," an older, more experienced cop said, making the suggestion that cleared both his conscience and the drunken kids' likely crimes.

The cops strolled past all the commotion to the front door, banged on it, and waited. A moment later, it slowly opened and a tall, thin guy swayed in the doorway, looking hesitantly over his shoulder at those behind him.

"Are you hosting this party?" the cop asked, but the kid glanced behind him as if to seek counsel from his friends. "Face me—not your friends! I'm talking to you, not them!" growled the cop.

"Uhhhhhh. What do you mean—hosting?" The kid scratched his head, bewildered as his friends laughed behind him.

"Alright, real funny. Whose house is this?" the cop asked, pushing open the door and glaring at the boys.

"Uh…"

"Tell em!"

"Shut up!"

"You shut up!"

The kids began to push each other so the cop stepped forward and shoved them apart. "No more games! Whoever belongs to this house, I want him front and center, right now! In fact, I want all you clowns out here, lined up! That's right, all you guys who think this is some big joke! Outside here right now!"

The group of older Jocks anxiously stumbled outside and lined up on the porch.

"Now I'm going to ask you one more time and if I don't find out who's throwing this party–I'm hauling you all in for your parents to fish out! Now whose house is this?"

"Stubby, get out here!" one of the Jocks on the porch yelled. They waited. "He might be passed out."

"Go in and get him!"

An older, fat kid who looked almost retarded drunk and half in the bag was dragged outside and propped up by his friends. "Hey! I was sleeping. What do you want?" he complained before seeing the cops. "Oh, shit!" Stubby tried to uncross his eyes and focus on the cops.

"It took you long enough to get your butt out here!"

"Uh–yup. I mean, no?" the kid asked, looking nervously at his buddies who were either bracing him on his feet or bending over laughing. "Wait, what's the question exactly?"

"All of you shut up!" the cop yelled and then peered directly into the heavy kid's grill. "Is this your place of residence?"

"Huh?"

"Go on Stubby, tell em the truth," one of the more sober kids said.

Strengthened, Stubby turned, faced the cop and said, "Uhhh maybe. I mean yeah, yeah, whatever you want. I don't care."

The cop stood there, stone-faced with an icy cold stare. "I'm going to ask you one last time before I make your life a living nightmare. Now is this your house?"

"I mean, it's not my house, not exactly, you know? I mean it's my mom and dad's house."

One of the cops turned away and cracked a smile, which pissed off the second cop even more, while the third kept a poker face, flipping open a notepad.

"Where are your parents, son?"

"On vacation, I think."

"Vacation? What's your name, boy?"

The fat kid took a deep breath. "Stubby."

"Your parents named you Stubby?" the cop exclaimed as Stubby's friends continued to snicker into their fists.

"The rest of you shut your fat mouths or I'm going to drag you all to jail for interfering with a police investigation!" the pissed-off cop screamed, wiping the smiles off each of their faces. "Now what's your birth name, wise guy?"

"Earl. Earl Davis," the fat boy said weakly.

"Well Earl, this party is over. Do you understand me?"

"Yes, sir."

"So that means if we get one more call here tonight, we are holding you responsible. Is that clear?"

"Okay," Stubby said, focusing on the melee around him, his fear apparently sobering him up a couple of decimals.

"Are these your guests?" the smooth cop asked.

"Yeah, everyone's my guest!"

"You don't learn so well, do ya big boy?" the older cop said, shaking his head. "Everybody is leaving except for your personal guests, or in other words, these drunk, idiot friends of yours. Everybody else is gone! If this party doesn't stay broken up, you are spending the rest of the weekend in jail! Are we crystal? Now I want you and you, over here, emptying this keg into the leaves!"

The cops stepped off the porch, shoving kids along, while one got on a bullhorn and chased the remaining kids out of the woods. "Who are you, the special people who don't have to listen to police officers? Do you want to go to jail and get your parents' cars towed?"

Dazed, Stubby swayed on his feet, staring at the cop cars' strobe lights before running to the bushes to puke. The police found more stragglers behind the house, who ran out hysterically shouting, "POLICE RAID!" I cut across the yard, avoiding the crowds and began walking along the edge of the street. Carloads of kids flew by, howling out the windows. The cops had done what they were called to do and now almost every kid in Riverview was now out on the streets, driving around drunk.

A flashlight flicked on and a figure walked toward me, shining the light in my face. "Where are you headed?"

"Same as everyone else, back home."

"Oh yeah, where's that?" He got in my path, stopping me.

"Not far. I can walk there easily."

"I asked you where!" he snapped so I told him.

"How old are you?"

"Uh...fifteen."

"Come with me." The young cop sighed and marched me back towards the house. We approached another police officer, who busily shined his flashlight into every car that passed.

"I caught this one up the road, Sarge. He's fifteen, looks two sheets to the wind and says he has about a five mile walk ahead of him."

"You know we had a kid die that way." He looked thoughtfully over at us. "Hang on a second." Sarge was a heavy man with an almost pleasant face. He turned around and monitored the next string of cars that passed, one of them peeling out after driving by. The Sarge picked up his radio and keyed the mike, "Car 77, come in."

"Car 77, go ahead."

"We got a blue Chevy, SUV, four occupants. Let's see what their story is, besides the bad habit of burning rubber next to the law."

"10-4, Sergeant," the voice came back and then a cruiser lit up, pulling out of a side street and taking off down the road.

"You mind posting here for a minute, Brad? Just check out the drivers, make sure they don't look too out of it. I'll be back in five."

"10-4"

"You! Follow me!" Sarge pointed at me and walked back towards the party while speaking into his radio. "Dispatch, this is Unit 50. Do you copy?"

"Dispatch, go ahead."

"Do we have any available units? I need a minor shuttled back to the station so his parents can be notified."

"Standby."

"Please no," I begged him.

"Why?"

"Cause my mother will kill me!"

"You should've thought of that before." He frowned. "What street do you live on?"

"Stag's Point Road."

"Hey, Kelly! We'll give you a ride!"

The Sarge turned around and looked at the old, gray sedan that was parked across the street with its motor running.

"Oh hey, Rick. How's it going, fellas? Hell of a game you played last weekend, but it's been a tough season after losing so many players."

"Yeah, you're telling us."

Sarge smiled. "You're not planning on hanging around, are you?"

"Nah. We're just waiting for Kelly over there!"

Sarge turned around and glanced at me, and then back to Rick. "Are you serious?"

"Yeah." Rick smiled. "We'll bring him home."

"Have you boys been drinking? Cause this car smells 90 proof!"

"Those two clowns passed out in the back have, but I'm the designated driver."

The Sarge unclipped his pen. "Follow this without moving your head, just your eyes. He began moving it back and forth, up and down, in front of Rick's face when a car sped past honking its horn with a girl in the passenger seat, raising her sweater and flashing everyone.

"God-dammit!" Sarge grabbed his radio. "We got a green Honda that needs to be checked out!"

The radio sounded out, "Stand-by! Dispatch to any available unit. Please come in."

"Sarge, you look like you got your hands full," Rick grinned. "We'll take the kid home."

"Have you been fighting, Rick?" Sarge asked.

"A little."

"Looks like he got you good."

"Well, you should've seen him."

"That's what they all say," Sarge chuckled back. "I don't want you guys drinking any more booze. Rick, I hope you're not providing alcohol for these kids."

"Hell no! Most of these kids shouldn't even be here!"

"Yeah alright, but none of you should be drinking either. It's not good for you!" The sergeant turned and looked at me. "Alright get over here, Kelly. These boys have offered to drive you home."

"Why can't I just walk?" I protested, having no idea why Rick would want to drive me home.

"Cause that's not the way we do things around here!" Sarge stared angrily at me. "We had a kid die that way. A motorist accidentally hit him walking home in the middle of the night."

"Just get in, Kelly. I'm going right past your house anyway."

"No, I'm alright."

"It's not up for debate, kid! It's either them or you're taking a ride down to the station and waiting for mommy!" He stepped out into the road and shined his light at the next string of cars driving towards the party. "Turn around and go back where you came from! Party's over!" Thinking he was distracted, I tried to sneak away. "Hey you! Get back here!" He stormed over, grabbed my shoulder and shouted, "You don't run from police officers. Do you understand me?"

"Give the kid a break. It's not his fault he's a stupid freshman!" Rick called out.

Sarge snickered, and then a voice came across his radio. "Sergeant, we don't have any available units as of now. All officers are out on code."

"Alright, cancel that."

"Which call, sir?" Dispatch responded.

Then another officer chimed in, "Unit 77. Sarge, do you copy?"

"God-dammit!" Sarge swore and then keyed the mike. "Go ahead."

"The driver of the blue Chevy seems very intoxicated. Should we administer roadside tests?"

"I can see you from here. Stand by." Sarge began walking down the street absentmindedly before turning and glaring at me. "Get in that goddamn car!"

"Okay, I'm going, I'm going." I walked toward Rick's car as Sarge raised his radio again. I opened the door as Rick reached up and flipped off the interior light.

"Keep the bottle down!" Rick whispered to the big guy, slumped over in the front seat. Everyone wore hats or hoods and looked passed out but Rick, who turned around and grinned. "Close the door, kid. We got an open bottle in here!"

I glanced back at Sarge, who stood there watching, so I got in slowly and Rick hit the gas and we peeled out. His foot was on the floor and we sped off with my door still open. A cop shouted as we flew past, "Slow down!"

"Sorry!" Rick called out the window and then hissed into the back seat. "Shut that door!" as the large guy beside me suddenly moved, violently shoving my head forward as he threw his body over me to reach and slam the door. The pain from his weight shot through my neck as if it were about to snap. At the first stop sign, I tried jumping out, but he grabbed my shirt and dragged me back in. When he sat back up, he pulled back his hood and laughed. It was Marc.

The guy in the front seat spun around, "Boo!" It was Baldy, laughing hysterically.

"We got you now!" threatened the kid to the far left, who leaned forward and pushed back his hat so I could see it was my old buddy Sean.

I slumped back as they laughed their asses off and Rick glanced back.

"You're dead, bitch!" He hit the gas again, passed two cars while tearing around a corner and then swerved back into the right lane, narrowly missing an oncoming car. Baldy beat on his chest and howled, alcoholic fumes wafting throughout the car. He raised a half empty fifth of vodka to his mouth, took a swig, and then passed it to Marc.

"You want a nip?" Marc smirked. "Cuz ya gonna need it."

I sat back letting my fear play itself out, realizing that there was nothing I could do to stop this from happening. They were going to kick my ass sooner or later. At least now I was drunk.

"Now where do you live?" Baldy asked.

"There." I pointed to the next house we sped past as both Marc and Sean chuckled darkly.

Baldy turned around and snarled at me drunkenly, "You didn't really think we'd let you get away with that shit you pulled, did you?"

"No, I guess not," I mumbled.

"Let's see how tough you are without your nightstick, fag!" jeered Baldy.

"You're so fucking dead, man!" spit Marc. "Even the police don't give a fuck about you! We should just do the world a favor and get rid of you!"

"Fuck you!" I answered.

"What?" Rick turned and looked at me funny. "Now I see why you hate this kid!" He glared into the rear-view mirror as we skipped through a red light and swerved onto the entrance ramp for the highway.

"Take it easy Rick. We don't wanna get pulled over!" Baldy said.

"Are you kidding? All the Riverview cops are back there at the party!"

"What about the state cops?"

"Don't worry, nuthin's gonna stop us from whippin' his ass tonight! It's payback time and he deserves everything he's gonna get!"

Marc leaned forward. "Hey Rick, play it cool anyhow." His voice was edgy. "I don't want to get arrested or anything."

We stayed on the highway for what seemed like fifteen minutes before tearing off an exit ramp and skidding to a stop. Then we whipped down a dark wooded road. If not for the full moon breaking through the heavy tree branches, it would have been pitch black.

"Enough of this garbage!" Rick reached up, turned on the interior light, ejected the rap tape and blasted some metal. Rick howled out the window as Baldy began punching the roof of the car, glancing back at me from time to time to see how bad they'd psyched me out.

Just how far these clowns planned on taking this was anybody's guess. If I got lucky, they would just leave me out in the middle of nowhere but I doubted that. Baldy flipped on the light and turned to say something but the music was too loud.

"Come closer!" he screamed above the noise so I leaned in.

"What?" I asked as he clipped me in the mouth. They all laughed their asses off as Rick blasted the stereo again as we drove farther out into the country.

The songs grew faster and crazier, riling them into a frenzy. Marc slammed into my side. I bounced off him and into the door, trying to brace myself, but he grabbed my neck and pounded my head sideways against the window. I grabbed hold of his hands, caught one of his fingers, bent it backwards, and tried to twist it off his hand.

"Aaaaargh!" he groaned, his face contorting into pain. Marc was stronger but my adrenaline was kicking in. I brought my legs up and stomped the back of Rick's seat, slamming his chest into the steering wheel as his right hand cracked into the radio. Death metal switched to the oldies.

"Bastard's trying to get us to crash!" screamed Rick.

Marc head-butted me just as Sean swung across him, attempting to hit me but smashed the side of Marc's face with a badly aimed left. Marc howled and cupped his ear in pain. He elbowed Sean, who shot backwards into the corner of his seat, crying, "You moved! I didn't mean to!"

Marc turned and again belted Sean. Sean cursed, swung at Marc, and then they started going at it. For a moment I was free, but then Baldy rocked that giant body of his to gain enough momentum to turn himself around. He sat on his knees and began swinging his tree trunk arms. His fat fists rocketed into my chest, so I raised my legs and kicked the back of his seat. I barely budged him so I tried swinging back.

"What the fuck is going on?" Rick howled amid the confusion.

Baldy was now choking me and so I lowered my head and sunk my teeth into his wrist. He screamed and pulled back violently, knocking Rick's hands off the steering wheel, and the car began to skid. Rick grabbed the wheel and whipped it to the left, attempting to correct the car but it fishtailed instead. Rick struggled to regain control, ripping the wheel back and forth, the car zigzagging from side to side before hitting the shoulder and skidding fifty yards in a dust storm around us. We screamed as we plowed over bushes and small shrubs, narrowly missing a telephone pole and finally stopping, pinned between a maple and a bridge's embankment, only a few feet away from sailing over the ledge and onto the road below. We sat there for a moment, mute but breathing hard, checking ourselves for damage while the oldies played on...

"Is everyone okay?" Rick finally asked as the dust settled around us. "Is anybody hurt?" He leaned into his keys, hitting the steering wheel and talking to his car as he laid on the ignition. "Come on, man, don't do this to me. Just start up–just this one time, please, god dammit!" When it sparked up, Rick threw the gear into reverse and turned around to look over his shoulder. The tires whined and spun but still the car wouldn't budge. Rick leaned out the window to see what was stopping him from backing up. "We're hanging halfway off a cliff!"

"You see what you did, you asshole!" Marc screamed at me as Sean and Rick dug their doors into the dirt and began to wrestle their way out of the car. Sean couldn't get out but Rick rolled down his window and squirmed outside, where he bent down to see what the car was caught on.

I saw my chance and took it. I pushed open the back door and started to climb out but the car was angled down, so it was tough getting out. Just then, Marc grabbed the back of my shirt.

"Where do you think you're going, jerkoff?"

I let the door fall behind me. I heard him groan and he fell back, gripping his nose with both hands. I jumped through the weeds, hit the street, and booked away. I glanced back, took a wrong step, and twisted my ankle. I fell forward, extended my arms to catch myself, and then jumped to my feet. But not in time.

"No more fucking around! This is how you say goodnight!" Baldy ran forward throwing a haymaker, a wide, wild swing that could have knocked my head off if he had connected.

"Kick his head in, Baldy!" I heard Sean's voice, higher than the rest.

"You're gonna be reduced to dog shit!" shouted Rick.

"Reduce his ass!" screamed Sean.

"Mud! Make his name Mud!" shouted Marc.

"Mud!" They all screamed in unison. "MUUUD!"

A ringing sound exploded in my head as Rick stepped in with a colossal sucker punch, catching me off guard and connecting with my jaw. My head time-warped to the right. I was stunned but my wobbly legs still managed to hold me up as I staggered from side to side, trying to stay on my feet, their evil faces spinning around me, laughing like clowns on a carousel from hell. In and out of focus, they screamed and laughed at me. I caught a glimpse of Baldy, gritting his teeth and stepping in, reaching out with a hard left cross.

"Fucking pussy," he said as I spun around and tottered, not knowing if I was moving or standing still. I tried to make sense of my blurred surroundings before feeling the pain storm down from all angles. I realized that I had fallen when I felt the kicks blitz down. Everything was dull then, quiet and foggy, as if my head had been wrapped in paper and mailed away. A brutal wind raged through my head whenever one of them landed another cheap shot.

"Alright," I tried to tell them, "I get it." I didn't know if I said it or just thought it but the ruckus continued. Then the blows faded into the distance and a moment of blackness crept in, and when I came to, they were breaking off and running away, feet pounding the pavement.

"One-two-three-lift!" someone shouted and I heard the sound of metal scraping and then another crash as they managed to tilt the car off the cement block and drop it back onto the ground with a loud thud. The engine revved and they peeled out, screaming something out the window as the smell of burnt rubber filled the air. I struggled to stand but only got one foot underneath me.

The world was somewhere out there, through the blurriness. I heard a voice to my left and flinched away—maybe I imagined it. I concentrated on standing, pushing up on wobbly legs.

"Oh my God!" the soft voice exclaimed, maybe from somewhere in my brain. I steadied myself. Somehow my ears had been stuffed with cotton and all my senses numbed. My teeth were caved in on one side of my jaw and most of my face was scraped into patches. Then I heard the gentle voice again. "It's going be okay."

I tired to walk but then someone was in front of me. "Where has this crowd come from?" I said or I thought. I didn't know which but I squinted at the forms ahead. I stopped walking and focused in on the people, wondering if they were only apparitions.

"Take it easy, big guy. You are safe now," reassured a young man, who reached out to steady me. And then I heard the voice of the woman, and I turned and gazed, trying to make sense of her face and finally I saw her—long, brown hair and blue eyes, standing in her pajamas.

"Who are you?" I asked but forgot as soon as they told me their names. The woman instinctively tried to touch me but the man stood between us, nervous. The woman held out something for me and I found that it was a blanket. I tried to move away from them but they continued to walk along. She picked up the blanket and tried to hand it to me again. I walked a few steps more, gave up, and then crumpled down on the street.

"That a boy," the man said. "Just take it easy for a while."

"Who did this to you?" the woman asked. She stared with these huge blue eyes. I tried to smile but blood kept filling my mouth. Then I heard a siren in the distance. Moments later, I was surrounded. The EMTs held ammonia under my nose and placed a tight collar around my neck. They taped me to a backboard and even the cop winced as he got in my face to ask what happened. The EMTs went to work, shining lights in my eyes and asking me a bunch of questions. I listened to what the woman told them.

"We thought it was a car accident but by the time we came out to help, we saw this group of older boys ganging up on him until my husband shouted that the police had been called. They were vicious."

"Don't get me started lady. I've seen the worst," the cop said, pulling his hero card. "Did you happen to get a plate number or anything?"

"No, it all happened so fast. They were driving a gray Dodge."

"Well that doesn't narrow it down too much, nothing to start an investigation on but okay." The cop jotted something down and then looked back over at me.

"Alright buddy, who did this to you?"

"Don't know."

"Come on kid, nine out of ten times when something like this goes down, it's personal."

"They told me they'd give me a ride home from this party."

The cop sighed and clicked his pen, holstered his black note pad, and then turned back to the young couple. "I don't know why he's protecting them."

I didn't know either, except that I didn't want to be labeled a snitch and, after all, they hadn't exactly ratted me out for the billy club. "All I need is a ride home," I whispered.

"The only way you're getting home is by taking a ride in the ambulance or I can arrest you, make you take the ambulance ride, and then you'll go to jail instead of home!"

"Officer please," said the lady. "He's just a kid who had been through a lot, don't you think?"

He glared at her for a second and then turned to the EMT's. "Alright, get him out of here!"

Before they closed the door, I looked at the lady for the last time and noticed how beautiful she was.

Chapter 4: Jonah

"What did they do at the hospital?" Doctor Gildmore asked.

"They x-rayed me and gave me a shot."

"Were you seriously injured?"

"They said I fractured my mandible and my zygo something."

"They broke your jaw and your cheek bone."

"Yeah, I also had a concussion and like half of my face was sanded off."

"Were the other boys ever caught?"

"No."

"This is why I said you shouldn't have started any more trouble with that boy."

"So you think he won?" I asked but Gildmore didn't answer.

"It must have been difficult for your mother to see you like that."

"Yeah, I guess."

"What did she do?"

"She grounded me for a month."

"Hmm. That's all? Apparently she has a different recollection of what was going on. We'll pick this up next week. And Kelly," Gildmore called me back to the door, "I want you to think about some of this over the weekend. Especially how to avoid situations like these."

I walked out of the office and glanced into the day room. The tables were covered with old puzzles and beat up board games that must have been donated along with the worn out furniture. The games were missing pieces, which someone probably guessed us loonies were too crazy to notice. Or maybe the games had fallen victim to some kleptomaniac patient with an overwhelming urge to steal Monopoly hotels. A camera was rigged high in one of the dusty corners to keep an eye on the patients, reminding me of a gambling casino for mental jobs. A few mismatched sofas were lined up in front of the television, caged-off and bolted to the wall. The TV program was barely visible because a large streak ran down the middle of the screen, but nobody seemed to notice. One patient was lying on the floor, facing the corner. She gently rocked back and forth, whispering to herself while another kid grinned, bouncing back and forth to techno jams inside his head. He wore old glow-in-the-dark necklaces and a visor hat, turned upside down on his head like he was trying to catch rain. He sported baggy pants and fat laced sneakers, looking like he was still tripping hard from his last rave.

A young nurse exited the bullpen with a clipboard and walked into the day room, checking off names. Her cold blue eyes fixed on the girl lying on the floor. She sighed and then walked out. A door buzzed open and two orderlies entered the unit, pushing a stretcher. They walked over to the girl, picked her up, dropped her onto the slab and then strapped her in. She lay there with glazed out eyes but babbled quietly, looking at the ceiling as they rolled her out.

"Hey, come over here for a minute." A girl in the smoking lounge waved me over. "So did you get bored playing with the Couch Potatoes yet?" she asked and winked at the boy beside her.

"Couch Potatoes?" I repeated, smiling.

"The kids in Day Room. We call them Couch Potatoes. I think it's a much nicer name than calling them Vegetables, don't you?

"I guess."

"Yup, this place loves making Couch Potatoes. They'll be glad to make a Couch Potato out of you. Just let em know you're gonna take all the meds they want to feed ya!"

"Dr. Gildmore seems all right though."

"Yeah, I guess. Hey, I'm Lauren and this is Curtis."

"Hey," repeated Curtis.

An older nurse stood in the doorway of the smoking lounge. "Are you gonna just sit in there and inhale carbon-monoxide poisons all day long?"

"What else is there to do?" Curtis asked, but the nurse ignored him, checked off our names, and walked away.

"You want a cigarette?" Lauren asked. She was overweight but had a pretty face.

"No thanks. I don't smoke."

"That's what most of us said when we first got here." Lauren exhaled.

"I said it and look at me now." Curtis held up a cigarette.

"So they let kids smoke?"

"They think smoking is the least of our problems, but they won't let Ducky in here cause he's only eleven."

"They got Ducky in isolation right now," said Curtis.

"What's isolation?"

"It's the rubber room." A plume of smoke rolled from Lauren's lips. We were quiet and the only sound was the inhaling and exhaling of cigarette smoke. "Before they throw you in the isolation cell, they tie you up in a straitjacket so tight that some kids pass out."

"I heard a kid died that way," Curtis whispered.

"And then they dump you in a freezing cold room with blue padded walls. That's to chill you out." She nodded as she inhaled.

◆

It started with a twitch in my jaw. Then my chin began to pull to the left as though I had no control over it. I felt like Popeye. It pulled farther and farther left and began to ache. I tried to talk but couldn't move my mouth. I tried to fight it but my jaw locked in place. I ran out to find a nurse.

"Wha' the hell are you giving me?" I tried to say between clenched teeth.

"What's the problem, Kelly?"

"I can't move my mouf!" I lipped.

"So what's the problem?" The nurse smiled while her icy blue eyes remained hard.

I grabbed my lower jaw with both hands and tried to move it by force.

"Alright, that's enough! Go in and see the doctor," she said and nodded toward his office.

"This medication you're giving me is fucking killing me," I ran in and jawed the words to Doctor Gildmore.

"Hmm," he said. "How do you feel otherwise?"

"Horrible! Worst I ever felt in my whole life!"

"Let's take a look at your chart. Hmm. 400 milligrams of Thorazine and 1200 milligrams of Lithium. That sounds a little high."

"Jus' a little?"

"Do you hear voices in your head?"

"No," I answered, looking at him strangely.

"See things that aren't really there?"

"Uh, no, not unless I'm tripping."

"Are people chasing after you?"

"I don't think so."

"Okay, hold on!" He sounded irritated and picked up the phone. "Give Kelly a muscle relaxant and discontinue his medication for now. We'll try something else next medication module."

"Why do I need medication at all?" I tried to shout. He covered the receiver and turned away.

"Alright, go down to the nurse's station. I've written you a script for something to counteract the dystonia. Should work in about twenty minutes. Can you hang out for that long?"

"Yes," I said, feeling stupid with my jaw jutting to the left and stuck in place.

I walked to the station. The nurse unlocked the top half of the door and swung it open. I leaned on the ledge and looked at the tired and pissed off nurse who handed me the medication in a tiny paper cup. I dropped the pill in the side of my mouth and tried to swallow it with water.

"Open your mouth and lift your tongue," she commanded.

"I got lock jaw," I hissed.

"Fine. Go to your room and lie down."

✦

As the first bell rang on Monday morning, I was walking down the school hallway when Vick jumped out of nowhere and tried to snatch the conscious band from my neck. I grabbed his hand and tried to shove him away but, like a sly Kung-Fu master, he knocked my arms aside and threw a fast punch, catching me in the chest. I flew across the hall and collided with the far row of lockers. Through the melee, students bustled past, some holding books across their chests like protective shields, sweeping in wide circles around the action. Those who hesitated were quickly shoved or herded away by the Leech Mob and told to keep moving if they didn't want to catch a piece of the beat down themselves.

To my right, Casey stood in a black hooded sweatshirt, his arms crossed just below the nine-millimeter bullet that swung from a silver chain around his neck. His lieutenant-like presence took up one side of the hallway, cutting off that direction as a chance of escape, a maniacal grin slowly spreading across his face.

His head was shaved except for the top, hair foot long and dyed blue-black, with a few stray hairs flopping down the sides of his shaved dome. Both ears were pierced and silver hoops ran down each lobe.

Their two droogs conducted crowd control, both towering over the lot of us, seeming twice our height and three times as thick. Dave had a shaved head and a *DRUDGE* tee shirt stretched across his barreled chest, representing some underground hardcore band. His light blue eyes spread far across his face and his wide pierced nose took up much of his grill. The other boy was just as big but had more fat than muscle. Known as Lampy, he was a pothead with long afro hair and a dreadlocked beard, and he sported a tee shirt that read *POSERDEATH*.

Lampy and Dave moved at angles through the hall, organized and stepping menacingly toward anyone who paused to check out the action. Bumped along, nobody seemed that interested to stay in Leech Mob affairs for too long. It was an effective tactical maneuver that kept the hallway traffic moving so not to attract the attention of any teachers. After a moment, Casey whistled and Vick released my headlock and casually leaned aside, calmly grilling me with alert but cold green eyes. I stared at Vick, who readied himself to strike again, waiting for a teacher to shuffle past before applying the headlock again.

"Take that fucking rope off before I rip it off, jackass!" Vick growled in a deep but cracked voice and pointed to my conscious band. His appearance was intimidating. He wore a long-sleeve tee shirt with the hardcore band *STRAIGHT UP* printed across the front, and the words *FUCK DRUG ABUSE* scrolled down his left sleeve. His ears were a wreck of piercings, though my eyes focused on the nine-millimeter bullet hanging on his chest. Lampy pushed in beside me and looked down disapprovingly. The smell of cologne and skunkweed hit me in the face. His long kinky hair and beard gave him a Viking's appearance but his half-serious expression made me crack a smile.

"Check out this crazy, little, skinny shit—for real!" Lampy jutted out a thumb and then spit, "You're laughing! You, all, took too many beatings, dude." He smiled and clicked his tongue.

"Dude," agreed Dave and then squinted at me, "if I get suspended for kicking your ass, I'm going to kill you!"

"You think this is a fucking joke, smiley?" Vick snarled as two more kids rolled up—Obi, a musician and guitarist for the Hardcore group Despair, and Kit, once a preppy jock who dropped out of the football scene to join the Leech Mob.

"Oh brother," Kit smirked, pushing back his red hair and grinning through his freckles and matching orange goatee.

"Dude, this is the kid?" Obi exclaimed while shaking his head and pushing through the ranks to stare into my face before turning to glare at his boys. "Have you all completely lost your minds?"

"Shut up, Obi!" Casey snapped without looking at him.

"Yeah, get out of here, Obi," Dave snarled through his down-turned slit of a mouth. He then took a deep breath and flexed his chest.

"Yeah or what?" shouted Obi. "Or I'll be jacked up next?"

"Don't be stupid," Vick grumbled and, with the attention momentarily off me, I saw my chance and broke into a wild run. But Vick was right behind me, hauling me back and cracking my skull against the cement block wall.

Casey glared at his boys, "You see this? No respect, not for nothing."

"Yo, what the fuck are you hoodlums doing to this bum?" asked a seventh dude, strolling up and looking almost studious, a mix between a prep and a skater. He carried a sketchbook of what appeared to be graffiti.

"What's up, Zed?" Lampy grinned.

"So, this is the kid who is trying to overthrow the Leech Mob!" Zed stroked his blonde goatee. "Very interesting." Obi shook his head and rolled his eyes as the graffiti dude stepped forward with an entertained smile and examined the damage done to my face. "Looks like somebody already fucked him up, man!"

"So!" Vick shouted at the newest arrival. "What's your fucking point, Zed?"

"Sooooo," Zed drawled out, "give the kid a break, why don't you?" He spoke in some weird, invented, foreign-like accent as he continued to study my bruised and beat up face. "He's all fucked up," he muttered.

"You're all like losing it, for real," Obi repeated himself.

"Hmm...Just looking at him gives me a good idea for a new graffiti character!" Zed flipped open his sketch book to a blank page and began to draw something while glancing back and forth between the pad and me. Kit and Lampy glanced over Zed's shoulder and then snickered at the beat-up, cartoon version of me.

"Shouldn't you be in honors English right now, Zed?" Casey growled.

"And shouldn't you be in in-school suspension, dude?" Zed cracked back in a disconnected way. "Instead of playing the local Nazis."

"Oh fuck you, man!" barked Vick.

"Man, let him wear the stupid thing if he wants to look like a fool!" Zed argued before returning to his drawing.

"And this is what it's over? That thing!" Frowning disbelievingly, Obi pointed at the conscious band around my neck. "Ahh. Get out of my way! I'm going to class!" He pushed back through the group and shuffled away, still shaking his head.

"Have fun in Music!" Lampy called.

"Yeah and have fun at lunch, fat boy!" Obi stopped and returned the diss as the others cracked up.

"Yo. I walked past the music room the other day," Lampy began before interrupting himself with a fit of laughter. "I saw Obi playing some classical shit on the violin! And check this out. The music teacher, Mr. Hermes, was all sitting, like leaning back in his chair and listening to Obi, with his eyes closed as he played air-violin. I don't know dude, but it looked kind of perverted to me." The others burst out laughing as Obi stood there blinking, zipping and unzipping his beat-up hooded sweatshirt.

"So! So!" Obi responded.

"So, we didn't know you were such a cultured youth!" Lampy cracked up again.

Obi raised his voice, "At least I'm doing something besides smoking dirt every day!"

With an ear-to-ear grin and stoned-out eyes, Kit saw his chance to approach me.

"Kid, like, take it easy on yourself. Just lose the conscious band. Yo, I like rap too, dude but you're not KRS-ONE!" Kit started to giggle and Lampy joined in with some hysterical, stoned-out laughter.

"That's it!" Casey said. "Outside!" Besides him, Vick and Dave were the only ones to remain seriously pissed off through the whole ordeal. They picked me up and used my face to open the side exit door as Lampy, Zed and Kit followed close behind, laughing.

"Dude! Freshmen are supposed to be stupid! That's like their job! Remember?"

"Yeah, just drop him off at Hill Top Avenue wearing that conscious band and see how long he lasts!" Lampy added to more laughter.

"We warned you, dude, but you still have it on!" Casey snarled in my face.

"Yeah," agreed Vick. "We warned this little fucker and now we got to show him what happens when he fucks with us!" Vick began jumping and whipping these spin kicks around in the air.

"Like, whoa, man." Zed glanced up and then went back to his drawing.

"Uh-oh, you're in trouble now," Kit laughed.

His foot spun closer and closer as I retreated from Vick, who continued to jump and fly in circles through the air, clearing out everyone in his path. As we edged along the building, a teacher gazed out a window in disbelief, her piece of chalk held frozen in mid-air and her head cocked to the side with an outrageous look on her face. The Leech Mob didn't notice, too busy talking shit and debating amongst themselves while Vick performed another roundhouse, this time clipping my nose. The side door banged open as the teacher stormed outside with a surprisingly loud and deep voice, "What on earth is going on out here? Should I call the office? Casey! Vick! Zed! What the heck are you boys doing?"

"Nothing, nothing, I was–I I mean–this kid–just wanted to see what a roundhouse kick looked like," Vick stuttered.

"Is that true?" She looked at me.

"I guess." I shrugged.

"Where should all you boys be this period?"

"Uh, study hall," said Kit.

"Then get there, all of you, get to where you're supposed to be!" she yelled, but everyone still hesitated. "Move! Or your next stop will be the principal's office!"

"Are you sure you're okay?" She glared at me and I nodded, and then she twisted around to face the others.

"I'll keep this between us this time but the next time I see anything like this..." She didn't finish her threat. "Now get moving!"

At the door, Casey turned to face me and mouthed the words, "You're dead." He then complained to Dave, "After all that and look! He still like has it on!" Dave sucked at his teeth and Vick shook his head slowly as they all walked backwards, dogging me, and then disappeared into the school with the teacher on their heels.

Kit and Zed held back and fell into place beside me. "You got some type of guts, kid. I'll give you that." Zed nodded his head.

"Either that," Kit said, "or you're like borderline retarded cause this isn't over, for real!"

I shrugged and Zed frowned with a look of pity on his face. "Hey kid, check this out." Zed held out his artwork, a drawing of a little guy with a black eye and scrapes across his face. His arms were crossed and he was sneering up at his opposition–a gang of dark figures, three times his size. An oversized conscious band hung around his stretched neck, and his chin jutted out in defiance.

◆

Five chicken nuggets, six tator-tots and a glob of slimy applesauce that tasted like liquid can. "Damn, I can never get used to this stuff." I glanced over at Andrew, who was sitting with the Skaters, something he rarely did. Both he and Jonah kept quiet but looked as though they wanted to tell me something. "This tator-tot is hollow. They vaporized the center," I said, making stupid conversation as I picked up a chicken nugget. "What's the stuff they use in place of chicken, I wonder?"

"Squid," said Ezra, sitting down.

"No, that's too rich, probably cow intestines." Andrew grinned but Jonah elbowed him in the ribs. "Ow, you bastard! What?" he cried as Jonah tried to be slick and mouthed the words, "Tell him!"

I pretended not to notice but instead took a gulp of warm milk and swallowed the chunk of breaded silicone. "What?" I finally asked, becoming irritated.

"Go on, Andrew!" Jonah snapped.

"Let me have my conscious band back, Kelly!" he demanded.

"Why?"

"I don't know." Andrew took a deep breath then looked at Jonah, "See, he won't give it up."

"He's gonna get his ass kicked for wearing that! I thought he was your boy!"

"He is but," Andrew paused, "what do you want me to do? I don't even want it back now!" He raised his shoulders around his neck as if to support his head. I could tell he didn't want to get involved.

"Don't be a pussy, Andrew!" snapped Brody with an amused look in his brown eyes, hidden halfway under a flash of black hair. He wore an Independent Skate Industries tee shirt, baggy pants, and a pair of graying white Vans.

"Fine, if he doesn't say something, I will," spat Jonah. "Andrew wants his conscious band back because he's decided to go Black Power after all!"

"Yeah, so give the kid back his necklace," Ezra coached, pushing back his blonde spikes that had grown so long they fell over like a jester's hat.

"What the hell are you wearing today?" Sonny walked up and dropped his tray on the table, looking at Ezra's kilt.

Ezra shrugged. After taking a sewing class in school, all he wore were his own creations. He copped outfits from second hand stores, ripped them apart, and then sewed them back together in strange combinations. Being the only guy in sewing class, anything he learned to design, he'd show up wearing to school. This included dresses.

"So give it up!" Jonah snapped his fingers and redirected the conversation to me.

"I'm not scared of them. Look, I still have it on."

Ezra took a big swig of milk and then laughed, spraying the mouthful across the table. "Dude, they so took it easy on you!"

"What the fuck, Ezra, you douche bag!" Jonah raised a fist and Ezra pushed off with both legs, sliding his chair backwards across the floor.

"You got milk all over the place! Wipe it up, you fucking hyena!"

"Dude, I can't help it," Ezra grinned. "This kid has no clue. It's a killer!"

"I heard that Obi and Zed were like sticking up for you!"

"And you haven't even met the Landbury Leech Mob yet."

"So everyone's heard about this?" asked Sonny.

"Yeah," said Brody. "News gets around."

"Fuck the Leech Mob!" I said and the others jumped back.

"Wow!" said Ezra.

"Shh," Sonny whispered as the others looked around suspiciously. "Keep it down, Kelly. You're lucky like no one else heard that! Dude! You know I got your back. That shit you did in Mrs. Nowak's room was off the hook!" Sonny shook his head. "But I'm not stepping up to the Leech Mob!"

Jonah lowered his voice, "Do you even know who the Leech Mob are?"

"Not really," I admitted. "A gang or something."

"Not exactly." Brody looked at the others.

"You should listen up, Kelly," grumbled Jonah. "It started with these two dudes named Egan and Connor, who got tired of the way things were. You see, Landbury High School from the 70's on was a messed up place to be. There were like race riots, fires, and the school was always being shut down. This went on for more than ten years. There were fights like every day between all the gangs."

"Vietnamese gangs, Spanish gangs, Black gangs," Sonny piped in. "They always had each other's back. If one of them got in a fight, all the rest would jump in but for everyone else, it was like every man for himself."

"Anyway," Jonah cleared his throat, "around '85 there was a fight between this skater and a Vietnamese kid. They started throwing down but when all his Asian friends jumped in and started to beat this skater kid's ass, that's when Egan and Connor decided to even up the odds and that was the start of the original Leech Mob crew."

"From then on, anyone who proved they'd fight and stand up for themselves got a nine-millimeter bullet on a silver chain," added Brody.

"They didn't mess with drugs either," continued Jonah. "The Leech Mob didn't even drink. All they did was skate or go to shows where more kids wanted to get down."

"What shows?"

"Hardcore shows, you know, hardcore music?" Jonah looked at me funny.

"He's never heard of that either," laughed Ezra.

Sonny tapped me on the shoulder. "The Leech Mob grew to like a hundred kids, and they started wearing purple."

"But only the original members wore the nine-millimeter bullet." Brody drew a circle around his neck. "The Leech Mob isn't about race though. Anyone could be down. They have Chinese Leech Mob kids, Black Leech Mob kids.

"So just give the thing back to Andrew," Jonah interrupted. "Lampy said they'd leave you alone if you'd just do that." Jonah appeared to grow calmer.

"Thanks for looking out for me but I'm not going to take it off just because they say so," I told them as Jonah slammed his fist down.

"Yeah, Kelly's a hero!" Ezra said sarcastically.

"You know," Jonah frowned, "I don't even care anymore. Do whatever you want. Just remember, we warned you."

"Andrew doesn't even want it back, do you, Drew?" I argued.

Andrew shrugged apathetically but said, "Kelly, we got enough problems right here, let alone South Africa. Come on, let me get it back. My father bought it for me and I don't want it winding up in a garbage can." He smiled as the Skaters clapped their hands.

"Yeeeeaaaaayyyy!" crowed Ezra.

"Finally, the Black Man speaks!" Jonah announced.

"Fine, since you put it that way," I said, taking it off. "Where did you get it anyway?"

"At an African import shop."

"Don't tell him!" Jonah shouted, suddenly pissed off again.

"What? Why?" Andrew removed his glasses, wiped his watery eyes, and then put the conscious band on.

◆

The next Monday, in Science, Ezra, Brody and Sonny broke into a wild fit of laughter.

"You went to the African import store!" Jonah shook his head disgustedly.

"Yeah."

"Dumb ass."

"You better take it off when you walk down the hall!" warned Sonny.

"You know the Landbury Leech Mob are driving up here today," said Ezra.

"Shut up all of you!" Mr. Ryan snapped.

After school, Jonah met me at my locker and punched me in the shoulder.

"What the hell's your problem?" I lunged at him, swinging as he skipped back smiling.

"You know who just rolled up?"

"No."

"Well you better have a look."

I followed Jonah to the front of the school where we looked out the glass doors to the teachers' nearly empty parking lot. Besides a few secretaries and clerks, the school was just about deserted. I followed Jonah's gaze to see Vick and Casey standing in front of two stout youths covered in tattoos. One wore grey jeans, frayed around the knees, black Doc Martin work boots, and a plain black jacket, with his hands stuffed into the pockets. He must have weighed 250 pounds and stood six feet tall. His beer gut and rugged clothes made him look like an industrial worker. He carried bowling balls in his calves. His forearms were tattooed murals and his neck was a tattooed tree trunk. His short dark hair was shaved to a zero on the sides; his long goatee carved sharp and angled down his jaw.

The other was slightly taller though less stocky but dressed almost the same. He sported a tee shirt exposing tattoos riding up both his forearms and ending at his elbows, unfortunately revealing where his money had run out. His baseball cap was pulled down low above his eyes.

"Those two are Egan and Connor. Egan's the really big dude."

"Egan right," I gulped, my mouth dry.

I looked back at Jonah. "I tried to help you, dude, but now you're on your own."

"Yeah," I mumbled. "I'm used to that."

A beat-up Ford pulled up and circled the parking lot, riding low on blasted shocks and plastered with bumper stickers of hardcore bands, X's, and skate logos that read, *SKATEBOARDING IS NOT A CRIME.*

The doors swung open and four kids got out. They were small guys, especially compared to Egan and Connor, but appeared just as vicious looking on Riverview ground, wearing baggy jeans and tattoos. They wore black baseball caps with brims pulled down low, hiding their eyes. Their heads were shaved but for the top, which they grew long and dyed black or bleached blonde.

One short kid dropped his skateboard. He ollied a curb, grinding his board along the concrete bumper. He then jumped off, hit the street, and skated across the parking lot, kick-flipping his board several times, landing tricks perfectly while ignoring the posted sign:

NO SKATEBOARDING
ON SCHOOL GROUNDS

Two others began to spar, throwing quick flurries of punches and blocks, mixing martial arts into their own blend of street fighting. The Riverview Leech Mob walked across the parking lot to meet them. Casey and Vick still sported the fading black X's from last night's show, inked onto the backs of their hands with permanent markers to symbolize straight-edge.

"You better get out of here," Jonah murmured to me. "Go to detention early or something." He looked at me nervously. "It's a stupid thing to get a beat-down for."

"Yeah, what isn't?"

"I tried to warn you," Jonah said, looking as though it was the last time he was gonna see me alive. "I'll be around dude. I'm not leaving yet." He walked off.

I walked into the cafeteria and watched them through the window. They waited until the last few teachers got into their cars and drove away, messing with their radios and pretending not to notice the gathering. Then Egan whistled and shouted something, getting everyone's attention with a whirling gesture that led all his boys, marching or skating, up to the school entrance where they kicked up their boards.

A moment later, I heard them talking as they trudged into the school, crossing through the main lobby and through the cafeteria doors. "Hey! That's him, right?" someone shouted.

"Yeah, there he is," said Casey.

Egan led the crew across the tiled floor, beside a nerd who watched them nervously. Once they passed, he swiped his books off the table and hurried away, dropping one. He spun around and twitched, as his brain fought the instinct to not leave the book behind. But then he was gone, leaving the book abandoned on the cafeteria floor.

"What are you? In Hill Top, homey?" a short skater laughed as they strolled up.

"Why ya wearing that, stooge?" sneered Dave.

"Look, somebody already kicked his ass!" Egan said, tilting his head. "Is that from you, Casey?"

"No," Casey shrugged. "He's probably pissed off the world."

"Is that true, kid?" Egan asked. "Is it you against the world? You ain't even hardcore, so don't play that!"

"Get that thing off your neck, jackass!" Vick screamed but then laughed hysterically.

"Since most of the school knows about this," Casey stepped forward, "we need to kick his ass to set like an example. And since you guys were driving up here anyway, I thought you might want to see what this poser looks like!"

"Get that fucking thing off your neck, jackass!" Vick growled again.

Connor moved in, somewhat amused. "Look kid, you know who we are and why we're here, right? Are you trying to disrespect us?"

"No, it's not like that." I shook my head and began to say something when Connor hit me real fast, as the rest of the Leech Mob start howling.

"Take it off, punk!"

"Throw it in the can, bitch!"

"No! Throw him in the can!"

Connor spoke lower and more slowly than the rest, so I focused in on what he said. "Why are you wearing that? Are you retarded or something?"

"No, I'm alright."

"No, no you ain't alright. What do you think, Otis?"

Otis was a skater kid a few years older than me. His large blue eyes bulged out of his albino face, and a thin silver hoop pierced his nose. A black baseball cap partially covered his white hair that ran down his neck in greasy strands. "You're pretty far from alright! You hear me punk?" he yelled in my face, but before I could glare back into his beady eyes, he leaned to the side and uppercut me in the jaw. I fell backwards into some chairs, which scattered across the floor.

"Now even Otis wants to kick his ass!" Casey said.

"What are you waiting for, poser? Take it off!" Vick kicked me when I started to get up.

"You want me to play baseball with your skull!" a beak-nosed kid screamed, glaring from underneath the brim of his frayed black cap.

"Look! Jasper is going to hit him with that skateboard!" Casey laughed as the kid, held the skateboard over his shoulder and lunged forward to smack it against my head.

"Hit that kid for real, Jasper!" encouraged his brother Aaron. "No more of those baby taps!" Jasper looked like he was psyching himself up to bash in my brains when Egan leaned over, pulling me back on my feet.

"You know, that would be one lame way to go out, dude! Otis just get that off his neck!" Connor grabbed my jacket and slammed my head down against the table as Otis wrapped the band around his hand and tried to snap it off.

"That fucking rope is stronger than I expected." He flipped out a knife, held it to my neck, grinned, and then sliced the thin rope.

"Alright, let's get this over with cause we're going to be late." Egan gave them a nod.

There were only thuds and hollow impacts–no one said a thing. The Leech Mob were almost mute as they pounded and kicked. Just then, I heard an angel's voice.

"No! You got him enough! Just get out of here!" I squinted to see this girl standing between them and me, shoving them back as they snickered.

"See he's fine." I heard Egan laugh before he stood me up and shoved me to Connor, who shoved me to Casey, who stepped aside and let me crash to the floor.

"Like what the fuck is wrong with you, Krissy?"

"Look at him!"

"Would you relax?" Vick laughed. "He looked that way already!"

"Yeah right," Krissy said. "Did they do that to your face?" She stared into my eyes.

"Nah. It's been a rough couple of weeks."

"See, he admits it."

"Leave him alone!" Krissy screamed as Otis tried to run around her and stomp me in the head. "I don't give a fuck what he did! If you touch him again, I'm going to call 9 fucking 1-1!"

"Relax, Krissy," said Egan, walking out. "We were just leaving anyway."

"So are you coming or not?" Connor asked as he began to walk away. "Cause I know one dude who wants to see you!"

"I don't think so, you freaking psychopaths!"

"Call you later, Krissy," teased Casey.

"You love us!" Otis shouted from the door.

✦

"Now wait. Who was Krissy? Your girlfriend?" Doctor Gildmore inquired.

"Kind of, but she was more like a babysitter."

"So the Leech Mob roughed you up but took it easy on you because of Krissy, right?"

"Right, and cause Jonah, Flip, and the Skaters were looking out for me by then."

"How do you mean?"

"Well, whenever I saw the Skaters hanging with Vick, Casey and the Leech Mob, I went the other way, but Jonah decided to put a stop to that one day."

✦

"Kelly! Dude, get over here, man!" Jonah yelled over at me as I crossed through the cafeteria looking for a place to sit.

"I'm, uh, I'm going outside."

"You're going outside!" Jonah exclaimed and he, Brody, and Ezra began to laugh.

"Look! He's all paranoid now!"

"Nah, I'm cool." I started walking away but Jonah got up and followed me out.

"Kelly, just get over there and act like it didn't bother you."

"Man, fuck that."

Jonah lowered his voice. "You gonna sit by yourself everyday from now on?" He glanced back at the Leech Mob table. "Just walk over there and say what's up."

I hesitated. "Yeah–alright."

I followed him over and Jonah kicked out a chair for me, Sonny slapped my hand, and Brody threw a ketchup packet. Flip was off in the corner, making out with his new girlfriend Jenny, while Zed had his sketchpad on the table as usual.

"Hi," said Krissy.

"Hi," I responded.

"Sit down dude," said Ezra.

"Wait, what was I just saying?" Kit looked around the table.

"How should I know?" Vick growled.

"Something about your brother." Brody rolled his eyes.

"Oh yeah! I have study hall first period at 7:00. So I have to get up all early to go sit there and do nothing! I'd rather be sleeping but my brother grabs me by my ankles and drags me out onto the floor!"

"But you two, like, drive to school together right?" Krissy looked strangely at Kit.

"Yeah, so?"

"So, what does he have for class first period?" Krissy asked.

"Uh," Kit thought about it. "Hmm, I don't really know. I never asked him." His face brightened as he held up his finger. "But even if my brother had study hall first period, he'd still go cause he's a dumb ass like that." Kit blushed before deciding to laugh along with them. "Fine! I'm an idiot! But he didn't have to drop me on the floor!"

I smiled at Krissy who laughed, wrinkling her nose and pushing back her straight brown hair. Besides her baggy jeans, Doc Martins, and half of her bangs bleached white, she dressed almost preppy.

"Hey Vick, uh, Casey," Jonah said. "You guys all know Kelly, right?"

"Poser." Dave glared at me, scratching his beard, the same length as his bristled head.

"Yeah, you got some type of nerve showing your face around here."

"Shut-up Zed!" Krissy slapped him.

"Look what you did!" he yelled, gawking at his sketchbook. "You made me fuck up my line!"

"So, erase it!"

"Bite me."

"What's up?" I said quietly and reached out to shake hands but Casey squinted his eyes as if it was the dumbest thing he'd ever seen while Dave continued to stare blankly and pick at his teeth with a plastic fork. I lowered my hand and looked at Vick. "How's it going, dude?" I asked, and he shrugged but threw out a very generous "W-sup?" before grabbing Eve and pulling her onto his lap, copping feels and whispering dirty things into her ear.

"Euu Vick, get off!" she exclaimed after staring at him for a moment with her mouth hanging open.

"Get off?" Zed asked brightly. "That's exactly what he's trying to do!"

"Totally not going to happen." Eve shoved Vick's face to the side and stood up, her sky blue eyes perfectly contrasting with her black ponytail. She had no less than twenty silver hoops in each ear, two in her nose, and a larger ring pierced the center of her bottom lip. She showed off her long legs with a black miniskirt, torn fishnet stockings, and Doc Martins laced up to her knees.

Lampy raised his fuzzy eyebrows, adjusted the rubber bands in his beard, and then winked a bloodshot eye as he went back to rolling a joint, his huge Afro kept tucked under a white knit hat, though it puffed out the sides and back.

"Hey kid, check out these stickers. I just had em printed up." Lampy threw a couple down on the table. One said *SPLIFF TRIBE*, another *LEGALIZE WEED*, and others had famous logos in the shapes of pot leaves: *JOLLY GREEN* Buds and *WEEDIES* cornflakes.

Ezra got up, wearing a skirt, and shimmied back and forth to the trashcan to throw out his leftovers. He looked uncomfortable as he sat down.

"Damn, I forgot to bring pants."

"Dude, why do you wear those things?" Brody looked disgusted.

"Cause I made em, dude. But some of them are pretty damn uncomfortable." Ezra adjusted himself as he sat down.

"Ezra, what does your dad think about your new clothes?" Sonny smirked.

"It's seriously, like, really hard some times. My parents are both tripping. Like every five seconds they get pissed off at something! And I'm like, Mom, Dad, you don't even like know me!"

Krissy laughed. "What do you mean they don't know you? Ezra, they've known you since you were born!"

"But they seriously don't! And my dad calls me Missie and Sweetheart."

Macie put her arm around Ezra's shoulder. "Oh, don't worry about it, Ezra. A lot of men like to wear dresses–priests, judges." Her dark green eyes, blurred with mascara and eyeliner, made her look like she'd just finished crying. Her shoulder length, dirty blonde hair was dyed in purple strands and pulled back with an elastic headband. Today she sported baggy jeans and an oversized, purple Champion sweatshirt that she tucked her knees into. "How many dresses do you have?"

"Maybe fifty or so," Ezra answered as the others laughed at him. "I'm trying to sell them but nobody wants to buy them."

"Do you wear them around your house?" Lampy asked.

"Yeah, and my little sister steals em. You can have one if you want."

"Dude, I'm not wearing any dress." Lampy looked up through his eyebrows, licked his joint, and then expertly rolled his fingers, sealing it in one motion.

"How about a dress for your mom, then?" Ezra asked. "I'll just have to see if the school has enough fabric first." Lampy lunged across the table to smack Ezra as he recanted, "I didn't mean it like that!"

"Vick, I swear to god I will soo slap you if you touch my ass again!" Eve threatened him as she laced up her boot.

"Yeah, like Tank's seriously gonna trip, girl!" Macie said.

"Vick!" Eve turned around and slapped Vick, who froze in surprise as a deep red imprint of her hand slowly appeared on his cheek. Krissy covered her mouth as Macie laughed. "I totally warned you." Eve cracked a smile as she stood up and brushed herself off. Vick chuckled bizarrely as he rubbed his face and shoved her away with one arm. He then reached over and dragged Macie's chair closer.

"Let me tell you a little something about women, Vick," Macie sighed as she allowed him to pull her over.

"Women are all pigs!" Vick cackled. "You don't have to convince me."

"Girl," Krissy raised her voice, "you soo don't have to take that! Don't let him talk to you like that, girl!"

"Shut up, Krissy. She likes it!"

"Trust me, Vick." Macie frowned as she spun her legs to stand, but Vick playfully held her down. "You need all the advice you can get!"

"Yeah like basically Vick, you're the pig," Krissy said. "That's the first thing you need to know."

"And second, girls don't like to be all grabbed by you constantly and third, um, no girl likes to be grabbed like second best." Macie and Krissy both burst out laughing.

"And fourth, all piggies must shut up!" Vick cackled as Krissy wrinkled her forehead.

"Excuse me, asshole?"

Vick humped the air twice. "Yeah, take it like a woman!"

"You're such a pervert."

"Vick has to be a pervert cause that's the only way he can ever get any!" Violet said, strolling up with Remmy. She sang, "Like what's up everyone, for real."

"You tell him what's up, Violet," said Macie.

"What's up, Vi?" Krissy smiled. "Hi Remmy."

"Yeah!" Vick cheered, "You tell him what's up, Violet!"

Violet curled her left nostril. "Euu, Vick! Shut up!"

"Alright stinky!" Vick croaked.

"That's fine with me, boy!" Violet leaned away. "Keep your diseases to yourself!"

Violet was hot, stacked up top, and shaped like an hourglass. She had bright brown eyes and long curly hair. Like the other girls, she had an unusual look about her, something unique. A splash of light freckles on her cheeks, pursed, pouty lips, almost cat-like, with a nose that turned up just a bit made Violet irresistible.

Violet showed off, letting her spiked leather jacket and zip down hoodie hang off one shoulder really low. She wore ripped black tights under a short, preppy school skirt. She also had a reputation for dating most of the older Leech Mob kids but was now in love with Remmy.

Until high school, Remmy had been a prep. He was a good-looking kid who played all the sports. Now he wore baggy jeans, a thin, green hoodie hammered with holes, and a battered, black baseball cap on backwards that covered his bleached blonde, greasy strands.

"Violet, you're all flushed!" Krissy grinned. "Are you like breathing hard, too?" She enthusiastically nodded her head and panted like a dog.

"Yeah, where have you two been?" Macie bobbed her eyebrows.

"Remmy's been getting some," laughed Kit.

"Euu, in case anyone didn't get it!" exclaimed Krissy.

"Who wants to go for a ride?" Violet dangled her car keys.

"I don't go for seconds!" Vick cackled.

"As if I was even offering!" Violet squeezed her left eye.

"I'd rather jerk off than tag any of you anyway!" laughed Vick.

"Dude, aren't you leaving on vacation soon?" Casey asked, changing the subject and breaking his silence.

"Yeah, we're leaving like tomorrow for three weeks?" Remmy answered.

"Like don't remind me, Remmy." Violet ran her hand over her forehead. "You're seriously gonna make me cry."

"Why are you leaving in the middle of fall?" Krissy asked. "Aren't you going to miss like a whole month of school?"

Remmy shrugged. "I'm probably gonna drop out anyway."

"Oh my god, Remmy, why?" Macie asked.

"Leave the kid alone. If he wants to drop out, let him drop out!" Flip piped in, looking up from making out with Jenny.

"Nobody should drop out, Flip!" yelled Krissy.

"I just don't like being around these kids anymore. I hate going here now and

I'm not going into the Program and be treated like some retard."

"Hey!" shouted Vick. "I'm in the Program!"

"Sorry, Vick." Remmy grinned. "But I figure, why go through four years of school when I can get my GED by taking night classes for six months? So anyway, I'm gonna see you guys after school in the parking lot."

"You're gonna trust leaving Violet single to mingle for a whole month!" Vick exclaimed.

"You got a one track mind, Vick!" Krissy frowned.

"Euu, Vick, get away from me." Violet squinted her eyes. "You seriously like really scare me sometimes." Then she leaned on Remmy's shoulder and looked at him lovingly. "And my man knows he has nothing to worry about for real, and we already went through this so it's not gonna be like an issue."

"Where have you been?" Violet asked accusingly as Paula stormed up holding a huge bag crammed with books. She glanced at me through the corner of her eye and flexed her nostril ring.

"I've been in the library, finishing my next class' homework!"

"Nerd," insulted Vick.

"Loser," she snapped back without even looking at him.

A teacher strolled into Cafeteria C and pretended not to stare at us. Violet rolled her eyes. "Fuck this place. Who like wants to go for a ride?"

"I'm not going to miss my next class," said Paula.

"Don't look at me, honey." Eve looked away.

"Me neither." Macie shrugged. "I've missed soo much English already."

"I'll go," announced Remmy.

"Well, I already knew that, Goomba." Violet pinched his cheek.

"Do you like even go to this school anymore?" Paula drilled Violet.

"What's your problem?"

"Whatever," snapped Paula.

"Remmy's dropping out on us." Krissy frowned. "And his parents are taking him on a vacation! Like what the fuck, right?"

"So when are you leaving, Remmy?" Casey asked.

"He's leaving tomorrow and that's why I'm skipping with him!" Violet curled her lip. "Come on, let's get out of here." Violet grabbed Remmy's hand and pulled him away before he had finished slapping everyone's hands goodbye.

"Fucking bitch!" growled Vick. "Let me say later to my boy!"

Macie jumped up to give him a hug.

"Remmy, you suck!" snarled Vick. "Jackass! Dropout!"

"Casey's dropping out, too," added Dave.

"You dry, fucking snitch!" Casey shook his head.

"Might as well tell them now," Dave sighed.

"You're dropping out, too," Vick cried out, "and leaving me alone with, with this?"

"Sorry bro, I meant to tell you. I mean we're always talking about dropping out. So I went and finally did it. Well, it was mainly the school's idea."

"Violet always brings out the best in people," Zed muttered but continued to sketch.

"Like shut your mouth, Zed," snapped Krissy.

"I like heard that, Zed!" Violet glanced over her shoulder and raised her middle finger.

"Like good," he called back sarcastically, finally looking up.

"Hold on, Violet. Lampy, you got any smoke?" Remmy asked.

"Which type?"

"Either."

"Yeah, I got both."

"Then let's go." Remmy smiled and Lampy stood up to stretch.

"What? You guys are smoking? I'm going!" Kit jumped up.

"Weed suckers!" Vick shouted as the four of them strolled away.

"Hey do you mind?" Zed looked up at me leaning over his drawing. "Fine, if you want to check out the master at work, go ahead, but don't crowd me, man."

"You're too cool," beamed Krissy.

"I know, but don't make a big deal about it." Zed flipped through his book, showing off dozens of versions of the same four-letter word.

"What does it say?" I asked.

"SAKE," he snapped.

"What does *S.B.N.* stand for?"

"Don't tell him," said Casey.

Zed looked around suspiciously. "It stands for *Silent Bombing Network*." He looked up proudly. "This little scribble will soon be painted 1000 times the size you now see on a bridge somewhere nearby. Some fun, eh kid?" Zed sarcastically gave me the thumbs up.

"You are such a freak, Zed," Macie giggled.

"Look who's talking," Zed shot back. "Hey, uh, Casey, Vick, you game?"

"I don't have any money for paint," said Vick.

"So, I got three cases."

"Can I get down?" asked Ezra. "Check out the newest piece." He busted out his notebook. "Brody did that one but this one's mine."

Zed glanced over. "Not bad, you two are getting better. You fucked that letter up though."

Vick glanced over. "You suck! Ha ha!"

"Let me try to write one," I said.

"You don't even have a tag, shithead." Casey rolled his eyes.

"At least he's gonna have a high school diploma."

"Shut up. Krissy." Casey glared at her.

"I can make one up," I said, thinking.

"Why don't you write *LAME*?" Zed snapped his fingers. "Yeah *LAME* is a good tag! I was going to use that." He grinned at Casey.

"S.B.N!" Macie nudged Zed. "So is that what you're doing tonight?"

"Well, I'm not going to Images, so don't even ask for a ride."

"Why not?" Ezra yawned.

"Cause Images is probably one of the worst clubs in the world!" Jonah chimed in.

"Next week is the last show at the Anthrax," said Casey.

"Yeah, nobody better miss that." Dave shook his head.

"When that's gone, the only place left will be Images," said Macie.

"Shut up, Macie!" Casey said. "There's other clubs!"

"Not really. There's like bars but they're always like a hundred miles away!"

"Have any of you ever gone to Images on Saturdays, when they have Club Night?" Krissy asked, biting into the bottom of her ice cream cone.

"Guido Night?" asked Zed. "No thanks. I've only gone to Freak Night."

"Me and Macie went. Everyone was either homies or cretins. All the chicks had their bangs sprayed up, skirts all tight, they were all hookered out, grinding to that Top 40 club shit. I never want to see another gold chain in my life," Krissy laughed.

"We left like two seconds after we got there," Macie added.

"Images gives me the creeps." Zed scratched his goatee. "I always think the building is going to collapse."

"I always smell bad after going there, too," added Macie, and Krissy sighed.

"But there's like nowhere else to go!"

"We might go," said Eve, getting everyone's attention. "Tank said something seriously bad is going down tonight. Like everybody's going."

◆

I waited for Jonah to walk out of the store, wearing a red grocer's apron.

"You should wear that smock to Images, bitch!"

"You wear it, bitch!" Jonah snapped, taking it off and throwing it at me.

"You're in a bad mood!"

"Not yet," he said as we crossed the lot. "But I'm getting there."

"Look man, we don't have to go."

"Yeah right, we're going to Images, dude. Then you'll see why I hate it there!"

Jonah had a white Mustang with tinted windows and a Pioneer stereo with 200-watt amps connected to twenty-inch pyramid bass-woofers in the trunk. On every door and corner of the car, Jonah had installed tweeters and midrange speakers.

"Now I see why you have to work all those extra hours," I said as he fumbled through his collection of tapes, chose one, and pressed *Play.* "I didn't know you skaters listened to rap," I shouted over the music as Jonah glimpsed at me from the corner of his eye.

"What did you think I listened to, bitch?"

"Maybe you should try some meditation music."

He started up the engine and pulled out onto the street. "You know my system was stolen twice already, right on my driveway, too."

"That sucks. What did they get?"

"Almost everything, the amps, speakers… Now I got a Cobra Alarm System and lined the bottoms of the speakers with razor blades." He smiled. "If they try to rip me off again, they're gonna rip their fingers off first."

On the highway, Jonah dropped it into fifth and lunged forward, burning across the black top and making it to New York State in five minutes flat. We cruised into Bog's Creek, a rural town that bordered Landbury. Jonah chirped through the gears as he downshifted off the exit ramp and swerved past the graffiti-covered train station, marking the start of the main drag, lined with soaped up windows and *For Rent* signs. Aside from a beat up motorcycle or a rusty car every few hundred feet, nothing but empty parking spaces lined the barren streets.

Jonah whipped down a side street vacant with dark houses. Besides the rustling of dead leaves, everything was completely still. We drove farther out until Jonah grimly pointed toward the ancient, desolate-looking house that sat with its back to the woods. "There it is," he said as we turned into the large dirt parking lot, hidden from the road by a thick row of menacing trees. A couple of space lamps speckled with what seemed to be thousands of dead insects shined over the hundred or so cars. We exited the Mustang into the cold wind, and I gazed up at the ramshackle castle that leaned to the left and threatened to collapse.

"So this is Images?"

"Yup," Jonah said disgustedly.

It looked like a cross between Dracula's lair and a condemned tenement. Every window was pitch dark except for a small one near the entrance to the club, identified with only a blue *OPEN* sign and a blinking red arrow pointing down to the cellar stairs. As we crossed the dirt parking lot toward the joint, I pointed at the top four floors.

"What's up there?"

"How would I know? The club is only in the basement," Jonah snapped and then went into a coughing fit as a group of kids entered the glowing red interior of the otherwise abandoned building. We bought our tickets, the bouncer stamped our hands, and we descended into the club. After running our hands under the black light to prove we had paid, we were set free inside the maze of the catacombs, crumbling plaster, and cold stone walls, which created dozens of rooms and passageways.

We wandered through the dilapidated structure with low ceilings and even lower doorways marked with pink neon tape warning us to *DUCK* as the wooden planks creaked unevenly beneath our feet. We followed our ears as the music grew louder, blasting over the sound of our footsteps as we clunked across the hollow wood floor. Here strobes and colored lights disguised the graffiti-covered plaster walls, disintegrating and exposing the honeycombed chicken wire beneath. The largest dance room had a stage and nearby, glassed in, was the DJ's booth where the dude spun a mix of new wave and industrial with the occasional punk.

Smaller paint-splattered side rooms looked as though they'd served as old tool sheds in the past. In each of these divisions, a single light shined down upon broken chairs and ripped sofas, oozing stuffing. Bodies littered the place, heaped on the furniture and strewn upon each other's laps, indifferent to the filth and decay surrounding them. Gutter punks and homeless kids slept on the floors with their jackets stuffed behind their heads, or they propped themselves up in the corners and passed corncob pipes stuffed with cheap weed.

"Looks like a fucking rest home for punks!" I shouted into Jonah's ear, though not as loud as beat up speakers that piped in the sounds of hell.

"When the bouncers aren't looking, one of their friends opens the emergency exit door so they can sneak in without paying." Jonah nodded toward the characters who lay passed out on the floor. In another room, a clan of Goths dressed in black lace and studded leather sat on the antique furniture. The dudes held skull-tipped canes, and the girls wore black capes. Their faces were painted white, their mouths stained blood red, and their hair dyed black.

"Recognize that chick Eve from school?" Jonah asked, watching Eve leading a thug in black past us.

"Yeah, she's hot."

"Well, that's her boyfriend Tank."

"That sucks," I said, mesmerized by her jet-black hair and flashing blue eyes. She lovingly held onto her thug of a boyfriend, dressed in dark, baggy clothes and wearing a red NY baseball cap that covered half his face. He had silver earrings at the top of his ears and a black tribal tattoo crept up his left arm and etched up his neck. He kissed her as he lifted her against the wall.

"I guess I don't have a chance with her, do I?" I asked but Jonah shook his head.

"Now look over there." Jonah pointed. "That's Gavin and Liz. You know Gavin is Vick's cousin, but they're as close as brothers. He's a martial artist, black belt in like five different things."

"Gavin?"

"Yeah, he graduated a few years ago."

Gavin was a skinny guy, only slightly taller than me. He wore a white collared shirt under a black sweater, kept his hair short and combed over. The only thing that stood out was his silver chain with a nine-millimeter bullet. He calmly gazed around the club with curious eyes and the slightest of smiles.

"That's Gavin!" I exclaimed. "He doesn't look like he could whip anyone's ass!"

"That's because he doesn't have to!" Jonah said. "And that's Liz, his girl, and they're going to have a kid soon."

The two of them stood beside the chaos of the dance floor with both their faces glowing under the flashing lights. Gavin stood behind her with arms draped around her shoulders protectively. They both swayed in place to the industrial noise.

"Now, see that little dude?" Jonah pointed to a short but cruel-looking kid with short black hair and pitch black eyes. He wore a blue hooded sweatshirt, dark jeans, and a single gold ring in his ear that lined up with a thick three-inch scar that extended past his left cheekbone. "That's Bram," Jonah said.

"Bram, huh?"

"Yeah, Bram's a fifth degree black belt."

"He's in the Leech Mob?"

Jonah clicked his tongue, "Hell, yeah," and glared at me as if he were getting tired of my stupid questions.

"What's your problem?"

"I got to get out of here for a second. This music's killing me."

"I thought you liked this music."

"Fuck this."

We crossed back through the catacombs, squeezed past the creeps, and walked up the cellar steps. Outside, a couple dozen individuals had formed a line outside the club. One punk sported an orange Mohawk and a pair of overalls; another had blue spikes and a black denim jacket, ripped and covered with patches. After them in line was a girl sporting a bride's gown but she was covered in blood. Beside her, with hair dyed green and wrapped around blue hair curlers was a chick in a pink bathrobe with a noose tied around her neck.

Just then, a beat up hatchback fired up its engine and tore out of a parking space, almost plowing through a group of girls walking in. The car swerved at the last second, barely missing them and bottomed out when they hit the road.

"Fucking assholes!" One girl turned and flicked them off. She wore a puke green button up sweater and a grey wool skirt, a Wilma Flintstone necklace and cat-eye glasses. She shook her oval purse in the air. "Fuck you! Shit!" she screamed as the rest of her friends giggled. None of them looked over eighteen yet dressed like a crew of bingo players that just arrived from a seniors' convention, rocking old lady costumes that went out in the 60's. Her friends carried metal lunch boxes and dyed their beehive hairstyles green, blue and red. One even sprayed hers white.

"Little old lady punks. That's cool, right?" I asked.

Jonah sneered at me. "Maybe at a Tupperware party. It just makes me remember why I stopped coming here."

"They even walk like old ladies," I laughed. "They probably smell like mothballs."

Jonah shrugged. "You want to stay? Maybe you can dance with one of them."

"So, you want to leave, already?" I exclaimed. "Dude, we just paid to get in!"

"Yeah, don't remind me." Jonah looked away as the sound of an abused muffler howled in the distance, screaming toward us at an alarming rate.

"That car sounds like shit but they're flying!" Jonah listened as he gazed at the street through the blockade of trees that screened the road from the parking lot. The car roared closer until it whipped past the club, missed the driveway, and swerved. The driver hit the gas, spinning the bald wheels on the pavement before catching enough traction to fishtail onto the dirt lot where it spun 180 degrees out of control, plowing sideways into the back of a beat up station wagon and then stalling.

"Daaamn!" said Jonah. "Is that Vick's car?" He pointed to the four-door, beat-up blue Nissan sitting in cloud of dust. "Yeah, that's definitely him."

A loud but muffled voice shouted inside the car, "You're one of the worst drivers I've ever seen in my life! Let me out!" Egan shouted as he got out scowling and leaving the car door open. "I'll be amazed if you ever get that piece of shit started again." Egan took a step back and watched Vick lean forward, grinding his ignition while hitting the wheel and cursing, before the engine sparked and sputtered weakly to life. With the passenger door still open, Vick slammed it into gear and swerved around in a circle, using the momentum to slam the door shut and skid into the nearest parking space.

All the doors swung open at once. Vick angrily smashed the car beside him as he got out. Casey and Connor looked at him strangely.

"You're crazy, Vick. Your car can't take that abuse every time!"

"You better hope nobody notices the damage done to the other car," added Conner.

"And that's the third car you fucked up tonight," Casey sneered.

"They were all pieces of shit," Vick said, and Egan shook his head and led the pack towards the club, his thunderous voice echoing off the tall rocky embankment like he was holding a megaphone.

"What was I saying?" Egan started.

"Boo!" shouted Vick.

"Oh yeah, I was like, fuck it dude! Boo's had my bathroom door locked for like two hours. We were all banging on the door but he still wouldn't open up or even answer us. And I don't know if he was like dying in there, cause I knew he was smoking that dust. After a while I knew I had to do something so I just reached back and bam!" Egan slammed his fist into his palm. "I kicked open the door to see his big sweaty ass sitting on my toilet with no clothes on! And I was like Boo, what the fuck are you doing, and he is just staring around with this crazy look on his face. It stunk like gasoline in there, chemicals, ya know? People go insane after smoking that shit for too long." Egan chuckled as they walked across the lot.

"He must have been freaked out seeing you knock down the door!" said Connor.

"Not really. He seemed like he was even glad to see me, like someone finally came to help him out.

Jonah smirked as we continued to follow them back toward the club. "They don't even see us."

"Hey Casey, you know we got that show in two weeks?" Egan asked.

"So?"

"So you haven't learned the last song Obi wrote and Cecil hasn't bothered to come to practice all month. So this Sunday everyone swore they'd be there and you are, too. Right?"

"Yeah, I already told you like ten times."

"Alright, whatever! Just so you know it's real important!"

"What do you think, I want to sound like shit on stage?"

"Hey, wait up!" Jonah shouted as we sprinted toward them.

"Look at these two degenerates!" Vick cackled as he turned around. Their scowls turned to grins, except for Casey, who continued to walk toward the building ahead of us.

Egan squinted his eyes at Jonah, "Hey, look at this fucking kid! I thought you died!"

"What's up, Jonah? It has been a little while," Connor agreed, walking up and slapping Jonah's hand. "I saw you everywhere for like two months and then nothing." Connor glanced at me, trying to figure just where he knew me from before it hit him. He continued to smile, turning to Vick for some type of explanation. "What the fuck?"

Egan seemed the last to finally recognize me. "Now you're hanging with us? What are you, in the middle of a fucking identity crisis or something?"

Connor looked at me and grinned. "Yeah, shouldn't you be at a Back To Africa convention or something? We didn't rattle you too bad, did we?"

"No, I'm alright."

"Your name's Kelly, right?"

"Yeah."

"I personally don't care what you wear but Hilltop Posse has a big problem with white posers wearing those conscious bands and if they saw you . . . "

"Alright, leave him alone. He's taken enough shit." Egan glared at Casey as he walked ahead of the group. "Nice seeing you, Casey, have a good night!" Without turning, Casey raised his hand from the distance. "So where you been, Jonah?" Egan asked. "You got a girl now, don't you? What's the trick's name?" He laughed.

"No, I've just been working a lot."

"Every weekend?"

"I need money for that thing." Jonah pointed toward his car.

"I thought you were getting some."

"You still fighting in those Judo tournaments?" Connor asked.

"Yeah, the last one was two months ago."

"How'd you do?"

"I got a first place."

"That's my boy!" Connor punched him in the shoulder as we arrived at the door.

"What's new, Billy?" Egan asked one of the bouncers.

"Same ole, same ole. What about you guys? No show tonight?"

"Nothing," confessed Egan, "and you heard about all the problems The Anthrax is having with the zoning dispute."

"Yeah, I heard it was going to close down."

"It's been beat, but next month we're signed to play in Norwalk."

"Oh yeah, where at?"

"The Night Breed."

"Oh, I know where that is. It's a shit hole, right?" Billy smiled.

"Better than this place." Egan grinned, looking up at the building.

"I'll try to make it."

"Yeah, alright!" Connor grinned. "Your wife got you on a leash?"

"Maybe you should try bringing her," Egan suggested.

"Nah, she would kick his ass!" Connor laughed, his breath reeking of booze yet he didn't slur his words.

As we crossed into the center of the club, masses of bodies jumped up and down to the sound of steel drums, distorted guitars, and repetitive screaming vocals. Vick recognized some little vampire chick, hair dyed red and wearing black, so he ran to spin her off her feet while the rest of us shuffled along, filing into the smoking room.

"Well it's about time you fuckers showed up!" Bram jumped up angrily and gripped hands with Egan and Connor before jerking back when he saw Jonah and me. "Yo, what the fuck are these kids doing around?" Bram narrowed his eyes, whipping up his chin as he grilled Jonah and me.

"Bram, this is Kelly," Jonah said.

"So what?" Bram spit, mad dogging him. "And like who the fuck are you?"

"Don't be stupid, Bram. You know Jonah," said Connor.

"Yeah but not like that!" Bram scowled as Casey pushed through, grinning and and slapping Bram's and then Tank's hands.

"I don't really know you either, Bram," Jonah said, looking around Casey. "So what?"

"Yo! What!" Bram snapped. He flicked his cigarette that buzzed past my left ear but Egan stepped up, grabbing Bram in a playful headlock.

"After what I heard, you should be happy we're even here!" Egan dragged him away. "Take a walk with me! We got to talk about something."

After the dust settled, most of the sober freaks had evacuated the room, leaving only the most random or stoned out creeps who lined the perimeter standing still and silent, their eyes hidden behind tufts of mangy hair, only moving to bring their cigarettes up to their down-turned mouths. Eve sat on one sofa with Tank on one side and Casey on the other, while we sat facing them. Tank glanced over at Casey and they both began to crack up.

Connor stared at both of them with an amused look on his face. "I see what you're all doing and it's not cool."

"Yeah it is," said Tank grinning.

"Your name's like Kelly, right?" Eve asked.

"Yeah." I stood up and reached for her hand, staring into her hard blue eyes for slightly longer than I intended.

"Aren't you kids out late?" Tank finally said and Eve bumped her thigh into his and said something in his ear.

"Are you gonna tell Connor?" Eve stared at Tank who shrugged.

"Shut up, Eve," said Tank.

"Tell me what?" Connor asked.

"Remember those kids that Bram had a problem with?"

"Not really. I mean, like, which kids in particular?" Connor squinted his eyes.

"It ain't nothing we can't handle, especially now that like everyone's here,"

Tank said as Egan and Bram walked back in.

"Dude, you're seriously gonna tell me those kids you fought here like a month ago are back?" Egan incredulously asked.

"Yeah, the ones who said they're down with Hill Top," Bram answered, his eyes shifting between Connor and Egan. "Well don't get pissed off at me!"

"That doesn't mean nothing, I mean, everybody said they're down with Hilltop," said Connor.

"That's not what Billy the bouncer over there said." Egan shook his head and grinned. "Billy said those kids are back, head-hunting for Bram."

"Was Hilltop with them?" asked Casey.

"I don't know." Egan shrugged.

"It don't matter. Tank and I drove back to my house and I got this." Bram lifted his shirt and exposed a small revolver shoved in his belt.

"Oh my god, I knew you two were so lying about why we went back there!" Eve stood up. "Look, if you're all going to kill people, I want to leave, like right now!"

"I'll bring you home!" Jonah offered

"Fuck you, Jonah. Nobody brings my girl home but me!" growled Tank.

"So you got your dad's burner?" Egan grinned. "You know he's gonna kick your ass like the last time you stole his gun."

"And you can't stay at my house again." Connor shook his head.

"Are you kidding?" Egan exclaimed. "If Bram uses that, he'll have a nice little jail cell to call home. You better give that gadget to me before you end up shooting your balls off."

"Yeah, Bram, give me the gun," Connor said just as Liz and Gavin walked in. Eve gave Liz a hug. "Like what's up, Dad? Hey, Mom!"

"Uh, like what was that I heard about a gun, like for real?" Liz looked nervously at everyone over Eve's shoulder.

"You all got big fucking mouths!" Bram handed the weapon to Connor and then shoved his way out of the room.

"No, but you're gonna tell me!" Liz got in Egan's face "Or me and Gavin are leaving now!"

Egan grinned. "Chill! It's nothing. It's just those punks Bram fought last time. I don't know why Bram has to pull the bitch card and all like bring his dad's gun into this."

"It's just the same thing that's been going on for like months, remember?" Eve said as she pulled Liz down. "Those kids come here on Freak Night and they start popping shit. They see all the new-wavers and start clowning everyone. Then one bumps into Bram and you know how the rest goes. So have you two found an apartment yet?"

Liz seemed to relax though she stared at Egan for a moment longer. "We got total good news and bad news for real, like, what do you want to hear first?"

"Tell me the bad news."

"Okay Gavin got into a fight with his boss and got fired for real."

"Like a real fight with his boss?" Eve's eyes got wide.

"Oh no, not that bad but pretty close. Mm-kay, he just got into a really big like word fight with his boss and they started screaming at each other and everything. And then his boss goes, you know, you can't like work here anymore."

"So what's the good news?" Eve raised her eyebrows.

"We totally found an apartment! Yeah!" She nodded her head. "And I don't want anything to fuck this up, so anyways back to this. What's going on with them!" Liz twisted her lips.

Eve rolled her eyes. "I don't know but I totally want to get out of here."

Egan grinned at Gavin. "So when you gonna be a daddy?"

Gavin looked at him. "You've been drinking again, Egan."

"Yeah, I had a couple, so what? Straight-edge is over, man."

"Not for me. There's still a lot of straight-edge bands out there."

"Well Despair ain't one of them! Look! Don't worry about me, Gavin-"

"You better not show up drunk next week at The Anthrax."

"I can't believe it's going to be the last night. It's gonna suck when it's gone."

"So when were you planning on telling us you were having a kid?"

"I did tell you, Egan. You were probably drinking so you don't remember!"

"Yeah, yeah. Hey, Jonah!"

"What's up, Egan?"

"Next week, you better be at The Anthrax!"

"That place is closing, huh?"

"Yeah, so you better get there."

A loud crash echoed over the blaring music, followed by screams.

"What was that?" Liz asked.

"Where's Bram?" Connor stood up.

"It's starting!" Egan plowed through the crowds, kids ricocheting out of his way. We followed, running through the maze. The shrieks grew clearer the closer we got to the front bunker, where a couple of bouncers struggled with a gang of thugs who'd managed to grab hold of Bram and drag him up the stairs, bouncing his body up every step. Now the bouncers tried to squash the riot by shoving the whole mess outside.

Half way up the cement steps and breathing hard, a bouncer with a crew cut stood by while Bram was yanked up the last step and dragged outside into the parking lot. Crew Cut shrugged at his fellow bouncer, took a deep breath, and then reached up to slam the metal, cellar-style doors closed just as Egan raided the steps. He planted a gigantic forearm into Crew Cut's face as he raced up the stairs, throwing his whole body into the doors just as they came crashing down. With one shove, Egan busted them wide open. At the top step, Egan twisted around and shrieked at his army below to "MOVE!" as the fallen bouncers scrambled up, each grabbing hold of a door and straining to close them again.

With a three hundred pound bouncer hanging onto each door handle, Egan still held them open. He gritted his teeth and growled through his spit, keeping both doors pressed open as we ran out, squeezing past the bouncers who hung on the doors, trying to pull them closed.

Outside, I turned to see Egan straining under the weight of even more bouncers climbing over him, dragging his arms down. Finally, Egan collapsed under the weight and the metal doors slammed shut. Silence.

I turned to look at our enemies, who were stoned out of their minds on something. One wore sunglasses and was dripping sweat. He laughed uncontrollably as he and his boys dragged Bram backwards, pulling the back of Bram's shirt over his face. I saw the perfect outline of his screaming head as he took cotton blind swings at his attackers. Realizing he'd better do something quick, Bram twisted his body as the thugs desperately tried to keep hold of his shirt. Finally they had to let go, dropping Bram on the ground, who immediately catapulted off his back and landed on his feet like a Kung Fu acrobat. He spun around, spitting and taunting them to bring it on. Just then, Gavin appeared from nowhere, placing his hands into a Kung-Fu position.

"Motherfucker thinks he's Bruce Lee!" one guy said.

"Both of em do!" said another, gesturing from Bram to Gavin.

"I got you, fat boy!" Conner stepped forward.

From all directions across the parking lot, figures loomed in. Then the sound of steel doors crashed open behind us. Egan roared forth with a palm pressed down on one bouncer's grill while he elbowed another in the jaw, before whipping his head back into a third bouncer's face, knocking him off his shoulders and freeing himself. Egan lumbered out into the parking lot as the cellar doors quickly slammed shut and locked behind him. He grinned as he took labored breaths, his whole body heaving up and down as the others seemed to flinch at his appearance.

"What the fuck is this?" Egan looked around, pulling a purple bandanna from out his back pocket and wiping his sweaty face, while squinting at the crew in front of us. "Now, Bram?" he asked tucking the bandanna into his back pocket.

"Yeah," Bram said.

"Then get it!" Egan spoke agitatedly but then turned back to the cellar doors and screamed, "You gonna lock a kid outside to get his ass kicked! Fuck you! If I see you again, it's on!"

Bram cast an angry look at Egan before lunging forward, skidding his Vans in the dirt and bobbing his head from side to side. Bram and his enemy exchanged punches, but Bram was quickly hit in the mouth and stumbled back. Bram darted forward again, faked a left jab and dropped a foot to his opponent's knee, bending it sideways and causing him to scream out in agony as he fell to the ground.

"You okay, Marcus?" one of his boys yelled as Marcus grabbed his knee and howled. "Come on! Don't go out like that!"

"Remember me, punk?" another guy shouted at Bram.

"Yeah, how's the nose?" Bram taunted through a bloodied lip.

"FUCKING FREAK!" Javon roared.

"KICK HIS ASS, JAVON!" the enemy yelled.

"FUCK YOU, CRETINS!" Bram shouted back in his cackling voice.

Bram went after Javon, who stood his ground, timing Bram as he kicked through the air repeatedly with spin-kicks. Javon waited before returning a front snap kick of his own. Bram fell to the side, tucked in his legs and gripped his balls in pain. Both gangs squared off, picking out targets with clinched fists

"Is that who I think it is?" Egan squinted as he walked out to meet the other gang.

"That's right, Egan!" A short, black guy stepped forward, "This here is my cousin. I bet you didn't know that. They say your boy is foul, Egan, he foul!"

"What's up, Moses?" Egan reached out and shook his hand. "Yeah, but could we say they just handled that?"

"Just handled what?" Moses smiled.

"I don't know. You kicked his ass–stomped him in the balls."

Moses laughed. "That's why I like you, Egan. You smart but we didn't come all the way down here for nothing. We're gonna show you white boys how we do."

Egan pointed to the club. "They probably already called the cops."

"Stay out of this! It has nothing to do with you!" Connor yelled from the side to one of their boys who edged forward, as though he were ready to start swinging. Egan shot him a look but Connor just shrugged.

"Alright, if they handled it, then this is handled. Right, Moses?"

"What if I say it ain't handled yet, Egan?" returned Moses.

"Where's your brother been, where's Franklin?"

"He in jail."

"Oh yeah, too bad."

"You only talking your way out of this one way, Egan."

"We're not apologizing."

"Now you being stupid–even for a white boy."

"That's one of the mother fuckers who started this whole shit." Bram pointed to a guy with glazed eyes as Tank and Casey helped pull Bram to his feet.

"Listen." Egan pointed toward his ear. "Sirens."

"That could be anything," Moses said and then turned to look at his cousin. "Go on if you want it! Go and get your pound of flesh!" he shouted.

"Hey Bram!" Connor called out to him. "Leave it alone!"

BAM! The metal doors banged open, and Billy the bouncer ran out followed by Eve and Liz.

"The cops are officially on their way, boys!" he yelled out and then hoarsely whispered to Egan, "I told them I called 5-0, but when they saw the cops weren't coming, they called them for real."

"Sorry for pounding your face, dude," Egan said.

"It comes with the territory. But you should get out of here. You broke Evan's nose back there!"

"I'm not going to be your co-defendant, Moses!" Egan said, walking towards the car, yelling to the rest of us. "Alright! We're out!"

"Fuck you, Egan!" Moses cracked a shark-toothed smile.

"No, it's cool Moses. I'm not going to jail, not over some old dumb shit."

Moses glared at Egan and then shouted to his boys, "We out! 5-0 on its way. We'll settle with these peckerwoods later when no cops around."

Jonah and I hit the road and a minute later, headlights flooded our car as someone quickly drove up behind us, blaring the horn and then tearing up beside us. Egan leaned out the window. "Dude, don't follow us!" he shouted, and then Vick passed us and burned ahead.

"Don't follow them? This road only goes one way!" Jonah said as Vick's car disappeared from view. "Those fools are gonna get pulled over! They're flying!"

"Yeah, I can't even see them anymore," I answered as we turned onto a street.

A cop car flew by with lights and sirens—never taking notice of us. We passed the graffiti-covered train station and turned onto the main drag, lined with soaped up windows and *For Rent* signs. Then we heard an engine whining into life in the distance.

"Is that who I think it is?" Jonah shook his head, looking into his rear-view mirror.

With Connor laughing and flicking us off, Vick sped past us again, ran through a red light, and then tore onto the highway.

Chapter 5: Face

The flier from Landbury said,

CLOSING NIGHT AT THE ANTHRAX

with

JUDGEMENT, WAKE UP, GORILLAS, FUBAR...

Someone had drawn a graffiti character of a bald scumbag holding a forty-ounce bottle of liquor. His eyes were crossed, he was drooling, and below his beer gut was written *BODY BY BUD*.

The Anthrax was a gutted warehouse, painted in zebra stripes and covered in graffiti and fliers from past shows. Immense cast iron columns supported rusty beams, while exposed ventilation ducts formed a haphazard network overhead. A red light shown down on the band of seventeen-year-old kids with black X's inked on their hands. The MC from the band Wake Up looked out at the crowd.

"If most people just want to get drunk, get fucked up, and slowly die off, I'd like to say I don't give a fuck, but I do and that's why I'm so fucking pissed off! When I first got into straightedge, I lost a lot of friends but now I got nothing... TO HOLD ME BACK!"

The music kicked in and kids jumped on stage as the MC paced back and forth, letting the masses of stage divers run across the front of the four foot high platform and then dive into the crowds of jocks, nerds, punks, and freaks, all moshing to the music like the lost generation. He raised the mic to his lips and began to scream as kids jumped on stage and swarmed in circles around him. Another wave of kids then jumped on stage and onto the backs of the first group, all fighting for a chance to scream the lyrics they knew by heart.

They bunched around the singer until we couldn't see him anymore. The crowds seemed to have swallowed him up, and I pictured him somewhere beneath their bodies, suffocating on the floor, but as the lyrics ended and the layers of kids peeled away, the MC stood there with the cordless mic. He screamed something and then jumped backwards off the stage, knocking a kid over and crashing onto the floor. Yet the crowd picked him up and threw him back on stage.

Between fits of moshing, the crowds seemed to relax but the stage diving was always constant. An endless flow of kids crisscrossed the stage, sometimes forming lines on either side, waiting for their chance to book across the platform and roll out onto the crowds. They jumped backwards off stage, while others dove headfirst, sometimes three at a time, like kids diving into a pool.

Then the band went off and shit got crazy. Even though it was chaos, aside from the occasional scuffle, nobody went out of their way to hurt anyone else. The singer spun around so his back was to the audience, and then fell straight back onto the crowd who faithfully caught him and pushed him back on stage. The set ended with the audience taking over the stage so there was almost no room for the band—the singer, again, lost under the crowds.

The place was dark except an oval ring of light that shown down on the next band, Judgment. The MC lifted the mic with a giant arm and said, "I know you're going through life with a thousand barriers in your way right now–and that's all drugs and alcohol turn out to be–barriers that get in your way, AND BARRIERS THAT GET IN MINE!"

The guitar whined to life and the drummer kicked in and the MC started to scream-sing, holding his thick forearm in front of his chest like a shield.

When Judgment began to play Hardcore Crew, I was almost trampled as kids scrambled to jump on stage, closing around the MC again. Others lined up behind the band, jumping on each other's shoulders, piling on for a chance to scream some lyrics into the mic. The stage became a mess of people pressing in from all sides, and eventually the crowd swallowed up the giant vocalist until only his voice remained. From opposite sides, two kids ran across the stage, jumped, collided in mid air, and crashed down onto the undaunted crowd.

✦

"Remmy should be back from vacation soon." Jonah wrinkled his forehead and stared across the high school parking lot. It was getting cold out and we didn't have much to do after school.

"Tomorrow I think," said Vick.

"I still can't believe what they did to his house," exclaimed Jonah.

"That's an idea," responded Vick.

"What?"

"Let's go see what happened."

Jonah shook his head. "No, we shouldn't go over there."

"Why not?"

"Because everything is fucked up there." Jonah kicked at the ground.

"That's the whole point," argued Vick. "The damage is already done."

"What are you talking about?" I asked.

"Did all that really happen?" Jonah looked at Vick, ignoring me.

"I don't know. It depends," Vick spoke slyly. "What did you hear?"

"I heard that something happened to Maxie." Jonah looked almost pained.

"Yeah, she died," Vick answered quickly and then looked away guiltily.

"She died?" Jonah exclaimed. "They killed her!"

"No! They didn't kill her, at least not on purpose or anything."

"Who's Maxie?" I asked but Jonah just glanced at me, slowly shaking his head like I didn't want to know.

"Let me guess?" Jonah's eyes grew narrow. "She just kinda died on her own. Nobody helped her or anything."

"Well she was like twenty years old!" Vick's voice cracked, so he cleared his throat.

"That's so fucked up," Jonah growled. "What did they do to her?"

"Nothing!"

"Nothing? Bullshit! They must have done something!"

"I heard it was the music," claimed Vick.

"The music killed her?" Jonah asked, raising his voice.

"I'm serious, the music gave her a heart attack or something—or maybe it was Egan's singing, cause they were playing Despair," Vick laughed.

"Who is Maxie?" I demanded.

"Remmy's dog," Jonah answered quickly and turned to Vick. "What? Nobody even tried to help her or anything?"

"What do you want, somebody to give CPR to a dog?" snarled Vick.

"They could've brought her to a vet or something," Jonah continued. "You're the animal lover Vick! You're the kid who won't eat meat!"

"Fuck you." Vick grinned. "Just because I don't support the millions of executions of cattle for mass consumption, doesn't mean I'm in the dog of the month club!"

"Unbelievable."

"So what do you want to do, jackass?" yelled Vick.

"I don't know, bitch," replied Jonah.

"Nobody is going to tell me what's going on?" I finally snapped.

"Somebody broke into Remmy's house and trashed it!"

"Who?" I asked.

Vick just laughed and repeated in a grungy voice, "Who did it? You did it! Ha-ha-ha!"

Jonah stood there frowning. "Who was the first to break in?"

"How would I know?" shouted Vick, always having difficulty controlling the volume of his voice. "Don't be stupid, Jonah. After what's happened, nobody's going to admit to anything! Unless they want to go down for everything!"

"And I heard the place is fucked up!" Jonah lowered his voice. "Hey, doesn't Flip live next door?"

"Why do you say that? Just cause he's Puerto Rican he broke in?" Vick laughed. "Sure, blame it on the Puerto Ricans, why don't you!"

"I didn't mean it like that!" Jonah frowned. "Maybe you did it."

Vick instantly stopped laughing and stared at Jonah for a second before looking away. "No, it wasn't me. Anyway, we should go over and take a look before they get back tomorrow."

"What needs to be cleaned up?"

"Uh-no. Don't get any ideas, Kelly," said Vick, looking over to Jonah for backup. "That place is too far gone to try anything like that and since I didn't do nothing, I sure as hell ain't cleaning anything up."

Jonah shrugged. "Alright, let's take my car."

"What I don't get is this," Jonah thought aloud as we drove out of the parking lot. "Everybody likes Remmy but his house got trashed by everyone!" Jonah glanced at Vick who began to laugh like it was the funniest thing he'd ever heard. Jonah knowingly looked through his mirror at me. "I keep thinking, what if that was my house, you know?"

"Who was over there, Vick?" I asked as Vick spun around angrily.

"I didn't make a list!" Vick snapped. "I don't want to be blamed for anything that happened in that house! I only went over there once!"

"Bullshit!" snarled Jonah.

"Just don't mention my name if anyone says anything, alright?"

"What happened over there, Vick?" Jonah continued to press.

"Lots of shit!"

"Yeah, like what?"

"I don't know! Someone disfigured his family's portrait," Vick answered like it was fresh on his mind.

"What do you mean *disfigured*?" Jonah asked.

"I don't know—with crude markings."

"Crude markings?" I laughed.

"Yeah!" Vick cracked a smile. "They painted horns and a tail on Remmy, big tits on his mom, and then a cartoon guy pissing on his dad's head. Some asshole even lit the couch on fire and shoved it through the sliding glass door."

"And to top it all off! Poor Maxie!" Jonah glared at Vick.

"Well don't look at me!" Vick said defensively.

"So what the hell really happened to her, Vick?"

"I already told you she died of a fucking heart attack or something when they were blasting music one night!"

"Who was taking care of the dog?" I asked.

"No one did!" Jonah exclaimed. "That dog had a little door and this huge, self-feeding food and water dispenser. It was trained to do everything, fetch the paper, play dead, stand up, speak. She could've run for governor."

"Yeah," Vick added, "She could roll over, shake hands, turn in circles–all that crazy shit." Vick grinned at Jonah who continued to glare.

"When did she die?" Jonah questioned.

"It happened like a week or so ago!" Vick snorted back some snot and spit out the window. "Maxie got more and more pissed off as the days went on! Who could blame it, with all these assholes ripping its house apart! Right?"

"She was getting aggressive, yeah," agreed Jonah, "but protecting her home."

"Then it got to barking so much, if anyone went near it, it would start attacking them! So we had to start locking it up in the back room but then someone would always go back there to fuck around and open the door and Maxie would get back out!"

"It knew you all weren't right!" Jonah shook his head. "And then what happened?"

"It just, you know, went yap, yap, YAP! YAP! YAP! YAP! YAP!"

"Yeah, and then what, you fucking moron! How did it die?"

Vick shrugged and leaned forward. "So we just turned up the stereo, blasting hardcore and playing video games, and let it bark its head off! We thought it was funny. Then somebody put on Despair's newest demo tape and then the dog went fucking ape shit! Especially when we turned it all the way up. Dude! It started running around the room in circles, going berserk, trying to bite itself in the ass, around and around, faster and faster, and the bulldog ran until it fell over, and then just its four stubby little legs were going at it, beating the air like this." Vick tucked his hands in and used his wrists to bat the air. "Then it started twitching and let out this huge, nasty dog fart that stunk up the whole room and just, fucking–died, dude."

"Why didn't you try to take it to a vet or something? I asked.

"Yeah right," Vick yelled at me. "There ain't no vets open at one in the morning!"

"And we are talking about the Leech Mob," said Jonah, "not the Salvation Army. So what did you do with her? Bury her?"

Vick snickered. "No, they just, uh, dragged her to a back closet and shut the door.

"That is so wrong," I said and looked down.

"If that was my dog, I would want to kill somebody!" Jonah agreed, staring straight ahead as he drove. "Did someone really bomb the inside of Remmy's house?"

"Yeah, markers and spray paint everywhere!" Vick nodded. "No tags though. No incriminating evidence. Someone even spray painted a tombstone on the closet door."

"This is pissing me off!" complained Jonah.

Remmy's front door was hanging off the hinges and when we stepped in, the first thing I noticed was the smell, a combination of paint fumes and rot. Vick strolled into the house while Jonah and I stood there, surprised at how bad it was. Graffiti covered the walls. His family's photos were all drawn over. Somebody had killed the kitchen, trying to cook. Burnt pots and pans were left in the stopped-up sink and on the stove with globs of rotten green eggs and pools of grease with white hairs growing out of the goo.

"They are going to bug when they come home to this."

"Tell me about it," Jonah said, kicking a stained burnt pillow out of his way and looking around disgustedly.

"This could be like a TV show," Vick laughed.

"Vick, how many Leech Mob kids were here?"

"I don't know. All of them. Landbury, too," Vick answered as Jonah pointed out the singed path across what otherwise might have been green living room carpet.

"This is where somebody accidentally set the sofa on fire and then, trying to keep the house from burning down, pushed it through the living room and dining room, smashing everything in its way!"

Dirt from overturned potted plants lay in piles all over the carpet. The glass coffee table was shattered and the dining room table had two legs broken off, slanting onto the floor. We traced the path of the burning couch straight through the sliding glass door, also shattered. There hanging outside and nailed to the house where the glass door had been was the shower curtain, flapping in the wind. We stepped out onto the deck, crunching the broken glass, and peered over the railing to where the burnt sofa fell to the ground below.

"Who lit the sofa on fire, Vick?" Jonah asked.

"I don't know but at least they saved the house from burning down."

"Yeah," Jonah shook his head. "He's a fucking hero, whoever *he* is." Jonah glanced at Vick who stared off in thought.

"I heard it's gotten worse since I was here last."

"Oh yeah? How did you hear that, Vick?" Jonah asked.

"I don't remember," he mumbled.

We walked toward the back of the house, stepping over a puddle of dry puke in the hallway. The walls had been smeared with stuff that looked like mustard and relish; cigarettes had been stamped out on the rugs and on the linoleum floors. I glanced in the bathroom and saw that the toilet was clogged with nasty toilet paper and water had flooded the bathroom, spilling out into the hall, only to be absorbed by the carpet. Inside the TV room, Jonah found two kids watching a TV that now had a crack running down the middle of the screen. They nervously stared up at us as we stopped by the door.

"What's up?" I asked. One barely nodded. "What are you doing here?"

"Who are these assholes?" Vick pushed me aside.

"We're like Stan's friends."

"Who the fuck is Stan?" Vick raised his voice.

"Just get these retards out of here. Enough's enough," Jonah said to Vick and moved on.

"Jonah, you want to see if Maxie is still there?" I asked, opening his parents' room door.

"Well, it didn't walk out of there."

We went in and instantly covered our noses.

"Oh my god, it reeks!" Jonah said. He walked over to the closet, where spray painted were the words *R.I.P. ROVER.*

We opened the door and smelled another gust of putrid air.

"Yup, she's still there," Jonah winced.

"Maybe we should bury her."

"No, I'm not getting wrapped up in the middle of this mess," Jonah shook his head. "If the police catch me in a defiled house with a dead fucking dog, I'll be called a Satanist."

"They didn't even get her name right," I mumbled.

"Let's get the fuck out of this hell hole!" Jonah said and then walked past Vick into the TV room where the two kids were still sitting.

"Who told you about the party?"

"Stan did!" one guy shouted. "I already told you, man!" The kid began to get loud, crossed his arms, and stared at the TV.

"Party's over! Get the fuck out!" Jonah raised his voice.

"You get out! I'm not bothering you, so fuck off! I'll leave when I feel like it."

Jonah lunged, grabbed hold of the kid, dragged him across the couch, and began pounding his head against the armrest. "Do you feel like leaving now?"

"What the hell is your problem!" the dude sat up and cried.

"Get the fuck out of here!" Jonah screamed again and while I tried to hold him back, the two kids ran down the hall and kicked the front door open, knocking it completely off its hinges.

"Let's get out of here," Jonah urged.

"Dude, what happened last Friday?" I asked Vick when we got in the car. "I thought you were going to pick me up."

Vick stared at me, his green eyes narrowing. "Do you know how many kids want me to pick em up so they could roll with me? Do you know how many plans I have to make each weekend?" Vick looked out the window grimly.

"No, not really," I answered dismally.

"Everybody! And a hell of a lot more!" Vick said with an insane smile. "So then you know what happens, right?" I shook my head. "They get fucked—

hahahahaha!" Vick snorted and turned up the radio.

"What did everybody end up doing anyway?"

"Doing? What did everybody end up doing?" he mimicked me strangely.

"Yeah," I said and he instantly grew serious.

"I just went to practice and then to Images. Then Saturday we played a show in New Haven."

"Damn! I got to get to a show! Anything happen?"

"I met some girl and sucked some face," Vick shrugged.

"Who?"

"I don't know, some hog!"

"A hog?"

"Listen, jackass! How am I supposed to remember every pig's name I slap in the ass—ha ha ha."

"You're in a hardcore group, right?"

Vick sighed as we drove along. "Yup."

"What do you all call yourselves?"

"The Hog Suckers. Ha ha ha."

"Really?"

"No, not really, jackass. We're called Horseflesh. You ever heard of us?"

"Horseflesh? No."

"I'll get you a tape, make a few copies, get it out, okay?"

"Who else from Riverview went to the show?"

"Most of the girls, Casey was there, Dave, Obi, Zed and Lampy. Kit, Flip and uh, Face was there."

"Face?" I asked.

"Yeah, he's always around," added Jonah.

"I don't know him."

"Face is that weird kid who missed the first couple months of school," explained Jonah. "He's the dude with like yellow dreads and round, uh, John Lennon glasses."

"He's hard to miss. He's annoying—even worse than you!" Vick snickered. "You won't see him much cause he's in the honors' wing and always skips lunch, leaves school, and smokes pot. Fucking druggie, ha ha. Besides that, he's okay. Yo, here's a flier for tonight's show!"

Vick dug through his backpack and shoved a sheet of paper into my hand. It was done mostly in graffiti lettering:

Desperate Bob Presents
FAST DRAW
POSERDEATH
DESPAIR
STRAIGHT UP
HORSEFLESH
At: THE NIGHT BREED
November 13th ALL AGES starting at 7 pm

"I wanna go but I don't have a ride, man!"

"So it's all my fault?" He looked back, shrugging.

"Don't look at me, man," said Jonah, pulling back into the school. "You know I have to work weekends."

"I'd seriously drive, dude, but I got to get to practice first," Vick explained. "After we load up all the equipment, there's no room for anyone else." Vick opened the door and then leaned back into the car. "Ask the girls if they'd give you a ride. Alright? I'll check you, later." He spun around, slamming the door.

"Even if he says he'll drive, Vick always disses."

"That dude is retarded." Jonah looked at me. "Get in the front seat."

◆

I missed the show. And I kept on missing shows. So I decided to see this Face kid but he turned out to be crazier than Vick. I saw him digging through his locker on the second floor. Hardly anyone had lockers up there.

"Hey, you're Face, right?" I smiled and reached to shake his hand. He slammed the locker shut and backed away slowly.

"I'm Kelly, dude. I keep on missing the shows, though I hear you manage to get there from time to time."

"Either you charge me with a crime or you let me carry on with my business. I'm warning you, I know the law, mister!" He lunged away, breaking into a wild run.

"Wait up, man! I just wanted to ask you..." I yelled while he sprinted away, peering back with bloodshot bugged out eyes as he booked through the school. "Yo! What the hell is your problem, man?" I hauled after him as he jumped the stairs, slipped and smashed his knee. Face sat on the bottom step and leaned against the wall, gripping his leg in pain. He took a deep breath and went limping away.

"Face!" I called.

"What?" he snapped, instantly stopping dead in his tracks, keeping his back to me. "Haven't you caused enough trouble already!" A teacher walked out into the hall, gave us a dirty look, and then shut the door. "I see how it is! Paid off by Nicodemus to look the other way!" He pointed at the closed door and started limping again. "Doesn't anybody see this? An illegal interrogation is taking place. Help!"

"Dude, you're not making any sense."

"You stay the hell away from me!" Face howled.

"Fine." I started to walk the other way but then he began to follow me.

"Alright." He looked both ways. "Follow me and don't say a word—it's not safe around here." I thought he was nuts, but I followed him toward the in-school suspension room. He checked the nearby corridor in case it might have been bugged and then whispered, "You want to get to a club or a show or out into the world, damn you!" He shook his fist into a corner. "That is what you're asking me, right?"

"Yeah."

"I already told you but you weren't listening. So, I'll say it just one, more, time. When you're out there in the parking lot after school, you gotta jump into somebody's ride." Face hopped to the side, demonstrating. "Like jump, jump, jump! Damn you! Jump into somebody's car! By any means necessary!"

"Okay, I got it."

"Then, like–you just–don't–ever–get out of that car. Not ever. Cause if you do, they'll probably leave you right there. And never, ever, never ever, never ever, ever, ever let them drop you off at home." Face shook his head crazily.

"Why not?"

"Why not? Cause they'll never come back for you!" Face stared into space, his eyes agape. He raised his eyebrows and flared his nostrils, "Not even if they promise they will! They'll tell you they'll come back for you! They always say they will!" Face paused. "But they, by god, are lying!" Face looked around the hall and mumbled. "Even if they want to go have sex with each other–you must wait in the car. If they want to have sex in the car–then you, my friend, must get into the trunk."

"No way."

Face raised his hand to silence me. "That's precisely how I got stuck in the trunk and they forgot about me until I made a big fuss Monday morning in the school parking lot! It was other kids who heard my screams and then Vick, who will remain nameless, was paged to the office and forced to unlock my cell. I couldn't breathe and I had messed myself. They wanted me to press charges but I refused. It was a terrible event but totally worth the sacrifice of staying mobile."

"You're making that up!" I chuckled. "You're really not serious."

He dropped a hand on my shoulder. "Is it true, or is it legend?" He suddenly grinned ear to ear with an insane gleam in his eyes, did a little tap dance, gave me the thumbs up, and winked. I stared at him and he stared back, frozen.

"Oh, there's Macie!" Face suddenly dropped his act and bumped into me as he ran past. "Oh Macie! There you are, my love! Macie! Macie! Macie! God knows I love Macie!"

Macie walked by with her green eyes blazing. Her dirty blonde hair was slightly greasy with a few strands dyed purple. "Oh give me a hug, Macie!" Macie saw him and began to walk faster but Face caught up and grabbed her, placing his cheek gently against hers while lifting one of his legs and wrapping it around her like he was about to do a pole dance. Macie paused and rolled her big eyes as he caressed her head.

"Okay Face, easy Face," she coaxed him while gently pushing him away. "Face, I'm late, honey!" she said sweetly before soon raising her voice. "Face, I'm late! Get the hell away from me!" She shoved him. Face instantly fell over dramatically and rolled across the hallway as if he'd been hurled aside, staring horrified.

"Well you didn't have to hit me!"

"Oh God!" Macie complained and then quickly sprinted away but Face followed her, crawling on his knees, pleading.

"Macie, I'm sorry! I'm sooooo sorry, come back to me! OH GOD, PLEASE COME BACK TO MEEEE!" He wailed until Midge walked out of the in-school suspension room and stared at him as though he'd completely lost his mind. Yet Face just stuck his thumb into his mouth and continued crawling on his knees past the stunned lady, and then stood up and shuffled after Macie, turning to look at the old woman with his thumb still stuck in his mouth.

Midge shook her head and moved on, exclaiming to me as she passed, "They're not even on drugs and they act this way! Oh, I just don't know with you kids anymore!"

"Macie! Macie! Wait up," Face continued to call after her.

"Face!" I shouted.

"You stay away from me!" He started to run. "I can't lose her!"

I followed him around the corner and saw him standing in the middle of the next hall, holding his hands up in the air. "That rat bastard Nicodemus took her!" Face shook his fist and threatened the walls around us, "Nicodemus, you haven't seen the last of me!"

"Face, what are you doing after school?"

"Going out with Kit for a little of this." Face held his finger and thumb up to his lips like he was smoking a roach.

"You think that will do any good?"

"Well it doesn't hurt to try."

◆

The last bell rang on Friday afternoon and, even though I had no ride, I followed Face's retarded logic, skipped the bus, and walked out to the student parking lot. It was a grey day that had threatened to rain since morning but still hadn't. The late November sky was covered with dark clouds, and the pines and hemlocks shook in the damp winds that grew colder day by day.

Casey sat in his car with Dave scowling out the window.

"What do you want?" Dave stared at me as I approached.

"Nothing."

"Then get to stepping."

I spotted Face a few cars over and expected him to freak out again, but instead he leaned over to say something to Kit, who glanced up but then shrugged his shoulders.

Face rolled the window half way down, "Psst Kelly, get over here."

I walked over to the old silver Oldsmobile, a big rectangular block of steel.

"Hey, what are you guys doing?" I asked.

"We're going to attack. Nicodemus has risen again."

Kit laughed. "Going for a drive. Got any money for gas?"

"Yeah. I can get you like four or five bucks.

"Sooooooooo?" Face asked. "Are you just going to stand there all day and get us busted for vagrancy or are you going to get in the car? Quick, they see you!"

"Close the door. It's getting fucking cold out," commanded Kit.

Face messed with the radio and began playing a strange song.

"This is Clam." Kit patted the vinyl top of the sun-cracked dashboard. "She's a beast."

"Except in the snow. Then Clam likes to crash into trees," explained Face.

"You should show some respect, at least you're riding cause of her," Kit giggled his high-pitched laughter.

"Yeah-yeah, go ahead and throw Clam in my face." Face then turned and looked at me. "Well, what are you waiting for–tell Clam you love her."

Kit chuckled, threw the gearshift into reverse, barely glanced in the rear view mirror and swerved backwards at a 90-degree turn, almost hitting a couple of girls in their parents' flashy car. The driver laid on the horn and they both sat there horrified as Kit slammed down on his brakes, nearly colliding with their car

"Didn't see ya, sorry-hee-hee." He crept forward, laughing his high pitched giggle out the window as we passed the other Leech Mob kids who stood pointing and laughing at Kit's driving. One spectator simply held out his middle finger, following us with the gesture as we drove out and circled back around to the front of the school.

"Oh man, where is she?" Kit complained as we rolled along until seeing Macie walk out the front door. Then he slammed on his brakes, throwing me and Face forward.

"Nice driving, iron-foot!" Face shouted at Kit, who yelled back, "Put your damn seatbelts on! How many times do I have to remind you?"

Macie walked over as Face jumped out to open the door for her, bowing gracefully as she slid in beside me.

"What's up, Face? That's like sooo nice you got the door for me."

"After the way you behaved, throwing me around in the hall, you should be ashamed of yourself."

"Oh god, Face, I barely touched you."

"What's up, Macie?" Kit asked reaching back to grasp her hand for a second.

"What's up, Kit, and you're like Kelly, right?" she asked but Kit slammed on the gas and tore back through the parking lot, chattering on like a maniac before slamming on his brakes halfway into the street as a car veered past, leaning on its horn and swerving around us.

"Oh my god, chill out, Kit!" Macie leaned forward and hit him. "You're going to get us into an accident."

"What! I didn't mean to!" he said, looking at her through his rear view mirror as he pulled out onto the road again.

"CAR!" she screamed as another raced past, also blaring its horn. Immediately Kit slammed on his breaks, throwing us all forward again.

Macie took a deep breath. "Just don't start driving like Vick, please promise me that at least." Macie sat back and buckled her seatbelt. "I didn't think you were going to stop for real!"

"Either did the other guy." Kit smiled.

"I didn't know you smoke." Macie looked at me.

"He doesn't. Do you, Kelly?"

"Not really."

"That just means more for us!" Face took out the dime bag and stuffed half of the contents into a Masterpiece Theatre style pipe and lit it up.

"Please don't tell anyone like you saw me all smoking," Macie pleaded.

"Your secret is safe with us." Face turned around before raising the pipe up to his lips and began taking puffs.

"Dude, you're wasting it!" Kit complained, smacking Face's arm.

"Chill out!" Face hollered. "You're gonna make me drop the bud. Then where will we be?"

"You'd be picking it up off the floor," Kit answered.

"No way! Never again!" argued Face.

"Yeah, you would," Kit chortled.

"Nope, not after last time. Worst mistake I ever made!"

"You're a trip, Face." Macie lit a cigarette and rolled down her window.

"No listen. I was smoking some kind bud up in my room and dropped my damn bowl so all the pieces flew out of my pipe and went everywhere on the floor. So there I am, picking up the burnt pieces and sticking them back into my pipe! So I'm finding all this bud, green pieces and burnt black pieces and I'm packing it all into my bowl and then I start to light it up again."

"Face, you better have a point to this story."

"Listen, I'm sitting up there, smoking and listening to some music and then I realize, hey, this shit tastes funny! So I look in my bowl and see this half-burnt fly, lying in a nest of green bud." Face tried to do his best impersonation of a half-burnt fly.

"Eeeuuuu!" shrilled Macie.

"Oh god!" Kit grinned and began cranking up his window. "Kelly, roll yours up too so we can clambake the clam."

"That's how she got her name." Face winked at me as he passed the pipe to

Macie. They smoked it until it turned to ash and then Face packed it up and sent it around again.

"Hey, I think I feel something," I mentioned to the others.

"But you didn't even smoke!" Macie giggled.

"I think I feel something anyway!"

"Yeah, you have a buzz from just the contact smoke in the car."

"It takes a couple minutes before it really kicks in," Kit agreed, "and then I bet you couldn't even put your socks on right!"

"So what do you guys want to do?" asked Macie.

"You're looking at it." Face lifted the bowl.

"We can go over my house," I suggested.

"Won't your mom know that we're stoned?" Kit looked worried.

"Not unless you tell her. Besides," I said, "she might be out somewhere."

Once we pulled up to my house, the three exited the car nervously and followed me inside. They all relaxed when they saw that my mom was out. Kit walked into the kitchen and opened the fridge, "Oh my god!" His eyes gaped open wide.

"What?" I asked.

"You have WHOLE MILK!" he exclaimed.

"Yeah so?"

"God, I love whole milk! My mom only buys skim. She says it's healthier but it tastes like water to me."

"Do you want a glass?"

"Oh, wow, yeah, really, can I?" His eyes were astonished.

"Yeah," I said, looking at him funny. "Go for it. Glasses are over there. Macie, Face, get whatever you want. If you like milk as much as Kit, knock yourselves out."

"Nah, no milk for me," she answered. "Can I just have some water?"

"Oh my Lord!" shouted Kit as he opened up the freezer. "Your mom's got microwave chicken pies! Those are the best! My mom NEVER buys microwave chicken pies. She says they're bad for you!"

"How are chicken pies bad for you?" Macie asked. "What do you eat?"

"Barley, broccoli, and fish," Kit said.

"What the hell is barley?" Face asked.

"What the hell is broccoli and fish?" laughed Kit.

"Heat up four of em," I offered.

As we ate, Kit found more and more food that had been outlawed at his house and seized the opportunity to indulge, while Face rummaged around my room and found a pair of electric hair clippers.

"Can you cut hair, Kelly?" He held them up.

"Yeah, I guess."

"Can you cut mine, too?" Kit asked. "Just shave the sides though."

"Yeah, don't touch the top," agreed Face.

"Lazy Mohawk," I said.

"A what?" asked Macie.

"The Leech Mob style. It's kind of like a Lazy Mohawk."

"Yeah, I like that," repeated Kit, "a Lazy Mohawk."

We went back into the kitchen and pulled a chair into the middle of the floor, where Kit pushed Face out of the way, shouting "Shotgun" and sat down.

"What the hell? It was my idea!"

"Yeah, whatever," he mumbled, as I threw the nylon sheet around his shoulders and snapped it behind his neck.

"So you cut hair, Kelly?" Macie asked.

"Yeah sure, I mean, I do now."

"Wait! You've never done this before!" Kit hollered, clutching his head.

"How tough can it be? I'll just snap on the attachment, dude!"

Kit looked up at the others. "Alright, but if he starts to mess up my hair, like real bad, I want you guys to promise to tell me before it gets ruined!"

"Look, do you want me to cut it or not?"

"Yeah, okay, fine…"

"You worry too much!"

Macie stayed on the phone, talking to Krissy before asking, "Do you guys want to go over to Krissy's house for a little while, cause I might be staying over there tonight."

"Yeah sure, can we sleep over, too?" pleaded Face.

"It's cool with me but I don't think her mother would go for it."

"Does she have anything to eat over there?" Kit asked, keyed up again.

✦

Krissy met us at her door, gave Macie a hug, and then motioned us in. She looked mad pretty, I thought, even though she wore a sweatshirt.

"Where's my hug?" Face flirted.

"You want a hug, fine, come here," Krissy offered.

Kit squeezed past Krissy and walked into the kitchen.

"Uh, hello Kit, nice to see you, too." Krissy added sarcastically, "I'm fine, how have you been?"

"Oh hi!" Kit said as he opened the fridge. "OH MY GOD!"

"What?" Krissy asked, concerned that something was wrong.

"YOU GOT BAGELS AND CREAM CHEESE! MY MOTHER NEVER BUYS BAGELS AND CREAM CHEESE!"

A half hour later we all sat around her dining room table, watching Kit stuff his face. It was going on six o'clock. After the bagels, Kit had seen the bag of Wonder Bread and went crazy, stacking ten slices on a plate saying, "I LOVE BREAD, GOOD OLD BREAD, BREAD, BREAD, BREAD." He stuffed slice after slice of bread into his mouth, guzzling it down with his beloved whole milk.

"Kit, are you like alright?" Krissy asked and glanced at Macie, who shook her head and shrugged her shoulders.

"Yeah why?" he grunted with his mouth full.

"Don't you get enough to eat at home?"

"My mom only buys whole wheat bread and skim milk and I think it's disgusting!" Kit explained. "And she puts bean sprouts on my tuna fish sandwiches!"

"Oh." Krissy raised an eyebrow at Macie.

"He went crazy at my house, too," I added.

"He always eats like this," Face piped in. "He's going to weigh like 500 pounds when he hits thirty, and have lamb-chop sideburns, and sit on the porch all day with an ugly dog, and his wife will have a beehive hairdo and move around with a walker." Face laughed, high pitched as he pointed at Kit.

"Did you just say hair *DOO*?" Kit asked and then burst out laughing.

"So, what's going on tonight?" Macie looked at Krissy.

"What do you mean? With the Wonder Bread boys over here?" Krissy tucked her chin in.

"Oh god no! After we kick them out."

"I haven't heard about anything. My mom says I can take her car but I don't want to go out, just to go to Images," sighed Krissy.

"Oh why not! That place is the coolest!" Kit interrupted her but was ignored.

"I wouldn't mind renting a movie and getting take out, like Chinese."

"Chinese food!" Kit exclaimed.

Macie shook her head. "Yeah, I don't want to go to a club either. I d▨ feel like going to a party. I'm just like sick of the whole scene."

"Well, I wouldn't mind going to a party," admitted Krissy. "What about y▨ guys?"

"What?" Kit looked up, poking the last piece of bread inside his cheek. He gulped the wad of bread down. "Face, what are we doing?" They both began laughing again.

"First, we shall partake in a bag of marijuana." Face took a gulp of soda, letting out a belch. "And I'm always willing to share."

"Eeeuuu. Face, you pig! Get some manners!" complained Krissy.

"So nobody knows what's going on?" asked Macie.

"Who cares?" Kit chimed in, getting up and opening the fridge again as Krissy rolled her eyes. "All I know is I want to get more weed. Hey! You got like seven dollars so I can get us a dime bag?" He turned and looked hopefully at her.

"No way, Kit."

"Oh." He dropped his shoulders and turned back to the fridge.

"Kit, get the hell out of my fridge. You've eaten enough."

Kit shrugged and sat back down. "Remmy and his parents came home the other day."

"So tell us what happened," Krissy whispered.

"Well his parents flipped out, of course, and let's just say that Remmy isn't living at home right now."

"He isn't?" Macie seemed more worried than the rest of us. "But it wasn't even Remmy's fault."

"Yeah, it's not his fault his friends are assholes!" Krissy said.

"Where's he staying? At Flip's house or something?"

"I don't know. His parents called the cops but there is like nothing they can do," Kit explained.

"But where's Remmy?" Macie repeated.

"Yes, she desperately needs to know," Krissy laughed.

"Oh I get it," Kit giggled. "Macie has a thing for Remmy, eh? Eh? Eh?"

"Shut up, Kit. See this is how rumors get started!" Macie frowned. "I like somebody, but not Remmy."

"Please, please, please. Let it be me!" Face crossed both fingers.

"Oh shut up, Face. You have a girlfriend."

"Yeah, but she's not you, Macie."

ted Kit, "but Face never sees her and if he does, he's
it!"

us old girl." Kit leaned back and crossed his arms.

c, they broke up a decade ago." Macie squinted her eyes.

"Well Otis doesn't seem to think so," said Kit.

"Well fuck Otis," retorted Krissy. "Tell him to get over her already."

"Easy for you to say."

"Why?"

"Cause you're a girl. Ask Kelly how Otis would act if we told him that."

"Yeah okay, I see your point." She looked at me. "I was so mad, I screamed at them, saying how lame they were for jumping you!"

"Yeah, I remember." I smiled.

"Everybody has to earn their colors," Face quipped.

"Yeah, they do," agreed Kit.

"Oh yeah, big time gang-banger Kit! Weren't you just saying how scared you were of Otis! And when did you get your ass kicked by the Leech Mob?" Krissy shouted.

"Like every day!" Kit bellowed.

"He does have a point there," agreed Face.

Krissy grinned and looked at me. "You don't like say too much, do you?"

"Yeah I do," I argued.

"No, you don't," she snapped back. "How old are you anyway?"

"Fifteen."

"You're only fifteen?" She wrinkled her forehead in surprise. "Do any of you boys know how to play cards?" Krissy leaned back in her chair, reached into a drawer behind her, and produced a deck of playing cards. "I bet I'll kick all of your asses at poker!"

"Krissy does know her cards," Macie chimed in.

"I can't even think straight right now." Kit sat with blood shot eyes and a stupid grin on his contented face.

"That's what I thought," said Krissy.

"Not so fast, sweet feet," joked Face, with one eyebrow raised. "Are you willing to put a wager behind your skill? If so, you can deal me in. That is, if you're not scared of playing against one of the all-time best."

"Yeah right," sneered Krissy. "I doubt you have fifty cents though."

Face stuck out his tongue as he began rifling through his pockets, then held out his fist, palm down, and dropped about three dollars in dimes, nickels and pennies on the table.

"But we need that!" Kit cried. "Cause we're out of bud."

"Oh please, Kit," sneered Macie. "How much bud can you get with three bucks in change anyway, dude?"

"That's why we're playing for money, cause we're gonna win!" announced Face, shaking his head as though Kit were a complete idiot for missing the point.

"Cards are boring if there isn't any skin in the game." Krissy smiled slyly and reached for a coffee can, which rattled with a few loose coins.

"How about strip poker?" suggested Kit.

"Please." Krissy rolled her eyes. "Why would I want to see any of you naked? Besides, I'll kick your asses so bad you won't be able to buy any more pot for the rest of your lives."

"Yeah, she's right, Face!" Kit appeared distraught.

"You're on, hot pants!" snapped Face, leaning forward and making a face at her. "Put some real money where your mouth is, slick stuff!"

"You're on!" Krissy roared. She split the deck and shuffled the cards, forwards and then bridged. The cards whirred.

"You see that!" Kit exclaimed. "You see how she did that!"

"So?" grunted Face.

"So, you don't stand a chance!"

"They're so lame. They only want to play for pennies!" Face reached into his upper pocket and slapped two one dollar bills on the table."

"Where did you get that?" Kit yelled, glancing at the money and then at Face, who gave him a furtive wink.

"Fine! I'll be right back." Krissy slid her chair back and stood up. "But remember, this is for keeps!"

"Yeah, for keeps," Face repeated. "Just show me the damn quarters!" He picked the deck of cards up and began examining them.

"And I'll hold those." Macie leaned forward and snatched the cards out of Face's hands. "I don't trust you. You'll mark the deck or something."

"Yeah, keep an eye on them, Macie," Krissy called from the back room.

"What? I don't even know how to mark a deck," confessed Face. "I was just going to shuffle them."

"Fine, shuffle them." Macie handed them back. Face broke the deck in half, held them against the table, stuck out his tongue, and began shuffling the cards, which flew all over the table and onto the floor while Macie giggled.

"Oh my god!" groaned Kit, sitting back and shaking his head pathetically. "We are so dead!"

"The game is all up here, my friend." Face tapped the side of his head.

"Did I mention how dead we are? And the pot is wearing off!" Kit buried his face in his arms on the table.

"Alright, I'm back." Krissy entered the room, now wearing a green poker visor hat. She dropped a large jar filled with silver coins on the table and sat down, all business. "And since I'm the house, I deal first. Do any of you not know how to play Five Card Draw?" Krissy shuffled the deck again.

"Does a duck know how to dance?" asked Face, as Krissy quickly dealt the cards to each of us. She peeked at her cards, moved two around, and finally looked at Macie, who tossed down two quarters to get things started.

"Very interesting play." Face fumbled with his cards, until he began dropping some onto the floor. He bent over to pick them up, hitting his head underneath the table. "Ow!" He squinted his eyes, holding his head in pain as he sat up. "Nicodemus, I'll get you for this!" he threatened the walls, waving his fist in the air.

"Who the hell is this Nickageemus you keep talking about?" Krissy asked.

"NICODEMUS!" Face corrected her, leaned closer and whispered, "He's an old rat but he was given chemicals to become a super genius."

"Nicodemus," repeated Kit. "You know, in that movie ..."

"SHUT UP!" commanded Face.

"Alright, I don't care already. Just place your damn bet. And how many cards do you want, Face?" Krissy asked in frustration.

"Whatever I can get from Miss Hot-Poker-Ass!" returned Face, with a crooked smile.

"Dude, what are you talking about?" Macie leaned back with her cards.

"I fold," Kit conceded, dropping his hand.

"You're beyond help, Face," fumed Krissy as Face stared at her crazily. "Well! What do you want?"

"Well, what can I get?" Face shouted back.

"Three cards but you haven't even bet yet!"

"Fine, give them to me already!" Face dropped the coins on the table. "And don't ask me any more questions!"

"But you got to throw in three cards that you don't want!"

"Oh, I see how you are! Nothing's ever for free. I always got to throw in a card or something."

Kit dropped his head with a thud on the top of the table. "There is no weed in our future," he wailed.

About an hour later, Krissy's mom walked in wearing a blue suit, a short corporate haircut, and gold-rimmed eyeglasses. She set her briefcase down and then stood in her kitchen, eyeballing us suspiciously.

"Hi Mom," greeted Krissy. "How was work?"

"Hello, Mrs. Thomas," chimed Macie.

"Well hello everyone. I'm Krissy's mother, to those of you I haven't met."

"I'm Kelly. It's nice to meet you."

"Hello Kelly."

"Hi, I'm Face."

"I'm Kit, remember me?"

"Yes, fine. So, kids, what's the plan tonight?"

"Actually I got to get the car back home soon," stammered Kit, standing up. "I'm going to be late for dinner."

"Yeah, Mom. They were just about to leave," Krissy explained.

"You need a ride home, Macie?"

"No, I'll hang around here."

"Alright later," said Kit.

"Well it was nice meeting you all…"

"Yeah and thanks for the poker tips, toots!" Face winked and then aimed his fingers like a gun at Krissy, who scowled at him before getting up and following us out.

"I know you were cheating, Facc," she whispered as we walked out.

"I was not!"

"When I figure out how you did it, I'm going to kick your ass!" She then slammed the door shut.

"I can't believe you took her for all that."

"Yeah, I hustled her real good," bragged Face.

"How did you learn to play cards like that?"

"Watching my uncles. That's all they used to do."

"Shit, how much money did you get?"

"Altogether, like 13 dollars in change. Did you see her? She was getting so mad that she kept throwing in more dough but that's how you do it. You let em win a couple times straight, and then get em used to losing. So now we have enough for a dime," Face sang out.

"You keep on forgetting that Clam's been running on fumes!" Kit pointed to his gas gage as we got in the car.

"And then to the mall!" I cheered.

"Yes, show some respect for your local mall. The only place that we can score weed, any time!" Face then snapped his fingers and we sped off.

✦

"There's no weed anywhere and I've looked everywhere," Face complained after we'd been hanging in the food court for over an hour. "Any luck, Kit?"

"No, beside some little Puerto Rican dude who just tried to sell me a bag of oregano," Kit laughed. "That shit didn't even look like weed and I was like you must think I'm pretty stupid, huh?"

"I bought fake weed a couple times," confessed Face. "What about that fat dude you know?"

"What fat dude?" Kit scratched his beard.

"That Biggie Smalls-looking kid."

"Are you talking about Boo Landers?" Kit laughed. "The Dust Head?"

"Yeah, Boo—"

"Boo's always been my last resort, cause his dimes are like nickel bags, but if we can find him, any weed is good weed now."

"Cause he's right over there!" Face exclaimed.

"Where?" asked Kit.

"He just walked off the escalator!"

"Well shit," exclaimed Kit, looking around.

"Take the money! I got ten dollars!" Face stuffed the money into Kit's hand.

"I got a better idea." Kit stood up. "Let's all go up."

We followed Kit up to Boo, an eighteen-year old black kid who towered over all of us.

"Like how's the view up there, Boo?" Kit shielded his eyes and looked up to Boo.

"Little white dude got jokes. What's up, Kit?"

"What's up, Boo? You got a dime bag?"

Boo looked around, "Fo show! Let's take a walk. Follow me." Boo led us down the escalator while warning his friends, "Keep your eyeballs on!" He walked toward a small side exit where he turned around, suspiciously checking in all directions before grumbling, "Let's see yo dough!"

"Where's the weed?" Kit asked nervously.

Boo smiled and then poked out his tongue where, stuck on the end and glistening with spit, was the small green bag. He wagged it back and forth, and Kit reached into his pocket and pulled out the ten-spot so Boo could see it.

Boo leaned over him and whispered, "Open yo mouth!"

"Wh-what?" Kit stuttered.

Boo raised his voice. "I says, open yo mouth!"

Kit glanced at us and then hesitantly opened his mouth, when suddenly Boo swiped the dime bag out of his own mouth and dropped it into Kit's, while snatching the ten-dollar bill out Kit's hand. Instantly, Boo disappeared through the doorway, while we took off toward the mall's main entrance, where shoppers sat on benches and waited for the bus. Face and I glanced at Kit who was turning green, though struggling to appear normal. We couldn't hold our laughter back, but laughing was the worst thing we could have done. Kit began to snort and before I knew it, he was choking on the dime bag, grabbing at his throat with both hands. His eyes bulged out as he desperately gasped for air.

"Holy shit! Do something, Kelly!" Face screamed, terrified.

"LIKE WHAT?" I wailed.

Frantically, I pounded on Kit's back, so hard that the dime bag came flying out of his mouth and landed on the floor, ten feet in front of us, right in front of the shoppers waiting for the bus! Two old Hispanic women, surrounded by several young children, saw it clearly: a postage stamp-sized, see-through bag, filled with buds, all glistening with saliva and reflecting the mall's lights.

As Kit sucked in air, Face raced over and scooped it up right before two curious children could get to it first, and we hurried away. We dropped all casualness and booked up the escalator, knocking into a lady.

"Hey, watch it, junior!"

We whipped around the railing, running back through the food court, and headed for the exit to the parking garage.

"God, I almost died choking on a dime bag!" Kit cried when we made it outside.

I was still laughing while Face kept repeating, "We're gonna get busted! We're gonna get busted! Those people saw everything!"

"Oh shit, we're dead! I can't even remember where I parked!" Kit howled as we ran circles in the parking garage, looking for the Clam.

"There it is!" Face shouted.

We jumped in. Kit turned the ignition over and sped down the spiraling ramp, down five floors, finally bottoming out with a snap-on hubcap spinning away.

"Go! Go! Go! A mall security truck!" Face screamed.

"Where!" Kit asked, looking around.

"Don't slow down! Those little kids were informants for the FBI! No! For *Nickodemus!*"

Chapter 6: Violet

"Some of you have already met Kelly, our new resident."

"Hello Kelly. I am Barbara and this is Rueben. We're both counselors here at the institution. We're going around the room introducing ourselves. . ."

"You don't give a fuck about what I've been trying to tell you!" shouted a short chubby girl with tears streaming down her face. Every so often she sniffed back the snot.

"Jody!" Barbara said sternly. "This is certainly not Level 4 behavior!"

"I don't give a shit! This place sucks!" she wailed, dropping her head into her hands. "Fuck!"

Barbara leaned over to whisper in her ear as she yelped, "I know but I can't. . .I can't! I fucking can't!"

"Alright, who's next?" Rueben asked and then pointed toward a kid who gestured to himself.

"Me? You want to know why I'm here? Well, that's not always easy to say! I mean, why are any of us here! Anything I say can or will be used against me. A police officer told me that and he wasn't lying!"

"Okay, thank you Stephen, and Lauren, you're next."

"I'm Lauren and I'm in here because of alcohol and aggression." She leaned to the side, weaving her hands together and smiling embarrassedly.

"Yes go on," Barbara coaxed her.

"What?" Lauren began to laugh. "I told you enough! Stephen didn't even say anything!"

"Fine Lauren," Barbara fixed her with an annoyed look. "Then we'll have to talk about this before you go to dinner."

"Alright fine!" Lauren stamped her foot. "Promiscuity! There I said it!"

"Henry, look's like you're up," directed Barbara.

"Uh, what?" A kid looked around, his face covered by long greasy hair. He reached up and parted the strands like a theater curtain. "What?" He stared around the room with crossed, blue eyes and then scratched his bristled face.

"Good Day, Henry. Would you be so kind to state your name and why you are here?"

"Drugs," Henry said, causing the group to chuckle.

Barbara sighed. "Thank you, Henry. You're up, Dianna."

"I'm Dianna," the girl whispered, "and I'm in here for depression and low self esteem." She curled her shoulders inward as though she were trying to roll herself into a little ball.

"Thank you, Dianna."

"JOE, VIOLENCE," a big kid with a shaved head announced proudly.

"Thank you, Joe. And Curtis."

"Curtis and I'm here for anxiety and paranoid thoughts."

But before Barbara could speak, the next kid screamed out.

"MY NAME IS DUCKY AND I'M HERE BECAUSE MY MOM IS A FUCKING ASSHOLE, MAN!" At eleven years old, Ducky was the youngest kid in the ward. Crust still lined his eyes, half of his hair stood straight up, and the other half stuck to the side of his head.

"Ducky loses a level, which puts him back on Level 0," Rueben sighed.

"NOOOOOO!" Ducky howled and then held his breath. His face turned from red to purple to blue.

The counselor ignored him. "NEXT!"

Ducky began to hit himself in the head. We silently watched as the slaps got louder. Then he gritted his teeth. Finally, he released the breath he'd been holding and bleated, trembling and sounding like a furious sheep.

"Ooooooohhhhhhh!" His voice shook as he vibrated with rage. At any moment, it seemed, Ducky was going to blast out of his chair and smash through the roof.

"Ducky, are you going to have to be restrained in the blue room again? Because that can be arranged," Rueben warned.

Ducky jumped up with his hand gripped firmly into a tiny fist and wheeled his arm around as he slowly walked toward Rueben. Barbara fished into her pocket, removed a small device, and switched it on. A split second later, Bunny crashed through the doors, holding the patient restraints.

"Alright! I give up!" Ducky pleaded from the center of the room as Rueben stood up behind him and Bunny approached from the front. "But I gave up!" Ducky cried. "I just want to sit back down!"

"This isn't a game, Ducky. Your actions bring consequences."

"You keep the hell away from me!" Ducky warned the two men as they closed in. "Stay the hell away from meeeeeeeee!" he squealed in a high-pitched, girlish scream and then dove headfirst between Bunny's long legs, causing him and Rueben to crash into each other. Ducky jumped to his feet and ran around the outside of the circle, tapping the other patients on the head. "DUCK! DUCK! DUCK! GOOSE!"

"Everyone get up and stand on this side of the room!" Rueben commanded, and we all shuffled to the wall as Ducky stood by himself in the middle of the room, caught somewhere between tears and laughter. Bunny and Rueben extended their arms and began to stalk Ducky. He faked left, ran right, and tried to get past them once more as chairs flipped over. Finally Rueben grabbed Ducky by the back of his shirt and slammed him down. As he squirmed on the floor, they wrapped him in a straitjacket. Then Bunny picked him up and carried him through the doors where his screams faded down the hall before the door slammed and echoed into silence.

"Alright, please take your seats. I believe that you are next, Edquina," Barbara said.

A girl stood up, holding a copy of the LOST DOG poster. "As you all probably know, Bowser is still missing." The others groaned as Barbara noted something down. "Anyone with any confidential information will be appreciated." Edquina sat back down. A few kids began to laugh.

"Fine, fine, is that all Edquina?" Barbara asked.

"Yes."

"And Kelly, why don't you introduce yourself?"

"Kelly, and I'm in here for getting arrested a few times and…" I paused, not knowing what else to say.

Dr. Gildmore shifted in his seat. "Yes…it was either jail or here, wasn't it Kelly?"

"Yeah…"

✦

Ezra stood up with his test and strutted down the aisle, wearing a dress as usual. He stood by the teacher, raised his skirt a few inches, and scratched his hairy legs.

"What are you doing, Ezra?" Mr. Ryan slapped his notes down as Ezra released his skirt.

"I just have a question about Number 3."

Ryan glared up, annoyed as usual, peering through his coke-bottle, magnifying-lenses. Ezra dropped the test down and then flipped through the pages, asking more and more questions.

"I'm not taking this test for you, Ezra," Mr. Ryan said angrily. "I have this strange feeling that you didn't prepare yourself for this little quiz one bit! What's your question exactly?"

"I don't understand Number 3."

"What is not an example of a symbiotic relationship?" Mr. Ryan read the question. "What don't you understand? It clearly asks which example given is the *wrong answer*! This should be your specialty."

"What should it be my specialty?" Ezra leaned back.

"Giving wrong answers," Mr. Ryan snickered to himself.

PRRRRRRRVT. Mr. Ryan looked up at Ezra, who squinted and farted again. "That's about as wrong as you can get," scowled Ezra.

Mr. Ryan trembled, working himself into a scream that was heard all over the school. "GET THE HELL OUT OF MY CLASS AND GO TO THE PRINCIPAL'S OFFICE TO TELL HIM WHAT YOU HAVE DONE!"

"What? It wasn't my fault!"

"YES IT WAS! Your flatulence problems—you tell him—never mind! I will tell him myself!"

"But I knew this guy who had to fart once but he held it in, and his stomach busted open and he died!"

"JUST GET OUT, YOU DISGUSTING IMBECILE!"

Ezra turned and walked out of the classroom as Mr. Ryan fixed his rage on the rest of us, who were hysterically laughing.

"Real funny, eh? Then you can all laugh your way down to the office, too!" Mr. Ryan stood up. "Now I'm going to give each of you three seconds to stop laughing or you can play follow the idiot down to the office! Sonny, you're first!" Mr. Ryan began to count. "ONE! TWO! THREE!" Sonny failed to stop laughing. "YOU'RE OUT OF HERE!" Like an umpire, Ryan wound his arm in the air and pointed to the door before moving to his second favorite person to kick out of his class. "You're up, Brody! Are you ready to stop laughing? No? ONE! TWO! THREE! NOW YOU'RE OUT OF HERE!" Mr. Ryan strolled over to Jonah. "You're next, Jonah! ONE! TWO–"

"But I can't help it, Mr. Ryan!" Jonah cried out between convulsions.

"THREE! YOU'RE OUT OF HERE! Last but not least–Kelly!" He strolled past me. "You also get till the count of three even though technically you've had the longest time to compose yourself. ONE! TWO! THREE! AND YOU'RE GONE!"

When Mr. Ryan was finished, he'd kicked all five of us out. We walked down to the principal's office in a single file line, all three seconds apart, intermittently cracking up. Teachers came out to the halls, shouting their lectures over our laughter as they slammed their doors. I was the last to enter the principal's office. Mr. Murphy stood behind his secretary, his hands raised in disbelief, while his eyes bugged out a little more with each new admit to his office. Thick beads of sweat formed across his forehead, as he waited for the last of us to sit down on the familiar row of chairs outside his office door.

"So, is this the last of you, or are there any more coming?"

"No, that's all," I answered.

"I was just saying to myself, I haven't seen the Leech Mob in a whole two days and thought that maybe there'd been a new world order."

"Me, too," said Sonny.

"You watch it, mister! There're plenty of good kids who want to learn and I will not stand idly by to watch the rest of you get in their way of receiving the proper education they deserve!"

"Yeah!" Ezra agreed, leaning forward and frowning at us.

"And you, SHUT UP!" Murphy glared at him and then down the line at the rest of us.

Principal Murphy had at one time been a Riverview High School student himself and, in his heyday, a star football player. Every time the jocks won a big game, you could catch Mr. Murphy in the cafeteria, swapping football stories before warning them to focus on the upcoming game.

"Ezra, you get in here first!" Murphy snarled as Ezra stood up, almost causing Murphy's eyes to tumble out of his head. "Nice dress, missy! What are you getting ready for–the prom?"

"Why?" blushed Ezra. "Are you asking?"

Murphy spun around, "Not another word, mister!"

"Maybe I can ask your daughter then," Ezra said, admiring the family photo on Principal Murphy's desk.

"Close the door!" he commanded, as Ezra turned to grin at us before slamming it shut.

"So, what did you do this time, boyos?" The old secretary peered over at us.

"Bad gas." Brody shook his head.

"Oh, that's not good."

"Yeah, it is," Brody disagreed and nodded his head. "If you don't fart when you need to, you could die! First thing I really learned in science class."

"Hmm." The secretary straightened up and slammed her fingers onto the keyboard and flew into typing.

After a minute, Ezra walked out of the principal's office and headed straight for the hallway door, followed by Murphy, who glared at us as though he'd never been more disgusted. "Alright, let's go!" he snapped, holding the door open with his foot and then clapping his hands. "That's right, follow the leader! That's what you all seem to know best!" And again, we followed Ezra to the new and improved, In-School Suspension Room. "No more smooth sailing now," Mr. Murphy informed us, "hanging out in the attendance room with Midge."

"What?" Sonny exclaimed.

"Yes, I've personally seen to putting an end to that cake-walk," Mr. Murphy gloated as he entered the new and improved prison block. He directed us to sit at separate tables and then turned to the teacher.

"Good Morning, Mrs. North. If any of these–hooligans–say just one more word, or decide to start laughing again, they'll each get a one-week home suspension and be well on their way to being expelled!" Everyone was silent as he stood behind us, breathing down our necks. "I dare any of you to try me!"

We heard his footsteps fade down the corridor as Ezra let out another PRRRRRRRVT.

We started cracking up and I glanced over at Jonah, who scowled back, shaking his head as though I lost my mind to even think about laughing now. Mrs. North was already wound so tight she was the perfect woman for the job. "You're lucky that your first move isn't straight to a home suspension. Didn't you all hear what your principal said?"

"What the hell are you doing?" Jonah grumbled out of the corner of his mouth.

"I can't help it," Ezra whined. "I got bad gas today."

"Then go visit the restroom like any normal person!" she said before covering her nose and mouth with her shiny pink fingertips. Gasping and standing up, she squeaked, "That was not there before!" She marched over to where Brody was sitting and pointed to the wall next to him where someone had written: *I hate this school!*

"Do you actually want to get expelled?"

✦

"Back through Riverview history, the only group that had ever been feared were the Jocks. And the only guys the Jocks had ever feared were the random kids who would drift into the small town from time to time but soon get kicked out of school after causing some minor havoc. So when the Leech Mob came into being, no one knew quite what to make of it, especially Principal Murphy. Whenever I saw him, I could almost hear what he was thinking: a whole gang of mutants had rained down on him all at once but, even worse, the Leech Mob virus seemed to be contagious and was spreading to other students.

"For a while there was this unspoken treaty between the Leech Mob and the Jocks, you leave us alone and we'll leave you alone type of thing. Besides that, they just called us Freaks in general. We dressed a little different. Ezra sometimes wore his fucking dresses. And we made them kind of nervous. But I don't care what anybody says, the girls we hung out with were just hot."

"Hmm." Doctor Gildmore scribbled something down.

"Yeah, we lucked into having the hottest group of punk rock chicks in one school. They didn't even dress that weird but the Jocks would stare at them, and the preppy girls didn't like it and gave the freak chicks dirty looks. And then the incident happened…."

✦

Lunch. Violet had been bawling but now only tears glistened on her cheeks. Every so often she would shut her eyes and squeeze out another teardrop, making sure the others noticed before wiping it away. Macie sat next to her, along with Eve, Krissy, and Paula, massaging her shoulders. Nearby, Flip, Vick, and Casey provided moral support for Remmy, who appeared equally lost. In the background sat the skaters with Dave, Lampy, Zed, and Kit, all who were quiet today.

"What's wrong with Violet?" I asked, joining the others in Café C. "Somebody die?"

"Not yet," Sonny exhaled, whistling through his teeth.

"I thought Remmy had dropped out," I said.

"He did," Brody answered. "Remmy and Casey showed up today when they heard the news."

"What news?"

"Shh," Jonah hushed me.

"It's real messed up," Brody explained as everyone got quiet and listened to Violet.

"It's seriously like really hard sometimes," she said weakly. "I'm just having a really hard time talking about this right now and it's like a major struggle for real, but I don't want anyone like doing anything crazy. Let's just like put the past behind us and treat it as a learning experience, okay? I know that I totally will."

"But Violet, you said that you were raped," responded Krissy, puzzled.

"LIKE, STOP, FUCKING, REMINDING, ME!" Violet shook her hands in the air. Vick leaned over and whispered to Remmy and Casey.

"Come on, let's go check it out!" Dave glared at the others.

"Not yet, Dave," said Casey.

"Why not?" Dave raised his voice.

"Cause Casey wants to wait for Egan." Vick rolled his eyes.

"Fuck you, Vick!" hissed Casey.

"Fuck this shit!" Dave grumbled. "The Jocks are stepping and we're not doing shit! Look at Ezra already!"

Ezra held up his arms where the skin had been torn off. A wad of bloody bandages was taped to each elbow. "Football players."

"Who was with Gary when he hit you, Ezra?" Sonny asked.

"I don't remember. I wasn't even paying attention. I was skating behind the school and before I knew it, Gary clothes-lined me off my board, fucking asshole!"

"What does everyone have against skateboarding?" asked Brody.

"I don't know." Ezra shrugged. "Maybe cause we do it."

"Cause it isn't like a normal sport to them," Sonny began. "No rules, no matching uniforms–"

"No bending over and slapping each other's asses," added Brody.

"They never had a problem with skating until we showed up," Ezra said.

"There was no skating until we got here."

"Then those signs went up," Sonny said.

"They fucking hate us."

"Will you all shut up?" Jonah snapped as he leaned forward, trying to catch what was being said at the far end of the table where Remmy, Vick, Casey, and Flip had now begun to plot with Dave and Lampy.

"I know how you can fix this for real," Eve was saying. "Cause like my friend went through this, and I have some for real good advice, okay?"

"Like what?" asked Violet, her pouty bottom lip hanging out so I could see her bottom row of teeth.

"Well, first you have to go and talk to like your guidance counselor." Violet looked at Eve strangely. "I know, *like what's a guidance counselor?*" Eve continued. "But really, you should go and talk to her and they'll seriously, like really, probably even call the cops."

"Yeah, you really should," Macie said slowly. "Like seriously girl, you shouldn't have to take that! You're totally like breaking my heart, girl." She began to get misty eyed but Violet appeared to dry up.

"And if you don't," said Eve, "then everyone's gonna trip!"

"No way!" Violet glowered at her friends. "I fucking already told you no cops. I'm not going through all that shit. The cops will call my parents and they'll send me to the hospital or something and all these people will ask me all these questions and run like tests, then I'll have to go to court for like months, and I couldn't even handle that for real!"

"It's not exactly like TV, Violet," argued Krissy.

"But I'd like help you, girl! Dude, I will. I really will!" Macie spoke breathlessly.

"No!" Violet snapped.

We got quiet and stared at her.

"Jonah?" I said, lowering my voice to a whisper.

"What?" he barked.

"What the hell is going on?"

"Violet said that Rob Keller raped her."

"Who's Rob Keller?"

"One of the captains of varsity football."

"Where did this happen?"

"At her house I guess–after they went out on a date or something."

"Like a date rape," Brody suggested.

"Dude, why did Violet go out with a jock when she's Remmy's girl?"

"Cause Violet and Remmy break up like ten times a week." Zed looked up from a book. "She probably went out with him so it *would* get back to Remmy."

"And it looks like Violet and Remmy are back together again," Ezra remarked.

Zed faked a look of sympathy. "I hope, for everyone's sake, that this just isn't another one of her famous stories."

"You're cold, man!" Ezra grinned.

"Either way," Jonah sighed, "something's got to go down now."

The bell rang. Immediately Violet's expression instantly went blank. She tossed back her long curly brown hair, wiped her eyes, and strolled away without looking back at the chaos in her wake.

✦

Last class of the day and I was stuck in Mr. Walden's jock-infested math class. Mostly older jocks who had as much trouble in math as the kids in the Program took the class with Flip and me. They'd all signed up for Walden's class, or Wally as they called him, who was known for putting his math lessons into wrestling terms, which was eaten up by them faster than spaghetti dinners on game nights. You might think this sort of sportscaster lingo wouldn't work past the fifth grade, yet Wally found a way to put a spin on it, winning the hearts and minds of the jockstraps and whoever else joined his Math Wars Cult along the way.

Since Wally loved professional wrestling, it should go without saying that he wore a mullet hairstyle and a walrus mustache. His single-color ties always matched his polyester pants, although over the decades his once cutting-edge 1970's fashion had faded and fuzzed. Yesterday, Wally pimped his two-tone green slacks/green tie combo while today, he wore his wannabe brown clip-on tie and matching pants getup. Covered with chalk and clothing burrs, Wally scratched a few equations on the chalkboard and then turned to face us with his eyes burning.

"WHO WANTS TO GO FOR THE TITLE SHOT IN A STEEL CAGE / NO HOLDS BARRED MATCH? THE INTERCONTINENTAL CHAMPIONSHIP BELT IS AT STAKE HERE AND YOU'LL HAVE TO TAKE ON THE CURRENT CHAMP WHO HAPPENS TO BE–," Wally scratched his head as though he'd forgotten.

"WEN-DY!" everyone groaned in unison.

"YES! THE EBBERDORFER!" Wally glared. "THE CURRENT HEAVY-WEIGHT CHAMPION OF MATH WARS WITH A RECORD OF–" Wally cuffed a hand behind his ear and leaned toward the class.

"Twenty-one and none," the students moaned.

"Yes! Twenty-one straight undefeated title matches. What a reign! With that in mind, who will be the first to step into the ring with this athlete of epic proportions?"

"Yeah!" Stubby Davis shouted out excitedly, caught up in the moment. Stubby was the jock who threw the keg bash earlier in the year and looked like the wide-eyed Michelin tire man.

"Stubby?" Wally's eyes brightened with excitement. "STUBBY AGREES TO TAKE ON THE CHAMP! Come on up, Stubby. You're the next contestant on MATH WARS!"

When all the Jockers finished beating on the tops of their desks and howling, Stubby still hadn't moved as he gripped the sides of his table for security, leaning forward, pressing his big gut out and over his tiny desk, squinting at the equations on the board.

"Come on, Stubby, stop trying to buy yourself time and just do it!" urged Wally.

"I...I..." he stammered.

"Spit it out, junior," yelled P.J., a Clark Kent-looking Catalog Kid.

"Shut up P.J," Stubby grumbled and then looked up at our teacher. "Hey Wally, I was just saying *yeah*. You know like–*yeah*!" Stubby weakly rocked his fist and then dropped his hand upon his desk with a thud. Wally stared at him oddly as Stubby sat there, fiddling with his fingers as the fat rolls on his sweaty neck turned red.

"Come on, Stubby, give it a try." Wally held out a piece of chalk but Stubby shrank back.

"B-B-But I don't stand a chance against her, Wally," he stuttered as one of his friends began to cluck like a chicken. "SHUT UP!" Stubby growled at his boys, scrunching his embarrassment into the toughest face he could make.

"That's enough, that's enough," Wally insisted awkwardly, holding up a hand to silence the class. "So is that all you have to say for yourself?"

Stubby took a deep breath and tried to put it into Wally's wrestling terms. "I'm at, uh, a severe disadvantage," Stubby began as his friends chuckled harder. "I haven't, uh, been training properly and I'm not ready to take on her, uh, ranking. She's the champ, man!"

Wally appeared to seriously consider his words as Stubby glanced anxiously over at THE EBBERDORFER, The Champ, The Monster, someone no one wanted to go up against when math and war were at stake. She pushed back her glasses nervously, hiding behind her perfect disguise of a mousy little nerd girl.

"Well, I agree with you on the training part," Wally spoke very seriously. "So alright," he sighed, "you got off easy this time, but next time," Wally warned, "nothing can save you! No more excuses! I'm just not going to take this crap anymore!" Wally dramatically banged his head in the air as he said each word, "What-more-can-I-do-to-get-this-material-to-sink-in?"

He turned toward the chalkboard and muttered something before facing the class again. "Now that Stubby Davis has backed out of the match with brain injuries, I mean training injuries, WHO HAS THE GUTS TO TAKE HIS PLACE?" Wally exclaimed as several hands shot up. "HANDS DOWN! HANDS DOWN! WE KNOW YOU LADIES GOT IT!" Tonya lowered her hand, letting out a whoop while Lauren, a cheerleader, did a little dance at her desk. The females looked about victoriously, gazing around the room at the guys who squirmed in their seats. "I'm looking for one of the boys to step into the ring, preferably one of you guys." Wally pointed at the Jocks.

"You do it, Bucky!" P.J. said and pushed his pal, a big linebacker, sitting in front of him. Bucky turned around and stared at him. His wide block of a head sat neckless upon his broad shoulders, and his tiny, half-circle eyes sank far apart on his face.

"You touch me again P.J. and I'll rip your arm off," Bucky threatened as the jockstraps began to turn on each other.

"Relax Bucky, save it for the game," coaxed Baldy.

"Why don't you step up there, P.J.?" demanded Tony, a tall, thin football player.

"I went last time, and you never go!"

"Yeah, stop acting like such a fucking pussy!" hissed Bucky.

"Hey, easy, easy," Wally said nervously, shoving the air forward with his hand. "It's alright, alright." The Jocks laughed. "P.J., I seem to be hearing your name a lot over there so let's have it. You're up!"

"No, not today, Wally!" P.J. grinned.

"P.J., make her see what she gets when she messes with Varsity 93!" Bucky chanted like he was on the football field.

Wally stood back and let his boys rip into P.J. as he sat rigidly with a self-assured, amused look.

"NOW I'VE SEEN IT ALL FOLKS!" announced Wally, holding a finger in his ear, as if he were sports-announcer receiving information though an oversized pair of headphones. "THIS JUST IN. P.J. DEAGAN IS NOT, I REPEAT, IS NOT COMING OUT OF RETIREMENT TO FACE WENDY'S CHALLENGE! P.J. IS CLAIMING OLD INJURIES BUT THE WORD ON THE STREET IS THAT HE'S JUST PLAIN YELLOW!"

"SHOW EM YOU'RE NOT YELLOW, P.J!" Stubby grinned, safely off the hook.

"Why don't you, Stubby? You fat fuck!" P.J. exclaimed.

"I know, I know, but hey! Clean it up guys!" Wally twitched.

"Cause I'm in training, P.J.!"

"Bullshit!"

"You're bullshit!"

"Okay, okay! That's enough. I know, I know but–that's enough." Mr. Walden changed back to his usual demeanor as he paced back and forth and said calmly, "I'm sure that there are many disappointed fans out there in the audience as well as those viewing this on pay-per-view at home. This would-be monumental battle, THIS CLASH OF THE TITANS, will never be seen and we can only speculate on the outcome!"

"Ralph would have done it but he is out sick today," rationalized Stubby, trying to save face.

"WHAT DID YOU JUST SAY?" Wally roared, suddenly angry again. "You guys in this class are an embarrassment to Math Wars! You think these equations are tough?" Wally spun around to stare down the problems on the chalkboard.

"Take em down, Wally!" clamored P.J.

"Own em, Wally!" yelled Baldy.

"Are you ready?" Wally picked up a piece of chalk. "Start counting!"

"One, two, three," the class began as Wally's hand began flying over the chalkboard as if he were the Bionic Man, scribbling his figures a thousand miles a minute and jumping from one equation to the next, distributing numbers, canceling some out, moving faster and faster until his hand became a blur. Suddenly, the small piece of chalk shattered in his hand, exploding into powder. He turned to glare at the class, as if to make sure we'd seen his chalk-shattering power. The Jocks cheered and Wally grabbed a new piece of chalk, finished the last equation, and then slammed the yellow stick down.

"DONE!" He spun around, with glory in his eyes after completing his feat. "How long did it take me?"

"13 seconds!" the Jocks cheered.

"13 seconds," Wally repeated. "13 seconds. If we were in the Federation right now, I'd put your whole league out of commission!" The Jocks cackled again, snorting as they tried to muffle their laughter at Wally's total seriousness. He turned, erased the board, and then wrote a new series of equations in their place.

"Alright – LAUGH IF YOU WANT, I'M SICK OF THIS CRAP! NOT ONE CONTENDER FROM THE GUYS! YOU'VE LET THE WOMEN'S MATH WARS ALLIANCE HOLD THE TITLE FOR TWO MONTHS!"

"SHUT UP, DUDE!" Bucky shouted at Baldy and P.J., who continued to crack up.

"What? I can't help it," Baldy laughed.

Wally threw his hands up in disbelief as he marched back and forth, muttering to himself. "Don't I try to teach them, Lord?" Wally looked up toward the ceiling for an answer but then gritted his teeth. "OKAY, HAVE IT YOUR WAY! BY DEFAULT–EACH AND EVERY GUY IN THE MEN'S MATH WARS LEAGUE WILL BE MADE TO WRESTLE AT ANY TIME, AT MY DISPOSAL!" He pointed wildly around the room and then quickly added, "CONTRACTS BINDING THEREOF!" Wally nodded his head stubbornly as the football players continued to squabble.

"I want to talk to my manager!" shouted P.J.

"What the hell, Wally!" laughed Baldy.

"That's not fair!" cried Bucky.

Wally's voice rose over all. "FURTHERMORE, I HAVE DECIDED THAT STUBBY WILL HAVE TO ENTER THE RING AND FACE OFF AGAINST THE CHAMPION, EBBERDORFER, NO MATTER WHAT EXCUSE HE HAS!"

The class cheered as the blood drained from Stubby's face. Still his buddies slammed their fists down upon their desks and shouted, "NA! NA! NA! NA! NA! NA! NA! NA! HEY-A-A, GOODBYE!"

Wally glanced at Stubby. He crossed over to the blackboard and picked up his chalk, raising it up to his mouth like a microphone. "WELCOME TO ANOTHER NIGHT AT MATH WARS FOR THE BATTLE YOU'VE ALL BEEN WAITING

FOR. RIGHT NOW, THE TWO WRESTLERS ARE MAKING THEIR WAY DOWN TO THE RING!" Hesitantly, Stubby squeezed out from behind his desk and sauntered up to the blackboard as Wendy picked up a piece of chalk and stood next to one of the equations. "IN THE RIGHT CORNER, WEIGHING IN AT 105 POUNDS AND HAILING FROM RIVERVIEW, THE REIGNING CHAMPION, WENDY, THE TERMINATOR, EBBERDORF!"

The girls went crazy, pounding on their desks and cheering as the Jocks all booed. "And in the left corner, also by way of Riverview, weighing in at an even 285 pounds with a record of four wins and twenty losses, STUBBY, THE PAPER BOY, DAVIS! ARE BOTH CORNERS READY?" They nodded yes. Wally clapped his hands. "LET'S GET IT ON!"

"Go Wendy!" Lauren shouted as the competitors went to work, scrambling to solve the equations as Wally rumbled on.

"THE BELL RINGS AND BOTH WRESTLERS TIE UP, TRYING TO GET A FEEL FOR THE OTHER'S STRENGTHS AND WEAKNESSES AS THEY PUSH EACH OTHER AROUND THE RING AND WOOPS! STUBBY GOES FOR THE OLD FOOT STOMP BUT WENDY IS TOO QUICK! SHE SHOVES STUBBY BACK BUT HE REGAINS HIS FOOTING AND SHOOTS IN, DUCKS WENDY'S HOLD, AND GRABS HER IN A BEAR HUG, LIFTING HER OFF THE MAT AND ATTEMPTING TO SQUEEZE THE LIFE OUT OF HER!"

"Yeah!" Bucky screamed. "Get her, Stubby!"

"BUT WENDY GRABS HIS LOCKED HANDS AND PUSHES THEM DOWN, TRYING TO BREAK HIS HOLD. THE EBBERDORF LOOKS LIKE SHE MIGHT RUN INTO A LITTLE TROUBLE BUT SHE TAKES THE UPPER HAND BY PULLING A REVERSAL AND WASTES NO TIME PICKING STUBBY UP AND BODY SLAMMING HIM ONTO THE MAT!"

"AH MAN!" Bucky swore. "THIS SUCKS!"

"NOW WHAT'S THIS? SHE PICKS HIM UP, HAS HIM UPSIDE DOWN, JACKKNIFES STUBBY, AND GOES FOR THE PIN!" As usual, Wally acted out the move.

"One! Two!" the girls chanted.

"BUT NO, STUBBY BUCKS HER OFF!" Wally jumped back, wiping the sweat from his brow." "THAT WAS TOO CLOSE FOR COMFORT! STUBBY STAYS DOWN WHILE CRADLING HIS HEAD. HE MAY HAVE RE-

INJURED HIS ALREADY DAMAGED BRAIN." Wally's eyes appeared to glass over.

"Just don't lay there, Stubby!" grinned P.J. "Do something!"

"Yeah!" Baldy chuckled. "Try sitting on her!"

"WENDY PULLS STUBBY TO HIS FEET AND CHOPS HIM ACROSS THE CHEST." Wally slashed out at the air. "YOU CAN HEAR THE SLAPS FROM A MILE AWAY! AND HERE COMES THE BIG DROPKICK AND THE STUB-MAN FLIES INTO A CORNER AND HANGS THERE, STUNNED ON THE ROPES WITH A GLAZED LOOK IN HIS EYES AND WHAT'S NEXT? OH MY GOD, A D.T.D! AND THE AUDIENCE GOES WILD!"

"No way! Stubby didn't even execute any maneuvers!" Bucky cried, but Wally lowered his voice and pointed to Stubby's barely worked equation.

"EXACTLY, HE HASN'T DONE A THING! NEXT WENDY GRABS THE STUBSTER BY THE BACK OF HIS HEAD, DRAGS HIM TO HIS CORNER, AND SLAMS HIS HEAD AGAINST THE TURNBUCKLE!" Wally grabbed the back of his mullet and illustrated the maneuver.

"One, two, three!" the class chanted along.

"THE GOLIATH IS HELPLESS AGAINST THE LIKES OF THIS DAVID! WENDY IS HANDLING THE STUBSTER AS IF HE WERE NOTHING MORE THAN A RAG DOLL IN THE HANDS OF A CHILD, A WORM IN THE BEAK OF A SPARROW! WENDY RIPS STUBBY UP AND THEN THROWS HIM ACROSS THE RING! STUBBY'S LEGS CARRY HIM HELPLESSLY AS HE BOUNCES OFF THE FAR ROPE BUT WENDY MEETS HIM HALFWAY WITH THE CLOTHESLINE! THE WHOLE STADIUM GOES CRAZY!"

Wally slowly turned in circles with arms raised and eyes gleaming as the class erupted into cheers. Even little Wendy rocked her fist in the air, taking her time to complete the problem. She only had the last step but waited. Meanwhile Stubby had abandoned his problem and stood staring at Wally instead.

"WENDY HAS STRUCK THE STUBASAURUS LIKE A BOLT OF LIGHTNING. STUBBY LIES THERE MOTIONLESS, HELPLESS, AS THE TERMINATOR TAKES A STROLL AROUND THE RING, WAVING TO HER FANS.

"Stubby!" P.J. shouted. "Just combine the like terms. It's 8X plus-"

"He's cheating!" shouted Lauren.

"NO WAY!" Wally shouted at P.J. "A SNEAK ATTACK IS ATTEMPTED BY STUBBY'S TAG TEAM PARTNER BUT IS TAKEN OUT BY LAUREN, THE SHE-WARRIOR, WHO HITS HIM WITH THE FOLDING CHAIR! P.J. DUCKS AND RUNS FOR THE LOCKER ROOM AS LAUREN CHASES HIM DOWN, CHALLENGING HIM TO A MATCH!"

"Yeah!" Lauren cheered and raised her hands. "Any day, any time!"

"MEANWHILE WENDY SIGNALS TO THE CROWD TO LET THEM KNOW WHAT'S GOING ON AND UNREMORSEFULLY CHOKESLAMS STUBBY! NOW THAT HAS GOT TO HURT!" Foam oozed out the corners of Wally's mouth, yet no one noticed for they were too busy booing and shouting.

"There's going to be nothing left of him once she's done!" cried Bucky, caught up in the narration. "Someone throw the towel in!"

A couple of kids walked past the classroom, looking in and wondering what was actually going on as Wally's voice boomed above the rest. "THEN WENDY PICKS STUBBY UP AND FLIPS HIM UPSIDE DOWN. I CAN'T BELIEVE IT! WENDY IS PREPARING TO…" Wally looked at Wendy, smiling and holding her piece of chalk but refusing to finish the last and easiest step of the problem. "OH MY LORD! SHE CLIMBS UP ON THE TOP ROPE WHILE HOLDING THE STUBSTER UPSIDE DOWN." Wally climbed up on his desk and then jumped off. "AND THEN PILE-DRIVES STUBBY INTO THE GROUND!"

"Are you trying to kill him?" Bucky cried, falling from his desk and sliding down the aisle, running his fingers through his hair.

"OH MY LORD! WHAT A ONE-SIDED MATCH. WHAT A DISGRACE!" Wally pointed at Stubby and cried, "IT'S ALL OVER FOR STUBBY! THE PUNISHMENT HAS BEEN MORE THAN ONE MAN SHOULD HAVE TO ENDURE." Wally dropped his voice and stared out into space as he spoke, almost whispering. "We can see Stubby's family in the crowd with alarmed expressions on their faces as Stubby is wheeled from the ring on a stretcher. He is going to have to do a lot of math therapy to recover from this beating."

Back at the chalkboard, Wendy had finally written the answer to the equation. With sweat streaming down his face, Wally raised her hand in victory. "THE WINNER AND STILL REIGNING CHAMPION, WENDY THE TERMINATOR EBBERDORF!"

Suddenly something got Wally's attention from the back of the room. "IF WE WEREN'T IN SCHOOL RIGHT NOW, I'D SUPLEX YOU OFF THE TOP

ROPE!"

Flip was listening to his walkman and flipping through a Hood Art graffiti mag. Wally stormed over and snatched the magazine out of his hand as Flip dropped his headphones around his neck and looked up.

Flip laughed. "Come on and get you some! We can wrassle! This ring ain't big enough for the both of us, you crazy, pay-per-view watching asshole!"

Wally was stunned. "You just bit off more trouble than you can chew, mister!"

Dramatically, a few of Wally's fans stood up nervously to face Flip. Wally saw he'd better calm things down and quick. He held his hands up and gestured toward the football players.

"Okay, okay! That's enough. I know, I know, but that's enough." Then he turned to Flip and shouted, "AS FOR YOU, PUNK, GET YOUR BOOKS AND GET THE HELL OUT OF THIS CLASSROOM!"

"Yeah and go where?" Flip snorted back, seeing that almost every student in the class had now turned against him for pissing off the cool teacher at school.

"IF YOU WANT MY ADVICE, GO FOR A WALK DOWN THE MIDDLE OF INTERSTATE 84!" Wally replied as the Jocks howled with laughter and beat on the tops of their desks.

"Go whack off to your wrestling magazines," Flip chuckled, causing Walden's eyes to pop out of his head, when suddenly a scream filled the room.

"Just get the fuck out of here, motherfucker! Nobody even wants you here! You're not funny! Everybody hates you but you're too stupid to see it!" Baldy leapt up, turning as red-faced as Wally. Being a junior, he was one of the oldest in the class and Wally's number one fan.

"You think I give a shit what any of you fake Riverview punks think about me?"

"We don't give a shit about you. You're nothing but a fat loser!" Baldy screamed as he stepped between Wally and Flip. "Why don't you do us all a favor and just drop out of school like the rest of your friends!"

"What, bitch?" Flip's smile slowly faded from his face. "This ain't over, me and you after school," Flip said calmly.

Everyone in the class seemed nervous, even Baldy, for fear of being suspended for fighting on school grounds. For a while, Wally glanced back and forth between the two youths as if he were just another student, caught up in the moment before realizing his place.

"YOU FOLLOW ME RIGHT NOW!" Wally roared. He dashed past Flip and sprinted outside to the hall, but Flip didn't budge and stood his ground, grilling Baldy as though he wanted to kill him. "GET OUT HERE RIGHT NOW, FLIP!" Wally stamped his foot and shouted again but Flip still didn't move. "I SAID NOW!" Wally screamed and marched threateningly back toward Flip.

"If you touch me, I'll knock you out!" Flip snapped.

"You throw one punch and I'll crack your face open!" shouted Baldy.

"Get back Baldy, I know, I know, but just get back! T-Take your seats, eh-everyone get back to your desks!" Wally stuttered nervously as Baldy's friends guided him back a few steps. "AND YOU GET YOUR BUTT INTO THE OFFICE NOW! OR I'LL HAVE YOU EXPELLED FROM THIS SCHOOL!" Wally pointed down the hall.

"I'm still gonna kick your ass," Flip promised Baldy, who stood there frozen and silent as the slimmest smile returned to Flip's lips before he followed Wally out of the room.

Instantly, the room broke into whispers. The Jocks crowded around Baldy and all talked at once.

"You believe that asshole!" shouted Stubby.

"You got to be a big time fuckup to piss Wally off!" spit Bucky.

"They don't care," Stubby mumbled.

"The Leech Mob doesn't give a damn about anything!" replied Baldy.

"Freaks!" Stubby agreed before Bucky lightly nudged him, gesturing toward me.

Baldy turned and glared, even though I pretended not to pay attention.

"Okay, Mr. Walden wants everyone in their seats." A secretary stood in the doorway of our classroom. "He'll be back in a minute." Everyone sat down but still huddled in groups.

"We all have to relax," said P.J., trying to be the voice of reason, which started another argument.

"Forget that. I'm not taking their shit anymore!" boasted Baldy.

"You heard what that freak Violet said about Tim raping her?" asked Bucky.

"Fucking liar!" Baldy shook his head. "I can't believe he even touched that dirty bitch!"

"She's so full of shit!" said Stubby.

When I stood up, all the Jocks shut up and stared at me as I walked past them and into the hallway.

"Where the hell does he think he's going?" Stubby asked.

"Mr. Walden wants everyone in their seats," the secretary repeated.

"I have to use the bathroom," I said, trying to look around the corner to see what was happening in the glassed off, main-office.

"No, class will be over soon, so take your seat."

I could see Flip sitting there, resting his head in his hands. They were probably going to kick him out for this.

"Did you hear me, young man?" the lady raised her voice.

"What are you doing out in the hall, Hayes!" Wally snapped as he rounded the corner. "Would you rather be in there with your friend?"

"No."

"Then get back to the classroom, NOW!"

After Wally entered classroom, his face got calmer. "I don't think we'll have the services of Flip Rodriguez in this class anymore, or in any class if I get my way."

The Jocks clapped, and soon everyone was clapping, except me. Wally smiled. "Okay, okay, I know, I know, but that's enough."

"Is he getting expelled?" Baldy asked.

"God, I hope so," said Bucky, raising a murmur from the other students.

"I really don't know yet." Wally raised his voice, "He'll probably just serve a suspension. At Riverview, we take it way too easy on these characters."

"Hasn't that kid been suspended like nine times already?" Stubby asked but Wally just shook his head.

"Okay, okay!" Wally smiled, patting the air in front of him to keep the room somewhat neutral. "We're now moving on to Chapter 68. I hope everyone–"

"I don't know why these kids even bother showing up!" said Stubby. "They don't care about school or anything!"

"Yeah, why doesn't he just stay home? Nobody will miss him!" agreed Bucky.

"Why don't they **ALL** stay home?" asked Baldy, looking in my direction.

"Alright, alright, we all have our opinions, but every student has a right to be here, even if they want flush their futures down the toilet. That's their choice. Now back to the drawing board." Wally sighed, "For the rest of the week, they'll be no more Math Wars."

"What? Why?" the Jocks complained.

"Cause it's getting out of control."

"What? Just cause of him!" Baldy shouted.

"I hate that kid!" Stubby shook his head.

"I know, I know," said Wally. "But it's—it's too much, maybe, maybe later—" Wally looked around lost, not really knowing where to go from there.

✦

After school, there was a teacher/staff meeting. Flip had suggested a good day in the eyes of the football kids. The hallways were almost empty. Some Leech Mob kids and I walked through the old lounge and outside to the back of the school, where the side entrance of the gym was open and an army of Jocks stood waiting.

Flip had been suspended, but he'd never left school. Instead he'd hid and waited to meet Baldy as promised. Remmy was also there, currently monitoring Rob Keller as he paced among his friends, trying his best to lose himself in a sea of football numbers. Even though Rob was twice his size, he'd glance up at Remmy and then go back to pacing.

"You still gonna SUPLEX me off the top rope?" asked Flip, as he approached the team and glared up at the huge Baldy.

"I'll do a lot worse than that!" Baldy grinned back.

"What? Like go and rape some girl, cause all the cheerleaders will laugh at that shriveled up steroid dick!"

"No," grinned Baldy. "Violet just wanted a real man for a change."

"You guys suck! When's the last time you actually won a game?"

Baldy laughed. "No! you suck! None of you give a shit about anything. That's why you'd go down for these stupid fights in school. I have to miss games, miss school, cause of assholes like you! While none of you got nothing to lose!"

"Did your coach tell you that?" asked Ezra.

"Where should we handle this?" Casey demanded. "Name the place, if you don't want to fight in school!" He grinned at them. "We don't want to get you in trouble!"

"Outside of school we'll settle this!" shouted Bucky.

"Yeah, no shit, you dumb ape!" blasted Casey. "I asked you where, shithead!"

"AT THE PARTY!" Stubby shouted over everyone.

"What party?" asked Vick.

"Mill Road, Friday night!" Stubby said, then realizing he'd stuck his foot in his mouth when all his buddies turned, wanting to kick the shit out of him.

"Why the hell did you tell them that?" Baldy shouted.

"I don't want these losers there!" yelled Tony.

"Yeah, what about his parents, man!" reminded P.J.

"SHUT THE FUCK UP, P.J." Baldy yelled. The Jocks argued as the Leech Mob laughed. The one place they hated seeing the Leech Mob more than anywhere was at their parties.

"Major buzz kill, huh boys?" Lampy laughed.

"Your parties are always lame anyway, bro!" smiled Dave.

"See, you all are just scared!" Flip screamed.

"Scared of losers like you? I don't think so! I'll whip your ass anywhere!" shouted Baldy.

"Then do something!" Flip began to shadowbox around the larger boy who raised his basketball-sized fists and turned in sloppy circles to stay lined up with the smaller Flip. Instantly, both sides stopped arguing and began shouting for their boy.

"Get em, Baldy!" bellowed Stubby.

"Stomp him into the ground, Flip!" coached Casey.

"Duh, don't listen to the freak show, Baldy!" called out one of the football twins, in a deep, borderline-retarded voice. "Just land one good shot, put this punk to sleep, and, duh, let's go play some football!"

"Duh, shut the fuck up, you genetic mutants!" Lampy roared back at them.

Flip wound back for a swing as Baldy shoved him, knocking him backwards. A scream rose up from the Jocks. At once, both groups began closing in, shouting at each other to stay out of it. Flip scrambled to his feet, dusted himself off, and began to circle Baldy again. He faked a left and then landed a right jab to Baldy's grill as they tied up again. Baldy held onto Flip's shirt as he windmilled his other arm. A loud popping sound rang out and Flip's nose began to bleed. The Jocks cheered and Baldy raised both hands in triumph as Flip scuttled away, smearing the blood with the back of his hand.

Baldy panted for breath. "Your nose is already broken. You better quit before you really get hurt!"

Flip charged forward while Baldy reared back and took a swing. As the fist fell, Flip lowered his head and Baldy cried out in pain as his fat knuckles met the top of Flip's skull. Baldy bit down on his lip to keep from howling and then held his hand out and began shaking his fingers and blowing on them.

"Get em, Flip!" shouted Jonah as Flip charged in, grabbing Baldy in a bear hug. Flip desperately tried to lift him but only managed to stretch his rolls of fat instead. Baldy's feet stayed planted on the ground and he began to drop elbows on Flip's back.

"Hit him, Flip!" we shouted.

Flip dug his fists into Baldy's soft gut. Baldy started to blow smoke rings while Flip continued to fire cannonballs.

"That's the weak spot!" spat Vick, skipping to the side. "Get him in the gut, Flip!" Baldy's thick arms dropped to his sides and he desperately tried to break free, shoving Flip aside and staggering away.

"Don't let him out of there!" shouted Kit as Flip tagged the sides of Baldy's face and jumped back.

"Stay on him, Flip!" we yelled, but Baldy had gained enough room to throw another swing. The two collided and traded punch for punch, both moving slow and out of breath. Baldy toppled over, grabbing Flip in a headlock, and they both hit the ground. Flip was pinned underneath as Baldy hammered down punches, squeezing off Flip's air supply and smothering his face against the ground.

"Are you finished?" Baldy gasped after whaling Flip a dozen more times, yet before he could answer, Baldy began hitting him again. Slowly Flip's struggle died down. His eyes rolled back in his head and he kicked his legs less often. We pressed in anxiously, nervously staring down.

"Yeah! That's how you do it!" Bucky smiled viciously, breathing hard and muttering calmly to his overweight friend. "Put his face in the MUUUDDD!"

"Duh, it's all over!" One kid grinned as his twin brother bellowed idiotically, "Yeah. Good night!"

"You got to let him up. He can't breathe!" I shouted, thinking of Flip slowly suffocating underneath. "Let him up, that's enough!"

"Yeah, let him up, Baldy!" Vick yelled.

"Hell no, it's over when it's over!" Marc responded, inching forward.

Everyone closed in, staring at the sweaty fat rolls glistening on the back of Baldy's neck. He lay there, with missing teeth, panting and squishing around on Flip like a human rolling pin. The painful image of Baldy and Marc flashed through my head, kicking me until I lay there motionless, waiting for someone to scrape me off the road.

Baldy's face would be an easy target. All I had to do, I thought, was step back and aim. I had to do it before Flip suffered anymore, before I lost the chance. I brought my right foot back and then punted his grill. I kicked Baldy harder than I expected to and my shoe dug underneath his chin. His fat head had barely budged but then blood began to drip down his chin like a leaky faucet. Everyone screamed as Baldy groaned and rolled off Flip. On his back, he gripped his face with both hands and jawed the words, "Who da hell kicked me?"

Flip lay there for a moment, breathing heavy, slowly recovering from having the life pressed out of him by a three hundred pound linebacker. Stubby, snarling like a mad dog, bounded towards me, but suddenly there was a crack, and he seemed to hang in mid air. Before he had a chance to hit me, Dave had swung and knocked Stubby to the dirt.

"Who the hell kicked me?" Baldy repeated, as Principal Murphy booked out with the assistant principal, followed by the security guard. The giant cro-mag football player Gary was the last to run out. His face was beet red and scarred with steroid acne; his eyes sunk deep into his head underneath his shelf-like forehead. He glared around as the school officials spread out into the fight, looking everywhere at once but not knowing where to start. Everyone tried walking away, the Jocks towards the field and the rest of us toward the parking lot.

"Alright freeze! And you two! Break it up!" Mr. Murphy announced, ignoring Flip and running up to Baldy, putting an arm around him and waving his free arm, looking like a referee breaking up a boxing match when a fighter was too dazed to continue. "Someone go and get the school nurse!" Murphy pointed to Face, who stared back with a moronic look. Murphy changed his mind and then pointed to a Jock. "You! Get the nurse! Now!" He nodded and ran toward the gym. "You're on suspension, Mr. Rodriguez! And here you are fighting at school!"

"You got a fucking problem, tough guy?" Gary roared as he stalked Vick. "Look at me when I'm talking to you, freak!"

"Fuck you!" Vick doubled his fists but the assistant principal got between them.

"That's enough, Gary!" he shouted. "Get to practice! And you," he screamed pointing to Vick, "get out of my sight!"

The assistant principal patted Gary aside. "Save it for the game, big guy."

"What is this fight all about?" the security guard asked P.J. and Tony, trying to remain calm.

"The Jocks are sticking up for a rapist!" Sonny glared at the football players.

"Bullshit!" said P.J. "It's all lies!"

"What's this about a rape?" the security guard asked.

"These fucking dirtbags are saying that Rob raped some freak bitch!"

"Enough!" shouted Mr. Murphy.

"You see these kids are crazy! Look at them. They're nut cases! Freaks!" Gary looked as though he didn't know if he were going to bust someone's head or bust out crying.

"That's enough. I've had it up to here with all of you!" Mr. Murphy finally screamed.

"Who was fighting? I want names or all of you get suspended!" Assistant Principal Goodpants slashed the air with his hand.

"I was fighting Baldy," Flip said, slowly standing up.

"But he attacked me!" Baldy tried to make an excuse, but with blood covering both his and Flip's faces, he dropped his shoulders and unhappily nodded in agreement.

"And who else?" Murphy glared around. "I want names! Now!"

"Stubby was...sort of."

"What's happened to Stubby?" Murphy cried. "Why is he in that condition?"

"Dave hit him!" Tony said.

"Yeah, but Stubby was going after Hayes."

"And Hayes kicked Baldy!" shouted P.J.

The nurse ran out, glancing at Flip and Baldy, but ignored them and headed straight for Stubby, who currently snored on the ground, surrounded by his buddies who had tried but failed to stand him up.

The principal glared at the group of us standing there. "I want all of you lined up in front of my office! Then he turned and commanded the football players, "The rest of you go to practice!"

"This is bullshit!" spit Jonah and pointed at the Jocks. "Why aren't you busting any of them?"

✦

I was waiting outside when Jonah swerved to a stop in front of my house. He was about an hour late but I was the last to be picked up. "I see you wore pants for the occasion," I said to Ezra as I ducked into the back seat. We all had on dark clothes, hoods, and baseball caps.

"Shut up, Kelly."

"I told him the same thing." Brody cracked a smile but Jonah stayed silent and hit the gas. We met the others at Food World, where a beat up hatchback with tinted windows blared its horn and pulled into a parking space beside us.

The standard shift grinded into place. Big Dave and Lampy got out, grinning and slapping our hands.

"Me and Dave had a five dollar bet going but he won!"

"Yeah, what was that?" Ezra asked suspiciously.

"I bet him you would show up in a fucking dress!" Lampy grinned.

"That's getting old. It's the third time I heard that," mumbled Ezra.

"That tell you anything?" suggested Lampy.

"Yeah, like nobody wants to see you in a fucking dress, Ezra," Jonah said.

"I'm not wearing one, asshole!"

"Damn Jonah, looks like you want to kill someone!" Lampy patted his shoulder.

"Yeah, that's the plan, right?" Jonah's blue eyes flashed. "I got arrested and suspended for no fucking reason!"

"Yeah, as soon as I saw the cops there, I broke out," said Lampy. "I had weed on me and I can't get arrested again."

"Tonight, I bet the jockstraps call the cops!" Dave said.

"Not when they're drunk," replied Lampy.

"Yeah, maybe," Dave spit. "I left a bail bondsman's card out on my kitchen table, just in case."

"Shit, why didn't I think of that?" said Lampy, grasping the leather bag that hung around his neck.

"How much weed you got?" questioned Brody.

"Enough to smoke before we get there." Lampy patted the bag.

"Well, bring it on."

"Don't smoke that shit now!" Dave complained. "You'll get all high and go pacifist on em."

Egan, who had arrived first, was leaning against the payphone and looking more pissed than usual. "Glad some of you bothered to show up!" he snapped at us. "Anybody heard from Remmy or even Vick?"

We shrugged and he turned back to the pay phone, dialed another number, and then slammed the receiver down. Kit and Face were there, stoned out of their minds and each listening to one side of a pair of earphones, while Sonny practiced sparring with Gavin. A dozen kids, girls and guys I didn't recognize, had driven down from other towns. Obi walked out of the grocery store, holding a bag of potato chips that Egan snatched out of his hand.

"Hey!"

"That's what you get for missing practice." Egan grabbed the payphone and dialed again.

"Whatever." Obi frowned and then saw us. "Hey, did you guys see that Landbury newspaper article about the fight?"

"No," Jonah said.

"They wrote about it in the paper?" I asked.

"Check it out." Obi grinned. "You guys are famous."

"Yeah, world famous fuckups," Egan said over his shoulder as we leaned in to read it.

LANDBURY TIMES

LEECH MOB ARRESTED
AFTER FIGHT AT SCHOOL

A classroom argument at Riverview High School this week erupted into fistfights that ended in the arrests of five students. Students say an organized rebel clique calling itself the Leech Mob was responsible for the fighting, but police and school accounts do not confirm such involvement. The students, Jonah Camps, 17, of Senior Road, Kelly Hayes, 15, of Arrowpoint Road, Vick Banks, 17, of Ward Drive, Dave Bale, 18, of Still Creek Road, and Flip Rodriguez, 17, of East Lake Street, were charged with Breach of Peace. Another student, not associated with the group, was injured after he was kicked in the face.

Fistfights began after school during staff meetings, Riverview Police Captain Will Tanner said. Police provided few details but students interviewed yesterday state the Leech Mob forms a distinct presence in school and many students steer clear of its members. Many are recognizable by trademark dark baseball caps and dark baggy clothing. They color their hair either blonde or black and have distinct haircuts, often shaved around the sides and long on top.

School Superintendent Craig Paul said when they have a fight of that magnitude, kids can hurt themselves and others. "Youngsters need to know they will be disciplined not only by the school but also by the police as well. It's something that we don't tolerate at all."

"Organized rebel clique!" Lampy grinned and took a hit off his pipe. "And then they make the other guys sound all innocent."

"I can't believe they wrote about us." Jonah shook his head.

"That was so fucked up nobody got arrested but us, right?" asked Dave.

"They're not going to send their star football players to jail, make em miss games and shit. How would that look?" Lampy shook his head.

"Whenever you get done jerking off to that, we got business to discuss," Egan called over to us, unimpressed. He then turned and stared over our heads as another car rattled in, honking its horn. Rook and two girls got out. Egan hung up the phone and turned around to eyeball Rook, the closest thing to one of his lieutenants.

At around twenty years old, Rook was a tall, wiry kid with a silver nose ring and short black hair, shaved down to almost stubble.

"What's up?" Rook asked, as he strolled up with a winning smile and a girl on each arm. "I read about you boys in the newspaper this morning–surprised the hell out of me!" He grinned at us. "So when Egan told me what was going down, I had to get your back."

Egan frowned, "Only you would bring chicks to a street fight."

"Hi, Egan," they said in unison.

"Hi Katlyn, Tonya." Egan looked at them. "So you know what this bum is getting you into, right?"

"Sure. We got to stand by our boys," gushed Kat.

Egan grinned.

"So where's everyone else?" Rook asked, but Egan ignored his question.

"You plan on stretching those fuckers out anymore?" quipped Egan.

"Chill out, they're only quarters." Rook reached up and gripped one earlobe.

"So far." Egan shook his head. "If you stretch them anymore, I'd be worried they'd get caught on something."

"Yeah, right. So where is everyone, Egan?" Rook asked again.

"Like who?"

"What do you mean, like who? Like everyone."

"You're looking at it."

"Where's Connor?" Rook looked around as if he were hiding somewhere.

"They think it's bullshit." Egan glared at us and asked, "And where's Remmy and Vick?"

"They're not here either, huh? Yeah," Rook agreed, "this doesn't make sense."

"You think Violet's telling the truth?" Katelyn asked.

"Who knows? Ever hear of the girl who cried wolf?"

"Wasn't that the boy who cried wolf?" Katelyn looked confused.

"Well, you heard of Violet now," said Egan.

"They'll be here," Gavin said as he and Sonny walked up. "I spoke to Vick about two hours ago, and he was about to pick everyone up."

Rook looked at him. "You believe her?"

Gavin shrugged. "I think that's what Remmy wants to figure out tonight."

"Jasper and Aaron are here." Lampy looked over his shoulder at a spray-painted trash heap roaring across the parking lot. Two tall, thin, menacing youths got out, looking grim in their prison-denim jeans and matching jackets, with black knit hats pulled low. Jasper reached through the window, into the backseat to retrieve a skateboard, which they began to argue over. This turned into a tug-of-war, as they each gripped a side of the skateboard and pulled it back and forth.

"Look at these two idiots," Egan growled. "Hey! Stop fucking around and get over here!" Aaron pulled the skateboard away from Jasper, threw it in the backseat, and they strolled over, bumping shoulders and talking shit to each other.

"Alright, let's go!" Egan snapped his fingers and motioned for everyone to gather around and listen. "Look, the Landbury guys think that Riverview kids should learn how to handle their own shit," Egan began. "Still, I decided to bring some justice here and let Remmy confront this rapist.

"What about Cincity?" Face asked.

"Are you serious?" Egan suddenly became angry. "If Cincity rolled down here, I'd expect kids to wind up dead! They don't fuck around with stupid shit!" Egan squinted at Face, who shook his head. "Dumb ass!"

"Where's Violet," asked Rook.

"Another good question!" Egan shook his head. "Nobody's seen her. Why has Violet stopped hanging around?"

"Does she know what's happening tonight?" asked Sonny.

"I know for a fact that she does!" exclaimed Kit. "All the girls know but they don't want a part of it."

"You think she's telling the truth?" Dave asked.

"So, none of you even know if Violet is telling the truth or not?" Egan waited for a response as we shuffled nervously. "Great! Now I see why nobody else wants to get involved!"

Rook began to laugh.

"What? What?" demanded Egan.

"Nothing. Just thinking." Rook smiled. "Didn't most of you Riverview kids like date Violet at one time or another? Besides Remmy, I know Casey did and–"

"Vick," said Kit, grinning.

"And Zed," Dave added.

"Zed went out with her?" Kit cackled. "I didn't know that."

"And Nickodemus!" shouted Face.

Egan clamped his jaw shut and glared at Face.

"Uh, shut up, Face," Kit mumbled out of the corner of his mouth.

"They call you *Face*, right?" Egan glared at Face, who gawked back with insane eyes. "Where the fuck did they find you? You know, I never saw you hanging around until those Fair Hills patients escaped." Egan frowned. "Is that just a coincidence or what?"

"He's always talking that Nickodemus crap," Jonah tried to explain.

Egan turned back to us. "If you all think this is a big fucking joke, I'm about ready to say I'm leaving, and the rest of you can handle it with fucking Nickodemus over here." Egan pointed at Face, who stammered incoherently.

"Shut the fuck up, Face!" roared Dave.

"Listen!" shouted Lampy. "Everyone knows this isn't just about Violet!" We grew quiet and listened. "The Jocks have been stepping to us for as long as I can remember! This is some straight up vendetta shit!"

"Yeah!" Dave shouted. "I know I got a few to waste."

Finally Vick arrived, bottoming out over the speed bumps and throwing sparks as he raced up with Casey, Remmy, and Flip, all looking uneasy. Behind him was Zed, driving up with a couple of graffiti guys.

"And where the fuck have you been!" Egan shouted at the car.

"I had to go pick everyone up," Vick yelled back.

"Gavin said that was two hours ago! You think I don't have anything better to do?"

"No," said Vick. "We already drove by the party."

"Yeah and what happened?"

"What?" Vick snorted back, turned his head and spit.

Egan raised his voice. "I said did you fucking do anything?"

"There were like ten thousand Jocks!" Vick exclaimed.

"Bitches." Egan grinned. "You still want to go?"

"Yeah."

"We'll follow you! Let's go!" Egan shouted, and everyone ran towards their cars and fourteen engines fired up. A Leech Mob caravan made its way through the wooded back roads, with Vick leading us straight to the keg party. As we drove slowly past the house, we looked up the hill at the drunken Jocks and Preps who stared back down, confused by what they were seeing. We rolled by in a parade of dented hatchbacks and old trucks, missing headlights and mufflers; cars covered in spray paint and bumper stickers, blasting punk and hardcore.

Some partygoers realized this wasn't a friendly sight. The ignorant looked amused, as if it were some kind of joke, while others retreated inside, knowing exactly who we were. Still others raised their arms as if to say, "what the hell," and threw down their plastic beer cups and stepped forward, shouting, "PRIVATE PARTY! NO BEER!"

Much farther up the road, we turned our cars around so we could burn out of there when it was time and parked in the dark shadows of the towering hemlocks. We waited quite a while before we began the long hike down the rutted road, quietly, stealthily. Without streetlamps, the country road was pitch black, so we arrived at the bottom of the driveway undetected. From the darkness, we silently peered up at the house and its well-lit front porch. The Preps and Jocks bunched together at the railing and cupped their hands above their eyes for a better view.

"The freaks are here!" someone shouted.

"Who?" another voice asked.

"THE LEECH MOB!"

When we emerged from the darkness, some kids screamed as if we were the walking dead. A gang of Jocks stormed forward like drunken warriors.

"WHAT THE FUCK DO YOU WANT?"

"THIS IS A PRIVATE PARTY!"

"GET THE FUCK OUT!"

We marched up the driveway as they held each other back at the top of the hill.

"What do you guys want?" a more sober voice called out.

Then another slurred, "Shh should I I go call 9-1-1?"

"I knew they'd call the pigs," Dave muttered to us.

"No!" a Jock shouted. "They'll just bust up the party and take our beer!'"

Egan squinted and spit toward them before turning around and searching his crew, "Remmy! Remmy!"

"What?"

"Get the hell up here! Vick! You, too!" Egan commanded and Remmy sauntered forward, followed by Vick and Casey.

"Where is he?"

Remmy looked up. "Rob? I don't know. I don't see him."

"Pussy is hiding!" said Casey.

"WHERE THE FUCK IS ROB KELLER?" Egan bellowed up the hill where Marc, Baldy and Stubby had joined the other Jocks up front. Marc said something to Gator who took off running into the house.

From the shadows, a couple of younger fools snuck up, carrying an empty keg and rolled it down the driveway. It came bouncing down toward us, while the Preppies cheered. The idiots then ran back toward the garage, tripping over themselves, red faced and laughing.

"You're fucking dead!" Egan promised.

Gator returned, dwarfed beside a giant kid, an older dude I'd never seen before. His fearless presence made the Jocks brave as he charged down the long driveway toward us, followed by his gang.

The giant peered into the night, sizing us up and taking a quick count, before asking in a loud, southern accent, "What the fuck do you freaks want?"

"They think they can trash our party, Red!" shouted Baldy.

Red stood looking down at Egan, standing on an incline and towering over us. The cold wind blew across the Jocks, and their ninety-proof breath whipped our faces.

"Take your act on the road, before one of ya'll turds gets squashed out here!" Red warned Egan.

"No," he shook his head, looking almost bored. "Get that fucking rapist out here before I make an example out of your wannabe country ass."

"Rob didn't rape anyone!" a high-pitched voice rang out.

"Violet's a lying fucking whore!" snapped Marc but flinched back when Remmy flew forward, only to be dragged back by Vick and Casey.

"Let Rob say that!" shouted Casey.

"Why's he always hiding?" Sonny stepped forward.

"Yeah. Why's he always being a bitch?" shouted Remmy.

The Leech Mob mumbled in agreement.

"Who the fuck is this little midget!" Red laughed as Sonny was dragged back.

"See, they're all fucking crazy!" Marc shook his head.

"We're done with this god damned press conference!" Dave roared. "You always talk shit but never back any of it up!!"

"Bullshit!" shouted Baldy.

"You said we'd handle this here!" Sonny said, breathing hard. "So what's up now, bitch?"

Red shot a pissed-off glance toward his boys. "You told them to come here?"

Stubby was shoved forward. "Yeah, but we didn't think they'd actually do it," he stammered as Red shook his head in disgust.

"What's with this *we* shit?" asked Marc.

"Shut up!" Red growled, folding his big arms and turning to us again. "And now we're telling you to hit the pavement, bud!" His drunken eyes glared into Egan's sober eyes.

"Well if nobody's gonna get this started, I sure as hell am!" Flip pointed at Baldy. "Come on, bitch! Round 2! Right now!"

"What?" yelled Baldy. "How many times am I going to have to kick your ass?"

"All you did was sit on me, you fat fuck!" yelled Flip and everyone began to shout.

"Shut the fuck up!" Egan shoved Flip back. "Look!" he began again. "It's real simple. We're not leaving here until Rob answers for what he's done!"

"But he didn't do anything!" the same high-pitched voice yelled out. "It's that girl who's lying!"

"Then let him come down and say that for himself!" Remmy yelled back up.

"Fuck," Red spat, turning around. "This garbage is seriously cutting into my drinking time. It's real simple. You want these guys out of here, Tony?"

"Uhhh–yeah!" Tony caught an attitude. "I didn't want these scumbags anywhere near my house to begin with!"

"Come on, let's go." Red was out of patience. "Move!" He took another step forward but Egan still hadn't budged.

"You're getting real close to crossing that line, dude."

"Dude, you don't wanna do that!" Rook shook his head, trying to warn Red but it was too late.

"You might have these guys fooled, but not me!" Red shoved Egan down the driveway. The bowling balls in his legs flexed as Egan propelled his body into a single right hook that pulled Red's feet off the ground. As Egan stumbled across the driveway, trying to keep up with his momentum, Red soared across the hill, hit the ground, and started moaning.

"What the hell is going on?"

Another platoon of older jocks spilled out of the garage and ran down the driveway toward us. Our two groups collided, but we pressed forward, struggling up the driveway while they tried to kick us down. As soon as Egan clambered to his feet, Gary was on him, picking Egan up by his legs and toppling him over on his head. Gary got him a third time and then a fourth. He grabbed Egan around his waist and roared, going off on some roid rage, as he strained to pick our huge leader up and over his head.

Turning almost purple, Gary accomplished the feat and carried Egan a few steps before dropping him on his back, but Egan held on, dragging Gary over. The two began brawling. Egan's first punch deformed Gary's nose, and the second fractured his jaw (we found out later). Gary slowly slid forward and dropped to the ground on his face. Egan stepped over him and limped back toward the driveway. Then the light caught his face, exposing half of Egan's mangled grill.

Things began to slow up. Most kids retreated up the hill, but two preppy girls rushed down the driveway, holding up their hands and shouting, "Don't hit us," as they struggled to pick this one kid up. He'd been fighting Gavin but now was fumbling around the ground, bleeding.

"Oh, Georgie, why do you do this to yourself?" His girlfriends strained to pick him up and carry him off the battlefield.

"Remmy!" Egan yelled, squinting into the crowd. Remmy limped up with a split lip and a puffy eye and glared up at the party.

"Now get Rob out here or there will be more trouble!" Egan shouted. The jockstraps carried away some of their wounded, leaving a few others to crawl up on their own. We were in no better shape.

A group of Preps, led by P.J., walked down the hill looking sober and passive, holding their hands out in a gesture of peace. "Okay, they're looking for Rob right now! We just want to see if our friends are okay."

"Fine," said Egan. "Let em through!"

The kids spread out, some stopping by Baldy, others by Red, and the rest walked over to Gary where he lay on the grass. Red was snoring until they slapped his face and tried their best to wake him.

Red started coming around. "What was that? What hit me?" he mumbled, looking up at all the friendly faces. "What are ya'll doing? Shit I had a bad dream." He looked around confused until seeing Egan. Slowly some recognition came to his drunken face. "Youshunofabitch," he slurred, pointing at Egan. "You dirty son of a bitch," Red said again, as they turned him around and walked him up the driveway, the crack of his hairy ass jutting out. Red took a few steps but then started to sink down again, and the kids struggled to keep him on his feet. Egan ignored him and kept looking up at the house.

When they found Gary, they gasped.

"We got to get Gary to the hospital, now!"

"Fuck that," Gary mumbled with a cracked and swollen jaw. "No hospitals! My dad will kill me!"

A moment later, P.J. walked over, trying to look as calm as possible as he approached Egan.

"Look guys, we don't want any more trouble. What exactly happened anyway?"

Egan glared at the kid. "Don't play stupid with me."

"They're just biding time, Egan!" I said. "They're calling the cops."

"No," P.J. laughed guiltily. "We don't want this party broken up."

"This is the last time I'm going to ask. Get Rob down here, now!"

"But he didn't rape anyone!" the familiar female voice yelled down the hill once again.

The crowd parted and a short, thin, little female walked over, shivering and holding her arms crossed over her chest, and stared up at Egan with large, brown eyes. Egan squinted down at the small girl. "Let me guess. Rob's your boyfriend and he told you that."

"No, I'm Rob's sister," she said confidently to the buzzing of voices.

"Oh, so you were there when it happened?" Rook said to her.

"No! But my brother wouldn't hurt a fly, let alone rape a girl!"

"Let him come down here and say that for himself!" said Remmy.

There was a pause. "If I get him, do you promise you won't start attacking him?"

"Look!" said Egan. "You all started this. All we wanted to do was talk to Rob!"

"We started this?" Marc shouted. "We didn't trash your party!"

"Oh shut up!" Flip shouted.

"Are you Remmy?" the girl raised her voice.

Remmy looked at her and then slowly nodded his head. "Yeah."

"Look, I'm sorry but that girl is a liar." She glared at Remmy who looked away.

"Go get Rob and let's hear him say that," commanded Egan.

"And you're not going to beat him up?"

"Not if he's telling the truth."

"Hold on." She didn't have to walk far as he must have been listening the whole time. Rob Keller walked out of the crowd. We were quiet for only a moment that seemed to draw out forever.

Then Rob spoke up, "Look Remmy, I didn't rape Violet." Everyone grew quiet. "Yeah, we went out that night. Yeah we had a few drinks, but she kept telling me that you dumped her, man!" Rob's voice remained calm. "So, one thing led to another and–I'm sorry man but, uh, when I heard her parents coming home that night, I freaked out and snuck out when everyone was asleep. Then before I even could talk to her again, she starts telling everybody I forced her to have sex! That's just crazy man!" Rob looked sad but not guilty. No one said a thing until the sirens sounded.

"Fucking assholes!" Egan pointed at Rob and then at Remmy. "The both of you!"

With the cops on their way, half of the Leech Mob had already run down the long stretch of cars, looking for their ride as the Jocks shouted, "Look at the criminals run!"

"That's right, call your buddies, the piggies, for protection!" Vick yelled out from somewhere.

I ran past him, dazed, while I searched for a familiar car as everyone swerved around me, flying down the street to evacuate. I recognized faces as they burned past me. I shouted for them to stop but they didn't listen. I could see that I was running out of options as I reached the end of the line but then spotted two skaters driving past. I didn't know them but I ran alongside their car, pounding on the roof and screaming. They came to a rolling stop, pausing just long enough for me to jump in.

We were one of the last to drive past the house, when the crowd got braver and ran down the driveway, chucking half-empty beer bottles at us as we tore past. The cops swerved up, just in time to see them throwing shit. By the time the cops got the story from them, we'd disappeared into the night.

✦

Dr. Gildmore slowly shook his head. "It sounds like Egan knew that this fight wouldn't solve anything."

"I think it did."

"What did it solve?"

"We stood up to them."

"But did it really change anything?"

"I don't know. At the time it seemed like it did."

"I hear that a lot," Dr. Gildmore said. "At the time it seemed like a good idea, at the time it seemed like the only thing you could do. Right?"

"Yeah, yeah, yeah."

"Yeah, yeah, yeah. Alright Kelly, go to dinner."

Chapter 7: Vick

"Dude! Vans?" Ezra asked. "What types?"

"Like this," I pointed at my shoes. "But one pair's green, one's blue and then a pair of high-tops that are purple."

"Like, how much?" Ezra asked.

"I paid thirty in California."

"Yeah alright," said Ezra. "I got the purple ones for real."

"No way, dude!" snapped Brody. "Those are mine!"

"I already, uh, called em!" said Ezra as Krissy walked past. "Hey Krissy! Where are you going?" Ezra asked as we caught up with her.

"I sooo have to go straight home today. My mom like needs the car for work."

Because it was snowing, most kids had ditched the parking lot scene early but a few hung in cars, yelling across to each other through half open windows. I dusted the snow off my cap as I watched Vick trudge out of the school. As he got closer, I could tell he was pissed off.

"This sucks! I hate it when it snows!" Vick held up a hand as he walked past me, headed toward his car.

This might be tricky, I thought, as I fell in step with him. "Hey Vick, what are you doing?"

"I don't know yet." He walked faster.

"You're not going out tonight?"

"Yes, I am."

"Then it's cool if I go with you, right?"

Vick looked at me over the roof of his car, shaking his head and then asked, "Hey, you still got them purple Vans?"

"Yeah, they're all yours."

"Alright, get in." Vick swung inside his car and then unlocked my door, allowing me to fall into the passenger seat.

"Where did you get all those sneakers anyway?" he asked as he tried to start the engine. Vans were near impossible to find in Connecticut.

"I told you I went to California over winter vacation."

"Shit!" He hit the steering wheel. "What ja do?" The car finally sparked, ran for a second, and then stalled.

"Skated, went to the beach once but it was cold."

Vick sneered. "Yeah, California is real cold."

"Are you gonna start the car, Vick?"

"Alright, pussy." Vick fired up the engine and planted his foot on the gas pedal to keep the car from dying, as freezing cold air shot out of the air vents.

"There's Kit," I said as the Clam rolled in, crunching through the fresh snow. A moment later, Macie and Face hustled past us and got into the Clam.

"What's up with them?" I asked.

"They're druggies," Vick said and rolled down his window to yell across to Lampy. "Hey! What's going on tonight?"

"Show at the Night Breed. We might skip it though."

"You better skip it! Druggies don't belong at straight-edge shows!"

"It's not straight-edge anymore, Vick! Anyway, me and Remmy might go snowboarding at the golf course!" Lampy grinned and took a hit off of a pipe before passing it over to Remmy, who then passed it to Obi in the back seat.

"You got an extra snowboard?" Vick asked.

"No chance, dude!" Lampy took another toke off his bowl.

Vick narrowed his eyes. "Why are you smoking that shit around here, stupid?"

"What?" Lampy shouted across.

"So what are we gonna do, Vick?" I asked.

"Well, first I'm gotta see my girlfriend and–"

From out of nowhere, Face ripped the back door open, letting in a blast of snowy air as he sat down, red-faced."

"Did I fucking say that you could get in, dipshit?" Vick growled. "Where the fuck did you come from?"

"Nickodemus sent me!"

"Asshole," Vick smirked.

"What's up?" Face winked at me as Vick turned back around.

"You're stupid, that's what's up! All toking up in the student parking lot, just asking to get narked on for real."

"We're smoking here cause nobody wants to drive in the snow and they're all crying about going home." Face made a sobbing face as he dug through his pockets and retrieved a red plastic wallet.

"What's that? Your superman wallet?" Vick cackled as Face rolled down the window. He held out a $10 bill and yelled out to Lampy, who nodded and started digging through his car.

"Where we going, Vick?"

"We aren't going nowhere if you don't have any money for gas, Face!"

Lampy knocked on his window, and Face jumped out and ran over to make the quick transaction and then jumped back in the car with us.

"Did you hear me, Face?" Vick asked.

"What?"

"I hope that wasn't your last ten bucks."

"Relax, man." Face patted Vick's shoulder but his smug grin suddenly changed to fear. "Here comes the security guard!" Face almost jumped into the front seat. "Let's get out of here!"

"Get the hell back!" Vick shoved Face into the backseat as he threw the car into reverse and then swerved backwards, hitting the brakes and then throwing the gear into first, peeling out on the snow, tires spinning but with no traction.

"Shit! Let's get the hell out of here! What are you doing, man? Let's go!" yelled Face, leaning into the front seat again.

"Sit back, you fucker!" Vick threw the gearshift back into reverse and looked over his shoulder as the giant guard trudged across the parking lot. Instantly the tires caught traction, and we sped backwards, leaving the others behind.

"You're driving backwards! You're driving backwards!" Face leaned into the front again, screaming.

"I know that, you druggie!" Vick hollered, pounding on Face, who screamed out in pain and crawled into the corner of the car. "Put your seatbelt on, jackass! I'm not getting arrested for you, hippy!" Vick threatened him as we drove backwards out of the lot and then out onto the road. A driver blared on his horn, swerved around us, and then skidded onto the school's lawn. Vick threw his car into drive, with wheels spinning again, as we made our escape.

"How bald are your tires, man?" Face complained.

"You want to walk?"

"Where are we going, Katie's house?" Face asked.

"Yeah."

"Aren't there any shows?"

"Why?" Vick growled. "Do you got a hardcore flier hanging out of your ass that I don't know about? Is your fucking band playing or something?"

"No," Face said glumly.

"Alright then," Vick said as he slammed on his brakes, sending us all jolting forward. "Just testing my brakes. Let me get a drag off that cigarette, Face."

"No more of your damn tricks, you communist!" Face shouted.

"Just give me a damn drag off that cigarette!" Vick screamed.

"Fine, I'll just put it out."

"Give me that fucker if you know what's good for you!"

Face sighed and handed the smoke over to Vick, who slowly brought it up to his mouth, but then tossed it out the window and laughed.

"That was almost as funny as the last ten times you did that!" grumbled Face as Vick smirked.

Vick began rifling through his glove compartment filled with tapes, throwing some of them onto the floor and tossing others into the backseat, hitting Face in the head. He laughed and continued sifting through the stash, even throwing some tapes out the window in aggravation before finding the Gorillas' tape.

"Did you install this stereo system yourself?" I asked, looking at all the wires dangling out of his stereo onto the floor, some cut and twisted together with black tape.

"Yeah and the speakers." Vick gestured to the two five inch speakers jiggling around on the back window ledge.

"Didn't the Gorillas break up?" asked Face.

"Yeah, genius, what straight-edge hardcore band hasn't?" Vick began screaming along with the lyrics as the music became more and more distorted. When he realized the tape was being eaten, Vick howled, punched *Eject*, and fished out the tangled strands of crumpled brown tape. "Motherfucker!" he swore as he pulled out the last of the mess and threw the whole disaster out the window. We continued to race down the winding back roads to Dilford, a town farther out in the sticks than Riverview even.

I picked some of the dirt-crusted cassette tapes off the floor, wiped them off, and read them. They were all old hardcore demos and mixes. "Can I borrow some of these?"

"I don't give a shit!" Vick said agreeably.

As we drove north into Dilford, the snow fell thicker, covering snow dunes from the last snowstorm with a fresh layer of powder. Freezing air blew out of the car vents, and Vick swore and beat the top of his dashboard. "My damn heater's broken!"

We caught up to an old geezer, driving twenty miles an hour through the storm.

"What the hell is this bullshit?" Face exclaimed. "He's driving all–*safe*."

"Why don't you go home?" Vick shouted out the window and honked his horn as he swerved back and forth behind the guy.

"You're going to give him a heart attack," I said.

"Fuck this shit!" Vick shouted as he tried to pass. Just then, a sand truck came barreling around the curve, blaring its air horn and downshifting gears.

"GET BACK!" I screamed but Vick stepped on the gas. I clawed around for my seatbelt and had it halfway across my chest when Vick managed to swerve in front of the old man's car, narrowly missing the oncoming truck by inches.

Finally, fishtailing up the driveway, we arrived at Vick's girlfriend's house. Vick hit his steering wheel. "Shit! Her mom's home!"

"What?" I asked. "She doesn't like you or something?"

"No, she loves me," Vick answered. "It just means that I won't be able to slap any ass till she's gone."

Katie met us at the door, tiny but real cute, all pierced up and neon red hair, angle cut three inches longer on one side. She wore a purple headband, purple lipstick and a HORSEFLESH tee shirt, Vick's band.

She stood with a mischievous grin. "What took you so long?"

"Ahh, I like your shirt!" Vick said. "Where did you get it?"

"Trash," she said. "Actually it's Tina's but it makes me looking like raging, so I stole it cause she was being like a real skank and got in my face and I was like, bitch, get over yourself and I seriously almost even like hit her, like kind of."

"Come here," Vick growled at her playfully and chewed on her neck. "Happy birthday, baby!"

"Hello Vic," came a woman's voice from the inside somewhere. "Why don't you boys come in?"

"Yeah Vick, are you just gonna stand there and let the heat all out?" Katie asked, knowing that she was just too damn cute for her own good. She sounded as if she'd taken a drag off a helium balloon, and she rolled her big, brown Kewpie Doll eyes while she spoke. Her little act seemed to tickle Vick all to hell. He started cracking up, nuzzled her close, and they danced to where her mother stood.

"Do any of you want something to snack on?" she asked.

"No, I got all I need right here." Vick playfully nibbled on Katie's shoulder while her mother raised her eyebrows.

"Are you sure, Vick? Now that I know you're a vegetarian, I have some food to accommodate you."

"No, I'm good." Vick stood with his arm around Katie's waist and smiled as her mother looked at Face and me. "Oh, these are my two friends, Kelly and Face."

"Hello boys."

"Hi, Kelly," Katie giggled and then looked at Face, "What's up, Face?"

Face nodded at her with a crooked smile, gave her the thumbs up, did a small tap dance, and then displayed his hands palms up as if he was waiting for applause. Vick started laughing and leaned into Katie.

"Are you into the theater or something, Face?"

"Well, now that you mention it, why yes," Face agreed. "Finally, someone who appreciates fine art." Face bent forward and reached out for her hand, which she reluctantly turned over for Face to kiss.

"Aren't we all full of surprises today." Katie's mother smiled and walked into the kitchen, opening the refrigerator door.

"You boys aren't hungry after school?" her mom asked disbelievingly.

"Do you have any chocolate covered seaweed?" Face asked.

"Shut up, Face," laughed Vick.

"No," Katie's mom smiled. "We happen to be out of that at the moment."

"Then I'll pass, thank you," said Face really politely.

"And how about you?" She looked at me. "I'm almost afraid to ask."

"No, we're leaving now." Vick looked at Katie. "Right?"

"In the snow?" Katie's mom exclaimed. "But it's terrible out. Where on earth would you go?"

"Like, Trash," said Katie.

"Yeah, Trash America," agreed Vick.

"Well, I don't think you kids should go anywhere in the storm. And it's already getting dark out."

"Oh, I always drive carefully," Vick promised and then smacked Face when he began to squirm.

"Since it's Katie's birthday, I guess, but it's going to get really bad out. And Katie, nobody over when I'm gone tonight!" she warned.

Katie pulled on her jacket and, as we started out to the car, she squeaked, "Hey Kelly, Face, there's something I want to tell you."

"Yeah, what?" Face asked.

"Shot gun!" she answered in absolute delight, calling the front seat.

"I was going to let you have it anyway," I said.

"I wasn't!" Face began to run.

"Oh no you don't!" Katie yelled, breaking away from Vick to book after Face, who slipped on the ice and fell. Katie gleefully ran to the car and got in the front.

"Well, you didn't have to kick me!" Face lay there in the snow while we got into the car and began to back down the driveway, leaving Face at the top. When he saw how it was going to be, Face started chasing us down the hill, screaming for us to stop as Katie and Vick giggled in the front seat. At the bottom of the driveway, Face climbed onto the hood and held on for life as Vick tore in circles around the cul-de-sac. After a moment, Vick hit the brakes, sending Face rolling onto the road, softly cushioned with fresh snow.

"Do you have it?" Katie asked, looking at Vick as Face slowly stood up in the headlights, his glasses crooked on his nose.

"What?"

"You know, the tape, our tape."

"Oh yeah." Vick reached over and rummaged through his glove compartment, again throwing tapes all over the car, before finding it and pressing play as Katie bounced up and down with excitement. Face walked around and opened the back door, breathing hard as the music started, the soundtrack to *The Little Mermaid*.

Vick laughed at my expression and began singing along.

Face collapsed onto the seat and groaned. Vick threw his gearshift into drive, spun once more around the cul-de-sac, and then slid down the hill, coasting through a stop sign and crashing into a snow bank while Katie squealed in her helium voice. The country roads were getting worse as we drove through the sticks, past Riverview and into Landbury, where the snow was just beginning to turn to rain.

Trash America was a punk rock junkshop run by a wise old hippy who bartered clothes, weird shit, and music. The offbeat shop held the largest supply of rare hardcore records anywhere. Katie wanted a video of the punk band Burning Flag but Vick didn't have the fifteen dollars to cough up for it, so while the hippy wasn't looking, Vick shoved it down his pants. When the store got crowded, the four of us slipped out.

Vick reached into his pants and pulled out the VHS tape and handed it over to Katie saying, "Happy birthday, sweetie." She wrapped her arms around his neck real tight.

"Oh thank you, Vick. I've been wanting this for so long!"

Snowplows were at work on Riverview streets, but we still had some trouble getting up to Katie's house atop the hill in Dilford. We gave up trying to drive up her road and walked instead. Back at the house, her mom was now gone. Katie switched on the TV, and then she and Vick went upstairs. A few minutes later, we heard the bedsprings bouncing up and down and Katie squeaking.

"We should have all stolen her something," moaned Face.

"I like that dude who runs Trash," I said. "You don't steal from someone like him."

Face shrugged. "Vick steals from everyone," he said, while nosing around, going through all the drawers and cabinets. "He doesn't discriminate."

"What are you looking for?"

"I'll know when I find it." After a moment the squeaking stopped. "That was quick."

"Did we come all the way back here for Vick and her to have sex?"

Face looked at me funny. "Probably."

"So now where?"

"The mall." Face rummaged through another drawer. "One time I found a whole ounce of weed that my friend's dad had."

A minute later, Vick stood at the top of the stairs looking at us with a silly smile. "Get out of her things, dumb-ass," Vick hissed. "Come on, let's go!" He walked to the door, opened it, and stood there waiting for us.

"Shotgun," I said.

"Shit!" Face closed the desk drawer.

"I'll see ya Katie," Vick yelled up the stairs and shut the door behind us.

"Why isn't Katie going with us?" I asked, but all Vick did was look at me funny, as though I were stupid for asking. We walked back down the hill, got into Vick's car, and he started it up, when *The Little Mermaid* tape started playing again.

"Ha-ha-ha!" Vick laughed before ejecting it and throwing it behind him without looking, hitting Face in the face again.

"Ow! Watch it!" Face hollered. "I bet that after they listen to *The Little Mermaid*,

Vick goes upstairs, gets naked and straps a plastic fin to his head and chases Katie around the room with a trident."

"Do you have enough dough if we go to a club?" Vick abruptly changed the subject.

"I have like seven dollars," I said. "Is that enough for all of us?"

"We don't all pay to get in, dude," Vick explained, "Only one of us has to get a stamp. Then we'll press all our hands together."

"Does it work?"

"All the time."

✦

Each weekend, the Leech Mob gathered at the food court in the Landbury Mall. Along with the other gangs, the Leech Mob hovered around the arcade games, under the watchful eye of the Landbury police, who stood grinning and chewing gum while talking out of the sides of their mouths. We crossed the glass-enclosed cafeteria to the section of tables reserved for the Leech Mob. The closer we came to our section, the fewer hard stares we got from the other gangs.

"What's going on tonight?" Kit asked, walking up with Lampy.

"We just got here," said Vick. "I have no idea."

"Nothing but the clubs," yawned Connor. "I might go home. I'm beat."

"You suck, Connor!" said Egan. "You said you'd go to Belly's. It's Freak Night." Egan continued, "Since I got the new job, I'll buy the beer. They never card us there anyway."

After another hour of killing time, we got in the cars and drove a few miles into New York. As we pulled into Belly's, I saw the bouncers toss a drunk out the door. We parked the cars and walked in with the girls leading the way. The drunk stumbled up to us as we walked past him.

"Don't go in dere!" he slurred. "A bunch of assholes. Can you believe dey kicked me out?"

"Get out of here, freak!" Vick turned around and snarled, kicking him and cackling real loud when the drunk crashed to the ground.

"Vick!" Egan turned around. "Get over here!"

At the door, Egan said we were all eighteen and, even though the bouncers frowned, they took our money and let us by. Inside must have been 90 degrees and stunk like a mix of alcohol and sweat. Industrial music blared across the dark dance floor. Ultra low ceilings, surrounded by mirrors and racked with all sorts of lights and gadgets, sprayed a mist. We pushed through the crowds back to another room lined with booths, lucked into grabbing two big tables, and all squeezed in. A moment later, a waitress strolled up, looking at us suspiciously.

"What can I get you?" she asked.

"Four pitchers of beer, and plastic cups will be alright," Egan said and tipped her quickly, handing her a folded bill. She looked thoughtfully at us kiddies for a moment and then walked off. If anyone in our crowd was straightedge, they weren't that night.

Freaks in wigs and costumes bounced up and down to the music piped in from the dance floor. More and more kids walked into the club and made their rounds through the back room, all saying hellos and leaning over for hugs. Egan knew hundreds of kids—skaters, goths, freaks, and punks. Vick flirted with the cuter girls, hugging them and yelling over the music into their ears, kissing ass, and trying to secure some play.

"Now you know why Katie isn't with us." Face leaned over and winked.

It didn't take long for many of the girls to tire of Vick groping them and they disappeared onto the dance floor. Vick leaned forward and drunkenly slurred, "Sooner or later, I'll get one of these pigs to suck face! And then off to the ass smacking session-HA-HA-HA!" Face leaned back, fanning away the alcohol vapors that radiated from Vick's trap. Vick stared straight up, while he drunkenly chuckled out of the corner of his mouth, tipping his head from side to side, acting like a fool until the next two girls walked in.

One girl was Leech Mob but had a cousin with her, a cute preppy visiting from Minnesota. I watched as she glanced around at the club's inhabitants, shocked at the strange characters at alternative night at Belly's but, after a few drinks, she started to relax. With the constant flow of people, she moved closer to Vick, who instantly went back into smooth mode and stared at her until getting her attention.

"Hey, you're cute."

"What?" She smiled.

"I can't hear you," Vick said as he began to crawl over Face to sit beside her.

"Hey! Ow!" Face complained as Vick planted a palm to his face and shoved him aside, hissing.

"Move over, you cock block!"

"Oh my god!" she giggled as Face cried out in pain. "Are you okay?"

As the night went on, a party was mentioned, and Vick's ears perked up at the news, happily seeing that his plan was taking form. He looked deeply into his new girl's eyes and gently asked her if she wanted to check out the party. Later on, we all stumbled out into the parking lot and got into our cars. Somebody had directions to the party and we all followed them. Somewhere behind us was Vick's new chick from Minnesota.

"So are you going to hit that, Vick?" Face asked, sitting in the front seat and chuckling almost silently.

"Ha-ha-ha," Vick laughed in his deep, impish voice. "What do you think, moron?"

"What about Katie, Vick?" I heard myself ask and he grilled me through the mirror with a disgusted look.

"What's this?" Vick asked. "I got like Face sitting on one shoulder, and Kelly on the other! *What about Katie, Vick?*" Vick mimicked me. "SHUT UP! I don't get in your business!"

"You think Katie would be cool if she found out?" I asked.

"No. She would cut my balls off," Vick snarled. "That's why I don't like taking Katie to clubs anymore."

"Why exactly?" I asked as Face started laughing.

"Cause she almost caught me one night! I was at Images, sucking face with some pig in the back of the club, and Katie shows up."

"What happened?"

"I was lucky that Remmy saw her first and ran over and pushed me out the emergency exit. We got in the car and took off."

"Hey! I remember that night!" Face sat up angrily. "That was the night you left me stranded at Images! Nobody wanted to drive me back to Riverview so I had to wake my mom up! I was so stoned and had to drive with my mom at midnight!"

"Ha-ha-ha," Vick laughed.

"It's not funny!"

"Yes it is," Vick laughed. "It's real funny!"

"Just wait until next time Katie shows up!" Face promised.

"Yeah and what?" He glared at Face. "You better warn me!"

"Nope!" Face said. "Not after you left me stranded! I'm going to bring Katie right over to you and say, 'Look! Look at that nasty Vick, your dirty boyfriend sucking face with that hog!'"

When we got to the house, music was blaring out the steamed windows and we could see a small crowd of people inside. We walked in where Vick joined up with his new girlfriend, and it didn't take him longer than five minutes to schmooze her upstairs into one of the bedrooms. I didn't recognize too many kids at this party and I had no idea where we even were. Meanwhile, kids stumbled around, half-drunk off the random bottles that cluttered the dining room table. Others sat banging on the piano, until someone sat down who could actually play a song.

Face bumped into me, "You got a paper or a bowl?" he asked. "I lost my bowl."

"No, how long are we gonna be here anyway?" I asked, watching Vick lead his new girl upstairs. "It's already 1:00 AM."

"I don't know, maybe all night," Face answered,

"Really?" I asked, in disbelief.

"I got to find someone with a paper or a bowl. Nickodemus, you'll pay for this thievery!" Face shook his fist at the walls and then pushed past me, concerned more with getting stoned. I fell down on the sofa, leaned back, and closed my eyes, letting all the noises blend into one continuous sound.

The next moment, the morning sun filled the house with bright daylight. A few kids lay passed out around me.

"Shit," I said, feeling last night's alcohol like a knot in my skull. I then noticed the only other person awake. Sitting across from me was the Leech Mob chick whose cousin was upstairs with Vick.

"Hey," I said leaning forward. "Did they come out yet?"

"Not a chance." She stretched. "I knocked on the door once but your friend yelled at me."

I smiled, "What did he say?"

She tried her best to imitate him. "Room's taken, fuck off!" she rasped and shook her head.

"You sound just like him."

"Thanks, I try."

"Sorry–"

"For what?"

"For Vick being an asshole."

She shrugged her shoulders. "I'm more angry at my cousin!" She raised her voice to the rooms upstairs, stirring a few bodies around us. Her cousin must have heard, because the door cracked open and she slowly emerged. The girl jumped up from the sofa and stormed over, throwing up her hands.

"Do you know how much trouble we're in at home right now?" she whispered angrily.

"So, let's go already. I know we're here late!"

"Late! We're not late–*we're missing!*"

"Alright shut up. Just let me use the bathroom!"

They argued as I got up and walked into the bedroom where Vick lay, face down, pretending to sleep.

"Vick?"

"What?" he groaned.

"What's wrong with you?"

"I'm tired."

"Let's go man, I got to get home."

He looked up, "What time is it?"

"After five."

"Fuck."

"So we're leaving?" I asked.

"Yeah," he grumbled, going off in a coughing fit.

"Then let's go."

"Shut your mouth!" Vick looked up while blinking his eyes. "Where's Face?"

"How should I know?"

"Well go find him! Check outside," he snapped, and he whipped his legs out of the bed and started to pull his pants on. I walked down the hallway, hearing the girls talking in the bathroom and went outside to see Face, sitting on the porch, gagging on a cigarette.

"It's freezing out here," I said as I opened the door. He glanced up from the steps and held out his cigarette for me to take, still choking.

"Have some. I think the cigarette company laced it with cyanide."

Vick walked out behind me while slinging on his jacket.

"You say bye to your girl?" I asked him.

"Fuck her," Vick muttered.

"What?"

"I said, FUCK HER!" Vick glared at me.

"So, did you have your way with her?" Face stood up, bobbing his eyebrows.

"Yeah, but it took me all night," Vick complained while reaching back and slamming the front door. "Let's get out of here."

The three of us walked down the steps and out onto the driveway toward Vick's car. I called shotgun but Face didn't even react and collapsed into the backseat. Vick started messing with his stereo, ejecting and fumbling with his tapes again as the two girls exited the house and walked down the steps, both staring at Vick for some type of response as they headed to their car. I nudged Vick and waved at the girls who waved back hesitatingly, keeping their eyes on Vick, who just sat there with a blank look on his face, before throwing the gearshift into reverse and backing down the driveway without so much as a nod in their direction.

"So what took you so long in there?" Face asked sheepishly from the back seat.

"She didn't want to screw without rubbers..."

"What are you talking about?" Face exclaimed. "There's like 500 rubbers in the glove compartment."

"I hate using condoms-ha-ha-ha!" snickered Vick, dropping open the glove compartment where an economy box of condoms sat buried under his mess of tapes.

He pulled out a strip with flourish and whipped them at me as I tried to snatch them out of his hand but he held them out the window.

"Look, they're right behind us," I insisted.

"So the fuck what?" Vick sneered, staring at them in the rearview mirror, expressionless. Face sat up and glanced out the back window before letting his body drop back down and shut his eyes in silent laughter.

"Dude!" I exclaimed, "You just told her that you didn't have any condoms!"

"Yeah?" snapped Vick.

"Dude, don't let her see those."

"Why not!" Vick howled. "Do you really think I care if she knows!" he admitted, furiously grinning, enraged at something. Vick stepped on the gas and we turned left onto Main Street, the girls still behind us. I dropped my hands and sat back. Vick glanced over at me and sneered, making it absolutely clear in one look that he didn't give a damn about anyone's feelings, let alone some girl he picked up at a bar last night.

Face lay in the backseat, chuckling quietly as Vick went on to rip the strip apart and then chuck the rubbers out the window, two or three at a time, letting the wind pull them away and fly behind us, covering their car like confetti. I dropped my head against the window in embarrassment as Face continued to laugh idiotically.

"Shut up, Face!" I yelled.

Face sat up and looked at Vick. "I bet you told her that you were falling in love with her! That you would drive up to visit her every weekend!"

"That's right!" Vick shouted. "She was a pig and that's how pigs get treated!"

I reached into the glove compartment, where Vick continued to re-load, grabbed the economy box and held them away. Vick reached over, car swerving, and grabbed the condoms out of my hand. "Look out!" I shouted as Vick jumped the curb and headed straight for a telephone pole. Vick gripped the wheel with both hands and whipped us back on the road, barely regaining control of the car.

"Jackass!" he said as he continued to dig into the box and let them fly out the window. I glanced back and saw they were still right behind us. Together, we stopped at the red light at the intersection and both idled there. After Vick said he spent all night overcoming her rejections, promising love, devotion, and everlasting loyalty, he tossed every promise away, like the condoms he carelessly threw out the window.

"Dude, this is soooo wrong," I said, looking down and shaking my head as Face sat up, blew a strawberry, and then fell back down.

"Shutthefuckup!" Vick shouted with an amused face.

The light refused to turn as he ripped off more and more. He must have had dozens...until the grand finale hit. He dug into his pocket and pulled out her phone number, written on a folded slip of pink paper and, as the light turned green, he hit the gas and let that fly out, too.

He laughed into his rearview mirror as they turned left. Then we were alone and Vick began tampering with the radio again.

Chapter 8: Flip

Despair was on stage. Cecil, the guitarist, a black guy with dreads, had just finished tuning up and playing riffs. Hank, the drummer, the only metal-head in an army of hardcore kids, seemed misplaced. Obi stood still, silent and professional, on rhythm guitar, while Casey, somewhat nervous that he might screw up, was on bass. Under the yellow light, wearing his terminator sunglasses and staring into the crowd, Egan began screaming out his lyrics, yet calmly gesturing like a professor philosophizing to his class.

BAM! I got hit again, a headbutt to the face. My nose was crackling around. SHIT! I reached up and felt the cartilage in my bridge crunch. The other kid spun around, swinging his arms to clear a path for himself, a larger dude with a *Scorch* shirt on. My body twisted in mid-air and I felt someone catch me at the edge of the pit and throw my skinny ass right back in, which was the last place I wanted to be.

Scorch danced through the pit and clipped Tank, who turned around and tried to kick him but missed. He then chased the kid down before grabbing him, spinning him, and slamming him down. Scorch grunted, rolled to the side and tried to evacuate the pit but Bull, from the Cincity Leech Mob, was waiting for him there, gripping a pair of brass knuckles.

Behind shades, Egan screamed into the microphone, gesturing with his palm up toward the ceiling as if he were behind a podium, explaining some complex theory. The music kicked in and the pit exploded into madness. Vick took over the pit with his dreaded washing machine maneuver until Bull, covered in black tattoos, charged in and stomped Vick in his lower back, knocking him, arching forward.

Vick flew into Remmy, who tried to catch him, and together they glared at Bull before forced smiles spread across their lips. Bull strolled around the pit, twice, nodding his head to the music and smirking hatefully. He challenged anybody to get in there with him and his brass knuckles. Vick and Remmy grimaced, looking as if they didn't know if they loved or hated Bull. Then he walked out and disappeared into the back of the club.

At some point two skinheads showed up, gripped hands and began spinning around the pit, building up momentum and knocking bodies out of their way like two wrecking balls. Otis dove off the stage into them and they all crashed to the floor. Bodies rained down from above as kids jumped off the stage, three at a time. Some climbed up the seven-foot speakers and back-flipped off, while others swung from the rafters.

Clubs that hosted hardcore shows were becoming more and more scarce. The dive we were in tonight was a messy little joint called The Night Breed. The main room was painted black. The stage was small, not much higher than four feet, and to the left was a railed-in platform. Most of the cheap metal tables and chairs had been pushed to the back and sides of the room, opening the area around the stage. Off to the side, a narrow bar room was sectioned off by plexi-glass windows that ran the length of the club, with a bouncer posted at the entrance, checking I.D.'s.

The Night Breed used to be a music joint for country western bands before it changed owners. Now, with the local drug dealer Desperate Bob running the place, it hosted heavy metal, hardcore, and punk shows, so there were always other crews bopping around. Tonight, I'd already gotten two of my earrings torn out of my left ear and my nose was cracked and bleeding. To stop the blood, I shoved a wad of cheap toilet paper up my nose, which I guessed was broken.

I pushed my way back through the crowds and into the pit. I fought toward the front of the stage and then held on, looking up at the band as people crashed into me. When the music kicked back in, I climbed onto the stage, ran across, and jumped into the audience. For a moment I was caught and carried overhead but soon I found myself on the floor with shoes stomping all around me. Before I was trampled, I jumped up and smashed into someone going the other way. I grabbed on to keep from falling and saw it was Vick.

I started to say something but Vick just grinned and sprang off the floor with a jump kick that sent me flying. I watched as Vick vanished from sight as I flew backwards and sank into the crowds. When I met the wall of bodies, I was shoved back off the line and sent barreling forwards again. I collided with someone and spun past him, then caught a shoe to my face as another stage diver narrowly missed landing sideways on my grill. I stumbled backwards, falling into the edge of the pit, clinging to the sidelines to keep from being thrown back in. I glanced up at Egan, who laughed at me from the stage. Everyone was freestyling or throwing down spin cycles, windmills, picking-up-change, floor-punches, blindmans, and round houses. A thousand different actions rolled through the pit and, for a shining moment, all the chaos grooved like clockwork. Even the band seemed transformed into an orchestra playing a symphony of insanity.

Gavin flew into me and I pushed him back out. He ran, jumped in the center of the pit, spinkicking 360 degrees in the air, before crashing down on the opposite end of the pit, only to be caught and shoved back in to spinkick again. In the center of the pit, Vick began his trademark spin cycle, starting off choppy as he hit people who got in his way. Soon Vick had worked himself into the quickest spin I'd ever seen. His arms flung out to the sides and he became a blur. Even Gavin stayed out of his way–no one wanted to get close to the human blender. Kids ran past, guarding their faces blindly with one arm while swinging the other in a move called the Blind Man.

At first, nobody wanted to try to take Vick out but when he slowed down, somebody tried. The kid lowered his head and ran in to throw a shoulder into Vick, but when he got close, a barrage of spinning fists slapped his head. He grunted and spun away, holding his face where his left eye swelled shut. When his friends checked him out, he looked up and smiled, shaking his head. It came with the territory...

Eventually Vick was taken out by a stage diver who brought him down like a giant claw. When we pulled them up, they gripped each other in a death-lock trying to pry each other's faces off. We dragged Vick away from the kid and outside the pit until he calmed down. The tangle mattered little to the others, who instantly ran from side to side, jumping and colliding into each other as they danced through.

In the audience, a kid faithfully screamed all of Egan's lyrics, so Egan held out the mic. The kid tried to fight in closer to the stage and strained to reach it. With one arm, Egan reached over the crowd and curled him off the floor without any difficulty so he could shout Despair's lyrics. The kid hung in Egan's clutches, shouting the words he knew by heart. Egan dropped him, stood up to yell the last line, and the music suddenly stopped. The kids stopped moshing, and applause sounded around the room.

✦

"Good morning everyone and welcome to Music Appreciation Class."

Mr. Hermes stood quietly in front of the class, staring at us with a slightly annoyed look, waiting for us to finish talking and allow him the floor.

"Shhhhhhh!" A few brainwashed jobs turned around with scrunched up faces and hissed at the rest of us.

"After the semester break, I understand it's tough getting back into the swing of things, at least it is that way to me. So to help, I've selected some exceptional pieces to play for you today that I wasn't going to introduce until much later in the semester."

Mr. Hermes probably thought he spoke smooth enough to melt butter. He carefully pronounced each word like he had a big marshmallow dissolving on his tongue. "You might think this is a give-away class, an easy A. After all, it must be a breeze just listening to music for one semester but, I assure you, there is nothing easy about this experience. I expect my students to memorize almost every song I play, the band or artist who wrote or performed it, the year it came out, as well as some other important facts."

"How are we supposed to remember all of that? Give us a break man!" a voice sounded from the back of the room.

"Shhhhhh!" One of the same students who shushed us before was back at it.

"You shut up!" Flip snapped back.

Hermes paused, waiting for any other comments before continuing.

"I will play a selection of classical music, as well as jazz, rock, blues and even some opera." As Mr. Hermes spoke, he gazed upwards toward the ceiling with a comfortable expression on his face. "We will also be watching a selection of award winning films and, oh yes, I find it best to have all the lights off when I am fully appreciating a fine piece."

"Me, too!" agreed Flip.

Mr. Hermes snapped his head down and his eyes shot open as he glowered at the back of the room but instead of scolding Flip, he said, "You will find that I will continue to treat each of my students with the utmost respect. That way, I hope that each of you will show me the same respect."

Mr. Hermes went on, "When listening to the music, I suggest that you close your eyes and try to relax. You could put your heads down on your desks as long as you don't go to sleep. To help you relax, you will notice that when we are listening to the music and the lights are off, that I have covered the room with some glow in the dark star and planet stickers. It helps to set the mood. So don't be alarmed. No, you are not dreaming with your eyes open."

"Oh-ha-ha-ha-funny!" laughed Flip, his voice loud and sarcastic, booming from the back row of desks.

Mr. Hermes ignored Flip again and decided to cut right to the chase, turned out the lights, and then blasted some classical music on his surround-sound stereo, which piped in from every corner of the room. All of the stickers glowed a fake green as we sat in the dark listening to his music. Every so often, using a flashlight, Hermes would get up and change the CD. He made a small announcement of what he was about to play, told us what we were supposed to know about the song, and then bowed as he introduced it. He started off with classical music and played Mozart, then switched to Blues and went with Billy Holiday, then decided on some jazz with Louie Armstrong, and finally hit us with some Billy Joel. Because of the range of music, I quickly figured these must have been the teacher's favorite songs. Besides teaching choir and music, this was his steady day gig, not bad for playing his stereo system. After "We Didn't Start the Fire," Mr. Hermes got up and shined his flashlight at the clock.

"Well class, we have about twelve minutes left and I want to play two more pieces for you but they are somewhat lengthy so I don't think we'll have time to finish both but we'll try. The first is a piece from Beethoven, taken from the second movement of Symphony Number 9 in D minor. I hope that you all enjoy this. The sheer mathematical genius of this music, the ability and talent to write such work is almost beyond comprehension!" Then Mr. Hermes bowed, stuck his flashlight into his armpit and leaned over the stereo, squinting in the darkness for the play button. A moment later Beethoven's Ninth thundered into the room, and Mr. Hermes walked back over to his chair, sat down, leaned back, stretched out his legs, and closed his eyes. The music wasn't bad at first, but it seemed to go on and on and then, from the back of the room, a voice started to rise up over the music. I smiled. It was quiet at first but then became louder and louder.

"Oooohhhhhhh. Damn! Ohhhhhhh no! NO! NO! NO! STOP! STOP! PLEASE! ENOUGH! AAARRGHHHH!" The class turned around, squinting in the dark to see who had begun to wail. Mr. Hermes jumped up, ran over to the stereo, turned it off, and flipped on the lights.

"Flip! I'm guessing this disruption belongs to you!"

Flip sat there, like the rest of us, blinking at the bright lights after sitting in the dark for so long.

"Flip! Are we having a problem?"

"Yes!"

"Well, what is the problem?"

"It's the music."

"What about the music?" Mr. Hermes smiled.

"It sucks!" Flip said and chuckled weakly.

Hermes sighed. "Well that's life, Flip. Does all the music that I play, suck, as you most delicately put it?"

"Most of it, yeah!" Flip answered. "I mean I don't want to lie to you." Flip smiled. Mr. Hermes wasn't expecting that.

"There will come a day when one or two of you will be able to bring your music in and play it for the class." Mr. Hermes looked at us as though we should have been thrilled.

"Only two of us?" Flip said. "So maybe we get to hear some good music one day and for the other 100 days we got to listen to your old stuff?"

"Yes, Flip, the world is full of music and this class is supposed to give you an appreciation for all music, not just…What do you listen to?"

"Rap."

"Yes, Flip, there is more to music than just rap!"

"Yeah, I know."

"Flip, why did you sign up for this class?"

"I don't know! I wish I didn't"

"Well, give it a try, okay?"

"Yeah alright, I'll try."

The teacher bowed, turned back on the stereo and flipped out the lights. Then he leaned back in his chair and closed his eyes, thinking he solved his little problem by letting Flip have his say but less than a minute later, Flip couldn't contain himself any longer and began to moan again.

"AAAAHHHHHHAAHHHHH!"

I watched Mr. Hermes eyes bug open in the dark. He looked around insanely before running back over to the lights, switching them on, and killing the stereo again. This time Hermes looked enraged. Never before had he ever experienced such rudeness.

"Flip!"

"I can't take it anymore. This music is driving me crazy!" Flip said collapsing on his desk, panting hyperactively.

"Get out! Get out of here this very moment!" Mr. Hermes shouted, pointing to the door. Flip slid out of his desk and sauntered toward the front of the class. "And don't come back until you are grown up enough to act like an adult and not like a little baby!"

Flip was smiling but it looked like he wanted to start crying. "I can't help it Mr. Hermes. That music was hurting my ears."

Mr. Hermes sighed. "Then why didn't you say so, Flip. Do you have an ear infection or something?"

"Maybe." Flip sighed after a moment's thought. "Mr. Hermes?"

"What is it, Flip?"

"I just happen to have a tape on me right now that I can play to the class. And I know that you'll like it so much, that you'll probably wind up playing it to your other classes."

"Is that so?" Mr. Hermes looked impressed.

"For sure."

"You know I've never allowed this before. But I'll tell you what, if we play a portion of your song, will you be quiet for the rest of the semester? Honestly Flip, do you swear in front of all these witnesses?"

"Hmm?" Flip held the tape in one hand as he thought about the teacher's terms.

The smile began to fade from Mr. Hermes' face.

"Flip? Do we have a deal?" He looked at Flip strangely.

"Umm." Flip thought deeper.

"Now that I think about it, this truly isn't fair to everyone else."

"YES!" Flip cried. "I agree."

"Alright." Mr. Hermes began again, "If there are no objections, would everyone like to hear a brief musical selection that Flip will present?" No one said a word. "Well since there are no objections, go ahead, Flip. I'll let you play a minute of a song of your choosing."

"Why only a minute?"

"Don't press your luck, mister!" Mr. Hermes leaned forward, gritting his teeth and glowing red.

Flip laughed. "I got to find it first. Shucks, Mr. H."

"Then step right over here, young man." Flip walked over to the stereo with Mr. Hermes, who proudly began to explain to Flip what to do. Flip stared at him for a moment crazily.

"I know how to use a stereo, old man. Shoot! I got a newer one than this."

Mr. Hermes stared at Flip. "My, you really are a delight to have in class."

"No one ever told me that before." Flip grinned. He pressed *Play*, listened, and then pressed *Rewind* again. "Not there yet."

"Just pick any song on the whole album, Flip. I'm sure we'll get the idea."

"It's at the beginning." Flip pressed play and listened again. "Not there yet."

"Carry on, Flip." Mr. Hermes sighed as he returned to his chair and sat down.

"Alright," Flip listened a last time. "Almost there, Mr. H.!"

"Who is the artist, Flip?"

"The artist?" Flip looked at Mr. Hermes as though he were crazy.

"Who is the performer, the singer, Flip?"

"He don't sing, he rap!" Flip said. "And *Play!*" The bass track came on and Flip began to dance and then he turned up the volume. "Check it out."

"That's loud enough Flip." Mr. Hermes shouted, but Flip turned it louder. "I SAID THAT'S QUITE LOUD ENOUGH, FLIP!" Flip turned around and hit the lights off.

"LEAVE THE LIGHTS ON, FLIP!"

"It helps when you turn them off–to set the mood," Flip said and did an arm pop.

Then the stereo began blasting the artist,

"CUSS WORDS JUST LET EM ROLL

MOTHER FUCKING BITCH GOD DAMN ASSHOLE!

CUSS WORDS LET EM RIP,

SUCK MY DICK YOU MOTHER FUCKING BITCH!

CUSS WORDS JUST DON'T QUIT

WHY DON'T YOU STEP OFF

YOU LITTLE PUNK ASS BITCH!"

Mr. Hermes lunged for the stereo and began punching it to stop.

"Alright Flip! Will you please take your seat at once!" Mr. Hermes ran over and flipped on the lights.

"You better give me back my tape."

"Flip, take your seat," Mr. Hermes said, holding the tape. "You can have it back at the end of class because I'd like to have a word with you."

"I know that you really wanna play that for your mom," Flip said and began to slump back to his seat.

"What was that, Flip? What was that you said? Flip! Flip!" Mr. Hermes chased Flip down the aisle. "Hey get back here!" He grabbed Flip's shoulder, but Flip shrugged him off.

"Try it, old man, and I'll knock your old ass out. I ain't playing!"

Mr. Hermes drew back, pale white, with beads of sweat running down his face.

"GET OUT OF HERE! GET OUT OF HERE OR I'LL PHONE SECURITY!" Mr. Hermes ran to the phone as Flip sauntered toward the door.

"Give me back my tape first."

"You can get it back from the principal."

"I said give me my damn tape!" Flip lunged at Mr. Hermes who dropped the tape. Flip picked it up and walked out. Mr. Hermes stood there for a moment with his hand on his chest.

"I'm sorry for that, that interruption." Mr. Hermes fumbled nervously with his stereo system for a minute. "It's all ruined now," Mr. Hermes mumbled to himself as the music began to play. A second later the bell rang and we all spilled out into the hall, leaving Mr. Hermes and Beethoven behind.

Down at the office, the administration finally decided to take action against Mr. Flip Rodriguez. Flip was finally expelled for threatening a teacher. After his four suspensions, this was the last straw and Flip was history at Riverview High.

✦

Dr. Gildmore waited until I'd finished. "You know I've been listening to you for a while now and I'd just like to know, while this was all going on, wasn't there anybody–I don't know, special, who could have helped you out?

"Somebody special?" I laughed. "Like who?"

"I don't know, a teacher?"

"Yeah, all we had were special teachers."

"You know what I mean."

"You're asking me if we had a teacher like in one of those movies, who makes it their mission to set us all straight, right?"

Dr. Gildmore rolled his eyes and bent to note something down. "More or less."

"Does it look like there was anyone like that?"

"No," Gildmore stared across the table. "I guess not."

"No, I never met anyone like that."

"That doesn't mean they don't exist."

"To me they don't."

"Have you ever thought about being a teacher and working with kids?"

"Nope. Why do you ask?"

"It's called being the person you'd like others to be. We can't always wait around for someone else to do what needs to be done."

"But I wasn't waiting for anyone."

"Fair enough. We'll pick this up next time.

Chapter 9: Geo and the Poontang

Remmy and Vick had their Vans off and were taking turns winding back and belting each other across the face, leaving a pattern of tiny red diamonds swelling up on their cheeks.

"Oh shit, Remmy! You gonna take that abuse?" Flip cried, adding more fuel to the fire just when the slaps slowed down between the boys, breathing hard and staring at each other with twisted smiles.

Remmy faked with his left, then swung with his right sneaker, smacking Vick across the face.

"Oh shit, Vick!" taunted Flip. "You're not gonna let Remmy get away with that, are you?"

A knock downstairs at the side door to my garage caused everyone to turn dead serious.

"I hope it ain't your mom. Last time she said I wasn't allowed back ever again!" said Flip.

"A lot of good that did," said Remmy.

I went downstairs and opened the door to see a skinny kid standing there in a green raincoat walking a poodle. "What's up, Geo?" He was a tiny, quiet kid, the type of dude that was hard to notice. He lived down the street in Dilford, so he didn't go to Riverview High.

Geo was smart, got straight A's in school, and was a little bookish.

"I haven't seen you in months, Kelly. What have you been up to?" Geo smiled enthusiastically.

I shrugged. "Yeah, you surprised us!"

"Oh sorry. I was walking my dog and I saw the light on so I just stopped over to take a look."

"You want to meet some friends from school?" I asked.

"Yes, of course. But what should I do with him?" Geo frowned at the poodle at his feet. "It's my mom's dog," he said, almost apologizing for it.

"Bring him up."

Upstairs in the den, Vick dropped his guard and Remmy saw his chance, wound back and swung his sneaker with all his strength and connected with Vick's jaw, making a loud pop.

"Holy shit!" Geo flinched and pulled his dog back. For a second it sounded as if Remmy had snapped Vick's jaw in two, as Face and Flip cheered him on.

"You fucking whore," Vick stammered, rubbing his chin as Geo stood awestruck, his little dog running around in circles, yapping. Remmy stood wide-eyed and red-faced, challenging Vick who didn't take long to recover. Vick's sneaker buzzed through the air and hit Remmy in the face. Remmy never flinched. He just stood there, flexing all the tendons in his neck and insanely grinning at Vick.

Vick whacked him again, and again, and again, but Remmy stood fast, psyching himself up as he took the punishment, unfazed. Then from out of nowhere, Remmy swung his sneaker underhandedly and uppercut Vick, just about lifting him into the air and sending him sailing back. Vick hit the ground with a loud crash that seemed to shake the whole two-story garage.

Remmy raised both his shoes in victory. Geo's dog ran in circles, barking and getting tangled up in its leash. Geo stooped to unwind it and it broke away, growling nervously before jumping up on Flip, who began scratching its ears.

"I'm sorry if he's bothering you." Geo shyly walked over.

"What's its name?" asked Flip.

Geo started smiling. "Uh, I forgot."

"You just don't want to tell us!" Flip grinned.

"Why?" asked Face. "We won't laugh."

"Alright, it's Mr. T."

"Yeah right," I said as Geo wheezed with laughter. "Geo, this is Flip, Face, Remmy, and Vick. And meet Mr. Humper-fuck or something."

"Could someone please get Humper-fuck away from me before I kick its fucking ass?" Flip shook his leg as the dog held on, wrapping its front paws around his leg and pumping away. Geo embarrassedly yanked on the leash, trying to get it to stop. The dog growled.

"I better get him home anyway." Geo began shaking everyone's hand. "It was good meeting you all."

"So what are you going to do this weekend, Geo?" I asked.

"Well, my parents are gone for the month."

"Oh really, that's cool."

"That's what I thought, too. Then this ugly witch, the house sitter, showed up and she's worse than my parents."

"Aren't you a little old for that?" I asked him.

"My mom and step-dad got sick of my sister, being the spoiled brat that she is, throwing parties whenever they were gone, so now we got *the thing* bossing us around all month."

"Is you sister hot?" asked Vick.

"No," wheezed Geo. "She cut her hair so she looks like a boy and she dresses like one, too."

"Is the house-sitter there now?" I asked.

"No, she's actually been sleeping home for the past few nights, thank God! So, if you guys want to stop by later tonight, no one will be there." Geo walked down the stairs.

"Alright thanks bye." Remmy hung up the phone. "Well, the girls just dissed us. They already left to wherever they were going without us."

"Pigs will be pigs," said Vick. "What we should do is find us some real hogs, and then fuck them."

"Yeah, I'm down for getting some bitches tonight," agreed Flip.

"We can go to Images," Face suggested.

"I'm broke," said Remmy.

"You're always broke," Vick shot back.

"We can go over Geo's house," I suggested.

"That kid?" Remmy asked. "What's at Geo's house?"

"His parents ain't home."

"Can we throw a party?" Flip asked.

"That's an idea, but wait until you see the place."

"Why?"

"Just wait."

We caught up to Geo just as he was reaching the main road. A carload of kids slowed down and began yelling out the windows of their parents' Mercedes.

"NICE DOG, FAG!"

We looked at each other and then burned down the road towards the

Mercedes. "You wanna get out and say that!" Flip screamed but the driver just stepped on the gas and disappeared down the road.

Then the six of us walked the poodle the rest of the way to Geo's house that stood out like a mansion overlooking the river. Geo's house had so many windows and sliding glass doors that it seemed to be made entirely of glass. A huge deck wrapped around the house, with a hot tub and outdoor shower. An expansive lawn slowly stretched down to the river, with several patios and a boathouse along the way.

Geo made us take off our shoes in the sunroom before we walked into the house. Covered with white rugs, three living rooms were filled with antique furniture, and a fourth room had a pool table and bar. We walked downstairs to check out the workout room, tanning booth, lounge, and another bar. Vick began using the exercise equipment and Flip opened the door to the tanning booth.

"Can I get in here?"

"What for?" Remmy asked sarcastically.

Flip smiled at the jab. "Shut up."

"And back there is the garage." Geo pointed through a door, which led to two completely restored 1963 Corvettes.

"Damn!" said Flip. "Your parents are rich."

"Yeah, well kind of," Geo admitted guiltily and then changed the subject. "If you're hungry, we can find something to eat upstairs."

We filed up the back staircase and surfaced into the kitchen. Geo opened the fridge that was stuffed with white Styrofoam containers and doggie bags from a hundred different restaurants. "Some of it's edible, just avoid the stuff that looks like scientific experiments," wheezed Geo as everyone began emptying the fridge and microwaving leftover lobster, steaks, chicken, and a slew of other chow. After we had eaten our fill, we sat down at the bar.

"Could we drink some of your parents booze?" Face asked.

Geo walked behind the bar and started taking down bottles and placing them on the bar. "You can drink this, this, and some of this."

"For real?" Flip's eyes got wide. "I was just playing, but you're all right, Geo!"

Geo laughed hoarsely. "Hey, I can mix a good drink. I made the recipe up myself.

"Hell yeah, mix us up a whopper!" said Vick. "I just need a little bit, just a little whopper, ha-ha-ha."

Geo found a silver drink shaker, dumped in three types of booze, some fruit juice and ice, then capped it and shook it over his head, before pouring the red drink around.

"Yeah, this isn't bad!" Vick licked his lips.

"Are you kidding? This is great," agreed Face.

"You know what I'm thinking?" Flip leaned back. "We should get some girls over here, mix some drinks, and get in that hot tub!"

"But the girls dissed us," Remmy reminded him.

"Some of my sister's friends are hot, but I don't know where they are tonight."

"Can we like hit on your sister's friends?" Vick asked.

"Yeah, actually, maybe. Damn! Look at all the crap I got to clean up." Geo walked out from behind the bar and stared at all the leftover food scattered around the kitchen. He picked up a carton filled with old spaghetti in one hand and a carton of half-eaten meatloaf in the other and peered into a huge pot of chicken soup someone left on the stove.

Everyone tilted back their glasses and grabbed for the last drink in the shaker.

"I thought you didn't drink, Vick!" complained Remmy.

"I do now." Vick poured another glass.

"Save some for the rest of us."

"I'll make some more," Geo said, distracted, as he dumped the leftovers into the soup and began to stir the whole mess around.

"Damn! What are you making?" asked Vick.

"Are you gonna eat that?" asked Remmy.

"Now I'll add this chow mein."

Geo was just getting started. He tore through the frig, finding old lasagna, eggplant parmesan, fried calamari, and chicken broccoli Alfredo, all of which went into the pot. By then, the others had wandered over to get a good view as Geo mixed it all together.

With a smirk plastered on his face, Geo turned up the heat and began to cook the mess. When he ran out of leftovers, Geo got a can opener and began opening cans of cranberry sauce, beats, beans, oysters, and sardines, which also went into bubbling cauldron.

"I sense Nickodemus has his wicked paws in this somehow," cackled Face, looking into the pot of sludge.

"Just a little thicker still!" Geo began looking through the cabinets. "I know!" Geo lit up. "When in doubt, add a pound of flour!" He grabbed a bag of flour, spilling it all over the stove as he dumped it in. Then he flung open the refrigerator door, laughing like a mad scientist, and grabbed the catsup and mustard, which he squirted into the pot. Last, he dropped in a few eggs and leftover hamburger patties, which slowly sank to the bottom of the stinking mess.

"That's just nasty!" squirmed Vick.

"There's no way I'm eating that," Remmy quaked.

"I dare you to take a bite," wagered Flip, who flinched as Geo spooned portions of the substance into a large skillet, turned on the heat, and began to fry it up, releasing the most horrible stench.

"This will give it a better consistency," Geo said, staring as it bubbled in the frying pan.

"Ahh that reeks!" shouted Remmy.

"Turn on the fan!" cried Flip.

"What the hell is it?" asked Vick.

"My trademark POONTANG. No matter how much you make, you'll never have enough," Geo answered.

"Yeah, that was fun," Flip said dryly.

"What is it for?" asked Vick.

"You'll see." Geo twitched with excitement and was off, running downstairs and reappearing with two, five-gallon plastic buckets still crusted with batches of old poontang.

"No way, Geo," I said but he ignored me.

"Tonight," Geo addressed the group. "The Poontang Clan will strike again!"

"What are you talking about?" laughed Flip while Geo dumped the new batch into the buckets and carried them outside.

We crossed through two neighbors' yards to a section of woods that overlooked a narrow, one-way country road. Geo expertly selected a large fallen branch, too big to drive over, and dragged it out into the middle of the street and dumped some poontang around it. We then climbed a small slope and hid behind a barricade of shrubs.

"Now, when a car stops," Geo explained, "and let's say an old man gets out of a beat up pickup truck to move the large branch, we'll just let him go on without any further inconvenience. However, if some yuppie gets out of a Mercedes, smoking a fat cigar, we'll rain down on him with the vengeance of an exploding sewer!" Geo's eyes burned in the night, his personality completely changed. "The fried chunks are the best for throwing, and stuff like those hamburger patties!"

All we had to do now was take aim and fire at the first vehicle that stopped as we huddled behind the hedge and peered down at the street. A Dodge Neon drove up first, and a pretty young girl got out. "Hold your fire," Geo whispered, raising one of his hands as if he were in command.

"Fuck that," said Vick.

"No, don't hit her. Don't waste the poontang—you'll see!" I said and we let her move the branch, staring at the poontang.

"Euuu," she said, got in her car, and drove around it.

"We got to reset the branch."

"I got it." I sprinted down and back, just in time for the next car, a decked out Cadillac. The door opened and a middle-aged woman got out wearing a full-length fox coat, which infuriated Vick and all his vegetarian morals.

"I don't give a fuck what you say—hit her with the meat!" Vick cried, diving into the poontang and fishing out a large handful of dripping hamburger. "Have some meatloaf, bitch!" he shouted and whipped the chunk at her like a baseball pitcher. It sailed through the air and smacked her in the side of the face. The lady screamed and swatted at the sides of her head, wiping the gobs away from her eyes while dragging the branch out of her way.

Elbow-deep into the poontang, we fished out more the solid pieces, which were best for throwing.

"Have some food for your fur! It looks hungry!" Vick yelled, whipping some pork roast at her. "Meat is murder. You got a dead animal on your back!"

She glared up toward us and screamed. "You rotten sons of bitches! You're gonna catch hell for this! I'm calling the police at the next phone I see!" Then the others turned up the heat and pelted her with twice as many throws and she retreated howling, "The cops will arrest you little jerks!" She jumped into her car and slammed the door. She hit the gas and tore off, her voice shrill as she disappeared into the night.

"I think somebody heard that!" said Remmy.

"Yeah probably!" agreed Flip. "Loud bitch!"

"How much more do we got?" I asked Geo, who was kneeling down by the buckets.

"We still have enough for two, maybe three more cars."

"Go get the branch!" Vick told me.

"I got it last time. Send someone else."

"Face, get it!"

"Oh sure, send the fat kid." Face pulled the branch onto the road again. By keeping our eyes on the telephone wires, we could see the reflection of oncoming headlights from a quarter-mile away.

"Car's coming!" Vick shouted. "Get up here, Face!"

"What the hell is that?" I asked as a truck came racing up from the opposite direction and slowed to a stop.

"Oh shit! It's a Land Rover!"

"A what?"

A Land Rover," repeated Flip.

They put the truck into park and two guys got out. They were in their mid-thirties; one wore a tie, the other a leather jacket. The guy in the tie stood by his open door as the other walked over to the branch and began to drag it out of the way.

"Hey! What the fuck?" He stood up and wiped the side of his face and then looked at his hand.

"What?" asked his buddy.

"Something flew right past my head!"

I looked over and saw that Flip and Remmy had clumps of fried poontang in their hands and were both picking off smaller pieces to chuck. The men both froze and looked at each other. Poontang bounced off the second guy's back and he spun around and glared up the dark hill.

"Now something just hit me!" he said and began to search the sky for some type of clue. We started to chuckle.

"Yeah, I saw it, too. What the hell is it?" the other said, bending over and searching the ground. "Euuug…" he said, as splats rained down upon their truck. "Hurry up and get that damn branch out of here!"

"It's coming from up there!" the leather jacket said as he squinted up the hill. "You fuckers are lucky I don't come up there and whip your ass!"

"Shut-up, ass swabber!" Vick hauled back and let one fly. The slimy dough whizzed through the air and smacked the guy in the ear.

"Fuck them! Let's get out of here!" the tie said as the leather jacket continued to curse as poon-balls rained down on top of them and their Land Rover.

Just then, a van sailed past, speeding from the opposite direction, and the boys instinctively started slinging poontang at it. A moment later, we saw that it was an ambulance. The ambulance slammed on its brakes and hit its strobe lights as the windshield was splattered with vomit-like chunks. I paused but the others didn't.

"I always hated ambulances!" said Flip as he chucked a handful of sludge and pelted the side of the ambulance. They continued to dip into the bucket and throw at will. I started laughing hysterically and could barely get words out.

"Let's get out of here!" I grabbed one of the buckets and we cut through the woods. We tore across two dirt roads and ended at a private golf course.

"We'll hide in there!" I said, running across the green and taking shelter among a clump of trees. It was pitch dark as we ducked in the thicket.

Within minutes, we heard sirens heat up in the distance.

"The ambulance must have called the cops!" Flip said, breathing heavy like the rest of us.

"Yeah, you think so, genius?" asked Vick

"Shut the fuck up, Vick!" growled Flip.

"You know it's a felony to assault an EMT or a cop!" said Geo.

"With meatloaf?" asked Remmy.

"With anything, I guess."

"Wait, did any of you grab the other bucket?" I asked, squinting to see in the dark.

"I got it right there." Geo pointed to it, leaning against an ancient stone wall that stretched deep into the woods. "We still got some poontang left in this one." Geo combined the contents of the two buckets, flinging the empty one deeper into the woods. It flew through the air and bounced off a tree.

"Keep it down!" Vick hissed.

"Those cops are going to be looking for us for a while," said Flip. "We got to stay here for a minute."

"Yeah," I said. "I don't want to risk making a run for Geo's house right now.

"My house? Why my house?" Geo exclaimed.

"I don't know–cause it's the base of operations." I peered into the darkness at Geo who actually seemed proud. After a moment, we saw a car driving slowly down the road, shining its searchlight.

"If that's not 5-0, I don't know what is," said Vick, knowingly.

"No shit!" answered Flip.

"Shut up!" I said.

As it approached, we could easily see the red and blue lights illuminated on its white roof as the searchlight ricocheted off the golf course and surrounding yards as it crept slowly past.

"He's gonna see us!" I said. "Everyone, get behind the rock wall!"

We scrambled to our feet, leapt behind the wall and huddled against it, pressing our faces into the cold dead leaves and waiting for the cop to drive past.

The moment seemed to drag on forever as we sat there, listening to the cop car idling and watching the searchlight comb over every foot of the woods.

"I got to sneeze!" said Face.

"You better not!" I whispered.

The cop hit the gas and the spotlight jumped ahead and we all breathed a sigh of relief.

"What now?" asked Geo when the cop car disappeared from view.

"We wait!" Flip said and then looked at Geo. "How long does it take to drive back around the neighborhood?"

"Four minutes."

"He's probably gonna drive around again," said Vick.

"Yeah, at least," agreed Flip, looking at his watch.

"When did you start wearing a watch?" asked Remmy.

"It was a present from Jenny."

"She was sick of you being late, huh?" Geo smiled and Remmy grabbed Flip's wrist and squinted down at his watch.

"No, she bought it so Flip would know what year it was!"

"Shut-up!" Flip laughed.

We breathed easier and Remmy stood up and lit a cigarette.

"Let me get one?" asked Flip and Remmy tossed one over.

"Are you jackasses trying to get us all busted? They're gonna see those cigarette cherries for sure, if they don't smell it!" shouted Vick, lunging for the cigarettes that dangled from their mouths. "Are you trying to send a smoke signal to those pigs?"

"Who do you think that town cop is–Rambo or something?" asked Flip. "Besides, they won't be back around for another minute."

"Shut up! Here he comes again!" warned Vick and we all scrambled for a place against the rock wall.

"Nobody even breathe," said Vick. "I don't want that cop noticing our frozen breath!"

We were lucky that there were no streetlights, leaving only the crescent moon as the single source of light. Again, the cop's searchlight flickered around the perimeter of the golf course and reflected off the trees around us. He moved more quickly this time, but still we held our breath and waited another minute before sitting up and making damn sure he'd gone. We stood up, grabbed the last remaining bucket of Poontang, and booked back to the main road. As we got closer, we saw that two cop cars were now with the ambulance.

"Holy shit!" I said.

"They're on a mission to bust us!" said Flip, watching them conduct their investigation. One cop stood by the stop sign, shining his flashlight into the passing cars, taking a look at the occupants before waving them on. The other appeared to be interviewing the ambulance driver and the two men who'd rolled up in the Land Rover.

"What did you expect? This is the crime of the century around here," said Vick.

"I bet they're gonna have the poontang analyzed," Geo said.

"You got any more poontang in the bucket?" Flip asked.

"Yeah, I was going to wait till I got home to dump it," said Geo.

"Dump it now, Geo!" I said as Flip grinned evilly.

Knowing what I meant, Geo turned to run but Flip and Remmy chased him down, wrestled the bucket away, and scraped the bottom for more to throw. Before any of us had time to react, Flip and Remmy hurled two handfuls of Poontang each. One of them actually managed to peg the cop taking down the report. We all raced away, blazing through the trees, heading toward Geo's house. The cops shouted something and then stormed the hill, their flashlights bouncing towards us. We ran through a hedge of evergreen bushes, their branches scratching our faces, jumped over a row of rosebushes, and landed on the next yard over.

We plowed across that yard and jumped from a tall embankment, landing on Geo's driveway six feet below. I led them down the cement steps into the basement, and Geo locked the door behind us. We sat there, gasping for breath. As the cops ran past, we heard their voices.

"They're around here somewhere!"

"Look under there!"

"They got to be close!" A flashlight beamed down the cement steps and light leaked under the basement door.

"Car 17 on foot pursuit of suspects, north of Green River Road, near Green River Estates, approximately three adult males, on foot, further info to follow, over."

"10-4 Car 17 out on code. . ."

We heard the radio and cops' voices disappear behind Geo's house.

"Hey Geo, can you mix us another one of those drinks?" asked Remmy.

✦

The following night we were back in the room above the garage. Vick and Face were throwing darts, Flip and Remmy were playing ping-pong, and Macie was on the other end of the phone, complaining.

"Remmy, get me off the speakerphone. I know when I'm on it!"

Krissy was in the background laughing.

"Are they drunk?" Vick asked.

"Nooooo," Krissy answered sarcastically. "I don't drink!"

"Get me off speaker phone!" Macie demanded again.

"I can't! I'm playing ping-pong," laughed Remmy, with a cigarette dangling from his lips.

"So you guys are playing ping-pong. Great!"

"You dissed me last night," Remmy said.

"I didn't even see you last night!"

"Exactly! You said you'd pick me up!" Remmy sliced at the ping-pong ball but missed. "Shit!" he yelled.

"Come on, Remmy. I had no idea where you were!" Macie said as Flip slammed another ping-pong ball across the table that Remmy returned for a miss.

"Ha!" Remmy shouted. "My serve! So what ja do?" Remmy bounced the ping-pong on his paddle as Flip jumped from side to side like a ninja.

"Nothing much," Macie sighed. "We just went to the mall, drove around for a couple hours looking for this party, and then went to the diner."

"You dissed us for that!"

"Is that Kelly?" Macie started to giggle before cuffing her palm over the phone. "Someone wants to talk to you."

"Hey, Kelly. Whatcha doing!" Krissy bellowed before the two started laughing.

"Oh my god, Krissy. You're gonna be so sick!" Macie said in the background.

"Pigs will be pigs!" Vick snarled. "Bring me some booze, hog slap!"

"Is that Vick?" Macie asked angrily and then began arguing with Krissy, who demanded that Macie turn over the phone.

"That was Vick, right?" Krissy shouted across the line.

"What!" Vick cackled.

"Did you just call us pigs?"

"No, that was Nickodemus!" said Face, holding a dart up even with his eye, carefully taking aim–his tongue stuck out in pure concentration–before letting it go, missing the target completely and stabbing the wall about four feet away.

"Shut up, Face!" Krissy said. "And Vick, I want to tell you something, straight from my heart!" She burped and giggled a little.

"Was that it? Hahaha! Drink some more, you sloppy sow!" Vick chuckled, leaning towards the phone as Krissy roared.

"When it comes to pigs, Vick, you are a boar!" A loud crash sounded on the other end of the line. Then Krissy and Macie began fighting over the phone.

"Let go!"

"I need to tell him jus one more thang," Krissy slurred.

"Just let me finish!" Macie cried. She came back on, giggling and breathing hard. "So anything happen last night? Ow! You skank! Stop fucking punching me, bitch!"

"Nice fucking language, ladies!" Remmy bounced the ping-pong ball on the table.

"What the hell's going on over there? Would one of you guys pick up the damn phone, please?"

Flip served. Remmy dove for it but missed, slammed his paddle down, and swore as Flip raised his hands in victory.

"It's game point. My serve, bitch!"

"Bastard," Remmy muttered, glaring at Flip.

"Remmy, I'm going to hang up if you're just going to play ping-pong and ignore me," Macie said.

Flip lunged across the table, managing to clip an edge of the ball, and popped it up extra high, allowing Remmy to slam the hell out of it. Flip skipped back, swung but missed.

"Shit! Shit! Shit!"

"Serve's mine!" Remmy said. "Wait, did Macie hang up?"

"Just serve it, white boy!" shouted Flip. "Let's get this over with."

"Let me hit redial."

Instantly Macie picked up. "Look, if I'm still on speaker phone, I'm hanging up for good!"

"We have to keep you on speaker."

"But I hate being on speaker!" Macie whined.

"Hey Macie, what's up?" Flip asked politely.

"Hey Flip, what's up kid?" she asked. "So what did you guys do last night?"

Flip shook his head. "Oh, you don't want to know."

"That bad huh?"

"Nah. Hey, who's at your place?" interrupted Remmy, changing the subject.

"Only Krissy so far, but Eve and Paula are on their way. Why, who's over there?"

"Vick, Flip, Face, Kelly and me. What about Violet?" Remmy asked.

Macie paused. "Why? Do you miss her or something?"

"No, I just want to make sure she's not dead or anything," Remmy admitted smoothly.

"I haven't seen Violet in a while. She refuses to come out, thinks people are against her." Macie paused, "I want you guys to know that we all tried to get her to go to the police instead of to you guys. You know–if Rob really did that."

"Really did that?" Remmy repeated her.

"If he really raped her."

"Well, didn't he?" Remmy winked at us.

Macie sighed, "I don't know. Why? You're not thinking about getting back together with her, are you?"

"Hell no!" Remmy raised his voice, looking across the table at Flip, who humped the air with his paddle and stuck out his tongue, pointing at the phone.

Flip held the ball up to serve.

"Wait Flip, I don't have a paddle!" Remmy complained but Flip served anyway, whipping the ball across the table straight at Remmy's face. It ricocheted off his front teeth with a loud crack.

"Ow! You fuck!" Remmy yelped, gripping his front teeth, "That fucking hurt!"

"Game! Who's next?" Flip looked around.

"My tooth is all loose now. I can wiggle it back and forth!"

"Are you boys killing each other over there?" Macie asked.

"Are you driving over here or not?" Remmy snapped.

"And do what?" she asked.

"We can go to this party!" I interrupted.

"Where?" Flip asked.

"Somewhere nearby," I said.

"What, here?" Vick didn't look impressed.

"Hey Kelly!" said Macie.

"Yeah."

"I know someone who likes you–ow!" Macie cried out. Ow! Okay! Okay!

"Don't tell him! She doesn't want him to know," Krissy said in the background.

"So where's this party?" Macie asked.

"Will you girls go out then?"

"Yeah, if you're serious about a party."

"Cool," said Remmy. "I'll call you back and let you know!"

"All right, bye." Macie hung up.

"Kelly, are you serious?" Remmy asked disbelievingly.

"Yeah, at Geo's house," I answered.

"Who's Geo?" Flip asked.

"Geo from last night?" Remmy looked confused. "He said that he wouldn't be home tonight, remember?"

"Exactly! So it'll be an excellent time to throw a party, right?"

"What are you talking about?"

"His parents are gone. That's what he said, right?" I responded.

"What if his sister is home?" asked Flip.

"Or that babysitter he was talking about?" Remmy added.

"That's why we have to go check it out first."

"Not a bad idea!" said Flip.

"A little breaking and entering but all in the name of fun," Face smirked.

✦

In the darkness, I took a knife and cut a tiny slit in the screen of Geo's bedroom window. I removed the screen and jumped down. Just as I did, a neighbor's light turned on fifty feet from where we stood. Remmy and I crouched against the house and looked up to see an old fat guy walk into his bathroom. We held our breath as the man moved toward his window but he only lowered the blinds.

Remmy hoisted me up while I, stepping onto his back, pushed open the window, climbed through, and lowered myself to the floor. I looked back out.

"The house looks empty but I'm going to make sure," I whispered.

"What should I do?"

"Stay out of sight! I'll let you in the front when the coast is clear."

I crept through the dark house and headed upstairs, to the third floor into Geo's parents' room, when a stench hit my face. It wasn't just any smell. It stunk like something foul had been left in there to rot. I turned on a lamp, saw an old suitcase, and women's clothes scattered around the place. I walked back downstairs, unlocked the front door, and whistled for Remmy, who came trampling across the front deck, grinning. I called my house where Vick quickly answered the garage phone.

"Hello."

"Come on down."

"What about my car?"

"Drive it down and block off the driveway. I want people to park down the street."

I glanced over and saw that Remmy was in the bar, selecting a bottle that Geo had out the other day. "Call up the girls and tell em how to get here."

By the time Remmy was off the phone, Vick, Face, and Flip were already on the deck. They opened the door and traipsed into the house.

"Take off your shoes," I said.

"Are you kidding?" asked Flip.

"Dude, they have white rugs! This family is serious about the shoes, and I need you guys to be the bouncers."

"He's not serious," Remmy told Flip.

"Yeah I am. Make some calls to invite people over, but when they're here, everybody's shoes come off."

"I don't know, man. That's corny," Flip complained.

"If Geo walks in, do you want him to be cool about us breaking into his house and throwing a party, or would you prefer he go straight to the police?"

"All right fine," said Flip.

Remmy got on the phone and gave Macie directions to the party. Vick called the two brothers who played in his band and told them to bring the equipment. A half hour later, Macie, Krissy, Eve, and Paula drove up in two cars. Brody and Ezra showed up with Casey and his new girl friend.

"You guys are the bouncers? Please." Casey smiled.

"No cover charge, but take your shoes off!" Flip said.

Casey laughed, "There's no way I'm taking my fucking shoes off, bro."

"Then have fun outside," retorted Vick.

"What the fuck do you want me to take my shoes off for?"

"Cause that's the rules of the house."

"And what a nice house it is," added Face.

"You know, Egan heard about this party and is pissed off that nobody bothered to call him," Casey mentioned as he pulled off his shoes and dropped them on the pile.

"We didn't even think about it," explained Vick. "Anyway, since when do the Landbury kids call us about a party?"

"Egan did come down to that jock party and put foot to ass, dude," Casey reminded us.

"Who is he with?" I asked.

"Connor and Otis, I think."

"Alright, call em up, give em directions," I said.

Next, Zed and his crew of graffiti artists arrived, who opened shop around the kitchen table, which became a mess of colored pens and art pads. Sonny arrived, drunk out of his mind with a carload of females he appeared to have picked up at a metal concert. They strolled in, in all their metal chick glory, quickly moved to the bar, and demanded a double of anything from Face, the bartender. At first, he used the same bottles Geo had the night before, but thirty minutes later we had run dry, so I made the call on what to open next.

Obi soon drove up, followed by Lampy, Big Dave, and two girls I recognized from one of the shows. Then Kit arrived with Jenny.

"Hey baby!" Flip walked over, giving her a hug. "Did you bring your swimsuit?"

"Yup," Jenny said, smiling.

"Well put it on. We're going out in the tub."

"Hot tub!" Kit exclaimed. "Why didn't you tell me?"

"So I won't be the only one wearing underwear," Flip joked and went behind the bar and pulled out a bottle of champagne.

"Dude, don't drink that," I said.

"I'll pay Geo back when he gets here."

"How is he gonna buy a replacement?"

"Come on, they must have a dozen bottles of this champagne back here. They won't miss it, please?"

"Show me." I walked behind the bar and there was a whole case filled with the same bottles.

"Check it out, see?" Flip insisted.

"Yeah, Don Perry something. Fine, but don't let anyone else see you have it."

"No. I'll hide it under here." Flip draped his towel over the bottle and then escorted the tiny blonde outside.

Stepping outside, they both shivered. Their breath froze in the brisk air as they proceeded to wrestle the top off the hot tub, releasing steam and light from the swirling waters below. Flip pulled off his shirt bravely, as the rolls on his stomach jiggled, while Jenny, a Barbie Doll, nimbly slipped out of her tight jeans and sweater. They both sunk into the bubbling tub. Jenny leaned back while Flip uncorked the bottle.

"I guess nobody's watching the door!" I called out but no one paid me any mind except Face.

"Here Kelly, take another shot."

I drank it quickly and Face poured another.

"Dude, go easy with that stuff. That ain't our booze!"

"Kelly, whose house is this?" Kit laughed as he stumbled over with bloodshot eyes after toking out with Lampy. "I heard you just broke in and invited everyone over!"

"This kid named Geo."

"I never heard of him."

"And you don't think he'll care?" asked Remmy.

"I don't know. We'll find out when he gets home," I said.

"I knew it." Krissy overheard us. "We're all committing a crime by being here!"

The door opened and Rook, Jasper, Aaron and two girls entered and started talking shit when I told them to take off their shoes.

"Is this your house, Kelly?" Jasper asked angrily.

"No, but I oversee the party, man. Look, drinks are on the house, man, you just got to take off the shoes."

"Hell no!" Egan stepped in and shoved me aside, clomping through the house with his boots on and positioned himself at the kitchen table, after helping himself to Geo's parents' beer I'd tried to hide in the back of the fridge.

"How's it going Kelly?" Connor grinned as he walked past, pulling my cap down over my eyes, followed by Otis.

"What was that about shoes?" Jasper slapped my face twice and pushed past, joining the rest of the Landbury kids who took over the living room and started watching cable after blasting some Trance on the stereo. A minute later, Tank and Bram arrived, bouncing off each other and laughing.

"Is Eve inside?" Tank asked when I greeted them at the door.

"Yeah," I said, "but you got to take your shoes off!" Bram laughed hysterically.

"No way, man!" snorted Tank.

"Is that Bram?" shouted Egan. "You got it?"

"Yeah, but get this shoe-man out of here!"

Behind us there was a loud knock, and two black skaters stood by the door. "Yo, there's Cecil and Matty!" Remmy shouted atop other voices expressing familiarity, and he moved forward to welcome them as Cecil danced humorously to the music.

"So this is how you white folks got it!" Cecil announced as he strolled in cheerfully. "Now this is how I got it. Not bad!"

"CECIL!" Egan bellowed from the kitchen, causing Cecil to flinch playfully. He shut his eyes and then slowly opened one.

"Ah man, is that who I think it is?" he asked, looking at me. "What's up Adolph?" he shouted back.

"Cecil, get your ass in here!" Egan's voice sounded again. "And turn that techno-garbage off!"

"Oh shit! Alright Satan–I mean Egan."

"Why have you been missing practice?" Egan snapped as Cecil sauntered into the kitchen.

"My guitar strings all broke, uhhh, my dog ate my demo tape. Dude, when is the next show? Oh yeah, we don't have one!" joked Cecil.

"We do now!"

"Look man, my girl is coming here tonight!" Cecil folded his arms.

"So?" Egan frowned.

"So don't embarrass me, alright?"

"When have I ever embarrassed you?" Egan asked.

"Last fucking show when you started bitching at us over the mic!"

"Yeah, that was fucked up, Egan," Obi chimed in.

"Shut up, the both of you!"

Back at the bar, another bottle I'd hoped would last had already been drained so I grabbed another two.

"We all have to slow down on this stuff," I insisted.

"Relax kid, we'll replace it all," said Face and confidently made another drink and slid it over. I looked at it for a second and then gulped it down and he then filled it again.

"Face! Don't be so quick to pour drinks! We can't have everybody shitfaced cause of you!"

"But that's my style."

Vick was on the phone shouting at his girlfriend, angry that she was not able to drive over. He slammed the phone down and then went after Macie.

"Stop, Vick," said Macie, as he groped her. "We're not going to do this again."

"Yeah, Vick," giggled Krissy. "She's telling you one mistake was enough!"

"Shh." Vick ignored Krissy as he pulled Macie down on his lap and began massaging her shoulders.

She closed her eyes and smiled, "Vick?"

"Yeah baby."

"Play with my hair."

Vick looked at me and winked–a night without pussy for Vick would be like a night without air. Vick began lifting strands of her hair and letting it fall between his fingers as Egan continued to gripe.

"Dude, how can I help it if my guitar's all fucked up?" Cecil argued.

"Then don't get mad when you suck and I tell you about it!" Egan persisted.

"Tell me at practice!" Cecil shouted. "Not at a fucking show!"

"You never go to practice!" Egan snapped.

"Can we not talk about the band for one night?" Casey sighed.

"I heard Vick's band is bringing their equipment," said Egan. "You want to play a song or two?"

"Not really," confessed Cecil, curling his left nostril. Egan slammed his fist down on the table,

Cecil flinched. "What dude! My girl's getting here any second! You need to take some yoga lessons, Egan. Meditation, aromatherapy, something!"

"So what's up, Matty?" Egan turned to Cecil's brother. "What have you been doing?"

"I don't know, skating, music, girls, you know."

"Yeah right," Egan sneered. "You want to replace your brother as a guitarist for Despair?"

"Has anyone seen Violet?" Remmy asked the girls.

"See, you really do miss her." Macie frowned.

"Not really."

"Yeah, you do," protested Krissy. "That's the second time you asked about her."

"She lied about everything," said Egan.

"She knows she screwed up," added Eve.

"Then she should apologize," said Egan, "especially to me!"

"What about to Remmy?" Macie asked.

"I told her the same thing," sighed Krissy. "That's why she's not over here. She thinks everyone hates her."

"For once she's right!" snarled Vick.

Remmy smiled, "I don't hate her…I just…hate her, you know?"

Vick gestured to Face, tipping his hand for a drink, and Face gave an all-knowing wink before going to work.

"Hey Macie, try this, my own special concoction, on the house."

Just as Face was sliding her drink down the bar, Geo was sliding the glass door open and he teetered in, dressed in a shirt and tie, absolutely bewildered. "What the hell is going on? Is my sister here?" he squeaked in disbelief before seeing me sitting at the bar.

"Kelly, what the hell is going on? Why are all these people in my house?" He looked frightened.

"Surprise! I told everyone about ya," I slurred. "And everyone wanted to throw a party for ya!"

"But my parents are gonna kill me!"

"Not if they don't find out."

"Of course they are going to find out. Look at all these people. Who are all these people?"

"Look, everyone's shoes are off, and they're abiding by the rules."

"You drank all this!" Geo exclaimed, seeing the empties lined up.

"Here ya go," said Face, sliding him down a shot.

"But I don't want it," winced Geo.

"Why not? It's good for you."

"Oh my god, I'm so dead!" Geo sank down at the bar, shaking his head despairingly.

"Hey Geo, this is Egan. You heard of Egan, right?" Geo slowly turned and looked at Egan.

"What's up, dude?" Egan asked, and Geo got up and took a step forward, wordlessly, and shook Egan's hand with respect. Then Macie walked over to Geo and introduced herself. Geo smiled shyly, picked up the drink and downed it.

"Oh Geo, you have such an awesome house."

"Yeah, like thank you so much for having us over. That is sooo cool!" added Krissy.

"Well, you know," said Geo, "it's not specifically my house."

"I have an announcement to make!" I shouted. "This is Geo, the generous guy we have to thank for throwing such a terrific party! A toast to Geo!" I raised my drink and everyone cheered, some sarcastically so, but Geo seemed honored.

"Look, we'll take up a collection and hit the bootlegger and buy cheap vodka and refill your parents' bottles!" reassured Face.

"Okay," said Geo, beginning to relax the more Macie rubbed his shoulders. "Alright, but don't drink anymore of their stuff. I have something else for you to drink stashed in my closet, my own special mixture."

He returned with two large bottles, one clear, one brown. "Smell them." We all took a whiff. The clear bottle smelled like mint vodka and the brown like iodine. "I mixed together so many whiskeys that all you have to do is take three shots and you are blasted for the rest of the night!" Geo looked pleased with himself.

"What's up with you and mixing things together?" asked Remmy.

Geo shrugged, "Try some." Geo poured some over ice and then mixed in some juice and shook it up. The phone rang and Geo answered it, gave me a slightly annoyed look, and handed me the phone. "It's for you."

Vick started dancing in the kitchen to the Trance music. Kids sat on countertops, barstools, and the kitchen table as he flew around. Kit flipped the lights on and off for effect until Geo asked him to stop.

"Enough of this techno shit! Put on this tape!" Egan held one out.

"So you pulled it off?" Krissy walked up behind me and patted my shoulder.

"Yeah," I said. "Not bad, right?"

But more kids showed up at the door. They carried instruments and black cases. Geo met them at the door with Vick standing behind him with arms crossed.

"No trouble or you're outta here!" Vick drunkenly warned them. He smirked and gave them hugs. "Get in here, jackasses! Hey what's up? This is my band," he explained to Geo. "Did you get everything?"

"Yeah," they chorused.

"Where can we set up?"

"How about here in the sunroom," Geo said, pointing around to the glassed in porch filled with ferns and wicker furniture, along with dozens of shoes scattered over the white tiled floor. "You'll sound good in here."

We emptied most of the room. The group brought in their instruments and began to set up the sound. They tuned the guitars and adjusted the drums. Vick picked up the mic, as his friend Trevor plugged the cord into the amp and then switched it on. Vick fixed the room with a confident expression as his voice jumped out of the speaker and boomed through the house.

"Um, what's up everyone? As most of you know, we're called Horseflesh and we're going to play something new we've been working on–something different. One-two-three-four..." The music took off and Vick began screaming. Everyone started dancing, bouncing into each other and forming the beginning of a small pit. Face slammed into me and Remmy shoulder-checked me from the opposite side.

"Hey are you alright?"

I looked up to see Ezra standing over me.

"I think so," I answered as he reached out to grab my hand and pulled me to my feet. Geo ran over, looking as if the world had just gone crazy, and grabbed a hold of me, screaming over the music into my ear,

"Look Kelly, your friends are gonna have to calm down! This whole room is made of glass!"

"What do you want me to do?"

He glared, confused and speechless, as the music blared and the bodies spun around the pit. Seconds later, Remmy crashed into us, and we demolished the potted tree that had been left in a corner, spilling piles of white-speckled soil all over the floor. Vick stopped singing and kids hovered above us, staring down at the mess we'd made. Feeling responsible for throwing Remmy across the room, Connor helped us both up, me with a shard of pottery stuck into my bloody side.

"Stop for a second, please!" Geo finally screamed, reaching for the mic that Vick handed off. "We got to stop! Stop! Stop the moshing! Blood has been shed! Property has been destroyed!" He glared around and received a rallying cry of support and applause.

Geo suddenly grew pale as the band played on. I traced his stare across the crowd to the outside and saw a twisted old face pressed against a far window, peering in. Instantly, I knew who it was. I looked back at Geo, who handed the mic back to Vick and started to shrink away.

She marched across the porch with her black beanie yanked down upon her frizzy-headed face, her eyes deadened by some old constant rage. She whipped the slider to the right, letting it crash open, bouncing off the track as a gust of frozen wind blew in a murky smell.

Geo took off running across the sunroom, pulling his shirt up over his head as if he were hiding from news cameras, and then crashed into a wall. He hit the ground stunned, jumped up, and then tore off in a panic towards the back of the house. The band continued to thrash, taking little notice of the house sitter. Realizing her complete lack of effect, she raised a fist into the air and tried to shout over the music, but the three amplifiers drowned out her voice.

Her face was contorted with rage. She ran through the mosh pit, but Face accidentally slammed into her. She lunged out for him, grabbed a handful of greasy blonde dreads, and yanked him across the floor. Face bent over in pain as she pounded on the back of his head. Suddenly, Face tore off running, carrying her skiing across the smooth white tile before she eyeballed the power strip. The house sitter let go of his hair and shoved back through the room filled with kids, smacking at each one as she stormed through, screaming and thrashing out at them before sliding to her knees and tearing out the plugs.

One moment Vick's voice backed by electric guitars filled the room—the next was nothing but the drummer drowning out Vick's screams. From the floor, she spun around, possessed and growling, eyes red with hate. Quickly, she pounced upon the drummer, clawing for his drumsticks, but he refused to hand them over, syncopating on her hands instead. She backed off and, with fingers hooked, smacked Vick. He stood there shocked as she twisted and hissed like Grendel. She then sucked in a deep breath, filling her jowls, and blared out of her thin, slit of a mouth, "GET OUT! GET OUT! GET THE FUCK OUT OF HERE!"

"What the fuck is that shit?" Otis yelled from living room, rubbernecking on the sofa to get a better look.

"Dude, you're fucking scary!" laughed Rook and barked at her with playful yaps while his girlfriend dragged him to the door. Egan and Connor laughed hysterically from the doorway, so she chased them around in a circle through the dining room and into the kitchen before changing direction and going after Tank and Bram instead. They all continued to evade her but only to different parts of the house, not wanting to miss any part of the show. Meanwhile, most of the kids were in a frenzy, running in circles, trying to find their shoes, hopping on one foot, and then ducking the house sitter's next swat attack. Others ripped through piles of jackets or tried to find where they'd set down their keys.

"GET THE HELL OUT OF THIS HOUSE! GET THE FUCK OUT OF HERE! I AM CALLING THE GOD DAMNED POLICE! ANYONE WHO STAYS IS GOING TO FUCK!"

"Anyone who stays is going to fuck?" Casey mimicked, followed by laughter that she went snarling after.

"YOU SCAT! SCAT! SCAT! YOU DONT KNOW WHAT THE FUCK YOU GOT COMING!"

"She's speaking in tongues!" Otis laughed, zoned out on the sofa as the banshee assaulted every drunken kid within claws' reach.

"Who invited Medusa?" Bram called out.

"Somebody call The Exorcist!" Tank added.

"Here she comes! Go! Go! Go!" Connor laughed, dodging her attack and running helter skelter.

"Otis, you just gonna sit there watching MTV all night?" grinned Egan.

"Dude, this is lame, man."

"Now you can see why you never take your boots off!" Egan said, sliding open the nearest glass door and then shouting to the others. "Stop fucking around with that crazy bitch and let's get something to eat. I'm hungry."

The Heavy Metal girls flew out of Geo's sister's room, chased by Sonny, stumbling behind them and waving his car keys.

"NONE OF YOU FUCKING ASSHOLES SHOULD EVEN BE HERE!" she howled, as she ran through the living room, the dining room, and the kitchen chasing the Landbury boys in circles.

"All you fuckers I want in line! You! Get over here!"

"Who me?" Bram asked, "No fucking way! I'm not getting near you!"

Egan ducked out the nearest door and leaned against the rail, while the rest of the guys cracked up and fell over each other's feet whenever she lunged for them. Suddenly the basement door banged open, and Face shouted, "DUDE! WHAT THE FUCK ARE YOU?" and then slammed the door shut. She jerked in his direction furiously, going straight for the basement door when someone held out a foot and tripped the bitch, so she landed flat on her stomach and went gliding across the kitchen tile. She jumped to her feet and charged straight at Lampy, Tank, and Bram, swinging her arms. Lampy dove over the table and crashed into the stereo, and Tank and Bram went running. She lunged after Otis, grabbing his jacket.

"Come on, enough of this shit!" Egan shouted through the door.

"FREAK!" a voice called out and she spun to see Ezra, standing there with his fists on his hips, posing in a kilt.

"YOU! OUT!" She howled, letting go of Otis, who dashed outside and took off with Egan.

Macie and Krissy appeared, tiptoeing past the house sitter, trying not to attract her attention. Once outside, Krissy turned and shouted, "You're insane, lady!"

The house sitter clomped toward the phone, almost ripping it off the wall, and dialed. "Hello police, I want to report a forced entry! And a few suspects I'm sure you're searching for, vandals who strong-armed their way into an estate I am in charge of. The address is…"

Everybody began really moving then, trampling each other to get out first. Yet the band still sweated, packing up without much help from any of us. "I WANT ALL THIS JUNK OUT OF HERE NOW!" the house sitter screamed, so I took to winding a cord around my arm, trying to blend in with the band.

The house sitter ran to the bar. "Oh my god, they've gotten into the alcohol!" She examined the empty bottles. "Look at this bottle, and this and this AND THIS!"

"We got money to re-re-pl-place all of it," Geo stammered, who reappeared after realizing he couldn't run from this one.

"I highly doubt that!" Her eyes narrowed and she marched over to yell in his face. "YOU CAN SAVE IT ALL FOR THE POLICE!"

Geo held up the money we'd collected and she snatched him by the wrist. He began to pull away so she grabbed him with her other paw as well.

"Let go!" Geo shouted.

They struggled for a moment before hearing noises coming from upstairs. By now, only the band and a few intoxicated stragglers remained. The house had grown quiet so it was easy to hear the dull pounding coming from upstairs. Medusa stared up at the ceiling and we all listened. The pounding grew louder and faster. The house sitter let go of Geo's arm and ran toward the source of the thumping noises–Geo's parents' bedroom. Geo and I crept upstairs behind her, not knowing ourselves what we'd find as she swung open the door and gasped.

"OH MY GOD! WHAT THE HELL ARE YOU DOING THERE!" she screamed as she barged into the room. We peeked around the corner to see Cecil in bed with a punk rock chick straddling him.

"What the hell does it look like I'm doing?" Cecil looked up from underneath the girl, who snipped, "What the hell! Get your own room!"

"WHY YOU FILTHY LITTLE SLUT!" The house sitter began to stamp her feet. "YOU'RE IN MY BED, YOU WHORE!"

"What is this bitch doing here?" Cecil asked and then looked up at the chick. "Wait, get off me, baby." He sat up and looked at Geo and me. "What the hell is going on, Kelly?"

"Party got busted, dude."

"Yeah, that would be the understatement of the year!" He smiled and then looked at the house sitter. "Look, would you mind getting out of here for five minutes so we can get our shit together?"

"NO, I'LL WAIT RIGHT HERE!" she screamed. "NOW MOVE!"

"Dude, she called the cops," I said.

"Shit!" Cecil's girl jumped up, picked up her clothes, and hurried into the bathroom, and slammed the door. The shower turned off and Cecil's little brother Matty opened the bathroom door and peered at the house sitter.

"Euuu," he said and slammed the door again, this time locking it. The house sitter ran over and banged on the bathroom door.

"STAY IN THERE FOR ALL I CARE. THE COPS WILL BE HERE TO ARREST YOU ANY SECOND!"

"She called them like a minute ago," I said to Cecil, who pulled on his shorts and pants. He grabbed his jacket before heading down the stairs, leaving us behind.

"I hope you know your room reeks like shit," he shouted from the bottom of the stairs. "We had to light like 48 incense sticks to get that stank out of there!"

The house sitter screamed down at Cecil but stopped as three kids sprinted out of the bathroom, half-naked with their hair dripping wet, pulling on their shirts, and tearing past us down the stairs, where they paused to grab their shoes, before disappearing into the night.

Downstairs in the living room, she continued her tirade. "You have a hell of a lot of explaining to do, first to the cops and then to your parents, Geo! What the hell were you thinking having these criminals over? Your mom hired me so your sister wouldn't throw any parties! They never thought in a million years that it would be you!"

"Why are you screaming?" Geo finally yelled back. "Would you calm down, please? Everything is in control here, alright?"

"IN CONTROL? IS THIS WHAT YOU CALL IN CONTROL? YOU GOT STRANGERS HAVING SEX IN YOUR PARENTS' BED! A HEAVY METAL BAND IN THE SUN ROOM! A DOZEN EMPTY BOTTLES OF YOUR PARENTS' BOOZE! A BROKEN ANTIQUE PORCELAIN PLANTER! And— oh my god! someone has gotten into this case of two-hundred-dollar a bottle champagne!" she said, lowering her voice.

"Lady, the party was my idea," I confessed. "I invited all these people over and Geo had nothing to do with it. In fact, he was out with his dad the whole night. He just got back."

"Do you expect me to believe that?" she asked with scowling eyes before something grabbed her full attention behind me. Her pupils dilated as they fixed on something she had missed until now. Tearing between us, she smashed Geo and me to either side as she raged across the living room, out the sliding glass door, and to the hot tub. Geo and I winced at each other when we heard her gasp again.

"Shit! I forgot about them!" I said and we ran outside, skidding to a stop behind the house sitter. Still enjoying a romantic moment with champagne and candlelight, soaking in the warm, bubbling whirlpool tucked into a corner of the deck were Jenny and Flip. Long ago having separated themselves from the party, the mini-mosh pit, and the raging house sitter, they'd gone unaffected by the recent changes until now. Confused, Jenny and Flip looked from one of us to the next, their faces losing hope as they quickly sensed that their special moment was soon to come to a terrible conclusion. Flip leaned to the side to peer at the sputtering lady.

"Who's this bitch, Kelly?"

I took a deep breath but could only shake my head. For seven long seconds, House Sitter sucked wind into her lungs as this sensual French song 'Je T'aime Moi Non Plus' played on the nearby radio. Now psychotic with rage, Medusa tore across the porch like Attila the Hun, reaching out for Flip and Jenny who slid in circles around the tub to keep away from her, balancing their thin glasses of two-hundred-dollar a bottle champagne as the water bubbled ignorantly around them. Flip glared at us fanatically, as if hoping this was all some kind of sick joke.

"GET THE FUCK OUT OF THAT HOT TUB, YOU LITTLE SNIPS!"

"What?" Flip sputtered. "Who the hell are you?" Still he managed a smile. "You're destroying the…the…" Flip whirled his hand as he searched for the proper word, "…ambience."

"YOU SCUMBAGS HAVE STOLEN PRIVATE PROPERTY!"

"I haven't stolen anything! Tell this bitch to back off, Kelly."

"THEN EXPLAIN THAT EMPTY BOTTLE OF CHAMPAGNE?" she screamed and Flip's face dropped.

"Fine," he sighed. "but this ain't no peep show! Alright, we're leaving so just get out of my face!"

Flip helped Jenny out and began toweling himself off. "Go back to whatever dumpster you climbed out of! Crusty old bitch with nothing better to do!" snapped Flip. "You don't own this house! I was invited here!"

"I AM PAID TO PROTECT THIS HOUSE FROM SCUM LIKE YOU MOVING IN AND HAVING A FREE FOR ALL. I KNOW THE GAME!"

"Damn!" Flip swore. "Everything was cool before your ugly ass got here!" He looked at Geo, who raised his hands helplessly with a defeated look in his eyes,

"She called the cops, man. They'll be here any second."

"Miserable old bitch!" Flip laughed into the towel as he dried his face.

"YOU WANT A PARTY," she screamed, getting into his face. "HAVE ONE AT YOUR HOUSE, YOU FAT PILE!" He dropped the towel and stepped away from her, trying to get dressed as she continued to get in his face. "I WANT YOUR NAME!"

"Why?"

"CAUSE I'M HAVING YOU ARRESTED FOR THEFT OF PERSONAL PROPERTY!" she shouted as Flip bent over and pulled on his pants. He reached out for Jenny, and they started walking past the house sitter when she grabbed his arm. "WHERE DO YOU THINK YOU'RE GOING?" she snarled, and before I could even think it, Flip had already done it. Medusa let out a startled cry, swayed on her feet, then slowly fell back like a leveled old tree. Without warning, he popped the house sitter in the nose!

Geo's eyes all but shot out of his head. "Oh God! Oh no! This isn't happening!" he cried, looking down at the house sitter stretched out on the floor, motionless, a trickle of blood seeping from her nose. Flip dusted off his hands and, like a perfect gentlemen, took Jenny's hand, helping her step over the fallen body as the French song played on for ambiance.

"You did it this time, Flip!" grinned Remmy as he strolled from around the back of the house. "You killed the house sitter!"

"The cops are here!" Geo cried. "Listen!" We leaned over the railing of the porch to see squad car after squad car burning up Green River Road and swerving up the winding driveway.

"What should we do?" Geo asked fearfully.

"RUN!" shouted Flip and we all took off through Geo's backyard, up a hill covered with pachysandra that led to another neighbor's yard, and then around to my street. I turned to look at Jenny and Flip, barefoot, dripping wet and shivering in the freezing cold night, but they stayed right behind us.

As we neared my house, a carload of kids sped by us, screaming out the window, followed by another car and then another and another–their headlights glaring on our friends ahead of us, trudging up the street, misplaced and drunk, and all heading for my house.

"Stop and let us in!" We pounded on a car that slowed down. Flip and Jenny, shivering to death, jumped into the backseat. I began directing traffic, telling everyone to shut up as they parked around my house. "Turn off your lights!" I shouted and then corralled them into the garage.

"Did my band get our shit out of there yet?" Vick asked.

"Yeah, at the last minute they got out," I said.

"What about the cops? Did they get anyone?" asked Kit.

"I can't believe you did that, Flip!" moaned Geo, rocking back and forth and biting on his thumbnail in horror.

"What?" Krissy perked up.

"Flip knocked out the house sitter!" Geo cried out, before anyone else could answer.

"He did what?" Macie exclaimed.

"He knocked out Geo's house sitter!" said Jenny, sitting by the baseboard heater, shivering, drying her hair with a towel.

"Shut up!" said Vick. "You're not serious."

"You're joking right?" asked Kit.

"He hit that crazy bitch?" whispered Macie.

"Yeah, knocked her out cold. When the cops get there, they'll find her laid out on the porch, twitching." Remmy grinned proudly.

"Is she going to be all right?" Macie seemed to be the only one seriously concerned.

"Who cares?" said Flip.

"Uh, duh!" jeered Krissy. "What if you like killed her? Then we'd all be guilty of manslaughter or like an accessory, you know."

Kit burst out laughing. "Geo's gonna get so much shit for this!"

"Nice, Kit," scolded Macie, rolling her eyes. "Was she breathing at least?"

"I think so! Maybe! How should I know?" Flip shrugged his shoulders.

"Did she have a pulse?"

"I didn't hit her that hard," said Flip. "Not hard enough to kill her."

"But you really wouldn't know, would you?" pressed Macie.

"Chill out, Macie," snarled Vick. "If I was there, I would have kicked the stanky hog in the ass when she was down!"

"She'll be fine," said Remmy. "If she needs help, the cops are right there."

"Flip knocked out the babysitter!" Vick laughed hysterically while Geo hung his head and twisted his hands.

"Oh god, I'm sooo dead."

Chapter 10: Revenge

Images closed down. That basement club on the outskirts of Bog Creek was history but the owners opened a new place. Inside, the ceiling was two stories high on one side and had a loft on the other. The joint had been fitted with new lights and music equipment. They put in a juice bar, kept it underage, and played Alternative crap on Friday's and Top Forty club shit on Saturdays.

It was crowded by ten when Krissy stumbled in, flushed from liquor. Holding her up were Macie and Eve. The trio walked across the club, made a dramatic spin around, and headed straight for the restroom. I waited for them to carry Krissy back out, looking as green as the gum Macie handed her. They leaned her against a wall and Krissy slid down and appeared asleep. Eve giggled while Macie sighed, looking around the club before seeing me and motioning me over.

"Hey, Kelly!"

"What's up, Macie?" I asked, giving her a hug.

"Why don't you keep Krissy company for a little while?" Macie looked down at Krissy. "She's not feeling well tonight." Macie made the motion of tilting a bottle back. "A little too much of that."

"What did she drink?"

"Her uncle's Dago Red. You ever heard of it?"

"No, is it strong?"

"I had like three or four sips in the car and I'm already buzzing," Macie paused for a second, and then smiled. "Go sit with her, please."

"Why?"

"Just keep an eye on her while I go see who else is here, please, just for a while."

"I don't know," I said. "She looks kind of out of it."

"Come on, she's not that drunk."

"Look, she's already passed out," I argued.

"Trust me, she's not that drunk." Macie pushed me in her direction until I was standing over her.

"Uh, what's up, Krissy?" I asked, kicking the wall beside her.

"Who's that?" She squinted up, smiling sheepishly.

"It's Kelly."

"Hayes?" she asked and I looked away. "Help me up!" She reached out for my hand and stood up swaying, then her eyes fell closed again, and she smiled. "Okay that's enough. Let's sit back down." Krissy feebly giggled and slid down the wall again, holding my hand. "Well sit down, Kelly. I don't bite!"

"Are you alright?"

"Yeah, I got so sick in the restroom, where all these girls were staring at me and I was like, 'Do you have a problem, bitch?'"

"You did, huh?"

"Yeah, I can be tough when I need to be," Krissy growled and flexed her muscles. I smiled and then looked back towards the dance floor when they started playing Elixir's song, "Closer To You," and Krissy bounced up, tripping forward and grabbing onto my hands. "I love this song. Come and dance with me." She pulled me over to the floor where she threw her arms around my shoulders, pressing her chest into mine, and we danced. I looked at her face and noticed her pink freckles and eyes that weren't brown but hazel, and I could smell the sweet shampoo in her long brown hair with that small streak of snow white in her bangs.

"I like how your hair is white right here." I leaned back and let the strands of hair fall through my fingers. "It kind of makes you seem—you know, older."

"Really, like how old?"

"I don't know, pretty old—like 30 or something."

She laughed.

We danced for a while and Krissy moved slower and slower until she was only gently swaying.

"Are you okay?" I brushed the hair out of her face and she looked up, gently biting her lip and looking at me. She leaned forward and pressed her lips against mine. She bit my bottom lip softly between hers, slowly opened her mouth, breathed, and pulled me in.

Then Macie was back.

"Ooohh, am I interrupting something?" She grinned. "Come with us, please?"

"Where?"

"With Kit and Face to go smoke," she answered, just as Kit and Face crashed into us, idiotically dancing arm in arm.

"But where?" Krissy asked again.

"Up by the railroad tracks," Kit said and pointed in the wrong direction.

"It's out that way, Kit," laughed Macie.

"Oh yeah, I meant that way, duh."

We got our hands stamped and walked across the street where Face packed his old Masterpiece Theatre bowl. He lit it. "Have a little puff of this shit, mister," Face said as he passed it around. I balanced on the train tracks and walked back and forth as I took a pull, held the smoke until it stung my lungs, broke into a coughing fit, and then passed the pipe to Kit.

"Don't mind if I do," said Kit, who passed it onto Macie and then Krissy. Face put some more bud in it and sent it around again. By the time we walked back, I felt like my feet were sinking into the street. I tried stepping extra high.

"What are you doing?" Krissy laughed.

"It's hard to walk like this," I said, checking my shoes.

"Walk like what? Like stoned?" Macie smiled.

"I've never been stoned before."

"Kelly's a Ganja virgin!" chortled Face.

"Are you a virgin, Kelly?" Macie teased.

"Cause if you are, Krissy will help you with that," Kit giggled and Krissy hit him. Inside the club everyone moved like robots. All I could do was lean against the wall and stare at the lights, which mesmerized me. Krissy had left me zombified and was off talking to Zed and the graffiti guys. Face had found Clighty, his girl from Landbury. With long blonde hair, she didn't look like she usually hung out on this scene. She didn't look like she'd be Otis's ex-girlfriend either, but she was. While they danced, Face kept glancing at the front doors, paranoid that Otis would walk in and kick his ass for dancing with Clighty. Even though she broke it off, Otis was still in love with her.

High beams shined through the windows at the front of the club, flooding the darkness with light, as a beat-up Jeep pulled into an empty space in the front row outside. The car door swung open and a curvy figure emerged. Violet smoothed the front of her jeans and blouse, tugged her bra up, and then strolled toward the door, cruising past the doorman who'd turned to talk to a bouncer, and breezed right in.

She ambled down the front hall as the DJ spun "Vox." She sauntered past Remmy, making no eye contact as she crossed the club, pausing at the edge of the dance floor where she nodded her head to the music. Her face was tilted down but her brown eyes gleamed upward, measuring the exact moment when she'd step in and pick up the beat.

As the music changed, the lights cranked in, spinning and lighting the dance floor with a kaleidoscope of flashing colors. What had seemed dull before, Violet lit up. I wasn't the only one to notice. A kid edged up to her and she whirled around to face him. Instantly, she had my full-on and stoned-out attention. I noticed her every detail, a careless arm swing, runny mascara, tousled hair–small details that told a story.

She rhythmically shook her head, taunting an invisible enemy, and slowly her aggression faded as the slightest of smiles formed on her glistening lips. She then noticed some of the familiar faces around, laughed when she saw Krissy and winked at Eve. Nearby, Remmy leaned against a wall. Casey stood beside him with Rook and Bram, all staring at Violet and trying to look pissed off.

Casey must have noticed that Remmy was starting to lose it, for he nodded at Rook and together moved him to the door where Casey shook his head at Violet, who shrugged in return. Then she looked at me. Suddenly Vick crashed into me, catching onto my shirt to keep me from falling over. After I regained my footing, I shoved him back.

"What the fuck's your problem?"

"Checking her out?" He nodded toward Violet.

"She's hot." I smiled and Vick rested his arm on my shoulder so he could lean in and shout above the music,

"She also has a way of fucking your shit up if you get too serious. Only problem is everybody gets serious with Violet. Ask Remmy." Vick stared, slowly shaking his head. "I fucked her."

"I don't want to hear about it." I looked away.

"Yeah, but I told you anyway."

We both stood there staring at her. Violet noticed and began to flaunt herself playfully, and Vick danced out onto the floor, showing off his moves, grabbed her in a giant hug and spun her around as she threw back her head and laughed. Vick looked at me to make sure I was watching, as he pulled her close and grabbed her ass and danced her away. Having enough of that act, I walked toward the restroom where Face was guarding the door.

"No entrance permitted!"

I shoved him aside and walked in to see Flip standing on Kit's shoulders, halfway through a section of ceiling tiles. Kit whipped his head, relieved to see me and asked, "Face is still out there, right?"

"Yeah, but how much good is he? Like how's he gonna stop a bouncer from getting through?" I walked over to the urinals.

"Almost got it!" I heard Flip's muffled voice from above, his legs dangling out of the ceiling. Then he stepped on Kit's face.

"Oooofff!"

"Give me a boost. Push up my feet!" Flip yelled.

"Give me a hand, Kelly!" Kit grunted. I flushed the urinal, zipped up, and together Kit and I each took a foot and bench pressed Flip up through the ceiling and onto what looked like a large ventilation box.

"Put the ceiling tile back in place!" Flip said. Kit jumped on the toilet and tapped it back in place and then brushed off the dust and debris that had fallen on him.

"What the hell are you doing anyway?" I asked Kit as he wiped his shoulders.

"I'll tell you later. Let's get out of here."

We walked out, running into Face, and the three of us cruised into the arcade. "We're getting turntables so we can learn how to mix records and shit!" Kit said.

"You're gonna steal this place's turntables!"

"Shhh!" Kit looked around. "Like yeah! We can't afford that shit ourselves! Now Flip is gonna wait up there for the club to shut down and for everyone to go home. Then he'll just grab the stuff and walk out the back door! They have alarms everywhere but the back door!" Kit pointed toward the front.

I shook my head. "How are you going to get the stuff home?"

"That's where I come in," he spoke proudly. "I got my dad's truck!"

Suddenly, a loud crashing noise echoed through the halls, and we saw the bouncers running toward the restrooms. We followed. When we ran in, Flip was lying on the floor gagging for breath in a cloud of white dust and wreckage of smashed ceiling tiles. He slowly raised one of his hands.

"Heeelp. Heeelp," he cried weakly, but the bouncers got to him first, picking him up and dragging him to the manager's office.

✦

Gildmore shook his head. "So how was school going then?"

"About the same."

"Were you still getting in trouble in your classes?"

"Yeah, it was more than halfway through the year and we'd already lost half the Leech Mob, who either dropped out or got kicked out of school, but the rest of us hung in there." It was almost spring then, the weather was warming, the trees were blooming. The only thing we thought about was the summer ahead.

✦

After lunch was old Dr. Nooland's Ancient Civilizations class. He must have been seventy years old. We watched the old guy struggle pathetically with a stick of chalk as he scratched today's lesson plan on the board. His hand shook so bad that he had to reach up with his left and steady his right by gripping onto the chalk with both hands, but still we could barely read what he'd written.

"Dr. Nooland, you write just like my little sister, and she's four!" said Lana, a tomboy who could get away with comments like that because she did okay in class. Dr. Nooland just smiled as a few others chimed in and cracked on his handwriting, too. "There ya go!" Dr. Nooland grinned and pointed at Lana. That was his favorite thing to say. "Do you know why I have such bad handwriting, Lana?" he asked. "Because there is a reason I do."

"Uh, no," answered Lana.

"Well back when I was in the second and third grades, a century or two ago..." Dr. Nooland began by making a joke that most of the class accepted as fact. He cleared his throat and continued, "I went to Catholic school and had nuns for teachers, who were very, very strict old gals. They were so strict, in fact, that back then they forced us to write with our right hand, regardless if we were naturally left-handed. Since I was born left-handed, I was already at a disadvantage. Whenever the nuns caught me writing with my left hand, boy, they'd whack me across my knuckles with a ruler, and if they caught me doing it twice in one day, I'd have to stand up in front of the class and get spanked with a wooden plank."

"Oh my god!" Lana covered her mouth as Dr. Nooland continued speaking.

"So slowly, I learned how to get by, writing with my right hand but, as you see, I can't write too well with either hand now." Nooland grimaced, as sadness seemed to well up in his old eyes. The whole class was speechless.

"Those bitches!" I called out angrily. The class laughed but Dr. Nooland scowled.

"Mr. Hayes, you must watch that terrible language."

Dr. Nooland was a big guy, six feet tall even hunched over, two hundred pounds, and extremely hairy. He had bushels of gnarled hair growing out of his nose and ears, his eyebrows twisted into his eyes, and more of the stuff crept out of his shirt collar. Hair grew everywhere but on his head. When he sweated, his polyester shirts stuck to his hairy flesh and appeared as though he were wearing a fur coat underneath. And his body odor filled up the whole classroom, like a cloud of armpit right above our heads. We smelled it all class long, especially on warm days.

Those nuns had really done a number on him. He was an extremely dull teacher who used the overhead projector every class to show us charts and diagrams. Currently, we were studying the ancient Sumerians but, for the first half of the class, Dr. Nooland had to explain how to complete these charts he wanted us to fill in. I lost interest and began working on one of my new pastimes during his class, which was drawing dirty comic strips, and the next thing I knew, my name was being called.

"Mr. Hayes?"

"What?"

"Well, you're next!"

"Okay…" I said.

"There ya go!" he said encouragingly, but then slowly frowned when I didn't jump right in and help fill out the chart. "You do know what to do, correct Mr. Hayes?"

"Sure."

"Then go on."

"What's the question?" I asked and Dr. Nooland sighed.

"There isn't a question, Mr. Hayes," he said, growing perturbed, his eyes magnified behind his thick bifocals. "You have to pick a topic. Haven't you been listening while I explained what we are doing?"

"Yeah, of course I have," I lied.

"Well then good! Now, pick a topic."

I looked up at the chart and said, "Religion."

Dr. Nooland smiled good-naturedly, rolled his eyes and said, "You can't pick Religion, because Britney already selected Religion and has filled in the proper fields on the chart, see?" Nooland again rolled his eyes and shook his head.

"Well, it's not my fault that she chose the topic that I picked out and, uh, did my research on now, is it?" Ezra began laughing and I shot him a dirty look.

"Pick another topic!" Dr. Nooland raised his voice, no longer in a good mood.

"Tools," I said.

"There ya go!"

I looked at the chart and tried to decipher the meaning behind it, based on what the other kids had filled in, but I could find no rhyme or reason to it. Next to Religion were some dates and names, all meaningless to me.

"Well, go on!" Dr. Nooland urged.

"Tools," I repeated myself, "I'll choose the topic of Tools."

"Yes, go on boy!" He waved me on.

"They, uh, they made tools?" I asked but Dr. Nooland scowled at me, as Ezra bent over laughing his ass off. Nooland shook his head and called on the next student, who picked a different topic, so I went back to animating my X-rated comic book, *The Postman*. I decided to start from the beginning and read it again.

The first scene starts with a mail truck parked in front of a house in a suburban neighborhood. The sun is shining and the birds are out. The postman rings the doorbell and a well-endowed female answers the door.

"Here's your mail, dear," the postman states with a wide smile and hands over a fat stack of letters to the lady, who instantly begins rifling through them. She gets angry and throws the letters at the postman.

"It still hasn't arrived!" she shouts. "How long am I going to have to wait for my mail order?"

"What did you order?" the postman asks but the woman grows red and begins to stammer.

"I–I–well, I–"

The postman then notices a catalog sitting on the table with an advertisement circled in red ink:

DILDOS!
ALL SHAPES!
ALL SIZES!
ALL COLORS!

"Welly! Welly! Welly!" the postman says, grinning mischievously as he picks up the catalog. "What do you use these things for? A paperweight? A door stop?"

The postman holds the advertisement up, smiling, as the lady tries to snatch it back, screaming, "Give that back, you dirty old man! It's a massager," but he holds the catalog out of her reach. She jumps, trying to grab it back as her boobs bounce up and down, mesmerizing the postman.

"I'm going to give you one more chance to give that back!" the woman shouts but the postman is too busy staring at her boobs to absorb her warnings. "You asked for it, mister!" she shouts, pulling up her shirt. Her boobs shoot out death rays that knock the postman on his ass, as she stands proudly above him, hands on her hips.

"Well, two can play at this game!" The postman grins, undoing his belt and pulling down his pants. His penis detaches itself and flies out like a rocket that chases the woman around the room like a heat-seeking missile, poking her in the ass and blowing her across the room. The penis reattaches itself and they begin the battle, her giant, death ray boobs against his detachable rocket-fueled penis. Furniture flies everywhere, things explode, and before either of them realize, they are going at it from every position imaginable. In the melee, a burning candle is knocked off a counter and lights the house on fire but the two cannot be interrupted. The room burns around them while they continue to boink.

The story needed a proper ending, I thought as I began doodling again. I glanced over at Ezra, who also appeared to be working on his cartoon. When he was done, we'd trade them.

Back to my cartoon, I drew a car pulling next to the postal truck and a fat man gets out, holding his briefcase. Since he is drawn from the back, his identity remains unknown as he calmly strolls to his front door, past the white picket fence, whistling a tune and ignorant of the smoke pouring through the windows of his house.

"Honey, I'm home," he calls out as he opens the door but is knocked back at the sight of his wife and the postman having sex while the house burns down around them. Finally, in the last scene, I let the reader discover that the husband is none other than Dr. Nooland, who holds up a giant dildo and says, "THERE YA GO!"

Instantly, my comic strip was ripped out of my hand and to my horror, Dr. Nooland was standing above me, reading the animated story from page to page. I looked up at his eyes, bulging behind his lenses, amused yet enraged. I put my head down on the desk because the last scene was unmistakably Dr. Nooland, down to his thick glasses and famous catch phrase. How could I have missed his approach? Why hadn't Ezra and Brody tried to warn me? They both turned around in their chairs with grins on their thrilled faces.

"Now you'll never get to read it!" I said, angry they hadn't tipped me off.

"Quiet!" Dr. Nooland growled. "Now I see why you didn't hear me call you three times before having to walk down here!" He continued to flip through the pages, looking more and more bitter. When he reached the last scene, his eyes popped out in shock. He glared at me disapprovingly and opened his mouth to say something–but didn't.

I imagined him ripping the comic into a hundred pieces and then slamming it into the garbage can, but instead he folded it neatly and placed it in his jacket pocket. "Get out," he said quietly, raising one of his trembling hands and pointing to the door.

"Go to the principal's office where you can tell Mr. Murphy about your depraved hobbies."

I scooped up my books and walked out, my ears burning red as I walked into the principal's office and took a chair. The principal's secretary looked up from her typewriter. "Mr. Hayes, what brings you here?"

"Drawing pictures in class," I tell her.

"Oh," she said and went back to typing. I sat there until the bell rang and then I left for the next class.

The following day, I expected to catch hell but Dr. Nooland seemed to have forgotten all about *The Postman* incident and had wheeled in the TV /VCR stand.

"Are we watching a movie?" a kid asked, walking in behind me.

"There ya go!" Dr. Nooland said cheerfully and then added, "Nothing gets past you, does it?"

The same question was asked over and over, by each new group of kids that entered the room. When the bell rang, Dr. Nooland held up his hand to quiet everyone down. "As some of you have asked, yes, we'll be watching a documentary that I taped from the history channel last night. I hope you enjoy this as much as I did, because if it works out, I'll record more as they'll be presenting a different ancient culture every week for the whole month! So, with no further introduction, here is Ancient Rome." Dr. Nooland smiled as he pressed *Play*, switched off the lights, and took a seat at his desk.

Ezra tapped me on the shoulder, "Check it out!" He flashed the contents of his bag, including an Asian porno videotape.

"What the hell did you bring that in for?" I asked.

"I didn't. Face brought it in for a trade."

"I dare you to switch tapes on Dr. Nooland," I said grinning.

"What are you, crazy?" Ezra complained. "I'm not getting suspended again. You do it."

"I'll do it," Brody offered, leaning into our conversation.

"How do you plan to pull that off without getting caught?" Ezra asked.

"All we need is someone to get Nooland out the room for five seconds," I explained.

"Yeah, tell him he has to go to the office or something, and then we can make the switch." Brody nodded his head.

"But then he'll know who's behind it," Ezra argued. "We got to work it out better than that, but I'll bring the tape back in tomorrow."

Dr. Nooland cleared his throat. "I'm sorry Ezra! Is the documentary disturbing your conversation?" Ezra shook his head and then concentrated back on the video.

The next day before the bell rang, Dr. Nooland fast forwarded the videotape through the credits and then hit *Stop* and waited for class to begin. Ezra opened his bag and slipped the tape to Brody saying, "When Nooland's out of the room, you know what to do!"

Ezra got up, trying his best to look calm and whispered something to Dr. Nooland, who gave Ezra a look of warning and suggested he hurry up. "Class is about to begin, Ezra!"

Ezra ran out and moments later, as the bell rang, a secretary stood outside our classroom door. Dr. Nooland got up to speak with her while Brody sat on the edge of his chair, gripping the VHS tape and leaning toward the VCR.

Dr. Nooland turned to face the class. "I have an emergency phone call in the office. I'll be right back and then we'll watch the second half of our film." The secretary stood outside our door, looking in and waiting for his return.

"Damn, I can't do it with her watching!" Brody grumbled, so Ezra strolled to the back of the room and tapped the secretary on the shoulder. She turned her back to the door when Ezra began asking her dumb questions and he gave us the signal. Brody snuck to the front, ejected the history documentary and inserted the porno, turned the sound very low, and raced back to his chair.

Dr. Nooland appeared moments later, looking confused and told the secretary, "Nobody was there! I called my wife and she's fine! Oh well!" He looked at Ezra. "What are you doing, boy? Take your seat."

Dr. Nooland walked over to the TV, pressed *Play*, and then sat down at his desk to record grades. The first thing we saw was a little Chinese man and woman, outside in a field somewhere with factory buildings in the distance.

The film was in subtitles, and the girls gasped when the little Chinese lady pulled down the guy's pants and started bobbing her head, turning to remark to the camera with surprise, "LOOK! WANG CHIN'S DICK IS ALIVE!" The guys in the classroom cheered when the lady started to strip, exposing her big chest for such a little chick. Dr. Nooland continued to work on his grade book, happy that the class was getting so excited about his history documentary.

"Isn't the sound kind of low?" he asked, obliviously.

"No," answered Brody, and the room remained surprisingly quiet as we watched the video. Then the little Asian guy got so excited, he started to jump up and down in the middle of the field, doing jumping jacks as his little pecker bounced up and down. The girls began to giggle.

Dr. Nooland, still concentrating on recording grades, absently encouraged us, "You didn't know studying Ancient Rome could be so much fun, did you?"

Next was a close-up of the Chinese lady's amazed eyes, unable to stop staring at Wang Chin's bouncing wang. Everybody in the room started laughing, tipping off Dr. Nooland that something was amiss.

"Alright, settle down," he said as he got to his feet and leaned over his desk to peer at the screen. "Hells bells! Oh my lord! What the heck is that!" He raced toward the TV, tripping over the cord and hopping to win back his balance, finally catching himself on someone's desk, and then spinning around to hit the *Eject* button. "THAT'S NOT MY TAPE!" Nooland grabbed the tape and cracked it across his knee. Plastic shattered in all directions and this time, he dunked the porn tape furiously into the garbage can and stared directly at me.

"WHO IS RESPONSIBLE FOR THAT–THAT FILTH?" He instantly guessed me because of my record with *The Postman* comic book.

"I don't know." I shrugged, watching his anger quickly change to helplessness.

"Won't one of the ladies in the room please come clean and tell me who switched the tapes in my absence?" Dr Nooland looked at the girls, but not one said a thing.

"You kids today–kids today! I'd never–ever! In all my years!" he mumbled under his breath, giving me another dirty look. He decided it was best to move on and fumbled with his tape on Rome. "Whoever is responsible for that garbage, I hope you know what a filthy thing that truly is! I'm going to find out whose tape that was and when I do, they aren't going to know whether to sing, whistle, or spit!" He trembled as he pressed *Play* and then waited, making sure there would be no more surprises from Wang Chin.

✦

At lunch, Violet glanced over at me and smiled. When I smiled back, she winked. Zed looked up from his drawing pad and snorted across the table at her.

"There's a party at four-rights this weekend if anyone wants to go," Violet said.

"I got plans," Zed said without looking up.

"What about you?" she asked me.

"Didn't see that coming." Zed shook his head.

"Shut up, Zed. Just keep doing your little drawings over there and don't worry about what I'm doing."

"Little, my ass," retorted Zed. "Where's Krissy?" He looked at Violet who stared back icily.

"I can't believe I used to date you!"

"Don't remind me." Zed sketched on.

"So, what do you think?" She reached out and poked me.

"What's four-rights?"

"Those are the directions to the party. Out in the woods, they build a huge bon-fire and have a couple kegs."

"Doesn't four rights take you around in a circle?" I drew the line with my finger.

"Not if you take the *right* four rights," Violet said.

Zed looked up and rolled his eyes at her. "Jock party."

"So who else besides Jocks throw parties?" Violet snapped. "Definitely not you."

"Hell no!" Zed carefully drew a line with a ruler. "Why would I invite people over to destroy my house?"

Violet looked back over at me. "All right Kelly, I'll pick you up at about eight." She wrote her phone number on my textbook and kicked the table as she stood up, messing up Zed's artwork. She then strolled away as he swore and ripped out the page, crumpling it into a ball and throwing it at her. Without looking back, she held up her middle finger as she walked away.

I called Violet that night and we talked for over an hour. She told me her version of what had happened with Rob and how he'd pressured her all night. As soon as she gave in, he bumped her and then snuck out and didn't call her again. And after the fight with the Jocks, everyone hated her. Now I felt sorry for her.

She picked me up Friday night and we drove off to the party. She was quiet but blared the radio the whole ride there, chain-smoking cigarettes, and acting like she was my aunt or something. After twenty minutes of driving down dark country roads, we saw the line of cars that advertised we had arrived.

She parked and said, "Don't lock it," as we got out of the car and silently walked down a trail towards the fire-pit. Long branches stood on end, burning six feet high. The keg was on ice and kids stumbled around, drinking and babbling to each other. One of the hippies strummed away on his guitar.

Violet saw some older kids she knew and rushed over to give them hugs, but I made up my mind not to follow her around like some lost dog. I bought a cup, drank a few beers, and talked with the drunks. An hour later, Violet approached me again.

"You wanna ditch?" she asked.

"All right."

Again, we didn't say anything for the whole trip back, and a half-hour later, she pulled up in front of my house.

"So?" she said, looking over.

"So, are you really going home?" I asked her. "Or just trying to get rid of me?"

"Well, are you calling it a night?"

"Let's see," I reasoned, "you drove me home so I don't have much of a choice, do I?"

"What can we do?" she asked with a look of encouragement.

"You want to come in?" I asked. I pointed to the top floor of the garage.

"What's up there?"

"Nothing–a room."

"Okay," she shrugged. I got out and unlocked the side door to the garage. We climbed the stairs and headed over to the large window that overlooked the river. A full silver moon was out and the water was splashing against the docks and boats.

"You got a nice view up here." She then leaned over and kissed me. I pulled her close and then brought my hand up and cupped a firm breast. After a few minutes, she drew back, as if to stop herself. "I think it's best if I go home now."

I didn't call her for the rest of the weekend because I didn't want to look like

I was sweating her and she didn't call me either. On Monday, Violet seemed to make a point to avoid most of the Leech Mob. At lunch with Macie, Paula, and Obi, she'd talked to everyone but me. Then Krissy sat down and wouldn't look at me either and later, I had to chase her down in the hallway.

"Hi Krissy," I said.

"Hey," she said distractedly but kept walking.

"Krissy!" I had to stand in her way.

"What do you want, Kelly?" she snapped and tried to walk around me.

"Hey, what's wrong with you?" I asked, stopping her by touching her shoulder.

Krissy sighed and looked at me, somewhat hurt. "I heard you went out with Violet this weekend."

"Yeah," I said, trying to play it off. "We went to four rights. They had a keg."

"Oh really? You know, it doesn't even surprise me anymore." She tried to walk around me again.

"Hey, wait a second. What are you talking about?"

"She always does this!" Krissy shoved me aside. "I'm not stupid, Kelly."

"I don't think that. What's your problem?"

Krissy took a deep breath as we walked along. "Whenever I show interest in a guy, Violet goes after him. Almost like I have to give the okay before she wants him."

"I'm sorry."

"Don't be. It's like not even your fault really. It's not like we were going out or anything. She always does this pretty quick. That's the only good thing I can say about it."

"All we did was go to this party, really."

"Oh yeah, right. I heard that wasn't all that happened."

"What are you talking about?"

"Afterwards—at your house. Does that ring any bells?"

"All I did was kiss her."

"Whatever, Kelly, I don't have time for this."

We turned a corner and saw Violet standing there, talking to some other kids.

"I'll see ya later," Violet told them and then approached us.

"Uh, what's up, Vi?" Krissy stopped in the hall.

"Hello Krissy!" she snapped as she stormed past.

"See, what about that?" Krissy shrugged. "Look how jealous she is?" Krissy rolled her eyes and walked away.

Before last class, Violet grabbed me in the hall and said, "Meet me in the parking lot after school and we'll go have some fun." She bobbed her eyebrows and then playfully slapped my butt, twirled around, and strolled away.

Out in the student parking lot, Violet leaned against her Jeep, waiting by herself. I walked out to meet her. When she saw me, she jumped in and rolled forward.

"Get in!" she said and before I had the door closed, she swerved out.

"Wait! Wait! Please wait!" someone wailed.

"Who is screaming like that?" Violet asked, looking around.

"It's Face," I said as he booked across the parking lot. Halfway over, his one-strap backpack flew open and books tumbled out, sliding across the blacktop. He scooped them up and then ran toward us again. Violet giggled and accelerated, but Face ran beside us and jumped, throwing himself across her hood.

"Get the fuck off!" Violet yelled as she slammed on her brakes. "Face, you're gonna scratch my fucking paint!"

"Then let me in," he begged. "Hey! I have weed! I have weed!"

"Stop that vehicle at once!" We heard a loud, deep voice and looked to see a seven-foot tall security guard chugging toward us, holding his radio up to contact the main office as he bounced along. "You there!" he pointed at us. "Stop that Jeep!"

"Don't be an asshole, Face!" I shouted. "Get down!"

"Take me with you! Don't leave me out here in the middle of nowhere!"

"Fine dick, get in!" Violet slammed on the brakes, and Face slid off the hood and onto the street.

"Hurry up!"

Face jumped to his feet. "Holy shit!" he said and fell into the backseat as Violet hit the gas and raced off school grounds, leaving the security guard behind.

Violet hummed as we drove down the road. She rewound an old Smashed Pumpkins' tape as she blew through a stop sign.

"Is anybody home at your house?" She looked at me.

"No."

"Good."

"Yeah good," Face said and then stretched out on the back seat, raising a book over his face. He remained quiet until we pulled onto his street where he started to throw a fit. "You can't bring me home! Not home! You guys are possessed right now!"

"Where do you want to go, Face?" she snapped in frustration.

"Anywhere but here!" Face screamed until Violet drove past his house.

"All right, but you're gonna have to wait by yourself for a while," Violet said.

"Yeah, I'll wait in the car." Face winked at her and then stared at me, real goofy before lying back down and dropping the book back over his face.

We pulled in front of my house. Face waited in the car as Violet and I got out. "Your mom isn't coming home soon, is she?" she whispered as I unlocked the front door.

"No, not for a while," I lied. The truth was that my mom was due home any time now. We went into my room and closed the door, locking it. Violet didn't waste any time and stretched out on my bed.

"Come here, boy!" She patted the bed. "Take off your shirt. I want to take a look at you." I took off my shirt. She hugged me and slowly we started kissing. When I reached up to touch her chest, she sat up, undid her strapless bra, and slipped it off, but left her shirt on. "I'll leave it on in case someone surprises us!"

She then surprised me by sliding out of her baggy jeans, before unbuckling my belt and whispering, "Take these off, too. Your buckle is jabbing me." When I did, she began kissing my chest and then kissed me lower before pulling my shorts down, too. Then we were naked. "I want something else to jab me."

"Take your hair down, please."

"Since you asked so nicely." She smiled, rose to her knees, pulled the elastic band from her ponytail, and shook her long curly hair that fell to her waist. Then changing her mind, Violet crossed her arms and gracefully lifted off her shirt. I stared and she giggled again, swung one leg over and straddled me. She leaned forward, curls of hair falling in my face, and breathed in my ear, "You've never done this before?"

"Nuh-uh."

Violet began rocking back and forth, making little yelping noises and grinding her hips into mine. She looked down at me, flashing her eyes before closing them and breathing heavy. I pulled her down and started kissing her as we slowly rocked together. After the fireworks ended, I intently looked up into her gorgeous eyes, but then I caught a glimpse of Face, squinting through the window with a big grin on his face.

"Face! You fucking perv!" I shouted and threw a pillow at him. His eyes bugged open and he ducked down.

"Oh my God! Was Face really out there?" She gasped, looking not the least bit upset.

"Yeah, I'm going to kick his ass!"

She gave me a last kiss before hopping up and strolling into the bathroom. I heard the shower turn on. I quickly pulled on my pants and ran outside. Face had jumped back into the backseat and acted as though he'd been sleeping the whole time.

"Stop trying to front, you pervert. I saw you looking in!"

He grinned, so I let him have it, punching his stomach. He tried to flex himself but let out a fart instead and screamed in pain before laughing. I hit him once more in the arm before I started to forget how pissed off I was at him. He sat up, holding his arm.

"That hurt! You got a cigarette, Kelly?"

"Nope."

A minute later, Violet came outside with her hair dripping wet. She scowled at Face but then laughed and lit a cigarette.

"It's okay, we're all friends here," she said and exhaled.

"Can I have a cig, Vi?" he asked.

"Don't give him shit. He's a pervert."

"Come on, Violet, I didn't mean to," Face pleaded.

"What type of bullshit is that?" I asked.

"Honestly Kelly, I thought I saw your mom driving up the street. It was a car just like hers. I was going to warn you two, but it drove on past."

"So, was I the best you ever had?" Violet teased wickedly.

◆

After school the next day, everyone had already heard about me and Violet. Vick and Flip were grinning, and Remmy shoved me as I walked past them in the parking lot.

"Yo Kelly, I heard about you and Violet the other day."

"It's been months since you and her. . ." I began to say but Remmy waved me off as if that were unimportant. "Who told you? Face right? Did he also tell you that he was peeping through the window?"

They laughed.

"Yeah, ha ha!" Casey laughed sarcastically. "You know, I was just thinking back to when she started all that shit."

"Yeah, I remember."

"But you're acting like you don't remember." He glared at me.

"She made us look like a bunch of fucking jackasses!" Vick said.

"She wasn't the only reason for that," I said.

"Just be careful when you mess with that pig!" Vick warned.

"Leave him alone. He just wants to get laid!" Kit laughed as he walked over.

"So everybody knows?"

"Yeah, we've all gone through the Violet phase," Casey leaned back against his car, putting his arms behind his head, all-knowingly.

"We were all about to be dads, one after the other," added Vick.

"You know, I went baby shopping with Violet once," Zed said. "We bought baby socks." Everyone laughed.

"Wasn't Remmy going to be the father of Violet's love child once?" Kit asked.

I couldn't help smiling. "You guys are messed up."

"Don't look at me man," said Kit defensively. I'm the only person here who hasn't—"

"Sooner or later, Violet will fuck you over and that's just a fact, so with that being said, have fun, kid!" Zed smiled sarcastically. "In fact, she'll probably even dream up something special for you! I can sense it somehow."

"So I guess our date's off?" Krissy walked up, patting my shoulder as she stepped toward her car.

"What's up, Krissy?" I asked.

"Hi, Casey." She beamed and gave him a big hug, ignoring me. She kissed his cheek and started to walk away.

"I'll call you later, babe," promised Casey.

"Krissy!" I caught up as she got into her car. She opened the door, paused, and turned around. When I looked at her, I realized I didn't know what to say. She got into the car and rolled down the window.

"Don't let Violet make you cry." With that, she drove away.

✦

"Ooo, I hate how this oil feels, sticking to my clothes." She collapsed down on the sofa beside me. It was warm out, especially in the room above the garage.

"Just go down to the house and take a shower."

"No way! And what if someone sees me?"

"Tell them you just came in from sunbathing. What are you doing tonight?" I asked, changing the subject.

"You mean, what are we doing?" she corrected me.

"That's what I meant."

"Just as long as you don't pull your disappearing act again." Violet nestled against me. "Why are you always hanging out with those dumb asses for?"

"I don't know. They're your friends, too."

"Some friends. You always say we'll hang out later but then you dis."

"Last time we all hung out, you were the only girl there and you showed everybody your boobs," I said but Violet laughed.

"I was getting changed. It's not my fault they're all perverts and stared at my breasts." Violet had on her innocent, feel sorry for me look. Her little top lip curled like a cat's.

"No wonder they always invite you to all the keg parties!"

"Show me your tits!" Violet growled playfully.

"Shhh! You better be joking right now," I laughed.

"My mother and Barry are throwing another party." Violet stared thoughtfully out the window. "I hope it doesn't go till late."

"I don't like Barry. Where's your real dad?"

"He died when I was three years old." She yawned. "I think I will check out that shower."

She jumped up quickly and went down the stairs. I got up and went to the open window. A warm spring breeze of cut grass and barbecue blew in. I heard her Jeep start and drive away. The phone rang.

"Hello."

"What are you doing?" It was a distorted voice, probably Vick drunk off his ass or pretty close. "We're stopping by! See ya later, pig-spanker." The phone went dead.

◆

When Kit dropped me off, just before dark, we found Violet asleep on a lawn chair in my back yard. I woke her up and she began to cry gently and reached out for a hug.

"What's wrong, Violet?" I asked but all she could do was ramble on about how he kept on touching her. I looked over her shoulder at Kit, who stood there shaking his head. I glared at him and he turned away.

"Who are you talking about, Vi?" I asked, leaning back and looking into her eyes, trying my best to stay calm.

"Ronny! It was horrible! I had to like let him make out with me until I was able to run! And then I ran out of the room, past my drunk parents, and out the fucking door!"

I led her inside and got her some water.

This is how I heard it.

Violet threw down the phone in anger and then trudged across the second floor from her bedroom into the TV room. A blaze of laughter roared from downstairs. She turned up the TV, so she could hear it above the party's noise. Her parents were at it again.

Ronnie, a neighbor, staggered up the stairs, bouncing off the walls and knocking a picture down. He stooped to pick it up and then hung it back, crooked.

Next she felt cold damp hands on her shoulders, massaging her neck. She didn't especially like how it felt, but she didn't shrug it off either, but when the hands began to inch lower, she turned to face him.

The stench of hard liquor hit her. His eyes stared in two different directions at once, almost as if he were looking right through her. He gripped her shoulders again, rubbing them so hard it hurt. She leaned forward and tried to break free.

"Shhhh!" he hissed in her ear with sour breath and pulled her back down.

"Please stop. I don't like that," she had said, staring into his drunk, frog-like eyes. He dropped his hands and coldly surveyed her. His icy blank expression scared her. She grabbed her jacket and headed out of the room, but he stood in the doorway. She turned sideways and tried to squeeze past him.

"Where are you going, sweetie?" He raised his arm and blocked her path down the stairs. His breath was reeking of the booze he had drunk for days, smelling old and stale.

"Downstairs. Out," she had said, trying to duck underneath his arm but he blocked her again. She tried smiling it off and again tried to push past him, but this time he grabbed her harder and clamped a cigarette-stinking palm over her mouth.

"Shhhh!" he repeated, pushing her back into her bedroom and shutting the door

behind them.

"When I take my hand down, you be calm and real quiet." He slowly released her mouth.

"Don't make me scream!" she had warned him.

"Why would you do that? I know you want it. I've seen you looking at me, baby."

She was scared now—and the man's face had gone blank and cold...

"I want you to wait here while I go and confront this guy."

"No!" She started to cry.

"Look, I'll be cool about it. What else are we going to do? You want to call the police?"

"No!" she bawled.

"Then what?"

"I don't know."

"Uh, maybe I should leave?" asked Kit.

"No, I need a ride."

"Where?"

"To Violet's house."

I left her in my room and motioned for Kit to walk outside. He was quiet for most of the trip until I said, "I know what you're thinking, Kit."

"What?"

"Let's hear it."

"Look man, I really don't want to get involved. And I don't want to get arrested for anything either."

"Don't worry. We won't."

"But I'm already involved!"

"This time she's telling the truth. I know she is."

Kit rolled his eyes. "I knew something like this would go down."

"Shut up, Kit."

"Fine, fine, just don't go all ape shit on the guy. If you do, I swear to god, I'm just going to drive away and let you deal with it."

At Violet's house, her mother answered the door.

"Is Ronny here?"

"I don't know," she slurred and turned around. "Is Ronny still here?"

"No, he went home!" someone said.

"No, he went back home. Where's Violet? Is she with you?"

"Where does Ronny live?"

"Number 91, right up there."

We found him in his driveway, drinking beer and washing his Mustang. He didn't know what to make of us until I rushed him, "So you like raping girls?"

He cringed and retreated around his car.

"What?" His voice shook when he spoke. "Whoever told you that must be pulling your leg!"

"I knew we should've gone straight to the cops!" Kit said.

"Yeah, you're right," I said, backing off. "Let the police deal with this piece of shit!"

"If you're Violet's friends, then you've got it all wrong. I've known her since she was five years old. Her father is like a brother to me! You got the wrong idea!"

I cleared my throat and spit towards the car, when a pretty lady walked out the front door and waved at us.

"Oh, honey, my car looks great!"

Kit hissed, "How does such a dirt bag like you get such a hot wife?"

"Dinner is ready. Should I make extra for your friends?"

"No thanks," Kit said. "We're just about to leave I think, right Kelly?"

"Don't let it get cold," she said and went back in the house.

"Keep playing stupid and I'll tell your wife and Barry!"

"All I did was rub her shoulders. I–I didn't mean nothing by it." He stared fearfully at me. "You got the wrong idea."

"No, you got the wrong idea! You'll be hearing from us. You're lucky your wife is so nice."

When we got back to my house, Violet was gone and I didn't hear from her for the rest of the weekend. We drove by her house several times but her car was never there. By the time I saw her in school, I was pissed off.

"Where the hell have you been? We went to see that scumbag but he denied everything!"

Violet stared at me with an amused look on her face. "What's your problem? I went to stay at my aunt's house and hung out with my cousin. You need to chill the fuck out!"

"Don't you want to hear what happened?"

"I already know what happened," she said, distracted. "He came down to the house. He talked to my father and started crying, my mother slapped him, and now everything is back to normal." She turned to walk away.

"Hey, get back here."

"Leave me the fuck alone! I don't want to talk about this anymore." She stormed away.

I stayed angry for a week, which felt like a real long time. Then she called me up one day. "You want to go out with me, Krissy, and Face? Or are you still mad?"

"A little."

When she picked me up, she leaned over and asked, "So I don't get a kiss?"

"Nope."

She frowned. We then picked up Face next.

"Where we going?" he asked.

"To get Krissy."

"Going out with Krissy is like hanging out with my aunt or something."

"I'm sure she feels the same way about you," said Violet. "Only you're her little retarded nephew or something."

"Krissy isn't bad looking," I chimed in.

"Yeah, you liked her, didn't you, Kelly? Before I came and stole you away." Violet took a drag off her cigarette. "You know, that's like the fifth time I did that to her," she confessed with a guilty grin.

"What?" I asked.

"Stole her boy, that's what!"

"You say some skanky shit sometimes, don't you!" I gave her a dirty look.

"Fuck you!" She slapped the side of my head.

"Fuck!" I screamed. "I hate hearing shit like that from you, but you never seem to get that. And where the hell are we going? I thought we were going to get Krissy."

"First, shut the fuck up! Second, I have to go to my house and get money for gas!" Violet took another drag off her cigarette, then exhaled and mumbled, "Broke-ass kid."

She stared straight ahead at the road, clamping the cigarette between her teeth like a vice.

"I told you I had ten bucks!" I shouted.

"Whatever." She yawned.

When we got to Violet's house, Violet went inside and returned, smugly twirling a set of keys. She pointed toward the shiny Mustang convertible parked across the street and said, "It's ours for the night."

"What?" I ranted. "That's Ronny's car!"

I gave Violet a dirty look and she stuck her tongue out at me. "Look at it this way. We can beat the shit out of it by driving anywhere you want." Violet began crossing the street toward the car.

"I hate that asshole," I said, following her.

"What happened with that anyway?" Face questioned.

"My father invited him over and broke his nose. Then he cried. Then he blamed it all on the booze. Then they had a beer."

"You never told me all that," I said.

"Well, I'm telling you now." She smiled slyly. "Don't you just love happy endings?"

I shook my head.

"So where to, kids?" Violet asked, upbeat and changing the subject as we approached the Mustang.

"I'm not going anywhere in that scumbag's car." I glared at the thing, getting more pissed off the more I thought about it.

"Not even if you drive? How about New York City? Come on, drop the puss face. Ronny doesn't know you don't have a license yet. You drive!"

"So you're going to let this asshole buy you off?"

Violet made a face and then waved a twenty-dollar bill in my face. "He gave me this for gas money, too."

"Since you took money from him," Face leaned forward. "is this going to be a weekly thing from now on?"

"Here Kelly!" Violet held up the keys. "You drive."

"No way. I'll do something to destroy it, even if I don't mean to."

"Suit yourself," she said and slid into the driver's seat. Face jumped into the back, and I stood there, looking at them.

"Fine Kelly! Stay here! Take the keys to my car!" She started rifling through her purse.

"New York City," I said, opening the door and getting in the passenger's seat as I turned to Face. "Watch her baby it the whole..."

Violet dropped the car into gear and slammed on the gas. It fishtailed from side to side, screeching rubber and flying up the street, almost running into an elderly couple chugging around the corner in the middle of the road. They rode the brakes and laid on the horn as Violet ripped the steering wheel to the right and bounced onto her neighbor's lawn.

"Holy shit!" Face shouted and turned around, pushing his blonde dreadlocks back from his face and pointing at them, laughing.

"Oooops," Violet said sweetly. "My bad." Behind us, Ronny stood on the porch, running his fingers through his hair. I raised my middle finger and Violet laughed into the rear view mirror.

When we reached Krissy's house, she was already waiting out front. Her mother came to the door and waved goodbye.

"What's up, Krissy?"

"What's up, Kelly? Give me a hug."

I got out of the car to hug her, but she quickly yelled "SHOTGUN!" and jumped into the front seat. Both Violet and Krissy began laughing.

"Fine by me." I jumped into the back seat next to Face.

"I hate it when my mom has to wave good bye at the front door like she's stuck in the '50s."

"She probably is," said Violet. We caught eyes in the rearview mirror and she winked, real slick.

✦

The little black guy stopped screaming and, instead, sang falsetto into the mic, his long dreads falling over his closed eyes, "You'll be dead…cause I'm gonna hit you…and when you fall, we're gonna get you…" Then the music kicked in and the singer convulsed, throwing himself around stage as if he was having a grand mal seizure. Moments later, he dove off stage backwards onto the audience, who passed the skinny kid overhead before he was rolled back onto the stage. He sat there for the moment, appearing dumbfounded before he got to his feet and skipped in place.

Rook climbed on stage and onto a six-foot speaker and then jumped backwards, flipping in the air and narrowly missing the overhead stage lights that shined down on the hardcore group.

The song ended when a kid with black glasses said something to the M.C. and the mic was handed over. "Yo, is there a Mike Evans in the house?" the kid asked the audience. "Mike Evans, you got a friend, you got a friend that's really fucked up outside." The electric guitars continued to shriek in the background. "He needs you outside right now. He got banged up bad so please, just go outside. Thanks." He handed the microphone back.

"Hey, we're FUBAR, out of Washington D.C. This is our first gig at The Night Breed. Our next one is called – Street-Wise – ONE-TWO-THREE-FOUR!" The music blasted and the singer jumped up and down. Others crisscrossed the mosh pit, swinging their arms.

Egan sat with the Cincity Leech Mob, who were drinking beer in the back of the club. Pete, smaller than the others, didn't look the part of one of the most feared Cincity kids. Trash snorted something off his hand and then took a drink from a flask and squinted. He leaned back with dead eyes as the shadows hung on his gaunt zombie face. After taking a 45-caliber bullet in his leg, he walked with a noticeable limp. Sitting next to Trash, Doc towered over the group, the giant hulking shadow of the gang, seven foot worth and three times the width of an average man. He sported a crew cut and a pair of dark-rimmed specs, his vicious eyes peering out. But even Doc wasn't as intimidating as Ogre, who sulked somewhere in the bar, waiting for an ounce of white powder, courtesy of Desperate Bob.

Stanley sat in the back at his own separate table, a tall, muscular, hooded dude who gawked out into the world with bulging blue eyes. He was second in command of Cincity Leech—only Bull held more weight.

Egan sat, more quiet than usual, in their presence and ignored the bag of powder Ogre brought back and passed to Pete, Trash, Doc, and then to Stanley, who rolled it up his sleeve. After Pete got amped up, he went off in the pit, taking something personal and coming back swinging a meat-tenderizer into a guy's face. The guy stumbled around, clutching his forehead where neat diamonds of pulverized skin gushed blood.

"Come on guys, get the weapons out of the pit!" the M.C. shouted into the mic, but Pete raised the meat tenderizer again and this time brought it down on the back of the guy's neck, knocking him to the ground.

The bouncers flew from the sidelines, tackling Pete to the floor. One wrenched the weapon away, as Pete screamed underneath, red and gasping for breath.

More bouncers surrounded the hammered man. One knelt down and checked for a pulse. "Well, he's alive, but I don't think we should move him."

Desperate Bob ran up. "Oh what the fuck!"

"He hit him with this." The bouncer held up the meat tenderizer.

"Gimmee that!" Desperate Bob snatched the hammer and leaned over Pete, whose face still pressed the ground. "Now the cops are gonna be crawling all over the place!" He shook the tenderizer in his face. "Now get this fucking asshole up and in my office." A bouncer yanked Pete to his feet and dragged the clenched youth into the back of the club. Pete began to throw a fit, twisting in circles to break free from the bouncer's grip. When the bouncer let go, Pete dove into the crowds and squirmed under the waves of kids to get away. He ducked down and later reappeared halfway across the room, edging toward the door.

"Let him go!" Bob lowered his voice. "Let the cops deal with him if they got a witness."

The others stood over the thug who'd fallen at the edge of the pit. "What should we do with him?" a bouncer asked Desperate Bob. "We shouldn't move em, right?"

"Hell no, you shouldn't move him!" Bob shouted to his security crew. "Let the ambulance handle this but, meanwhile, nobody else in or out of the club! Bill, you stay with these guys, and I want you helping Charlie at the front–get those doors locked!" Desperate Bob pressed through the crowds and then jumped up on stage, grabbed the microphone from the singer of FUBAR, and said, "Attention everybody! We've had a serious, uh, injury. So just sit tight until we've had a chance to, uh, figure out what's happened." The plug was pulled on the band, the front doors locked, and Bob tried his best to treat the place like an accident scene before he ran off to hide the drugs.

At the doors, the bouncers were arguing with a group of kids who were told they couldn't leave. A howl rose up and a few larger kids decided to make a push through the strip of security but were shoved back. The guards started swinging, hooking one kid to the jaw and sending him flying sideways into a table. They weren't messing around.

Two lines then formed: one, the bouncers, and two, the crowds of hardcore kids. Every so often, a kid would lunge forward to challenge the security guards and then the punches would fly. The fights were scattered and quick. The bouncers weren't breaking their line, and nobody was getting through the doors that had been locked with metal deadbolts, which slid into braces on the concrete floor.

From the back of the show stepped Ogre. The floor seemed to shake with each of his strides, and the crowd stepped aside, allowing him room toward the front where the bouncers seemed to shrink under his shadow. Ogre swung his giant arms. The bouncers hit back. Their fists stopped dead on his chest until finally one guard landed a good shot to Ogre's chin. Ogre faltered for a second and then raised one of his redwood-sized legs and stomped out, smashing the guard into the door behind him. The door buckled as the deadbolts and hinges started to give way.

The kids pressed forward into the bouncers, who were growing frantic. In angry waves, the crowds hurled themselves against the bouncers, who fell back against doors that warped farther and farther out. The crowds pressed in from all sides, pushing against the doors and the bouncers were caught in between.

They hung there, pinned to the doors, their eyes drawn shut and heads hanging in exhaustion. One looked unconscious, the other's lips were silently moving as though he were praying–praying that the last of the deadbolts would snap and release them from their pain. Finally, doors gave way, and the bouncers were trampled as the crowd escaped into the streets.

✦

It was a warm spring day and we were hanging in the parking lot after school. Only a couple more weeks and we were out for the summer.

"Listen. You guys hear that?" Jonah asked, cocking his head to the side and listening to the approaching bass, sounding from a car stereo about a half-mile away. "Every poser in Riverview is getting a system now!" He stood up and spit. The bass continued to get louder. We paused, and looked out to the street, waiting for the car to drive into view. A small red pickup with black tinted windows appeared.

"It's Tank," Kit said nervously.

"What is he doing here?"

"Why don't you ask Face?"

"Ask Face what?" Jonah demanded as Tank pulled into the student parking lot, followed by two trashed cars covered with graffiti and bumper stickers. We nodded at them but were met with hardened stares as if we were strangers, enemies even.

"What's going on, Face?" I glanced at Face, who remained mute.

Kit shrugged. "Face keeps on hooking up with Otis's ex girlfriend."

"You're an idiot, Face," accused Jonah.

"Why? They broke up like a year ago. What do you want me to do?"

"Yeah, Jonah. Otis is tripping," Kit said.

Face looked at us as if to ask, "What should I do?" But I shook my head, keeping my eyes on the Landbury boys.

"Just be cool for now," mumbled Jonah as the older gang of scruffy, tattooed Leech Mobbers swaggered over.

"They're tweaked out on something. Check em out," I mumbled.

Tank grinned from behind Otis, who led his pack of wolves. Jasper and Aaron approached, taller than the others, hiding their thin frames under baggy flannel shirts. The albino-like Otis looked more strung out than usual. His fists were doubled in body language that said he meant business, especially since Bram, looking as vicious as ever, backed him.

"Which one is Face?" Otis growled.

"The one in the glasses," Bram spit.

"That's Face? What the fuck is Clighty thinking about?" Otis glanced at Tank.

"I asked her the same thing," Face agreed, with a crazy gleam in his eyes.

"You're gonna step off my girl, bitch! I've been with her since we were like kids and it's going to stay that way. So I'm handing you a court fucking order. I don't want you within two hundred feet of Clighty, motherfucker! You hear what I'm saying, you little bitch?" Face stared back with a mix of fear and anger. "Let me explain something to you," Otis said, dropping his tone. "She's gonna be Mrs. Otis Drenger one day. You got that, you fuck?"

"Not until she tells me that," Face answered defiantly.

"What did you say?" They all looked surprised.

"You heard me," Face said.

I would have been impressed if he hadn't begun to tremble.

Otis reached around to the back of his belt and then began swinging a pair of wooden nunchucks at Face, who at once went on the retreat, holding his backpack up like a shield.

"Why you got to bring fucking nunchucks to this!" screamed Jonah. "You're fighting Face, man!"

Cries rose up from the other students in the parking lot as Otis, swinging the chucks, chased him down. A moment later, Face screamed out in pain as one of the nunchucks clipped his hand, enraging him. Face began swinging his backpack by its strap. With the first swing, he knocked the nunchucks to the ground. With the next, he caught Otis under his chin and knocked him back. Otis fell and Face stood over him, raising the backpack, yet this time the zipper ripped and books flew everywhere.

"I didn't know you took calculus, man!" Kit remarked stupidly.

Otis grabbed the nunchucks before we could get to them.

"Why don't you fight fair?" I said, stepping up.

"You want a piece of me, bitch!" shouted Bram.

"No bitch!" shouted Jonah. "I got you, Bram! I think I can whip your ass!"

"Is that right? I say bullshit."

"You stay the fuck out of it, Jonah!" said Tank. "Face should have known better than to fuck with...

"My possessions!" Otis finished Tank's sentence.

I stepped up, raising my fists toward Tank.

"No way, you're mine, boy!" Otis snarled. "I'm gonna finish what I started!"

"What are you gonna do, Bram?" Jonah growled.

Otis turned away from Face and ran towards Jonah, raising the nun chucks over his shoulder and snapping them out, missing Jonah's face by inches. Otis swung them again but Jonah skipped back, moving parallel to Kit's gray Oldsmobile. He opened its door to put a barrier between them, but when Otis closed in, Jonah kick-slammed it, pinning Otis in. He hung there crookedly with the wind knocked out of him, dropping the nunchucks yet again.

"Oh man," yelled Kit from the side, "you dented the Clam, man!"

"Shut up, you bitch!" shouted Tank.

For five seconds nobody moved. The Landbury Leech froze, seeing their boy laid out like that, so I moved first, lunging for the chucks. Everybody else had the same idea, but Kit was the closest and got to them first. He grabbed them up and retreated, screaming and then throwing them. They took off like a helicopter, spinning through the air. They sailed over the fence, bounced off the roof of the equipment shed, and landed on the football field.

Kit turned around, raising his arms victoriously before seeing Bram, dead on his trail, who quickly punched him in the mouth. Kit's head snapped back. He staggered a few steps as Bram hopped around like a boxer, but Kit dropped to the ground.

Otis recovered and lunged for Jonah, who grabbed hold of him, spun him around in some type of Judo move, and threw him over the hood of the car. Otis jumped back up and attacked Jonah again, who then grabbed him in some type of contorted face lock. Otis's eyeballs rolled in his head as he blindly patted Jonah's thick forearms, trying to scope in on his enemy.

Tank didn't like seeing his boy like that so he made a move, but not before I cut him off and both of us crashed into each other. Then everyone ran in and soon we were in a circle, punching and kicking each other. I saw flashes of faces– Jasper's stepped on and Face's pulled down by an unseen hand that twisted a fistful of his dreadlocks. Face opened his mouth in a silent howl before letting out a bloodcurdling scream.

I pounded on the arm that gripped Face but had to defend myself when someone smashed my nose. I then felt teeth puncturing my arm and saw that Otis was back, like a mad-dog biting me with pointy, yellow fangs, so I dropped an elbow straight into his jaw. Then Bram flew above us, kicking Jonah and knocking us all over. All I could hear beneath the mound of bodies was grunting and swearing and hollow thuds. I caught another glimpse of Bram's face squished between Jonah's vise-like arms. I reached up and poked my fingers in Bram's eyes, and he shrieked. A second later, we heard Kit's voice holler out.

"Listen!" Face tried to shout, his head pinned under Otis's shoe.

"Chill! Chill!" Tank looked around, seeing Kit limping past, having quickly recovered from the TKO Bram had given him moments before. I felt the pile getting lighter until I was able to stand and see Jasper and Aaron pulling Bram to his feet, who staggered around in a daze. His face was bright purple, squeezed for the last minute in Jonah's head lock. They dragged each other to the cars and dropped Bram on the back seat.

"THE COPS!" Kit yelled again, pointing to the gargantuan security guard, racing up in his old Ford and talking into his radio.

"You boys break it up!" he shouted, getting out of his car but keeping his right hand on the steering wheel.

"THIS AIN'T OVER!" Tank screamed at us from across the lot, as blood streamed down his face.

"This is just the start of it! You guys are dead!" Otis' voice was shaky, but he hid it behind a drugged-out grin.

"FUCK YOU, BITCH!" Jonah yelled and gave him the finger.

Tank jumped in his truck and fired up the engine, holding his hat and exposing his new black eye. Tank looked into his rear view mirror, cursed at himself, and then tore out of the parking lot. The others followed Tank and raced away, their beat up engines screaming down the street.

The four of us jumped into Kit's car. After our first arrest for fighting, we weren't going to stick around and get cuffed again for sure.

"You think that security guard knows our names?" Kit asked as we raced along.

"I wouldn't be surprised," I answered.

"I'm going to drive towards the police station," said Kit. "They might catch up to them, but they won't expect us to drive right past em.'"

"There's one right there!" Jonah yelled. "Chill! Everyone just chill."

As the cop zoomed past, the older officer didn't even look at us. Kit took a hard right and sped down the street.

"He might turn around!" shouted Face, looking behind us.

"No he won't!" cried Jonah.

"Listen! He did turn around. That siren's getting louder!"

"No, that's another one!"

"Pull in there!" Jonah shouted, pointing at a curvy dirt driveway that led to a rundown house, obscured by overgrown weeds and vines. Kit pulled in, shut the motor, and we all ducked down and waited for the siren to get closer. The cop car momentarily slowed down but then raced past, searching for us.

"He went right by us," Kit whispered.

"Damn! They're all over the place!"

"We got company," Jonah said, pointing at an old woman who came shuffling out of her house in her bathrobe, holding a cordless phone.

"Just chill out and see what she wants," Kit said as we all sat up and watched her approach the car.

Lifting a crooked and boney finger incriminatingly at us, she croaked, "I know the cops are looking for you!" She held the phone up to her ear and said, "I got a bunch of high school punks hiding out in my driveway at 338 Maple Road!"

"Let's get out of here!" Kit put the car in reverse and started to back down the driveway when a cop car swerved in, with the crone shrieking and pointing at us.

"I can't believe this," groaned Jonah. "I don't go to school to get a record, man!"

✦

"And you were arrested yet again?" Dr. Gildmore asked.

"For disturbing the peace, yeah."

"Did they get the other boys?"

"No."

"So this is how the school chose to deal with you then?"

"Yeah, but after that, it was over. We had our last day and then we were out for the summer, thank God!"

"Let me guess. There was more trouble after that?"

"Yup."

"So let's hear it."

"It gets complicated."

"Try me."

"Remember Violet?"

"How could I forget?"

✦

Violet and I were always breaking it off and then getting back together, but this last time I hadn't heard from her in weeks. I found out that Violet had been staying at Paula's house, whose parents were away for the rest of the summer. Paula had an older brother, a drummer in the early hardcore scene, so she knew all the Landbury kids and the Cincity guys, too, who showed up for one endless party during her parents' absence.

Paula's house was nice—a renovated basement, guest rooms to crash in, and a half pipe her brother built for skateboarding in the backyard. It was definitely a straight place to party, but Paula hated me as much as she hated Vick, Flip, and most of my other friends—but she and Violet were tight. I didn't like Paula either because whenever I saw her, she gave me attitude. Then they'd go out with the Landbury Leech Mob kids who, at the moment, wanted to kill us.

So we sat around Vick's condo's parking lot, me, Flip, Remmy, Face, and Kit, without much to do. Violet was teaching me a lesson, I thought. Hopefully, I'd see her or she'd call me and we'd talk about getting back together, like we always had.

"So what did you and Violet break up over this time?" Remmy joked.

"She told the old men at the pizza parlor that she had a shaved bush. When they didn't believe her, let's just say she gave them solid proof."

Violet and I were always breaking up over dumb shit like this, like the time she decided to change her clothes in front of Vick, Kit, and Face when we went swimming. When I got back from taking a leak, she was standing in front of them naked, jumping up and down, her tits bouncing all over the place as she tried to step into her shorts. They were throwing nickels and dimes at her and cheering. We broke up for two days over that one.

But this time felt different. It had been two weeks since I saw her. I broke down and finally called her house, and her drunk step-dad happily told me he hadn't seen her in a week. Usually she'd get the message and call me back, but not this time. I couldn't act like I was sweating it either, especially around the boys. For the next hour, no one said anything more about Violet. Then I brought her up.

"Anyone see Vi?"

"Aah," grunted Face and Kit laughed nervously.

"What?" I asked.

"Not good, not good, not good," replied Kit as he paced back and forth, balancing on a curb and biting his fingernails, giggling to himself.

"Don't look at me, man," Flip smiled tensely.

"Uh, Kelly, remember that talk we had when you first started, uh, going out with Violet?" Remmy started to laugh.

"There's been a party for like two weeks straight at Paula's house." Vick cleared his throat and spit.

"I know. Yeah, so?"

"So that's where Violet's been."

"And all the Landbury kids who hate us," added Kit. "They're all chilling at Paula's house."

"I know that," I said. "Whatever. So?"

Vick shrugged. "We fucking warned you, dude."

"I can still talk to her."

"Dude, she's gone," said Vick. "You don't want that anymore."

"Trust us, Kelly," said Remmy. "It's better to leave that alone now."

"Why?"

Kit took a deep breath. "We heard, uh, Tank and Otis had their fun with Violet and when they were done, probably some of the Cincity boys did, too."

When I heard his words, my heart sank. How could I be so stupid to let her get away?

Remmy shook his head. "That's just the way she is."

"They've been fucked up, drinking and snorting shit for two weeks," quipped Kit.

They were quiet for a while and then started talking again. Vick had a skateboard and was getting pissed off because he couldn't land a kickflip. I knew they wouldn't lie about these things. Things like this happened or they didn't. There was no reason to make it up.

Still, it took me a while before it really hit me: There would be no getting back together. After what they told me, I couldn't get back with her no matter how much I wanted to. I slumped back over and heard Kit saying, "It's like speed... meth. They have mescaline and this shit called K. I heard it fucks you up!"

"Who has that?"

"Landbury kids, Cincity..."

"Fuck!" I yelled. "Fuck that bitch Paula!"

"Why Paula?"

"Cause she's always around when Violet and I start to fight."

"Forget about her," Vick said putting his arm around my shoulder. "Have the last 40! Drink up! They're plenty of other pigs left in the sea!"

"You guys hear about Mud?" Remmy asked.

"Who?" Kit asked.

"This nasty fuck they call Mud, cause he eats anything anyone dares him to. The more disgusting it is, the faster he gobbles it up. He's a real freak show," Remmy explained. "He's visiting from New Mexico. Someone invited him to Paula's party and he's been hanging around there even since."

"Uh, Kelly?" Remmy asked hesitantly.

"Yeah."

"You haven't heard the news yet." Remmy seemed to say it in slow motion, "Violet hooked up with Mud. He's like her new boyfriend or something."

"Oh shit!" said Kit and I shut my eyes in disbelief.

"What?" I asked painfully. I tried to convince myself that this wasn't happening. It was all just a bad dream and soon I'd wake up and everything would be back to normal again. They had been right. When it was my turn to go down, Violet would dream up something extra special for me. The grand finale, the boys said, was that Violet was moving to New Mexico with Mud.

"Look at the bright side, Kelly," smiled Remmy. "She wasn't raped this time."

"No, that was last month!" Kit cackled his stupid laugh and I glared at him.

I tossed the rock I was juggling at a tree. "She's moving to New Mexico with this weirdo?" I looked back and forth between Remmy and Vick, who sat on the curb on either side of me. This was as sympathetic as they were going to get. Vick never gave a shit about Violet but it wasn't any secret that Remmy had cared about her.

"Dude, don't sweat it," Remmy said. "Violet and I had been going out for like five months when she got drunk and cheated on me with a football player!"

"Uh, this might be a little worse," emphasized Kit.

"Just drop it," I mumbled.

"Why don't we hit the bootlegger before the old man passes out for the night?" Remmy suggested. "Kelly looks like he needs a drink."

"Fuck it, let's go," I agreed.

"Where?" asked Vick.

"The party," I answered.

"What, Paula 's party?" Kit asked.

"Yeah."

"Dude, do I need to remind you that everybody who wants to kill us is probably there right now? Tank, Otis, Bram…"

"If you don't want to go, don't go!" I shouted at him.

"I'm down," Flip said casually.

"But I need to take care of something first."

"What?" Flip asked.

"You'll see," I promised.

Two hours later, we had finished and loaded it into the trunk of the car.

"You're really fucking crazy," Remmy said when he caught my eye.

"No, this is genius!" argued Face.

"We're going to die!" said Kit as I shut the trunk.

Paula's house was on a cul-de-sac. We parked the car facing out for a quick getaway. Face and I opened the trunk and began unloading the supplies as Vick, Flip, and Kit furtively dispersed into the dark. We expected most of the doors to be unlocked, due to the built-in security force of hoodlums walking in and out, who were by now probably passed out downstairs.

The plan was to check the place out, taking note of who was where. Vick, Remmy, and Kit would go around back and Flip, Face and I would try the front doors. We stashed the supplies by the front door that was unlocked as expected. We snuck in and went downstairs, startling each other in the darkness of the staircase.

The basement had been renovated and transformed into one gigantic bedroom. Heavy breathing and the glow from the static TV urged us on. We stepped over bodies and blankets that littered the carpet.

"Where's Violet?" I whispered.

"I think she sleeps upstairs," mouthed Remmy, who then leaned forward and added, "There's a keg of beer over there! Gimme a hand!" Kit crept over and they each grabbed a handle and lifted it up out of the melted ice water and carried it to the door, banging it on their shins. They began cursing each other in tiny whispers.

"Stop swinging it against my legs, you dickhead."

"I'm not, bitch. Just pick the thing up, you wimp."

Then, from among the masses of blankets, someone began to stir.

"Shhh!" hushed Remmy and Kit responded the same way.

"Shhh!" Vick sounded from the bottom of the basement stairs, posed ready to run up.

A girl opened two big blue eyes and blinked at Kit and Remmy. Remmy smiled at her. "Paula wants us to take this keg outside cause, uh uh, it's leaking." We all froze, not breathing, hoping she wouldn't notice the lot of us and, sure enough, she turned to her other side and went back to sleep. Remmy and Kit hiked the beer up the stairs and lugged it out to our car.

Meanwhile upstairs, Flip took a fat paint-marker and wrote across the living room wall:

When Remmy and Kit returned, they cocked their heads to one side and then to the other as they stared at the words. Vick joined them in their evaluation of which graffiti letters were fucked up.

"The M needed to be wider," Vick told Flip.

"And you fucked that E up right there," offered Remmy.

"You try to do something better," Flip dared them.

"Give me that." Remmy grabbed the marker and began to tag all the walls.

"Where the hell is Face?" I asked the others.

"He went outside, I think," said Kit.

I walked out front to see Face standing by the supplies, smoking a cigarette. I picked the buckets up, one in each hand, and walked past my grinning buddies who held the front door open and followed me back in. I climbed the stairs and peered into each bedroom as I moved down the hall until I saw Violet, lying there next to the snoring Mud Man, who didn't look at all like I expected. He was going slightly bald and had a patchy beard, and wore tight jeans and a ripped Bud tee shirt.

I turned toward the others. "Hit the lights when I say when."

I raised one of the buckets filled with carefully-crafted Poontang, the recipe I had learned from Geo. My boys began to chuckle at the sight of me swinging the bucket back and forth like a giant pendulum over the sleeping kids who had no idea what was about to happen. "Hit the lights!" I shouted.

"It's showtime!" Flip said, as I let the chunky stew fly out of the bucket. For a moment, it seemed to freeze over Violet, as if it were checking her out before allowing itself to cover her like a blanket of filth.

"Ohhh euuuu!" Violet sat straight up, blinking through the poontang and the bright lights that stung her eyes. Completely baffled by the source of the attack or the reason why, she began to hit Mud out of instinct. My boys howled with laughter, tripping over each other as they ran down the hallway and then back again, wanting to escape but not wanting to miss the show.

"Arrghhh!" Mud shuddered and twitched but continued to snore. Being covered with Poontang was not enough to stir the Mud Man from his sleep. Meanwhile Violet whimpered as she tried to spit the Poontang out of her mouth and wipe it from her eyes.

"Oh my god, what did you do?" she asked and again hit Mud who groaned pathetically, "Leave meeee lone."

Paula shouted out from her bedroom, "Alright, what's going on out there? It's way too late for this shit!"

Violet pulled herself out of her stupor and peered up at me, blinking her eyes, just as I swung the next bucket over her head and let it fly, covering her and Mud with the next layer of Poontang. To my surprise, Mud chuckled, "Yo, what the fuck man! Who is fucking around, man?"

Violet wiped her eyes again, grasping the situation. "You fucking asshole, Kelly! I can't fucking believe you!"

Mud Man jumped up. "What the fuck, dude!" He then turned to Violet and screamed, "Who the fuck is that? Is that your boyfriend, dude?"

He then went for me but one of his legs got caught up in the soaked sheets and he ended up doing a face plant on the floor. He groaned when I began to stomp him, and Violet stood up on the bed and howled.

She was wearing one of my tee shirts and tears were streaming down her face, and when our eyes connected, it was as if she pulled the pain out from my drunken soul, and I wanted to start crying, too, but I tried my best to swallow it down and turn it into rage.

"WHAT ARE YOU DOING?" I shouted back at Violet, my voice shaky. "Why?" I asked, swallowing the huge lump in my throat and only managing to point at Mud on the floor, "With that?" I suddenly knew that if I hung around any more I would end up hugging her, crying and covered with poontang, and that would've fucked everything up. I backed up into Vick, whose expression went suddenly serious as he read my eyes.

"Let's go!" Vick shouted and shoved me into the hall.

Paula burst out of her parents' room, screaming, "WHAT THE FUCK ARE YOU GUYS DOING HERE!" Paula ran across the hall into Violet's room and screamed behind us, "OH MY FUCKING GOD, YOU ASSHOLES ARE GOING TO PAY FOR THIS!"

I jumped down the steps behind my boys, who laughed hysterically. I then saw Kit struggling to keep the Landbury kids, awaken by the screams, from breaking through the basement door.

"Come on!" I shouted as I leapt down the stairs and took off running through the front door. We charged down the long driveway, heading for our car. Halfway down, I heard a grunt and the sound of bodies hitting pavement, and I looked behind to see that Tank had caught Face and dragged him down. They crashed on the driveway and went rolling.

"Shit!" I skidded to a stop and spun around, just in time to see Otis jump over them and sail through the air. I ducked and let him flip over me. He groaned when he hit the drive, but before he could stand I booted him in the ribs. A few feet behind, Tank had draped an arm around Face's neck and was punching him. I ran over, stomping Tank down, giving Face the chance to get back on his feet. Then I was on my back, looking up at the stars because Bram had kicked me in the head. I tried to get up, but he kept on kicking me. I thought that I was done for, but then Bram was slammed away and Flip pulled me to my feet. I glanced back at the house, seeing more figures swarming out, pulling on shoes or pants, falling over in the process, tripping down the steps, and screaming for our blood. We were lucky they were shit-faced and moving like crap.

"Come on!" We jumped over the fallen bodies and took off running down the driveway toward the car that Kit had already fired up and was slowly rolling away with the doors hanging open.

"Hurry up!" Remmy screamed, leaning out the door.

From the corner of my eye, I saw more shadows, much larger, looming out of the basement door and running across the yard and down the grassy embankment to cut us off. They had a shorter distance to run and were quickly catching up. I recognized Trash out front, gritting his teeth in a murderous glare, followed by

Pete and two other Cincity boys I didn't even care to identify. I jumped into the back seat, where Remmy and Flip dragged me in, and then turned to reach out for Face who made it only halfway in, falling on his stomach on the floor with his feet still dragging the road. Suddenly, Cincity were running all around us, screaming and banging on the windows, smashing one. Finally, Kit picked up speed and we began to dust them when a single gunshot fired and shattered the rear window.

"They're fucking shooting at us!" laughed Vick from the front seat.

"Holy shit!" Kit ducked down and hit the gas, leaving his window and the Cincity boys behind.

"Hey, I lost my shoe!" Face cried out.

"Fuck your shoe!" Kit howled in fear, smashing down on the gas and cursing the old car as it got going. "My windows! My mom is going to kill me!"

"Shut the door!" Remmy shouted after we heaved Face in.

"Those kids are fucking crazy! We're all fucking dead, you know that, right?" Kit cried as we hit the main road. "What were you thinking about, Kelly? I thought you were going to throw some poontang at their house maybe! Not on them while they slept!"

"This isn't funny! They saw our faces!" added Flip.

"So what? We got their beer," smiled Face.

Chapter 11: Skinheads

"What's up Egan?" Flip asked.

"Don't give me any of that what's up shit. You know what the fuck's up!" Egan was sweaty and his eyes beady.

"Are you alright, Egan?" Vick asked.

"You better not worry about me!" He glared at Vick through squinted eyes and turned back to Flip. He picked him up by his throat and started screaming again.

"So what exactly were you idiots thinking when you decided to pull that shit and crash Shelly's party anyway? Didn't you know who was there?"

"It wasn't just me," Flip complained, his voice sounding elfish through squished vocal cords.

"I'm talking to all of you!" Egan bellowed. "Don't think for a second that any of you are going to get off easy." He then turned to Connor and Rook and yelled, "Get them up here! Line those clowns up!" Connor and Rook strolled up like cops and shoved Remmy, Kit, and Vick against the wall next to the crucified Flip.

"Whose idea was it to come up with this shit?"

"It was Kelly's deal!" Flip squeaked, trying his best to smile even though his face was turning purple. "He was all tripping about Violet hooking up with Mud!"

"Don't even mention that girl's name, especially when you are giving any type of reason!"

Egan let go of Flip, who dropped to his feet and began coughing, rubbing his neck, where Egan had tethered him two feet off the ground.

"You, get over here!" Egan shouted and pointed a finger at me. I moved forward, looking down before feeling myself ski across the floor. Then I was ripped off the ground, as it was my turn to hang on the wall.

"I stuck my neck out on the line for you morons! Everyone else wants to kill you! They can't just let this slide! You made em look bad!"

"Otis and Tank started it by driving down–" Kit tried to explain.

"What?" Egan screamed. "I don't give a fuck about them! I'm talking about Cincity! You stole Cincity's fucking beer! I'm talking about hospital bills that you won't ever be able to pay."

"Electric wheelchairs and baby food," added Connor.

"Do you understand what we're saying to you?"

I glanced at Vick and Remmy, who stood solemnly by staring at the floor.

"Egan!" Rook said.

"What?" he snapped.

"It's the mall cops. Drop the kid." Egan dropped me on my feet. Coughing, I was dragged down the nearby service hallway, a plain concrete walk that eventually led into the daylight. We were shoved through the parking lot toward Egan's van, a beat-up and ominous-looking vehicle with nothing but two front seats and a stained layer of red carpet stretching across the back.

We climbed in and the doors slammed behind us. Connor and Egan sat in the front, and Rook took the only folding chair in the back, shaking his head.

"So how you been, Vick? How's the band?"

"Sucks. I think we're gonna break up."

"Why?"

"We haven't been practicing and there's no place left for a show."

"Don't break up. Everyone breaks up and that sucks."

"Rook," said Connor.

"What?"

"Don't be cool to them. They're in a heap of shit!"

"Don't worry about what I'm doing, Connor!"

We drove onto the highway and finally Kit, looking like he was about to lose it, spoke up in cracked voice, "Where are we going?" Rook glanced at Kit and then shrugged.

"We're not going to New York, are we?" he persisted.

"You'll be straight." Rook stared ahead.

"Oh shit, oh shit, oh shit," Kit repeated.

"Hey Kit!" snapped Connor.

"Yeah," Kit answered meekly.

"Shut up!"

"Oh shit."

We drove for fifteen minutes along the interstate. Egan took Exit 19 and pulled into a gas station to use the payphone. After a brief conversation, he hung up, got back in the van, and drove to a run-down apartment complex.

"Rook, let em know we're here," Egan commanded.

Rook knocked on the iron gate numbered 237, and it opened instantly. A guy approached, seeming larger than the doorway, and signaled to the van.

"Alright, get out," Connor growled and, in single file led by Kit, we trudged through the gate. The giant glared down like he wanted to step on us.

Kit tapped Egan's shoulder and begged for mercy but Egan just shrugged him off.

"You're just going to make it worse on yourselves," Rook explained.

"What's up, Ogre?" Connor slapped the big guy's paw and blocked the sun with his hand as he gazed up at the beast. "I like haven't seen you in months."

"I just got out of the cooler," Ogre shrugged, his voice sounding like a set of bass woofers.

"What were ya in for this time?" Connor asked.

"Murder! I caught some kids stealing my beer."

Both Egan and Connor frowned down upon us, fixing us with a look of disgust until Egan shoved us forward.

Inside the dark apartment, it stunk like beer. I immediately recognized the Cincity Leech Mob: the big dude named Doc, then Pete, and then Trash and Stanley, who sat in the front room, sniffing lines. Bull walked out screaming from one of the back rooms, flexing his tattooed fingers in our faces and swearing how dead we were.

Egan slapped the back of my head as we were all propelled towards the cellar door. Kit began to hyperventilate.

"What's down there?" Vick asked, trying to mask his fear.

"Pain," promised Doc.

"We got to get rid of the bodies. They've seen too much," said Bull, shaking his head.

"Ah, they won't say anything," Egan promised.

"Egan, ya know I love ya, but I can't do it, not this time. We got to get rid of the bodies," bellowed Ogre. "Are the holes already dug downstairs?"

"Come on, dudes. We'll get you another keg—we'll get ya two, three," pleaded Kit.

Bull opened the cellar door and said, "Get downstairs!"

Nobody moved.

"Go on!" Egan said, pushing Kit, who was first in line.

"Egan, come on man," Kit cried.

Egan looked expressionless.

"Just get your asses down there!" Bull shoved us toward the cellar stairs. Downstairs, they ordered us to line up as they all cracked their knuckles and measured their fists to our faces. When we were good and terrified, they laughed till their sides split. They told us we had to clean out the cellar, taking trips out to the dumpster, and then paint the basement while they drank beer upstairs, stopping only to scream threats that we better be doing a good job.

Five hours later, when we were done, they checked out our work and then directed us upstairs. Doc counted what looked like prescription pills, before looking thoughtfully at us.

"Do these guys want any?" Doc asked.

"No," Connor answered quickly.

"They're all broke anyway," Egan said.

"I have K and acid, too. That's only five bucks a hit," offered Pete.

"Dude, these kids are like twelve, man," said Rook. "Don't sell em nothing."

"Check this out." Egan handed a record to me. "This is Despair's old album cover. Have you seen this picture?"

On the cover was unmistakably Violet, in Vick's car on the highway, lifting her shirt and flashing her tits. This time I started to laugh.

✦

By the time Despair took the stage at the Night Breed, Obi was the only one sober. Cecil and Casey forgot which song they were playing, and Egan zoned out on the mic. The band was playing like shit, and Egan took it out on the first stage diver who ran into him, picking him up and throwing him back into the crowd.

Vick tapped me on the shoulder. "Check out who's here."

I followed Vick's gaze to see Geo at the edge of the club. When he saw us, he waved and headed right over.

"What's up, Geo?"

"Hello, Vick," Geo said and then turned to me. "I was wondering if I would see you here."

"You get in trouble for that party?" I asked.

"Yeah, my parents had to pay that bitch like eight thousand dollars plus medical to keep her from suing us!" Geo wheezed with laughter.

"Come on, let's go over by the pit."

"No way I'm getting in there," Geo shook his head. "I don't think it's fun getting punched in the face."

"Just stand at the edge man," I said.

"Nah, I'm cool here!"

"Alright, Geo." We slapped his hand and shoved back through the crowd toward the front.

Egan scowled at the audience, wearing shades to hide his trippy eyes. "I'm sorry that my band is playing like shit tonight," Egan yelled into the mic, pacing back and forth. He then turned to Cecil, who glared back.

"What?" Egan exclaimed. "You are! And what the fuck, Casey?"

"And you aren't?" Casey argued back. "You're all slurring on the mic and I thought you said you'd get this shit fixed! It still sounds like shit!"

"All our equipment sucks!" Cecil yelled in agreement. "I can't play with all this feedback!"

"I'm not slurring!" Egan raised the microphone. "This next one is Death Camp 66! One, two, three–,

> The breaking point brings us down
> But for now we slowly drown
> Bowing down to the yellow crown
> The machine astounds
> Spitting out junk to be found
> To build the urban mound
> Letting ourselves be bound…"

Egan reached out the mic for the crowds, who shouted the next line,

> "Shit we don't want
> Shit we don't need!"

Egan nodded and then screamed the next verse,

> "And the cause is lost
> In the cost of our hearts
> Lives poisoned and burned
> Raped and turned,
> Cut and churned,

Tortured to death,

Waiting for that day,

When we'll be born…"

Egan reached the mic out into the crowds, who again who faithfully yelled,

"Into Death Camp 66!"

After getting the support of the crowd, Despair started to sound better until the feedback screeched out again and drowned out the instruments. Cecil and Casey stopped playing and stared at the amps as if they were about to explode, and Hank, the drummer, slowed down as Egan turned red and screamed "WHAT THE FUCK" into the microphone, causing even more feedback. Enraged, Egan picked up the mic-stand, an ancient iron thing that looked as though it had been rusting in someone's basement for the last fifty years. Egan threw the mic aside and whipped the stand around in circles over his head. Everyone stared in awe at Egan, center stage, swearing and swinging the mic stand around like a war club. Then he let it go.

It sailed high over the audience's heads before beginning its downward arch. I traced its path and saw Geo standing directly underneath its point of contact. Everyone moved out of its way–I don't know why Geo failed to see the missile coming straight at him. I yelled "HEY LOOK OUT!" but my voice was drowned out by all the feedback from the amps. At the last second, Geo saw it and tried to step aside but it was too late. The thing had flown halfway across the room and crash landed into his face!

A loud clanking noise sounded over the feedback and Geo's knees buckled and he sank in slow motion onto the floor. Tank and Otis started dying, falling over laughing. I walked over and knelt by Geo's side. His left eye was swelling shut as blood gushed from his gaping brow.

"Geo, Geo, can you hear me?" I asked and he started to groan. He saw us standing over him and tried to sit up, looking almost embarrassed and holding his head in pain.

"No Geo, stay put, man," I said, laying a hand on his shoulder. The manager ran up screaming at Egan who, enraged, kicked the amp over next.

"Fuck!" Egan yelled and stared out at the audience to where his mic stand landed.

"Yeah, fuck it all up!" some skinny idiot screamed from the audience.

Egan jumped off the stage and grabbed the kid's neck. He was choking the shit out of him until Gavin and Connor pulled Egan back and others wrenched his fingers away, loosening his grip on the kid's neck. The bouncers crashed into Egan, knocking him down.

"What happened?" Geo asked. "What hit me? Was I standing too close to the pit?"

"No man, the microphone stand hit you," I said, feeling bad.

"Hey man, are you alright!" Vick ran up beside us.

Geo squinted up at me, looking confused. "How did the microphone stand hit me?" he asked and then started to laugh, which apparently hurt, because he flinched.

"Egan was swinging it around and must've just lost control of it."

"He threw a microphone stand at me? Oh man," Geo said.

"He's been doing way too much of that shit," replied Vick, who looked over his shoulder at Egan, still going at it with the bouncers.

✦

"So kids were frequently getting hurt at hardcore shows?" Dr. Gildmore asked.

"Yeah, especially at the last one I went to."

"Where was this?"

"Dismay was playing at The Roadhouse."

"Is that a bar?" Gildmore asked.

"Yeah, everybody was messed up—drugs, too."

"Where is it?"

"In New York."

"Do you remember the date?"

"Around the end of July."

"So it was right before you were arrested and admitted as a patient here."

"I guess. Jonah called me for the first time all summer and I told him about the show at The Roadhouse and he wanted to go."

✦

The Roadhouse was set back a hundred yards from the highway. Marked on either side with two iron pillars, the narrow entrance was basically a bridge over the drainage ditch that ran down an embankment and along the highway. Isolated by woods on one side and the steep embankment on the other, the club was virtually cut off from everything–except for an old decaying brick factory that loomed at the top of the ridge.

Tonight, the dirt parking lot was packed with beat-up hatchbacks and pickup trucks. Jonah finally found a space at the back of the joint, in the last row of cars where a crew of skin-byrds wearing bowling shirts and cargo pants leaned against a rusty Ford pickup. The toughest chick had a black hooded sweatshirt zipped down the front, exposing a red bra through a sleeveless, wife beater tee shirt. Her head was shaved except for her bangs, ten inches long, dyed scarlet, and gelled back. They leaned to stare into our car as we drove by, trying to see if they recognized anyone as they glared inside.

"Skinhead bitches," mumbled Jonah.

"The red head is kind of hot, for a skin-byrd," I laughed.

"Then she's all yours."

We shut the doors and Jonah chirped the alarm. "Now don't go saying anything to them. I don't want my car getting fucked up tonight."

We walked along the lot, past the chicks who talked shit for us.

"Check out the studs…"

"What band ya here for, kid?"

Jonah ignored them and made it a point to walk quickly as he scanned the lot for familiar cars.

"There's Remmy," I said, seeing the kid stumbling toward the front doors.

"What's going on, Remmy?" Jonah asked. "Who's here?"

"Like everybody."

"Yeah, I see." Jonah glanced toward four skins standing at the outdoor payphones acting like they were waiting for an important call. Remmy turned his head and looked out at the street as a car bottomed out, sparks flying. The car roared into the dirt parking lot and came to a grinding stop. Its rusty doors squawked open, a beer bottle fell out and shattered, and a guy belched as the Cincity Leech Mob emerged.

"Look at these chumps, getting in line like good lil boys," Bull clowned us.

"I'm not in a rush to get in. I don't think I even want to," Jonah countered but the Cincity guys just laughed.

"So what's up?" Bull probed us with black, drug-ridden eyes. "Where's Egan?"

"I dunno," I answered. "We haven't been in."

"Seriously, you better be careful. Empire State Skinheads have been jumping kids all over the place," Trash warned.

"Yeah, I heard," Remmy said.

Stanley scowled at us. "Man, fuck these kids. Bull, let's go in."

"Hold on a second, Stanley," said Bull. "What did you hear?"

"Nothing much." Remmy frowned. "There was a fight or something."

"Some of you, uh, Egan's kids, got jumped by the Empire State Skins, that's what," Bull explained.

"*Egan's kids?*" repeated Jonah. "That sounds like a charity or something."

"It is," said Doc as the others cackled.

"Who from the Landbury Leech Mob?" Jonah asked.

"Some Chinese dude and that other kid Egan always hangs with. What's his name?" Bull snapped his fingers, trying to remember.

"Bram."

"Yeah, those two kids whipped their asses!" Bull spit. "Made the skins look real stupid."

"It was a good thing the skins were drunk," mumbled Stanley, running his hand over his shaved head. "Otherwise it might have turned out different."

"We can't get your back over this one. We run into the Empire State Skinheads way too much at the shows out here to start a war over your fucking problems." Bull slowly shook his head and looked at Trash, whose grin sported missing teeth.

"Let's go in, Bull!" Stanley said again.

"Shut up!" Bull snapped at his boy.

"The Empire has been head-hunting lately." Pete stepped forward and got in my face. "Beating little punks like you down all over the place."

"And four other Landbury skaters got jumped last night in New York," Bull added. "On the border of Bog Creek–got all fucked up."

"Maybe you all should stay in Connecticut from now on!" Stanley spit when he talked.

Bull lowered his voice, "Usually we'd help ya out–but only cause you're cool with Egan." He looked to the side. "Still we can't get in a war we can't finish. If we got involved, people would die, and then we'd go back to jail. Ogre, Doc, and Trash are still on parole." Trash glared at him but Bull laughed, "Look, just tell Egan that we need ta see em, can ya handle that?" Bull bumped into Jonah and then cut the line. The bouncers scurried, patting them down, and then stamped their hands. We watched as Cincity passed into the dark interior of the club.

"Did I tell you Bull gave me a black eye?" Remmy broke the silence.

"No, when?"

"Last show at The Nightbreed."

Inside the club, we saw that Egan, Connor, and Rook had already faced off against a group of older skinheads with Cincity standing between them. Bull did most of the talking and, after some coaxing, just about forced Egan to shake hands with a skinhead wearing a black trench coat. They stood, an army behind each, like emissaries initiating a temporary truce. The meeting quickly concluded and both gangs broke apart. The chief skinhead winked a scarred, film-covered eye at Egan, while another skinhead leaned forward to mutter something into his boss' ear.

Moments later, Otis bumped into me.

"What's up, Otis?" I asked.

"Egan wants to see everyone, now!" He motioned to where the Mob had already begun to assemble and shoved us as he shuffled past.

"Asshole," Jonah muttered and then looked at me. "Alright, let's go see."

"Look," Egan began. "We had a talk with the Empire and it's been agreed. We'll put whatever beefs we got on ice! At least until after the show! Nobody wants to get kicked out of here tonight, especially not Despair! We plan to go on stage and get paid. Now does anyone not understand me?" He glared around at each of us. "Good! I don't want anyone taking anything personal in the mosh pit! That's all. Fuck off."

Both crews kept things cool while the first band performed. Between the sets, all that was heard was the loud buzz of voices as kids snuck drinks from metal flasks or sniffed lines off tables. When the second band, Hate Craft, opened up, an explosion of sound razed the joint with their roadies still on stage.

A mess of bodies flew into violent motion and tried to take over the pit. Out of nowhere Egan appeared, plowing through the mosh pit and heaving bodies aside like he was the Juggernaut. Then, from the dark perimeter of the club, a tall, muscular skinhead shoved his way into the pit and made a beeline for Egan. He threw an elbow into Egan's grill. Egan staggered, cupped the side of his face, and checked his hand for blood.

"You want me to get this?" Connor asked.

"Nah, forget it." Egan smiled and passively stared across the club before lunging at the 250 pound skinhead. Ignited, both gangs began shoving each other. Rook,

Gavin, and Connor dragged Egan back before he broke any more of his own rules.

"What the fuck, Egan?" Bull screamed. "Get him over here!" he yelled to Cincity, who surrounded Egan and ushered him back to their table, supplying him with beer until Cecil, Obi, and Hank showed up.

"Where the hell have you been?" Egan screamed.

"Are you kidding, Egan!" shouted Obi. "You're lucky I'm here!"

"For real, Egan!" Cecil glanced around nervously, "I'm not hanging around here any longer than I have to."

"We're up next!" Egan shouted. "Jasper! Aaron! We're setting up!"

Despair then took the stage as the third band of the night. Egan staggered out, continuing to shout orders at Cecil and Obi. After a sound check, Despair was ready. A mix of boos and applause jumbled into one disturbing drone. The Empire stood glowering with arms crossed while others turned their backs on Despair. Egan rolled his eyes and adjusted the microphone as the crowds held up middle fingers and tried to boo them off stage.

"Check it out," Egan began by saying. "If we got some problems, it is what it is. But this is a hardcore show and nothing should be taken personal in the pit. We got to save that shit for the street!"

"Yeah, save that shit for the niggers!" shouted someone in the audience, and a cheer rose up that Egan turned his back on. He looked at Cecil and said something. Cecil twisted his lip and partially shrugged, not at all happy being the only black guy in a swamp of skinheads but he took it out on his guitar instead. Despair kicked in with their first track and Egan screamed into the mic. The pit broke into a frenzy. The Leech Mob crashed into the skinheads, who were hyped up on some shit and whipping their arms around. Combatants had to be pried apart from mangling each other. Some skinheads even kicked each other's asses, settling personal feuds.

Vick flew out of the pit and stood on the sidelines. His eyes were bugged out and he appeared dazed, like he'd just seen hell. He glanced at me with fearful eyes and touched the side of his swollen red face. "Someone hit me right here." Half his earrings had been pulled out of his ear, leaving a string of bloody holes. Vick momentarily clung to me for support but jumped back in, was knocked right back out, and finally crashed to the other side.

Instantly, a fat skinhead, sweating grain alcohol, plowed into Otis. Both fell over. The drunk took his time getting up, pressing Otis's face down as he slowly stood up. Connor ran over and shoved the drunk off his feet as some others jumped in. In the chaos, Egan dropped the mic and grabbed the skinhead from behind and threw him against an amp.

"Shit, what the fuck man!" Obi screamed as he jumped back to avoid the skinhead, who quickly recovered and taunted Egan on. Egan jumped off stage and the skinhead charged forward, kicking up a steel-toe boot into Egan's leg. Egan flinched back but then lunged forward, grabbing him and ramming his head into the stage, blood spewing from his forehead.

By then, bouncers had pried their way in and surrounded the bloody scene. One, a biker named Harley, grabbed Egan in a chokehold and dragged him back. Another skinhead saw his opportunity and attacked Egan, punching him in the face while his arms were held back. The bouncer defensively spun Egan around as another bouncer jammed the skinhead back.

"Ah shit! Get Marty!" the bouncer shouted. "You think you got him enough?" he sarcastically asked Egan. "Get the fuck back!" he screamed at the crowd. "Tiny! Get those kids back!" he commanded another bouncer, 500 pounds and wearing suspenders.

Cecil quickly unplugged his guitar and fumbled with the case while Obi copied, more than ready to get out of there. Hank, the drummer, stood up with a stick in each hand, looking stoned and confused. Two younger skinheads, mean and drunk, crept up toward Egan.

"You two get over here where I can see you!" Tiny screamed, manhandling them away. "You want to get 86'd?"

Suddenly, an electric current seemed to surge through the bloody goon on the floor and he began shaking. The audience pointed down at their fallen comrade, shouting in anger, while Bull loomed up behind Egan, shaking his head.

"I knew this was a bad idea!"

"This was the only show we could get!" Egan argued.

Bull patted him on the shoulder. "Now you deal with it."

"Yeah, it's your funeral, man," hissed Trash.

"Fuck you, Trash," Otis sneered as the Cincity Mob departed, leaving the skinhead crowd unchecked. More bouncers pushed in, nervously chewing gum and waiting for the next move.

"What should I do with this guy, Harley?" the fat bouncer asked.

"Egan's not going anywhere! Now, first things first! Make sure that guy is breathing!!"

"But he's on his face."

"Alright, get back and give this guy some room!"

The crowd barely moved.

"Tiny, you grab his legs. Chris, you grab his arms and I'll keep his neck aligned!" They counted to three and then flipped the skinhead on his back. Harley began lightly slapping him and yelling into his face. "Breathe motherfucker, breathe! WAKE UP DUDE!" He slapped him again and the skinhead sucked in some air and coughed.

"Marty is going to have to talk to you about this fuck up, Egan," Harley warned as a little man ran up.

"Coming through, hot stuff! Get the hell out of my way! Watch it buddy or you're out of here!" The club manager pushed his way through the crowds and walked up to Egan.

"What I *should do* is let the cops handle this. Kick your band out of here for good and not pay you a dime for all the trouble you caused!"

"All the trouble I caused?" Egan exclaimed in disbelief. "Marty, what the fuck? Didn't you see this asshole fucking with our shit the whole time? He was getting on the stage and tackling my friends so I had to put a stop to it."

"Wait a minute! That's all I see you kids doing! Jumping on the stage and beating each other up! Anyway, it's not your job to keep order! You wouldn't know how! That's what I've hired all these guys for!" Marty yelled. "For security!"

"But your bouncers weren't doing shit!" Egan argued.

Marty turned and stared at one of the bouncers. "What the hell is he talking about, Harley?"

"I was posted at the door. I couldn't see what was going on back here. I got here as soon as I realized something was up."

"Well who the hell was supposed to be down near the stage? Who wasn't doing their goddamn job?"

"We didn't see nothing!" Tiny said, holding up the bleeding skinhead.

"Look at this fucking guy. You want me to call an ambulance?"

Another skinhead charged in from the crowds, swinging at Egan.

"And get these crazy fucks out of here!" Marty shouted at the security guards. "I can't hear myself think!" He ran his fingers through his grey afro. "You kids act like you got two brain cells left in your goddamn heads and you're getting worse all the time!!"

"Let's go!" Harley shouted but to no one in particular.

"What are you doing standing there? Egan's out of here, too! I've made up my mind! And you won't be getting anything in the form of payment out of me! You get it? NO EL DINERO!" The owner rubbed his pinched fingers together and stormed off before spinning around and announcing, "Just be glad I'm not calling the fucking cops and shutting the club down!"

As the bouncers pushed Egan toward the doors, two guys moved out from the shadows—one with a ponytail and a swastika tattooed on his neck, and the other a skinhead in a black trench coat. The trench coat whispered something to Egan, who yelled back, and instantly both crews were back in each other's faces. The trench coat's left eye began to twitch. "Not now! Get the hell back, you fucking idiots!" he shouted at his boys. "We'll handle this later!"

"God dammit!" the manager screamed. "You want the cops down here! Enough of this bullshit! Harley! Tiny! Ed! I want these two gangs out of here!" He pointed at the Leech Mob. "Especially him, him and him, and where the hell did he go? Him over there! I want them all out!"

The trench coat grinned as they shoved Egan and the others out the door.

Aaron, who'd been elected roadie for the night, jumped on stage and asked Obi and Cecil what they wanted him to take out first.

"Just help Hank get his drums off stage."

"I don't know what Egan is getting us into!" Obi barked.

"And now Egan is getting kicked out! SHIT!" swore Cecil. "Where's the van parked anyway?"

"It's way in the back," said Casey.

"I know where it is," Aaron offered. "Let's hurry up and get the equipment out there!"

While Despair was packing, Chill Factor began setting up on stage. When they started their set, the skinheads roared into chaos. Moshing became suicidal as they turned on each other like a bunch of rabid dogs, kicking steel toes and throwing wild punches.

Aaron walked up to Jonah and me, wiping the sweat off his face. "You think you can help me carry some of this stuff out? Egan's van is way the hell across the lot!"

"Yeah alright," I said and followed Aaron behind the stage, where Cecil, Obi and Hank waited nervously with their equipment.

Carrying drums, amps, and duffle bags, we took trips all the way around the back of the club and across the parking lot to Egan's van, where he, Connor, and

Casey waited.

"You could at least meet us halfway." Aaron complained.

"Shut up, dude. Do you wanna get paid or not?" Egan snapped.

"Dude, you heard what Marty said! None of us are getting paid."

"We're getting paid, maybe not tonight, but we are getting paid! So I don't want to hear your shit," Egan argued. "You got everything fucked up back here anyway. I got to re-arrange the van every time you bring something out!"

Aaron glared at Egan. "What do you want me to do? Everything while you just stand around?"

"Give it a rest, would ya, Aaron?" sighed Connor. "You know it's been a messed up night for us all."

We went back into the club to get the last of the equipment. By this time, Chill Factor was just about to do another song, but the manager hit the lights, flooding the once pitch-dark joint with bright metal halogens. Marty ran up onto the stage clapping his hands, but Chill Factor flicked him off.

"Let's hear it for Chill Factor!" he exclaimed into the microphone. The crowd just stood there, shielding their eyes that were blinded by the lights, and scowled up at him. Now the darkness wasn't hiding their charming faces anymore and the little man gulped. "We're closing down, so I need everyone to proceed to one of the exits. Thank you for coming and we'll be reopened next weekend." He looked around anxiously but nobody moved.

"Fuck you, man, it's still early!" someone shouted.

"What time is it?" I asked Jonah, who looked at his pager.

"It's 12:20. They usually close around one."

Then the crowd began to chant, "WE WONT GO! WE WONT GO! WE WONT GO!" Then the chant morphed into "SUCK OUR ASS! SUCK OUR ASS! SUCK OUR ASS!" and continued until the manager ran back up to the microphone, waving his arms in the air.

"Everyone shut up, I mean, uh, please, we have to close a little early tonight! We're having some, uh, technical problems! But we'll be open next weekend for more heavy metal!"

A slow but loud *BOOO* sounded throughout the club as Marty stood there working his jaw as if he were trying to speak but couldn't get his mouth to operate properly.

"I mean, come back next time for some more Grunge!" he said triumphantly, holding his index finger up in the air.

The crowd really booed him then. Marty shrugged his shoulders, pausing at the top of the steps where one of the bouncers corrected him and he lunged back toward the microphone. "I mean HARDCORE! HARDCORE! HARDCORE! MORE HARDCORE NEXT WEEK!" Then he jumped off the platform and his little grey afro disappeared into the crowd, until he resurfaced at the stairway and climbed back up to his office.

Harley, the bouncer who looked like he'd ridden a motorcycle through hell, cuffed his hands around his mouth and shouted, "WE'RE NOW CLOSED! PROCEED TO THE NEAREST EXIT! THE SHOW IS OVER! I KNOW YOU ALL GOT SOMETHING BETTER TO DO! GET STONED! GET LAID! JUST GET OUT OF HERE!"

"FUCK THAT HIPPIE SHIT! WE DRINK, MAN!" a drunk shouted as another cheered.

"I DON'T GIVE A SHIT WHAT YOU DO," Harley roared. "IT ALL WORKS FOR ME, JUST AS LONG AS YOU DON'T DO IT HERE! THE ROAD HOUSE IS NOW CLOSED. WELCOME BACK TO THE WORLD. IT'S RIGHT THROUGH THESE DOORS! YOU ARE OFFICIALLY INVITED TO GET THE FUCK OUT!"

"Dude," I stopped the bouncer, "did you just make that up?"

"Yeah, I got a million of them. Ya want to hear another one?"

"Yeah, alright."

"Get the fuck out of here, you little midget! You're cutting into my drinking time! How did that one strike ya?"

"I liked the other one better," I admitted.

Aaron nodded toward the bouncer, "Well you can't argue with that," and then gestured to the last piece of equipment. "Come on, Kelly, let's get going."

I picked up the case and we cut through the waves of skinheads who funneled out the doors. Some dragged their wasted friends along, while other drunks stumbled past, with arms around each other and singing lyrics. Some gave us dirty looks while others grinned, as if they knew something we didn't. Outside in the parking lot, we could see how outnumbered we really were but, lucky for us, most of the kids were leaving and there was even a traffic jam as the skinheads raced to get out first.

"Hey!" Egan said as we approached the van where our small gang hung close together. "I'm going to go talk with Marty and see if he'll pay us anyway."

Meanwhile, cars drove by with skinheads howling out their windows, "FUCK

THE LEECH MOB" and the laughing hysterically.

"FUCK YOU WHITE TRASH!" Vick shouted as he flicked them off but Egan slapped his hand down.

"Chill with that."

"Yeah Vick, don't start any shit! Not tonight," Casey snarled, glancing at the last few groups of skinheads that hung around the lot. One group started their engine and swerved around Vick's car, narrowly missing it, as they raced their friends out.

"Vick, you should drive your car over here!" Connor pointed at Vick's ride in the middle of the lot.

"Yeah, maybe we should just go," Casey suggested.

"Relax, you're being paranoid, Casey." Egan glared at the passing cars. A group of females walked past staring hard but with little smirks on their faces. They got into the car beside Egan's.

"What's up?" Connor asked.

"Nothing!" One of the girls grinned back as they peeled out in a cloud of fumes.

"Where's Bram and Tank anyway?" Egan asked Connor.

"They left after everyone got kicked out," Casey added.

"And where are Obi and Cecil?"

"Waiting inside with their guitars," said Aaron.

"Fucking pussies!" swore Egan. "I'm going back in."

"I'll go with you," I said.

"A few of you have to stay with the van!"

"I'll stay." Aaron lit a cigarette and leaned against the wreck.

Back inside the club, Cecil pushed off the wall when he saw us walk in. "Are we leaving soon?"

"Do you want to get paid or not?" Egan answered.

"But Marty said we weren't getting shit, dude!" Cecil complained.

"Yeah Egan, let's just forget it and leave," Obi shivered. "I've got a bad feeling, dude."

Egan shook his head and walked past them towards the stairs.

"Where are you going?" Cecil called.

"To talk with Marty."

Harley and the other bouncers had already cleared the place out. Nobody was left in the building but the guy sweeping the floor and Chill Factor carrying out the last of their equipment.

"Hey Egan, I thought you were told to leave!" Harley shouted as he walked out from the restroom. "What, you don't understand English very well?"

"Is Marty still here?" Egan asked.

"What's it to you?"

"I need to talk to him."

"What the hell do you wanna talk to him about?" Harley glared.

"I just want to get paid."

"HA! You think you're getting paid after what you did? Playing half of a song and then knocking some guy's head in!"

"I got to pay for the gas to drive us back and forth to Connecticut! I got to pay my roadies to haul all this shit in and out of here! It's not my fault those kids are assholes!"

"Look, brother." The biker took off his shades, exposing his tired, bloodshot eyes. "You win some—you lose some!"

"Here ya go, Harley." Egan fished into his pocket and then held up a cassette tape.

"What's that?"

"It's a free demo tape of Despair."

"I don't want a free demo tape, Egan! I had to pawn my goddamned stereo last week!"

"Just let me talk to Marty," Egan pleaded but Harley shook his head. "For two fucking minutes, dude!"

"You already know what Marty will say," Harley argued.

"What?"

"He'll say, 'Fuck you, Egan!' Look man, just do as I say and give it a rest tonight and let me talk to him later on, maybe about booking your next show."

"At another Nazi training camp?"

"That's what sells up here in the sticks, bro."

"Could I just talk to that crazy fucker for one minute?"

Harley put his shades back on.

"I know. I'll be cool, man." Egan smiled.

"Alright, I'll go ask him but you better not give me any shit if Marty just tells you fuck off!"

"Yeah, yeah, yeah." Egan waved him off and then shook his head at Cecil who stared nervously out the door. "Dude! Don't you want to get fucking paid?"

Cecil turned around and flicked Egan off.

A few minutes later, Harley opened the office door and walked back down the steps with Marty behind him, carrying a briefcase. "I'll meet you at the door, Harley," he said and quickly turned the corner as the bouncer walked toward us.

"You should have listened to me, Egan,"

"Why, what did he say?"

"He said to fuck off or else he'll call the cops."

"He's full of shit! He would've done that already!"

Harley frowned. "Look, we're leaving soon and if you were smart Egan, you'd clear out of here fast. Some of those kids look like they want to kill you and they got Marty spooked. I have to see him to his car.

"NOW WOULD YOU KINDLY GET THE FUCK OUT! ALL OF YOU GUYS!" he shouted to all of us in the room. Anxious to leave, we walked out, and Harley locked the doors behind us.

"Come on, let's get the rest of this stuff loaded. I need a beer or something," Egan said as he led the way outside. "Fuck! I hate being broke! I was supposed to meet someone after this."

The parking lot was almost empty now and the exterior lights shut off.

"What the fuck took you guys so long!" Connor called out as we crossed the lot toward our crew, where Jonah and Vick were now parked on each side of Egan's van.

"They wouldn't pay us," Egan said and Connor shrugged.

"Let's get out of here!"

"Damn!" said Egan dropping his head.

"What's wrong?" Connor asked.

"Terry, I forgot all about her."

"Who's Terry?" asked Obi.

"You know Terry!" Egan scowled at him. "That chick I was trying to hook up with!"

"I saw her leave a while ago," said Cecil.

"When?"

"After you started bashing that dude's head against the stage, man."

"Shit!"

"Dude!" Casey said as he got out of Vick's car. "We're gonna get jumped out here! Look! Everyone else ditched!"

"Stop acting like a cheese dick." Egan shoved Casey aside and opened the back door to the van.

"At least we're here!" scoffed Casey. "We could've left like the others!"

"You're lucky you didn't." Egan frowned at the way Aaron had packed the equipment. "Where's Aaron! I told him to watch the van! Where is he?"

"He left," said Vick. "Everyone thinks we're stupid for hanging around."

"Shut up! It's all screwed up back here!" Egan started to unpack the van.

"WHAT'S UP NOW? SKATER FAGS!" a deep voice boomed across the lot.

"What?" Egan said, stepping to the side and squinting around the van.

The color drained out of our faces when we saw a handful of skinheads walking out across the empty lot toward us–followed by a mob swarming from around the building.

"Oh no!" yelled Obi, throwing his precious guitar into the van and then slamming the doors.

"Great, now look at this," Connor muttered, trying his best to hide his fear.

"Now what are we going to do?" breathed Casey. "I told you we should've left!"

"We got to get the fuck out of here, man!" cried Obi.

"Shut up!" Egan yelled.

"Yeah, hey Egan, this ain't cool!" Cecil nervously hit the van. "Let's get this fucker started and run them over!"

Egan shrugged. "Let's see what the hell they want."

"I can tell you what they want!" shouted Connor.

"They want to string us all up!" yelled Cecil.

"Shut up! All of you!" Egan snapped as the small infantry continued to merge and block our way.

"There's like fifty of them, and they all got weapons." Cecil threw his hands in the air.

Egan checked us out, read our fear, but turned around and grilled them. The back of his head moved slowly as he appeared to count the number of skinheads.

"Is that who I think it is?" Jonah griped.

"Empire State Skinheads," Connor stepped forward, staring nervously back and forth between the other gang and Egan. "Don't even think about it! There's way too many for this shit," Connor hoarsely whispered as we all desperately stared at the growing mob creeping up from behind the building. They were holding sticks, chains, and rocks.

Egan continued to squint, his eyes roving over the dusty parking lot, almost dazed out.

"Egan!" Connor shouted again. "I'm not going to the morgue tonight! Fuck these guys!"

But Egan stood motionless. An angry grin of defeat covered his face when he slowly realized that our only option was retreat. He shook his head slowly, staring at their leaders, front and center, the same ones Egan had problems with inside the club.

When Connor saw that Egan wasn't budging, he darted to the van and fished something from underneath the front seat before returning to Egan's side. Instinct pulled the rest of us toward the cars. We all stood sideways, poised to retreat to the cars, outnumbered ten to one.

"YOU'RE FUCKING DEAD!" the boss in the trench coat screamed. "TIME TO PAY FOR YOUR DISRESPECT!"

The first rush began. Younger skinheads skipped forward, hurling rocks and chunks of bricks. The first stones fell short or sailed overhead. But their next downpour of rocks stormed right down on us. Egan chuckled nervously as the bricks smashed against the van, hitting the windshield and gouging the hood with shards.

"Yeah, alright, let's bolt," Egan said, whipping his head to the side to avoid being hit by one of the rocks.

"Yeah, we're being stoned," agreed Connor.

A rock hit Obi's hand. "Shit!" he snarled and began shaking his hand as he spun around, biting his lip in pain. "That's my fucking hand, man! I need my hands!" He glared out at the enemy. A buzz rose from the skinheads and they threw more stones. As their aim improved, we lost what little cool we had and headed to the cars.

"GET THOSE FUCKAS!" the skinhead commander roared with a psychopathic glare in his eyes. He slashed a survival knife as if he were a sword-wielding colonel commanding the cavalry to charge. A few overzealous skinheads flew ahead of the rest, including the Frogman, horribly deformed from where Egan had pounded his face against the stage. The rest of the gang confidently strolled forward, taking their time while others held back, drinking cans of beer.

Jonah dug into his pockets for his keys and then fumbled to deactivate his alarm. We heard the chirp but, when he unlocked the door, he dropped the keys. Connor reached behind and produced a gun, pointed it high and let off four rounds into the air, setting a few grinding their heels and reversing their direction. A half dozen stopped in their tracks, scowling but refusing to charge, yet many still ran forth too drunk or high to care. Egan swung at the first one, knocking him down, wound back and hit the next, and then stomped him on the ground.

By then, both Casey and Vick were in Vick's car with the engine fired up. Vick yelled something over to Egan.

"Fuck it, Egan. Let's go!" Cecil screamed, grabbing Egan's arm, but he shrugged him off angrily.

Vick hit the gas. His tires spun and he fishtailed to the side, whipping up a cloud of dust before catching some traction. He headed straight toward the pack. They must have guessed that Vick was only bluffing until he barreled right into them, aiming to run them down. They dove to the sides, crashing into each other to get out of the way, hitting the ground and rolling as he plowed through. The smarter ones were ready, having maneuvered far enough out of his way but close enough to raise their bricks and bats overhead and bring them down upon his car.

Once past them, Vick slammed on his brakes and swerved around, revving his engine. Half of the skinhead crew, now enraged, turned and charged after him, which divided their herd and increased our chances to escape. Vick raced around the parking lot in figure eights, creating a diversion. Running, the skinheads stooped to pick up rocks, not bothering to slow down, causing more than one drunkard to fall on his face.

"Kelly!" I heard a muffled shout and turned around to see that Jonah had gotten in his car and was now screaming at me to do the same. I quickly jumped in as the next platoon was almost upon us and slammed the door.

Egan stepped back, reaching for the door handle on his van, and swung it wide open, straight into the face of a quick little punk who bounced off and fell on his ass. He quickly sat up, but only in time for Egan to boot him in the grill. Another charged Egan at top speed from behind yet before I could scream a warning, Egan ducked down and the skinhead sailed overhead, tumbling before landing on his ass.

More were instantly upon Egan. One skin jumped in the air, grabbing hold of Egan like some crazy little monkey, and the two of them crashed into the side of the van. He headbutted Egan but then fell back dazed against Jonah's car.

Egan grunted in pain and spit out some teeth. The next second, Jonah hit the gas, grinding the stunned skinhead and dragging him a few yards before flinging him onto the ground. Jonah raced into the oncoming fleet, making them dive out of his way. One bounced off Jonah's car, his ponytail flipping as he somersaulted backwards. They jumped to their feet and came after us, screaming, while we circled the lot.

Another pack chased Vick's car, throwing stones as Vick tore around in circles like Mad Max. From out of nowhere, a skinhead car roared in. The insane driver, either high or really pissed off, attempted a head-on collision with Egan's van. Gunshots rang out and I saw Connor aiming at the car that was barreling straight for them, but it swerved at the last second, flying into some trees at the edge of the lot.

The trench coat led his herd of skinheads at us with their boots beating the ground like a stampede of buffalo. Jonah flew forward, driving straight for the trench coat who, at the last moment, raised a gun and fired. Jonah screamed and swerved into another group of skinheads as a bat shattered a side window, hitting my face like a hailstorm. Jonah raced towards the exit, behind Vick and Casey.

I looked back to see that Egan had managed to get into his van, but with a skinhead hanging onto his open window. Connor, on the other side of the van, was surrounded. With no time left to spare, he fired his last round. As the skins ducked to the ground, Connor jumped sideways into his seat and Egan hit the gas, with both doors open and the guy still hanging onto his mirror. Egan punched him through the window, and the kid fell off.

As we turned down the driveway only yards from our escape, the Empire was waiting, hurling rubble at our cars and beating us with sticks as we gained greater and greater speed. We were almost around front when Jonah slammed on his brakes to avoid crashing into the back of Vick's car, while Egan's van skidded to a stop behind us.

The Empire had barricaded the only exit with their cars!

We sized up our predicament quickly. If we could get across the ditch at the far end of the parking lot and up the embankment, we could escape through the factory's exit.

Vick threw his car into reverse and backed up, and Jonah and Egan did the same. Immediately, we had our three cars going in reverse as the skins pounded down upon us.

One ran up with a brick and beat it against Jonah's window, smashing it. Another jumped on the hood of Vick's car with a crowbar and stomped on the windshield before losing his balance and falling off. A terrible raking sound tore across the top of our car. I spotted a little skinhead holding a long chain he'd swung from ten feet away, whipping one of his boys in the process and taking him out for us.

Vick hit the gas and sped for the ditch, with Jonah and me on his tail. He jumped the curb and bottomed out in the ditch. His wheels began to spin, fishtailing as he tried to climb the embankment.

Jonah jumped the curb and flew into the hill. The Mustang's wheels dug into the dirt, polluting the air with a storm of dust. Both cars screamed as they careened sideways, kicking up small rocks and almost flipping over as we tried to get up that embankment. Then we heard a crash and, as the air cleared, we found ourselves rolling along, bouncing through the old factory site atop the hill.

"Shit, Egan's not gonna make it!" Jonah cried and turned around to see that Egan's van was still in reverse—still flying backwards. They hit the ditch hard, sending missiles of debris as they bottomed out and tore up the hill.

"Christ! A tire blowout is the last thing they need," Jonah yelled as we watched their van struggle to make it up. They bounced around like crazy and I thought they would snap an axle or lose a tire, as they tore into the dirt and rocks. We could see the dark outline of Egan's and Conner's heads hitting the roof of the van, with Cecil and Obi somewhere in the back, getting thrown around with the equipment.

Then they were over onto the factory's lot, the van barely rolling along on tortured shocks. Our cars raced for the exit, as the skinheads swarmed over the hill, re-armed with rocks and bricks.

"Shit!" said Jonah, looking down. "I'm fucking bleeding!" He opened his jacket and saw a huge red spot down under his arm. "I think I've been shot." He slammed on the gas and burned toward the front, swerved onto the main road, and quickly caught up to Vick's car, which was slowing down, losing power, and sputtering to a stop. We pulled over behind them and waited for Vick and Casey.

"Someone better drive. Jonah's been shot!" I yelled as they came running up.

I jumped out of the car and helped pull Jonah over to the passenger's seat as Egan swerved up beside us.

"What the fuck are you doing?" Connor screamed out his window.

"My car broke down!" Vick shouted, getting behind the wheel.

"Hurry up!" Connor screamed again, as I jumped into the back seat next to Casey as Vick hit the gas with my door hanging open.

"Where should I go?" Vick punched the wheel, frantically looking at Jonah, groaning beside him.

"The hospital! Go to the fucking hospital!"

Chapter 12: Hill Top

"What is this? The whole Hill Top got out of jail at the same time?" Dave mumbled, looking over at the group of kids assembled on the other side of Broger Park's parking lot.

Tank tilted his hat. "Hill Top keeps on staring over here like something's up."

"Ah man, fuck those guys." Otis leaned on a nearby car with a frown, his blown out pupils making him look like a strung-out frog.

"They're probably watching us skate–who cares?" Cecil's kid brother Matt grinded his board to a stop and popped it up.

"No, they ain't. You're not that good," joked Lampy.

"What's up?" Jasper asked, skating up with Aaron behind him, spinning 720 degrees on the back wheels of his board

"Nah, something's up. I can tell," Tank responded, staring back and spitting.

"Yeah, that's Hill Top," said Lampy, squinting with bloodshot eyes.

"No shit, detective," grinned Connor.

"I'll skate past em. See what they do."

"No, Otis!" Connor yelled but he had already dropped his board and pushed off, skating across the lot, kick flipping in front of Hill Top, who began throwing up their hands and talking shit.

"Man, get that honky shit out of here!"

Otis turned as he glided on, spitting through his teeth, ollying like he didn't give a shit, and then rolled back over to our side.

"They called me honky!" Otis smiled.

"So!" Conner said. "They probably think you're all stepping!"

Too busy to notice Hilltop, Egan rambled on to Cecil and Obi. "You two have been skipping practice way too much. I don't want to hear anymore lame-ass excuses, dude!"

"Dude," Obi repeated quickly, "last time we had practice, it was at your house and *you* didn't bother to show up."

"Yeah, like always!" Cecil mumbled.

"Bullshit!" Egan said. "When was that?"

"Last week!" Obi answered as a look of realization spread across Egan's face.

"Oh, well, I had to go out and do something. Something came up," Egan faltered before raising his voice. "Everybody better be there next time though!"

"Have you heard anything about a show?" asked Obi.

"I have a couple of ideas. Nothing for certain but I'll let you know. What we need is studio time! We need to cut another record!"

Broger Park, a large chunk of real estate in Landbury, was wedged between the river and the highway. The parking lot was hidden from the main road by a strip of industrial buildings. Behind us, we had a wide view of the fields and the playground. By eleven o'clock that night, nobody else was out there but a handful of older men and women who sat on a picnic bench, sharing a box of wine until they staggered off to their car to buy more. Then it was just the two groups, Hill Top on one side and the Leech Mob on the other, each standing under the buzzing streetlights on opposite ends of the otherwise empty lot.

More and more cars pulled up and soon Hill Top outnumbered us, even if they were only smoking weed and blasting music.

"What did you say?" Obi asked Tank when Egan stopped talking to take a breath.

"Hill Top keeps on staring over here, like something's up," Tank insisted.

"Yeah, I've noticed," said Obi. "I thought it was just me."

"It is just you!" Conner grinned. "And Tank, you're being as paranoid as these Riverview kids!

Egan squinted in their direction and then gave us strange look. "I went to school with most of those guys. They live around here."

As the minutes ticked on, more and more black dudes pulled up in cars and gestured toward us as we subconsciously took a head count, becoming more and more outnumbered on our side of the yard. Eventually Egan shut up long enough to see two Hill Top kids get in a car and swing wide around the lot to take a closer look at us. I strained my ears, hearing phrases like, *the Leech Mob* and *somethuns goin down if Franklin shows up.*

"Yeah," another one agreed, "then it's def'nitly jumpin off!"

"Yo, Egan," said Casey, "they said something's jumpin off."

"Yeah, Egan," Tank agreed, "I'm telling ya. I heard them say *Leech Mob* like three times."

"Last I heard, Franklin was in jail." Egan looked over at Conner who shrugged real wide. "You hear anything, Rook?"

"Nope, but check the way they're acting."

Egan looked across the lot, straining his eyes as a car crept by with tinted windows and an ominous beat blaring through bass woofers. Slowly, some guys got out of the car. One was short and older, wearing a white tee shirt and red sneakers.

"Now that's Franklin," Connor said.

"Who's Franklin?" I asked.

"The president of Hill Top. Moses' brother, remember?" Jasper answered.

"He's coming over here." Bram glared at Egan. "I told you something was up."

"You didn't tell me shit."

Franklin and his friends approached us. Egan also stepped forward and smiled as Franklin strutted into view like he was nine feet tall and bulletproof.

"Where the fuck have you been? In County again or did you make it up the way?" Egan smiled as he moved out with Rook on one side and Connor on the other, meeting Hilltop halfway.

Egan and Franklin shook hands diplomatically though the Hill Top kids glowered.

"What the hell's up with you guys tonight? Somebody die?" Egan asked.

"Not yet," said one of the younger boys, but Franklin began to talk quietly so I couldn't hear what was being said. Then Connor spoke up.

"Dude, what we got over there isn't even the start of it."

Out of the corner of my eye, I saw Cecil bend over and groan, and then run his fingers through his hair like it was the worst shit he could hear. His brother Matty didn't look any happier; in fact, none of us seemed thrilled about fighting Hilltop, who were now pointing over at us and screaming who was going to get bashed first.

"Chill out, Connor," Egan said. He listened to Franklin for a moment before shrugging his shoulders and saying in his loud and clear voice, "I don't know anything about that. If I had a problem with someone, it would just go down and that would be all there was to it. But if I wanted to get all deep, I'd make a phone call to some kids who think Landbury's a fucking joke–but I'm not about that."

Franklin studied Egan's face carefully and then glanced over at Connor before allowing himself to grin. "No, leave all your daddies back home, getting drunk and watching wrestling where they belong and we won't have to…" but I couldn't make out the rest until Franklin stepped back, throwing up his arms with a crazy smile on his face. "Know what I'm saying?"

"Yo, fuck these punk ass crackers!" a skinny dude from the black crew said.

"Shut it, Clay." Franklin glared at his friend.

Egan turned, glanced at Connor who shrugged, looked back toward us, and shook his head. Egan spoke low again, so I couldn't hear.

"Hey Otis," said Connor, "get over here for a second."

Otis pushed off the car he'd been leaning against, looking mean and sketchy as usual. Recently, he had been continually drugged out, with a permanent tripped-out glint to his froggy eyes. Otis trudged out, limping in his sagging jeans and red hoodie, staring back at the black soldiers fearlessly, his white-blonde hair pushed behind his baseball cap worn backwards.

Egan looked at Franklin as he spoke, "Otis, do you know some kid named Danny?

Otis narrowed his eyes. "No. Who the fuck's that?"

"Franklin says he told em that he and the Leech Mob had problems with Hill Top."

"Nah, but if you point him out, I'll kick his head in myself," said Otis with a smile. "We done here? Cause I'm getting fucking thirsty." Tank and Bram laughed, but Otis's attitude created a disturbance among Hilltop.

"Ah man, look at this piece of white trash!" Clay spit at Otis' feet.

"Fuck you, nigger!" Otis sparred.

"What bitch? You wanna die out here, you grimy little punk!" Clay shot back.

"As grimy as you want!" Otis snarled at him.

Egan turned and glared at him. "Otis, shut your fucking mouth. I'm not in the mood for your shit tonight. We ain't about that racist shit!"

"Why? Homey America won't touch the pathology, bro! They're racist! Look at em!" Otis argued back.

Franklin turned to his outspoken boy. "You too, Clay, dead that cracker shit!"

"This shit is mad weak, man!" Otis raised a finger at the others. "These guys always got some bullshit drama! Now they gonna sweat us for every punk that claims Leech Mob!"

"We ain't sweating shit, white boy!" Clay responded.

"Look, we been hearing the Leech Mob name more and more lately," said Franklin, "and we getting sick of hearing it."

"So what?" Otis smiled. "I'm sick of hearing about Hill Top! Especially from you!"

"You think you're a little killer!" scoffed Franklin, grinning and raising his jaw.

"Fucking hell!" Otis shouted.

"The Leech Mob ain't shit! You never show us shit!" said Clay.

"Cause we don't need to show you shit!" Otis snapped back.

"Let's take a walk, Otis." Rook winked at Egan and draped a tattooed arm over Otis' shoulder and tried to steer him away, but Otis quickly spun away and snapped out the blade of a folding buck knife, whipping the handle and pointing it toward the others.

"I ain't playing."

"What the fuck is up with your boy, Egan?" Franklin laughed. "It looks like he wants to do this."

"He's just fucked up, Franklin. He took some bad acid. Man, get him the fuck out of here, Connor!"

"Inbred redneck!" hissed a Hill Top.

Connor pulled Otis back. "Man, now why do you gotta be all saying that, dude?"

"Alright, dude!" the Hill Top mocked him as Otis snarled, "Fucking redneck right!"

Rook pushed him back, speaking low in his face, "Put the fucking knife away, Otis!"

"Look, we'll take care of this Danny kid, alright?" Egan shrugged. "No dumb ass is worth us getting it all twisted. We'll deal with him."

"Nah. It's deeper than that cause we're finished hearing about the Leech Mob like they're some untouchable shit!" Franklin peeled back his eyes.

"We know you guys ain't all that!" said Clay.

"What happened to you, man?" Connor stepped back over, folded his tattooed arms across his chest, and looked at Franklin. "We used to be cool. We had like every class together."

"So what? Ya know, I remember that Leech Mob shit used to irritate me back then, too."

"What's on your mind, dude?" Egan asked, raising a single eyebrow.

"Yeah, dude," Clay mimicked him but Egan only smiled.

Franklin took a deep breath and then announced in a loud voice. "Hill Top has been disrespected and we expect each of you punk ass Leech Mobbers to apologize and then bend over and kiss Clay's ass. Then you pack it up and get the fuck out of here."

"And my ass, too," came a voice from somewhere in the crowd.

"They got to kiss all our asses if they wanna get out of here alive!"

"No, we're not going to do that." Egan shook his head.

Otis busted out laughing from twenty feet away as Connor snarled, "That's fucking bullshit, man."

"Alright then," replied Franklin.

"Alright what?" Egan said dryly. Then it was Franklin's turn to laugh.

"What do you think? Here and now, that's what."

"Dude, we're not even deep like that."

"A minute ago, you said you could fuck this place up!" yelled Clay.

"You got us outnumbered! And I don't want to bring heat down on this place!"

"Pshaw!" Franklin jeered, turning to his friend, "You hear this scary ass bullshit?"

"We'll handle this later on. That's all I'm saying."

The argument wore on as a blue beat-up hatchback pulled in, driven by Hu.

"What's up?" Hu asked us, stepping out.

"Nothing," answered Bram. "Hill Top came down here, sweating us, cause some asshole dropped the Leech Mob name on them–again."

"I'm going over there," Hu sighed.

"I'll go with you," Bram muttered, and they began to walk towards Egan.

"Man, fuck these earth babies!" Otis groaned.

"Shut the fuck up, powder!" Franklin said, as the others cracked up.

"What's going on Franklin?" Hu asked.

"What's up, Hu? You better check your boy over there, that's what. He's gonna talk you all into a blood puddle you ain't gonna be able to crawl out of."

"Otis is totally out of his mind. He's shot, okay?" Hu said but Franklin looked away. "Egan, what's the problem?" the Asian kid persisted.

Egan slowly shook his head. "So now what, Franklin? You want to fight me?"

"Hell no, I ain't gonna roll around on the concrete with your oversized ass, mother fucker! I'll let Booker fuck you up instead." Franklin gestured toward a silent, hooded, muscle-bound brute, who then cracked his knuckles by squeezing each fist. Nineteen years old and huge, Booker spent the last three years in confinement, lifting weights and planning his revenge.

"When did you get out, Booker?" Egan asked. "How's your brother?"

"Why you hang out with these crackers, Hu?" hissed Booker, ignoring Egan.

"Even though I don't drink…" Hu paused, "much, I'm going down to buy a case of beer. Then the six of us will go drink it, and we'll settle it like that."

"Yeah, I got some money for beer," said Connor.

"We don't drink your brand, bitch!" shouted Clay.

"Hell no!" Otis raised his voice. "I don't drink dog piss!"

"We drink Olde E, not your honkey shit," Clay smiled.

"Anyone ever tell you that Olde E is the shit left over in our cans, squeezed out and recycled," Otis sneered.

"Shut the fuck up, Otis!" shouted Rook. "We'll get Olde E then. That shit is straight with me."

"Shut the fuck up, white boy!" Booker said.

Rook's face faded into a scowl. "I never had a problem with you, Booker."

"You do now."

"This isn't going too well," Kit mumbled to me.

"No shit."

"We came to put Hill Top foot to Leech Mob ass and there is no way you're gonna talk your way out of it," warned Clay.

"We can take these darky sons of bitches!" Otis tangled while being held back by Connor and Rook.

"I'm about through listening to you, boy!" threatened Franklin.

"Your move, ace," said Egan. "I guess everyone's going to jail tonight."

"Hey, why don't you put up one of your boys to fight Otis?" suggested Connor.

"Yeah, come on!" Otis growled. "I'll kill the son of a bitch!"

Franklin's eyes lit up, "I got an idea. We'll see how hard your boy thinks he is. Bring them bats up here! We gonna have some gladiator-type shit going off around here!" Franklin snapped his fingers and a kid carried up two wooden baseball bats.

"Otis, since you got such a big mouth, you handle this!" Egan taunted but Otis didn't seem to give a shit.

"GIMMEE THE FUCKING BAT!" he screamed and a bat was dropped at his feet by a scowling Hill Top youth.

"Who want to fuck up the midget–I mean, the white boy?" Franklin jeered, and his associates all roared at once.

"I got this!" A Hill Topper stepped forward and grabbed the other bat. He was a short but stocky black youth with crossed eyes, giving him an unstable look.

"Clarence ain't the smartest motherfucker but he's hard as hell," Franklin explained, grinning and exposing his top row of gold teeth. He glanced over toward his crew. "Clarence gonna put a hurt on this albino midget for sure."

Clarence and Otis began to circle each other slowly as both groups gathered around the two. Each gang eyed each other suspiciously as the two gladiators faced off, expressionless and fearless.

"I'll split your face into a black ass!" Otis spit.

"Well, I'll knock yours clean off, chicken dick!"

"Kill em, Clarence!" shouted Booker.

"Whip his fucking ass, Otis!" screamed Tank.

Otis swung the bat but it came off sloppy, and Clarence easily chipped it aside, laughing, "Is that the best you got?" He then swung, letting go with one arm like he was trying to hit a home run. The bat sliced air in front of Otis' face as Clarence missed, but then he whipped the bat under-armed, aiming for Otis' chin. Otis grabbed his bat by both ends and blocked Clarence's swing. Otis charged, screaming and swinging the bat in a wild frenzy as Clarence operated like a trained sword fighter, blocking every strike.

Loud thuds sounded, reverberating across the parking lot as both gangs howled. Clarence wound back and then sliced low, trying to take out Otis' legs, but Otis skipped back instead, raised his bat overhead and shot forward, clubbing it down. Clarence ducked to the side, tried to swing but his grip was too high, so Otis caught a piece of his knuckles and Clarence yelped.

Otis grinned and whaled on, aiming for Clarence's bat, smacking it down and sending it flying out of his grasp. The bat bounced on the ground. Clarence lunged for it but Otis cut him off halfway, hitting pavement. Clarence faked in one direction but then rolled in the other, diving for his lost bat. Otis was faked out for a second as Clarence tumbled and grabbed his bat, but Otis stayed on him, clipping his heel. Tripping with pain, Clarence gritted his teeth and slashed out, whipping Otis in the guts and sending him stumbling back.

In the midst of the commotion, an old Chrysler pulled in and drove slowly past. The carload of older drunks, who had returned with a full box of wine, watched in horror. They stepped on the gas and swung a U-turn out toward the main road as the two combatants squared back up. Sobered by the pain, Clarence swung the bat wide and caught Otis in the side. Now they both were doubled in agony.

"Alright, enough of this shit. You're gonna kill each other. This is fucking crazy! Gimmee the bat, Otis!" Connor walked in and held out his hands. Otis held the bat out weakly, gripping his side in pain. Connor took it away and then approached the other fighter saying, "Clarence, lose the bat. This shit is stupid." Clarence looked at Franklin for a nod before handing the bat to Connor.

"So Leech Mob boys do got some heart." Franklin smiled and then gestured to Clarence, who instantly ran to attack Otis. Otis pulled his knife and slashed out at the kid, tearing his shirt and slicing his stomach. Clarence lifted up his shirt and saw the cut. "You motherfucker!" he shouted, throwing kicks and trying to boot the knife out of Otis' grasp.

"Cheap shot lying motherfuckers!" Clay screamed. "Lose the bat so that bitch can pull a knife!"

Connor ran forward to disarm Otis, who turned to slash out at Connor instead. "What the fuck, Otis!" he screamed but then it was on.

Chaos reigned. Big Dave chucked empty beer bottles at our opponents, which he had stashed under his armpit, sending amber glass shattering and sparkling on the ground. Then a hot streak of pain raced down the side of my head. Dazed, I kissed the street, seeing nothing but stars and size ten Jordans stomping my face. Booker knocked down Leech Mob kids like bowling pins, throwing these ham and egger punches that convinced us not to get back up again.

Booker and Egan worked their way through the rumble toward each other. Booker took aim, swinging his deadly right fist while Egan, a south paw, reached up with a left uppercut. When they hit, one unstoppable force met another, and they both flew backwards with an atomic, bone-crunching sound.

The two lay on their backs, thirty feet away from each other. Hill Top ran over and tried to lift Booker back on his shaky legs, as Connor did the same, dusting the splinters of broken glass off Egan's arms.

"Oh shit, it's the cops!"

"5-0, it's 5-0!" A few kids tore off into the playground, looking to hide, as others ran for their cars.

"Everybody freeze and get down on your knees!" a cop yelled over his loudspeaker as another cop car raced in and joined him in cutting off our only path of escape.

"Everybody down on their goddamn knees now!" The red and blue lights spun and the strobes flashed, and I wondered how anyone saw straight in these situations. As more and more units raced in, tension grew. Screams, cries, and groans rose from all over the parking lot. Kids from both gangs littered the asphalt. Some yelled, "I got stabbed!" but the cops didn't pay any attention to the cries and jumped on them all the same.

I felt a knee in the back of my neck and a cop growl, "Stay down, you fucking dirtbag!" They pushed us onto the shards of broken glass and tied our hands behind our backs with giant twist-ties. An endless flow of cops appeared on scene, followed by state troopers and ice-cream trucks to haul the masses off to jail.

When I could, I looked up and saw Otis halfway across the lot stumbling backwards, still clinging to his bloody knife.

"Drop the knife, druggie! AND GET DOWN ON YOUR FUCKING FACE!" Cops moved in methodically, with guns drawn and pointed at Otis.

"What the fuck are you doing, Otis?" Egan breathed through slivers of glass.

"He's been on those pills for days!" screamed Connor.

"DON'T DO THIS, OTIS!" Rook yelled before he was plowed over, tackled by zealous cops, who carried him to the ice-cream truck and shoved him in.

"Take it easy and drop the knife kid!" shouted the only sane cop, holding out his hands to show Otis that he held no weapon. But others moved in, pointing guns at Otis, who lunged forward, slicing in the air at them.

"YOU FAT FUCKING PIGS! YOU SENT MY FATHER AWAY!" Otis ranted.

Suddenly, he stopped and stared straight up at the sky, astounded by something that seemed to circle above him. He began to hop, flapping his arms at his sides as though he were trying to join the unseen entity.

"Hey Otis!" shouted Connor, who was pinned down on his stomach. "Just throw down the knife. Then you can fly away!"

"Shut the fuck up!" A cop kicked Connor in the back. "I'm not warning you again!"

"Take it easy, son!" the calm officer urged, but Otis glared over to the cops who were pointing their guns at him.

"Why did you let him eat so much acid?" Connor looked at Egan who, with arms tied behind him, stood and staggered toward Otis. The cops quickly spotted him and shoved him back to the ground.

"Take it easy kid!" the calm one coaxed. "Be smart and lower the weapon, son."

"Fucking listen to em, Otis!" Egan shouted.

"Give him a break. He's so gone he'll only listen to us!" Connor pleaded with the cops.

"Let go of me!" Egan roared, struggling with two cops who were trying to load him into a wagon.

"I can talk some sense into him! I know it!" Connor struggled to his feet and painfully limped out toward Otis.

"Otis, everything's gonna be alright! You just have to drop that blade!"

"DON'T YOU FUCKING MOVE!" shouted one cop. Now the guns were pointed at Otis and at Connor.

"GET YOUR FACE DOWN ON THE STREET AND CROSS YOUR LEGS!"

"But I know him!" Connor argued. "Otis is just having a bad trip. We can talk to him for you!" A cop ran up behind Connor and shoved him down again.

"What the fuck is wrong with you?" Connor twisted to look up at the cop. "It's only a stupid knife. It's not a grenade!"

"JUST DROP THE FUCKING KNIFE, OTIS!" shouted Egan from farther back. "JUST DROP THE KNIFE, DUDE!"

"Shut up, dirtbag!" The cops shoved Egan into the van. "We don't need your help with this!"

"Just lose the knife, son!" the calm cop repeated.

"DROP THE FUCKING KNIFE, ASSHOLE!" another screamed.

"YOU PIGS ARE FUCKING UP MY FRIENDS! YA THINK I'M BLIND, YOU BASTARDS! NO FUCKING WAY! If I drop it, you'll kill me! It's my only chance!"

"DROP THE KNIFE AND GET DOWN ON YOUR KNEES!"

"Otis, just do what they say!" Conner yelled.

"Listen to your friend, son!" the calm one encouraged Otis. "Everything will be just fine but you must drop that weapon!"

Another cop pointed a gun and howled, "Drop it now, you piece of shit!"

Otis, once more, stared straight up at the sky. Then he raised the knife and charged the line of cops.

We heard a single gunshot and Otis dropped instantly, as if some unseen pair of hands had reached up from the asphalt and pulled him straight down. I didn't even know which cop had shot him, so many had their guns out. Now one ran forward, kicking the knife. It skidded across the parking lot and came to a rest, twenty feet from Otis' motionless body. Only then did the cops begin holstering their side arms and unlatching their two-way radios.

"Can we get an ambulance ASAP at Broger Park, Veteran's Drive."

"10-4, we're notifying EMS, over," came the reply.

I watched all of Otis' muscles relax as he sank deeper into the street. One cop flashed a light onto his face, and I could clearly see Otis' glazed eyes, his pupils blowing out large and black as his lips peeled back, turning purple and fat, blown apart from his yellowed teeth. He began to spasm.

"Shit," said one cop.

Connor, breathing dust and lying flat like the rest of us, continued to call out to Otis. "Otis?" he seemed to ask before shouting, "OTIS! OTIS!" Connor tried to get to his feet but a burly cop stomped on his back.

"OTIS!" Egan howled, banging on the inside of the ice-cream truck.

"Otis, say something!" Connor pleaded and then,"GET THE FUCK OFF ME!"

"NOOO!" Bram screamed, flipping out on the cops who dragged him away.

"He's just a fucking kid!" Connor cried as they pulled him up. "WHY DID YOU HAVE TO SHOOT A FUCKING KID?"

The cops milled around confused but pretended to be expert. The others dragged us to the awaiting wagons. I saw two rip Connor to his feet. He struggled so they hammered him with batons until his legs went limp. Then Dave rammed one cop so they let him have it, picked him up by his arms and legs and carried him to the truck. The cops counted to three, as they swung him back and forth, gaining enough momentum to toss him in.

"Get up." Someone was pulling the back of my arms and then I was being pushed to the wagon. The doors opened where I saw Leech Mob kids smeared with dirt, blood and snot. We sat there breathing hard and barely speaking.

"Move down to make more room!" one cop shouted as he opened the back of our wagon to dump Jasper in. He held the door open long enough for me to see Cecil being carried off, his face smeared with blood, along with his brother, unconscious, to another truck filled with grinning Hill Top members who taunted the two black Leech Mobbers. Hill Top laughed at the cops' ignorance in putting the two in a van filled with the wrong gang.

"Check it out! It's Sid Vicious and Milli Vanilli!" they roared sadistically as the doors slammed shut.

"Did they shoot Otis?" someone in my van asked in the dark.

"Yeah," a voice answered.

"Is he going to die?"

"Only the good die young."

"Otis wasn't good."

"Shut up!"

"Egan would kick your ass if he heard that."

"I'm going to tell him you said that!"

And then we heard the scream of an approaching ambulance.

✦

Dr. Gildmore brought a handkerchief up to his face. "I'm sorry. I have this cold I can't seem to kick. So what happened with that arrest?"

"I don't know. I still have to go back to court."

"I see. So trouble became more and more serious, correct?"

"Yeah and after that, Egan and Connor put out the word–no more Leech Mob business. They said it wasn't started for this shit–that things had gone all wrong."

"You know what they say about best intentions right?"

"What?"

"They don't always justify the outcome."

"What are you talking about? What do you expect Egan and Connor to say? They lost one of their best friends, someone they wanted to protect."

"So they took Otis' death badly."

"All the Leech Mob did. And then Egan started hanging out with Cincity more and then…"

"Egan started taking more drugs." Dr. Gildmore finished my sentence.

"He might've. I mean, I think he did, cause afterwards, everything seemed, I don't know, different. The cops killed Otis, kicked our ass, and then made an example out of us so we were all arrested on rioting charges. It was a big deal because a similar thing happened in Landbury in the '70's."

Dr. Gildmore leaned back. "What happened?"

I sighed. "A race riot broke out at Landbury High School and the city cops had to call in the state police."

"That was a rough time, the 1970's. Crime was up, the murder rate was at its highest."

"So Egan said the only way to stop a punk from using the Leech Mob name was to end the Leech Mob. Kids had been dropping the Leech Mob's name left and right to get out of fighting their own battles. Then Connor said it would be like the Leech Mob never existed. We were never a gang, just a group of friends, and Egan said we know who's down and who isn't. And with that, the Leech Mob was gone, officially, forever.

Chapter 13: A Bad Trip

"Even though I was pretty out of it, I still remember most of the last night."

"You mean the night that you were admitted to Fair Hills?

"Yes."

"What do you remember?" Gildmore asked.

"That we all died."

"Who died?"

"I thought that all my friends were dead–and I was dying."

"You thought you were dying?"

"It seemed that way."

"And that was after you took the drugs, I assume."

"Yeah."

"And do you think this delusion might have had something to do with one of your friend's deaths?"

"I don't know."

"You don't know?"

"Don't start that repeating thing again."

"When did you find out the bad news?"

"It was that night."

"Then we should go through this again, until everything is clear in your mind, hmm, discuss what happened, put it to rest, and then move on."

"I can't be sure what actually happened, only… "

"What do you remember?"

I thought for a moment. "I can remember these little flashes, like scenes in my head, but I don't know what happened in any regular order. I kept blacking out."

"Well, give it a try. What's the first thing you remember?"

"The whole night was messed up."

"I see."

It started off bad and only got worse."

"I can imagine."

✦

Face had a camera and took a picture of me when I got into the car.

Click

It was one of those disposable cameras and Face said it was to gather photo evidence of Nickodemus. Kit had his parents' Navigator because the Clam had exploded. We drove to Flip's house where everybody was hanging in his basement den. "Wave of Mutilation" was playing on an old stereo with one speaker and they'd already taken the drugs and were waiting for them to kick in. Then somebody handed me two white paper squares rolled up in a cigarette pack's cellophane.

"When should I take them?" I asked but Flip only shrugged.

"They're Mindbenders," he said. "The same ones that gave Otis that bad trip. Conner tossed most of them, but Jasper and Aaron got these from Cincity."

"Are you taking them?"

Flip grinned, putting his arm around Jenny. "Yeah, we all are."

Macie and Remmy had finally hooked up and were smothering each other kissing. Face snapped a photo.

Click

"Face, you pervert!" Macie's dilated pupils made her eyes look black.

"Flip! Get up here!" Flip's mother stood in the doorway.

"Ma!" Flip cried. "What do you want?"

"You got a phone call! What da ya think?"

"Who is it?"

"I don't know—one of your fucking friends!" The old Bronx woman slowly shuffled in place as Flip ran past her and jumped up the stairs just as she reached out to whack him. The rest of us stayed in the basement den, waiting for the movie to finish rewinding in the VCR.

I twisted open the pack and emptied two tiny squares onto my hand and stuck them on my tongue. "When is it supposed to happen?"

"A half hour," answered Face.

I sat down and tapped Macie on the shoulder. She pulled her lips away from Remmy's.

"Are you tripping, too?" I asked.

"Yeah, me and Krissy split one."

"You too, Krissy?" My mouth hung open.

"I took half cause I was curious! Big deal. Everyone else took two!"

The sliding door whipped open and Vick stood there, breathing hard and looking pissed. "Did you hear about Egan?" Face snapped a picture of him.

Click

"Hear what?" Krissy asked.

"I can't fucking believe it!" He stood there gaping. "Egan might be dying."

"What do you mean Egan might be dying?" Krissy cried.

"What are you talking about, Vick?" Remmy stood up.

Vick shook his head. "I gave Connor the phone number here because Egan's in the hospital!"

"What happened?" Remmy stepped forward.

"Why is Egan in the hospital?" Krissy asked.

"I don't know. I heard he collapsed at a show last night!"

"Did he overdose?" asked Remmy.

"Maybe," said Vick.

Kit pressed for more details. "What did he take?"

"I don't funking know!"

"You'll think he'll be okay?" asked Macie.

Vick looked down. "I don't think so."

"Oh my god," gasped Krissy.

Flip trudged downstairs and looked at Vick. "That was Connor."

Face snapped a photo.

Click

"What did he say?" Vick asked.

"Egan probably won't make it."

Everyone got quiet and slowly Krissy started to cry and then Macie.

"Did Connor tell you anything else?" Vick raised his voice.

"He said Egan and him were at a show and Egan just collapsed."

Remmy closed his eyes. "That's so messed up."

I tried to imagine Egan on a stage and then falling over.

"Connor said he's moving with Bram, Casey, and some chicks out to California,"

Flip added as his thirty-year-old brother walked in with his arm strung around a chick with braided blonde hair.

"Great, you clowns are here!" He stood in the doorway, shaking his head slowly.

"Yeah, that's right," returned Flip.

"Are you gonna leave soon? Me and her were gonna watch this movie." He held up a videotape.

"So are we."

"We'll be upstairs, waiting," Flip's brother grumbled and started to leave.

"Fuck off, loser. Get an apartment, why don't you?" Flip turned and pressed *Play* on the VCR.

"What was that?" His brother leaned forward, gritted his teeth, and pointed at him. "If I wasn't with my lady just now, I'd whip your little ass in front of all your friends!"

"Mom!" Flip shouted up the stairs.

"Go fuck yourself, you little weasel!" he spit.

"Yeah, that's right. Go upstairs!"

"Fuck you!"

"Flip!" his mother shouted down the stairs.

"Yeah."

"Phone call!"

Flip followed his brother out as *The Hills Have Eyes* began to play on the TV. He was back down in a few seconds. "That was Aaron and Jasper calling for you, Kit. They said they're ready."

"Alright." Kit stood and opened the door. "I'm leaving."

"Wait up," Vick barked and then whispered something to Flip, who fished through a bag and then dropped two paper squares into his hand, which Vick quickly took.

"I hope you don't start freaking out tonight, Vick," said Krissy.

"For real, Vick, I heard these were strong and you like took two of them," Macie chimed in.

"Shut up, snaggletooth," said Vick and followed us outside.

"Where are we going?" I asked.

"To meet Aaron and Jasper for some weed." Kit started the engine.

"Damn! I can't believe that Egan's dying, man!" I said.

"First Jonah gets shot, then Otis gets killed, and now Egan!" blurted Face.

"Anybody talk to Jonah?" I asked.

"The bullet went in and out of his side like this." Vick turned and pointed under his arm.

"Did you go to Otis' funeral?" Kit changed the subject.

"Otis hated me," explained Face. "I didn't go."

"Me neither," said Kit.

"Who was at the hospital when Jonah's family got there?" Kit glanced over at Vick. "I heard they completely like bugged out in the waiting room."

"Casey, me, and Kelly were there," answered Vick. "When his mother started screaming, I went outside."

"His mom scared me," I said. "She walked in, all pale with her eyes bugged out, looking like somebody had died. Then she walked over to me and just stood there, trembling and staring at me, and when I reached out, she smacked my hands away. I guess she was really freaked out because he lost a lot of blood. First his father asked us what happened and then like Jonah's mom started screaming so his dad broke down and told us to leave."

The four of us drove into Landbury. Kit turned down a dead end road where every other house was boarded up. We stopped in front of a house that had been converted into several apartments and Kit ran inside.

"So what are we doing tonight, just like watching a movie?" Face asked.

"Well, I say we find some pigs, and first we fuck em and then we dump em!" Vick laughed so insanely that he looked like the devil.

"You'll anger Nickodemus with talk like that!" Face stared out the back window, brought up his camera and took a flash photo.

Click

"He's been following us since we passed the Food Barn!"

Kit swung open his door and jumped back in. "Aaron and Jasper said there's a rave in the city tonight." Kit turned up the stereo as we started to drive, bobbing his head and pointing his fingers as he bounced around to techno.

"Fuck a rave! What the hell is this techno shit?" Vick demanded. "Don't you got any hardcore in here?"

"Hardcore's dead, man. Techno's the new shit!"

Vick hit him. "Fuck you, man!"

"Ow!" Kit cried. "That hurt!"

"So what happened to the Clam?" Face asked.

"Dead," Kit said as he rubbed his shoulder. "The Clam finally kicked the bucket so my dad let me borrow his truck. It's real cool. You just can't smoke in here. My dad will kill me if he smells smoke in his Lincoln!"

"Why is everything dying?" Face wailed.

"With all this damn snow, we'll be lucky to stay on the road!" I grabbed Kit's shoulder. "Put this fucker in four-wheel drive!"

"Why are you talking about snow, Kelly?" Kit glanced back. "It's August for crying out loud!"

But outside, the flakes of snow fell everywhere.

"Don't worry about him. He's just tripping," said Vick.

"Yeah," Kit nodded his head. "You're tripping balls, kid!"

The passing headlights smeared across the sky, leaving trails of sparkling diamonds that whirled within the gusts of snow.

"You guys took the same shit that tweaked Otis out, huh?" Kit asked.

"I think so, yeah," grinned Vick.

"I took one of those last weekend and I thought my mother was trying to kill me with a pair of scissors! It was the worst experience of my life!" Kit flipped his mirror to night vision. "What the hell is this bitch doing tailgating me? I can barely see!"

"All this damn snow!" I shouted.

"Shut up about the goddamn snow! This guy has his high beams on and he's riding my bumper!" Kit thumbed toward the vehicle behind us.

Vick turned and looked around. "Gimmee that!" He grabbed an empty iced tea bottle and rolled his window down.

"No!" Kit yelled when he saw what Vick planned to do. "No! Not the bottle!" But it was too late. Vick let it fly, smashing into the car's grill, causing the vehicle to fishtail but stay on us.

"They're still on our tail!" yelled Face. "It must be Nickodemus!"

Click

Face lowered the camera.

"Pull over and we'll see what they want!" Vick shouted and Kit pulled to the side of the road where the car rolled to a stop behind us.

"He's just sitting there, doing nothing! You stupid bitch!" Kit shouted into his rear view mirror. "Go around me or do something!"

Slowly the car backed up and sped around us.

"Quick, after them!" shouted Vick. "They're getting away!"

Kit giggled, accelerated and quickly caught up, flashing his high beams into the car. "Now we'll see if you like it!"

"You're gonna die, bitch!" Vick screamed out the window.

"I think it's a woman," laughed Kit. "Look, she's pulling into those condos!"

Vick jumped up and down in his seat. "Give me that other bottle! Quick!"

"No! No more throwing bottles!" Kit yelled but Vick lunged for the bottle and wrenched it away from Kit when he tried to grab it. Vick leaned out the window and tossed the bottle over our roof. It sailed through the air and smashed against the top of her vehicle, shimmering as it shattered into a hundred jewels while she swerved left and we stayed straight.

Face snapped a picture, blinding me.

Click

Then we were back in Riverview. I recognized the landscape but now it had changed. Something terrible had happened. The buildings were crumbling, fiery trenches spread in all directions, and rusty barbwire lined the streets. Somewhere in the distance a bomb went off, flashing in the twisting sky. We slowly rolled through the war-torn land, surveying the damage as we cruised to a stop beside what appeared to be a supply bunker, constructed of sandbags.

"What are we stopping here for?" Vick asked.

"I need to get some Rolaids or Pepto-Bismol or something. My mother's health food is killing me," groaned Kit.

The bunker turned out to be an old convenience store, nothing more than a wide hallway lined with racks of magazines, potato chips and candy bars. The twenty-something ex-football player who ran the joint didn't see us through the window as we approached, too busy flirting with two preppy girls who'd come to visit. The Jock raised his sleeveless arms and flexed his thinly-developed muscles. He was just about to kiss each bicep when the chime went off and we walked into the store. He jerked his head to the side and glared around the chicks.

"We're closed! Don't you see the lights are out?"

"Come on," Kit tried to persuade him. "I just need some Rolaids, dude!" But the guy shook his head sternly, keeping his thin slit of a mouth stretched tight.

"Try the gas station down the road. They're always open."

"But I'm going the other way, man!"

As Kit argued with the cashier, Vick and Face roamed around the store. I walked toward the rear of the bunker to check on the supplies before returning to the front.

"Alright fine, we're leaving!" Kit said and shoved open the door. Outside, it had started snowing again. "What a fucking asshole!" he said as we got back in the SUV. Vick and Face were quiet as they dug into their pockets, taking out the chips and Skittles they'd stolen.

"Shit, why didn't you get me some goddamn Rolaids while you were stealing the rest of the store!"

"Here." Face tossed a roll of Tums up front.

"Oh thanks, man," Kit said and ripped them open.

Click

When we returned to Flip's house, everyone was wandering around outside.

"What the hell is going on here?" Vick exclaimed as he got out. Kit began to roll a joint on his armrest and then got out to smoke it as Ezra, Brody and Obi drove up.

"We have to leave," Remmy said as he walked down the hill with Macie.

"What for?" Kit asked and exhaled a cloud of smoke.

"Flip got into a fight with his brother and his mom kicked us all out."

"Like a real fight or did they just start yelling at each other?" Kit asked as Remmy reached for the joint.

"A real fight." He took a drag. "I think she might've called the cops so I'd be careful with this shit."

"Damn! When is he gonna get his own pad. He's like fifty years old!" Flip slammed the front door and walked out with a fresh, black eye. "We have to get out of here or my mom's gonna call the cops."

"Are you okay, Flip?" Krissy asked.

"That dick sucker punched me, so I stomped him in the balls and now he's in there lying on the floor crying."

"Where are we gonna go?" Macie looked at Remmy.

"Should we go and try to see Egan?"

"In a hospital? Aren't you all tripping on acid?" Obi asked as he walked up. "I don't think so. They'd call the cops! Anyway, who told you about Egan? I thought I would have to."

"Vick heard from Connor."

"Yeah, me too." Obi shook his head. "You know I warned Egan about that shit but he wouldn't listen. They're not letting anybody in to see Egan anyway. And they have him in a hospital in New Haven which is like a two-hour drive."

"Boy, this was a bad night to take acid," confessed Macie.

"Well, we can't just sit around here and think about it," Krissy looked at us.

"We'll end up killing ourselves."

"But where should we go?" Flip glanced back at his house. "We really have to get out of here."

"Aaron and Jasper said something about a rave tonight," said Kit.

"Where?" asked Remmy.

"In New York City."

"There's no way I'm going to a rave," said Obi. "I hate techno music."

"Do you even know how to get there?" Krissy asked Kit.

"I can try to call Aaron and Jasper, see if I can catch them before they leave."

"Good plan," said Krissy.

"Quick! Follow me to the pay phone."

We got in the cars and drove down to the local burger joint to find the place swamped with Jocks and Preps.

"Looks like there's no Jock party tonight," Kit laughed. He drove over to the payphones and started making calls as the rest of us stood around and waited.

Kit spoke to someone on the other end. "Hey, this is Kit! We need directions to that rave! There's a bunch of us hanging at the Burger World. Everyone's down to go!"

Face snapped a picture of him.

Click

Next thing, a flashy red car drove into the Burger World lot, with tinted windows and a loud system. They chirped past the Jocks and cruised into a spot near us. The limo-tinted windows made it impossible to see who was inside until they rolled them down, grinning and blasting techno music into the night. It was Aaron, Jasper, and a raved-out chick named Sleepy. They oozed out of the car and grooved to the hypnotic, repetitive music that blared out of their stereo.

"This is Sleepy, everyone." Aaron draped his arm around the girl, but she didn't respond, maybe because she had a ring pop stuck between her pouty, red-stained lips. Instead, she nodded her head as she gyrated her hips to the music; her pale and glassy eyes gawked thoughtlessly into the night. She had long jet-black hair and makeup plastered to her face, ready for the rave and dressed in new, designer baggy clothes with glow-in-the-dark jewelry wrapped around her skinny neck and wrists. Aaron's and Jasper's hardcore skater clothes had also been dropped for the new look, and they sported Kangol hats, yellow-tinted goggles, and windbreakers. Carelessly, they bobbed their heads, stuck in a drug-trance like the rest of us, rolling on acid and then shrooms. Jasper ducked into his car, reached under his seat, and produced a large bag of smelly dried mushrooms.

"Give me two bucks a cap," Jasper said as the others gathered around the car. "Keep the money hidden."

Kit handed him ten dollars and made off with a small handful. "Here, try a few of these, Kelly." He dropped a few pieces in my hand.

Now red-eyed, Kit danced along with them, bending his knees and bouncing as he pointed both index fingers, shooting foolishly. Sleepy wobbled her knees around, letting them buckle as she swiveled her ass in circles, jumped up, and spun around. She weaved her arms together like two dancing snakes, keeping her fingers interlaced as her double joints flowed in and out of knots. Face snapped a picture.

Click

Lampy and Big Dave rolled up next. Vick told them the news about Egan, and Dave started to kick his own car.

"Yeah, it sucks and all," said Jasper. "But Egan would want us to party."

A cop tweaked his siren and raced across the road from where he'd been hiding, watching us from a tavern's parking lot across the street. Grinning, he slowed down by the gang of Jocks first, who cozily gathered around the police cruiser. He flipped off his lights and leaned over to shoot the shit.

"Oh crap, I got weed on me," mumbled Kit.

"Yeah, let's get out of here." Remmy stood up and stretched.

"Relax," Macie said.

A second later, the cop waved for the Jocks to carry on and then turned on his flashing lights and sped over to us. Rolling to a stop, he flicked on his shades and raised the radio mic to his lips like he was pulling the crowd of us over.

"Where are you all from?" the cop asked as he lowered his window.

"Riverview," Krissy spoke nervously.

"What about those clowns?" He pointed toward the Ravers.

"They live nearby. They're friends of ours."

"Well, why don't you pack it up and call it a night?"

"Cause it's not 6 o'clock in the morning yet," said Face.

"Yeah, it's still mad early," agreed Ezra.

"Excuse me?"

"Shut up, Face," said Krissy. "I'm sorry, Officer. We're just about to leave."

"How about a ham sandwich!" Lampy suggested and then got in Dave's car. Dave turned up his stereo, blaring hardcore over the techno jams.

"What's his problem?" The cop pointed at Dave. "I saw him kicking his car."

"We just got some really bad news–about a friend."

"Is that right?" The cop faked a sympathetic look. "What are your names?"

"I'm Krissy. This is Macie."

"Hi," said Macie.

"I'm Nickodemus," joked Face.

"Sure." Annoyed, the cop stared at Face. "Can't you all read the sign?"

"What sign?" asked Flip.

"The no loitering sign."

"We're not loitering," Brody corrected him.

"Well, you're not customers!"

"Cause I don't eat meat slop!" Vick growled in a deep voice. "Meat is murder!"

"Then you can move out!" The young cop raised his tone.

"We've only been here ten minutes."

"Are we going to have a problem?" The cop rammed his gearshift into park.

"No sir," said Krissy.

"Then I don't want any more lip! Just take your act somewhere else or I can take you all to jail! Now, what's it gonna be?"

"Why don't you tell them to break out, too?" Vick pointed at the Jocks.

"Cause they are customers and they aren't bothering anyone."

"We're not bothering anyone either," argued Flip.

"You're blasting music and kicking things, so pack it up and vacate the premises!"

Face took a picture of the cop.

Click

"Hey!" the cop screamed. "You don't have my permission to take my picture! Now give me that camera!"

Dave and Lampy peeled out of their parking space and tore out towards the road where they fishtailed down the street.

"What the hell!" the cop shouted and raced after them, blaring his siren.

"Let's get out of here!" yelled Jasper and we all started moving towards the cars as the gang of Jocks jeered.

"Bye bye, freaks!" Baldy waved as the other Jocks laughed. Flip flicked him off.

"Yeah, fuck you!"

"Have fun at Burger World!" Brody jerked his fist in the air.

"Where are we going?" I asked.

"The rave," Kit said, distracted as we got into the cars, and followed Aaron, Jasper and Sleepy, who sat in the front seat working on her ring pop.

"That bitch Sleepy looks like a real fine slut," Vick laughed gutturally.

"That's Aaron's girl."

"So?"

"I'm just saying."

"Then shut your face, Kit! I know what all pigs want!"

"How far away is this place?" Face asked.

"I don't know. Outside Manhattan somewhere."

"Ruff! Ruff! Ruff! Ruff!"

I'd blacked out again and when I came to, we were waiting at a stoplight. I had my head through the window and was barking at the car beside us. The driver glared at me and rolled up his window as Vick laughed and Face took a picture.

Click

"You're gonna get us arrested, Kelly!" Kit grinned and hit the gas when the light turned green, and we raced to catch up with Aaron, Jasper and Sleepy.

"Ruff! Ruff! Ruff! Ruff!"

We must've caught up to them because the next thing I knew we're standing inside what looked like a huge warehouse. At its entrance, a long line led up to a table with black light. Krissy and Macie had gotten stamped, licked their hands, and then pressed them against the backs of our hands. We stood in line. I held my hand under the black light and then was turned loose inside the dome. The music grew louder as we walked through the dark tunnel-like entrance and into an immense coliseum. The DJ stood high above us, with lights strapped to each side of his head, spinning records on a tower of a stage.

A blur of bodies pulsated to the sound as huge images of blood vessels and lava lamps were projected onto the vast walls. The floor was packed with kids while the perimeter was lined with metal bleachers, like a sports arena. Some of the Ravers dressed like mutant preppies, wearing $1000 designer outfits. No more oversized jeans copped from the Good Will or Vans sneakers in this joint. No more hardcore tee shirts or torn hoodies.

"Check out these two jackasses!" Vick cackled in my ear and dragged me toward two kids, with 5 o'clock shadows, who went through their little act, clapping their hands, snapping their fingers, and slapping their pants.

"We're Geo-Geo in da house, with big fat pockets. Pockets are fat, SLAP!"

They clapped their hands. "$500 polo shirt, CRACK! $1000 pants, SMACK!" They slapped their pants. "$400 sneaks SNAP, ain't no thing, cause our pockets are fat, SLAP! CRACK! SMACK! What you want? GEO-GEO in the house!"

I turned away from the drug dealers and thought about little Geo. I hadn't seen him since he'd been hit by a flying microphone stand and before that, we crashed his house. The poor kid had a run of bad luck and I never apologized.

I wandered onto the dance floor and made a fool of myself trying to dance but moshed instead. I couldn't help it—old habits die hard. People cleared out around me, forming a ring as I slammed around. After getting enough dirty looks, I pushed back through the crowd and collapsed on the metal benches. Face ran by, slid to a stop in front of me, and snapped a picture. The flash blinded my eyes.

Click

I remember hearing a loud *POP* and smoke rising all around us. The police had capped us with exploding gas canisters that they rolled in, releasing tear-gas all over the place. Kids wrapped their shirts around their faces and began running, as cops in gasmasks circled the joint and herded them out the exit. Then we were back outside. Kids were everywhere, looking for friends and screaming at cops. I saw a few being arrested. Others were sick, coughing and puking.

Then I was standing in this courtyard, this wide alleyway that stretched out to the street. Crowds of kids swarmed around these double doors. I stood off to the side, talking with two kids with painted faces. They were dressed up like clowns and wore jester's hats. I was excited and rambling on about something and they were smiling, amused with whatever I'd been telling them, which I now have no idea what that was. It was like waking up in a dream and finding myself still dreaming. I had no idea where I was, how I'd gotten there, or what I'd been doing. Their happy expressions faded from their faces and I slowly backed away.

"Wait! Where are you going?" one of the jesters asked.

"I have to find my friends," I babbled. "I don't know where I am."

"You're at the 3010 Space Odyssey Rave." The girl jester stepped forward. "But it got shut down." She pointed toward the double doors. "Everyone's leaving!"

"Why?"

"Something about drugs and the wrong permits."

"I have to find my friends." I turned and walked out toward the street.

"But they told us to hang out with you!" the girl called.

"Wait!" the dude shouted. "You're gonna get lost."

I saw them running to catch me, the bells on their hats and shoes jangling as

I started to run.

"Wait for us!"

"You stay away from me!" I shouted and ran out of the alley but at the street I froze, staring at the cars flying past. Everything smeared together, especially the lights and I could barely see enough to cross the road. I stepped out and a car blared its horn as it whipped past.

"Kelly, what the fuck are you doing!" a familiar voice shouted and then Kit, Face and Vick were dragging me back.

"Dude! You're gonna get hit by a car!" said Kit.

"Some clowns were after me!" I said panicky and Vick laughed.

"I told those kids to stay with you while we found out where the other rave was!" Kit exclaimed.

"Why did you leave me with them?"

"Cause you were talking crazy man! Nobody wanted to tell us shit with you around, shouting about dead people!" yelled Kit. "I fucking introduced you to them. You seemed cool about it before you started freaking out!"

"It's alright, Kelly,'" said Face. "I understand."

"Where is everyone else?" I looked around.

"Around somewhere. I hope that acid wears off soon," Kit grumbled. "I'm tired of babysitting you!"

"There they are." Vick pointed toward Krissy, Macie, and Remmy who walked up with Sleepy, still dancing.

"Any luck?"

"Sleepy says there's another rave on the other side of the city," said Krissy.

"We just have to find out how to get there!" Remmy said as Face snapped a picture.

Click

We stood in what seemed to be a train station or bus station, but it was late and the whole place was deserted. I looked outside and saw that it had started to snow again. I walked over to a kid who'd joined our group along the way. His clothes were covered with name brands, as though he were a walking billboard.

"What?" He glared at me.

"So that's how you're living?" I pointed at his clothes.

The kid narrowed his eyes and glanced around at the others. "Who the fuck is this?"

"Kelly," Vick laughed.

"Don't mind him. He's just tripping balls," explained Remmy.

"My shit will fly anywhere–look at what you're wearing."

I had heard that before and it had pissed me off then, too. I shoved him and he shoved me back, but Flip and Remmy dragged me back. The mutant billboard began screaming, his face turning purple as he cursed and spit.

Click

"You have to chill out, Kelly," Remmy said.

"Nobody knows what's happening but I'm going to find out what's going on!"

"Yeah!" said Face. "We're onto you, Nickodemus. Do you hear us?"

"We're waiting for a taxi, Kelly," Kit sighed. "We've already told you a thousand times."

"A taxi where?"

"I give up!" Kit sighed, "Uh, can you like deal with this, Macie?"

"Kelly, look at me," she said and gazed into my eyes. "We're in the city, remember? Now we have to wait for a taxi to show us how to get to the rave."

"But no taxi is going to take us anywhere with you acting crazy all night!" Kit added.

The station began to shake as the last train pulled in with air-brakes hissing. The doors slid open and a crowd of people walked up the stairs and into the lobby where we stood.

"Do you know where we are?" I asked.

"57th Street Station," a man said. I tried to say something else but the girls pulled me back.

"Don't worry about him. He's just a little drunk," Macie apologized as they sat me down on a bench.

"Taxi's here!" Vick shouted and we walked out the doors toward the dark yellow taxi that waited by the curb.

Kit spoke to the cab driver and pointed to his truck. He turned to us and said, "Alright, some of you go in the taxi. The rest of you will follow with me in the truck."

"Come here, Kelly" said Krissy. "You probably shouldn't go with them."

"Why not?"

"Cause you don't need any more drugs."

Remmy, Face, Macie and Krissy squeezed into the backseat of the cab, and I got in the front. I looked at the driver, a short, black man with an African accent.

"Everybody's going to 5023 Grant Street?"

Macie leaned forward and tapped the driver. "Yeah, I don't know if he told you that our friends will be following us." She pointed back at Kit and the others.

"Yup," the taxi driver said. He pulled out into the empty road and sped off.

"Whoa!" we yelled as we raced through the streets, passing rows of crooked city houses leaning against one another with rusty garbage cans behind metal gates. The snow began to fall again and build up on the road.

I glanced over my shoulder at the kids in the back seat smashed together. "You're driving fast, dude!" I said to the driver. "Who are we on the run from?"

The driver laughed and when he did, he grew younger until he was a kid, about fifteen years old.

A kid driving a taxi? I thought. But how—unless he stole it? "Did you steal this cab?" I asked and he laughed again.

"Go right! Right! Right!" Face shouted as the driver turned right and glanced behind us.

"Someone's chasing us!" I yelled.

"It's Kit, you acid head!" Remmy laughed.

"No, it's Nickodemus!" Face shrieked, turned, and snapped a photo. Kit began honking his horn, pissed off at the camera's flash in his eyes.

We tore down the battered streets at 1 A.M. The city had been abandoned by all of its residents except the rats, which scurried along the cracked and crumbling sidewalks, scavenging waste from the heaps of trash. The fire hydrants had been emptied of water and now stood dry. Some of the buildings had holes blown into the walls and threatened to collapse. I tried to look where we were going but the snow made it impossible to see. We blindly flew around the next corner in this twisted maze of decomposing roads lined with barricaded homes.

"Is this the future?" I asked. "What happened here?" but the driver only shrugged.

"What happened where, man?"

"So, you won't tell me either." I rolled down my window, letting the snow fly in. I squeezed my body through the window and sat on the ledge.

"Hey! What are you doing, man!" the driver shouted as I banged on the roof and howled into the storm. The car slowed down and hands dragged me back in.

"You're gonna fall out and get run over!" Krissy screamed but I told her it didn't matter, cause we were already dead. "Sit back and put on your seat belt, right now!"

"Look man, I'm going to kick you out of my car."

"Damn, you're crazy dude!" laughed Remmy.

"Kelly, you got to get control of yourself," said Face.

"But we're dead man!" I exclaimed. "We're already dead!"

"Relax honey," said Macie and then whispered something to Krissy.

"Will it always be like this?" I asked. "I mean, you'd tell me, wouldn't you?"

"I know Kelly, just relax," said Krissy.

"How do you know?"

"I just know."

"Everything is alright, Kelly," Face tried to console me. "Look, we're alive man! See, we're alive." I watched as he glowed until I couldn't see his face.

"What happened here?" I asked, looking out the window at the passing dunes of dust that was once a city. "Are we in the bad section of town?"

"No," Macie laughed.

"It gets worse than this?"

"What are you talking about man?" Remmy asked.

"Krissy," I paused.

"What, Kelly?"

"Why won't you answer the question?"

"What question, Kelly?"

"Where are we going?"

"To a rave."

"Krissy…Krissy."

"What Kelly!"

"You've come to lead me across, is that right? I knew it! You're ghosts, man! You're dead—and now you're ghosts!"

Krissy leaned and said something to Macie and then they both giggled.

"See? You know what's going on!" I yelled. "Hey guys…"

"What do you want, Kelly?"

"You're in on it! And that's why you can't tell me, right?"

"Yeah, we're all in on it!" grinned Remmy.

✦

"In on what?" Gildmore asked.

"They knew they were dead, but they couldn't tell me."

✦

"You're ghosts, aren't you?" I looked at Face.

"Yeah, maybe!"

"How are we ghosts?" Krissy asked.

"Look at this place!" I said, pointing at the disintegrating streets. "It's the land of the dead! I've figured it out!"

Face stared at me, slowly brought up his camera, and snapped another picture.

Click

I tried to grab the camera. I pulled it away and then snapped a picture of Face.

"Hey!" the driver yelled. "Knock it off!"

"You're all out of your goddamn minds!" Krissy yelled.

"You're gonna get me in accident. Everybody calm down!" the driver yelled. "Especially you!" He pointed at me.

I slid back out the window and felt the wind sting my face. Then the car slowed down and they dragged me back in again.

"This is your last chance, man. I'm warning you," said the driver.

I turned around and looked at Krissy. "Cut the fucking shit, Kelly! You're gonna get the cops on our ass!"

"But we're dead!"

"We're all dead if you keep that up!" Macie said.

I watched a bug crawl out of Face's ear.

"Don't look at me like that," Face argued.

Macie pushed my face. "Kelly, stop acting crazy!"

They laughed and whispered and I could tell they knew something. The fifteen-year-old driver accelerated around a corner, sliding sideways and splashing up sludge.

"Slow down man! You're flying!" I shouted

"I'm only going forty miles an hour! What's wrong with you, man?" the kid asked.

"Who are we running from?" I asked him.

"The cops," he grinned back.

"I knew it."

The storm had gotten so bad that snow began to fly in through the air vents.

"Close those vents or we'll drown in the stuff!" I screamed over the static as I slapped them closed.

Strobe lights began to fill the car, flashing red, white and blue. Everyone was moving in slow motion. I spun around, looked out the back window and then I saw it.

✦

"What did you see?" Gildmore asked.

✦

"GO! GO! GO!" I screamed as we accelerated through the burning wasteland, flying around the corners with a cop car burning through the snow behind us. Only this wasn't an ordinary cop. We took a sharp turn that sent the cop car swerving sideways and that was when I saw it. Alongside of the cruiser, instead of *POLICE* was written *GOD*.

"God is a cop, man!" I screamed. "And he's right behind us!"

"The cops! Where?" The others looked around.

"Behind us! What are you, blind? He's trying to stop us! He's trying to stop us from getting to the land of the dead!" Face snapped a picture of me. The girls laughed and Remmy flicked a cigarette out the window.

Click

"He's gaining on us!" I shouted as we flew through the streets with the snow beating down on the windshield, past the burning buildings. The others chattered behind me, grinning yet ignoring the circumstances. "God is chasing us!"

The kid behind the wheel glanced back while God's cruiser stayed on us, burning rubber, fishtailing and flashing its lights, attempting to stop us from getting across. The siren grew louder and louder. We seemed to drive faster yet wherever we turned, God stayed right behind us. Macie and Krissy glanced back.

"Relax, Kelly," said Krissy.

"We're almost there," the driver told us.

"Almost where?" I asked, looking out at the burning streets. "We're in hell, man!" I yelled but they just laughed. The grin faded from my face as a little voice grew louder in my head, warning me to stop. Slowly the voice got louder until it was shouting in my head and then I was shouting.

"Stop the car! Stop! Stop! Stop the car!"

✦

"And why were you yelling for them to stop, Kelly?" Gildmore asked.

"Cause I knew if I didn't get out, then there was no turning back."

✦

Krissy leaned over the front seat. "What is wrong with you?"

"Let me out of here!" I screamed while opening my door. The driver hit the brakes, swerving up to the side of the curb and I fell out before he'd stopped.

"Kelly, what the fuck!" Krissy shouted.

The kid driver sighed loudly, "I'm going to leave you in five seconds, man"

"What's the problem, Kelly?" Remmy asked.

"I can't go with you! It's not my time yet!"

"It's not like that, Kelly," said Face. "Look, we're still alive man! Nobody's going to die." But they looked at each other, smiling like they knew something I didn't.

It was all a test. I had to make up my mind. If I missed it now, I'd never get another chance. My mind raced as I stood there, leaning into the car and staring at my friends. I had to make the decision to go with them and stay like this forever, or to stop it from happening.

"Kelly, you're like babbling, man," said Krissy.

"Quick, before Nickodemus gets here!" Face shouted.

"Look man, this is the only way to get back home!" Mickie said.

"Wait, wait." I gazed around as the others looked out of the car. "I don't know where I am," I sighed helplessly.

Krissy grew serious. She stepped out of the car, put her hands on my shoulders, and moved her face close to mine.

"It doesn't matter where you are kid—just as long as you know where your heart is."

I looked at her for a long time, thinking of what she said, as the others began blaring their horn.

✦

"And what did you decide?" Dr. Gildmore asked.

"I went with them."

"Even though you thought it would cause your death?" Gildmore asked.

"Yes."

"Well, I'm glad they didn't leave you there," the doctor almost laughed. "A little later, the police brought you to Crisis Intervention. Do you remember the Emergency Room at all?"

"Why did they bring me here?"

"You were delusional."

"What about my friends?"

"They went home, I guess. I take it that you haven't talked to them."

"No–," I paused, confused. "What do you mean they went home?"

"They went home, Kelly. What don't you understand?"

"But they were arrested!"

"Only you were arrested, Kelly."

"But I remember…I remember…"

"A little out of order, Kelly, but yes, I think you do.

"I remember the rave."

"I'm going to recommend for you to increase a level soon."

"I remember the cops crashing it!"

Gildmore sighed. "When the club was raided by the police, you began attacking them, shouting about dead people."

I looked down.

"Now do you understand why you came to stay with us?"

"When will I get to go home?"

"Just keep on making the progress you have been, and you'll be out of here before you know it."

"Where are my friends?"

"From the Leech Mob?" Gildmore smiled. "Moving on with their lives, I guess, not as a gang, but as *a group of friends*, to put it into Egan's terms."

"Right." I cracked a smile.

"So you *do* remember what happened to Egan?" Gildmore asked.

I looked up. "I don't know what you mean."

"And Jonah?"

"I don't know either."

The doctor leaned back and stared at me and neither of us said a word for a time. "I think you do…"

After leaving Gildmore's office, I walked down the hallway and waited for the next group session to begin. The kids were talking about Ducky's latest escape attempt. He had tried running into the woods while the group walked back from the mess hall. The counselors commanded everyone to sit down on the walkway, while Reuben and Bunny tackled him, and then carried him into Ward F and threw him into a padded cell.

But it was business as usual for the rest of us.

Bunny ushered in a new girl, a walking skeleton looking nervous and out of place. At first I didn't recognize her. Her face was now pale, zitty, and gaunt. Bluish veins webbed through her flesh. Her blonde hair was straw; her eyes red circles.

"This is Carlie, our newest patient," announced Bunny. "Let's make her feel at home." Carlie glanced around the room and we caught eyes. There was no warmth or life in her expression, but this time she had looked at me. I was sure of it.

"Okay, let's go around the room and, hmm, introduce ourselves and let Carlie know why we are all here," said the doctor.

As we all took turns introducing ourselves, I watched her. She made faces from time to time until it finally came to her turn.

"I don't think I'll be here for long. My father is making arrangements for me to stay in a home for people who have problems more like my own." She glared around the room. Curtis chuckled, almost to himself, with his chin resting on his chest and his hands folded on his stomach.

"Is there something funny?" Barbara, the counselor, snapped at him.

"Yeah, I guess she's just stuck here like the rest of us but she doesn't know it yet."

"No way," the girl scowled.

"I got news for you, pumpkin!" said Lauren. "My issues will eat your issues for breakfast!"

"Excuse me!" Barbara raised her voice. "Curtis. Lauren. Maybe you should take a time-out in your room and think about why we don't attack new patients. She has made a giant step coming here and needs all the support she can get."

"I'd love to." Curtis got up, walking like he had a stick jammed up his ass. At the door he turned, making a stupid face. "My dad's gonna hear about this!"

"That's enough, Curtis!" said Gildmore.

Carlie sat there horrified, yet I couldn't help but smile. I hadn't seen her since last September when she was the prettiest girl in our class. Now I knew why she hadn't been around.

"Something funny, Kelly?" Bunny asked.

"No, I was just thinking about something else."

"So Carlie, what issues will you, uh, be working on during your stay here, no matter how short it may or may not be?" Dr. Gildmore sat up straight.

"I have an eating disorder. I imagine I'll be working on that."

"Fair enough. So would you elaborate on the events just prior to your coming here?"

"Is this really anyone else's business?" she asked, which made Gildmore's smile quickly sour.

"Discussing your issues is the only chance you have to get better and then go back home. I hope you understand that, Carlie." Dr. Gildmore looked unimpressed. "And next we have Henry."

"What? Oh yeah. Drugs." Henry scratched his head and looked over to Carlie. "Pleased ta meet cha. Have a nice day." Henry then reached out with both his arms like he wanted a hug.

'No-no-no! No physical contact, Henry," reminded Barbara.

"Is your new medication helping with the hallucinations, Henry?" the doctor asked.

"Oh yeah," replied Henry, smiling. "I see lots of em."

"So hmm, it's not helping."

◆

Riverview High School was back in session. It was a beautiful September day. In PE class, the coach had paired off students who stood on the sidelines and threw footballs back and forth. The coach walked between the lines, up and down the middle of the field, twirling his whistle on a silver chain. As a coach, he'd done this exercise hundreds of times before, walking up and down the field as the kids carefully threw the footballs around him while he shouted instructions.

As he passed between Face and Vick, Vick reached way back and then threw the ball high, aiming for the sky. He had a hell of an arm. The football arched through the air, sailing halfway across the football field before beginning its downward spiral. By the time the coach saw it, it was too late. The football crashed into his head, smashing him in the side of the face and knocking his sunglasses off.

THE END

LEECH MOB
SOCIAL

Get educated!
Take a seat in Homeroom:

LeechMobNovel.com

Wanna hang out?
We've got your back on Facebook:

Facebook.com/LeechMobNovel

Wanna see us in action?
Catch us on YouTube:

YouTube.com/user/LeechMobNovel

What's the 411?
Read our blog:

LeechMobNovel.blogspot.com

Made in the USA
Middletown, DE
29 April 2022

65008746R00196